Love Calls Her Home

Mended Hearts Series

An Anchor on Her Heart
Love Calls Her Home

Love Calls Her Home

Mended Hearts Series

By
Patricia Lee

Love Calls Her Home
Published by Mountain Brook Ink
White Salmon, WA U.S.A.

The website addresses shown in this book are not intended in any way to be or imply an endorsement on the part of Mountain Brook Ink, nor do we vouch for their content.

This story is a work of fiction. All characters and events are the product of the author's imagination. Any resemblance to any person, living or dead, is coincidental.

Scripture quotations are taken from the New King James Version of the Bible. Public domain.

ISBN 9781943959-43-3

The Team: Miralee Ferrell, Jenny Mertes, Nikki Wright, Cindy Jackson
Cover Design: Indie Cover Design, Lynnette Bonner Designer

Mountain Brook Ink is an inspirational publisher offering fiction you can believe in.

Printed in the United States of America

Dedication

In special recognition of the unselfish sacrifices made by friends Amy Rodman and Roger Jones, Craig and Julie Murphy, Kurt and Melissa Blair, and to all other foster parents who have opened their homes and their hearts to hurting children.

Acknowledgments

Giving credit where it is due always makes me cautious, because I'm certain I'm going to leave someone out. This book required talking to a lot of individuals about their personal stories involving cancer experiences, foster care, military service, and horse rescue operations. That's a lot of ground to cover.

First, and foremost, I give thanks to my Lord Jesus Christ who has held my hand on this journey and found a place for *Love Calls Her Home* in the publishing line-up. Without daily check-ins, my creative spirit would have run dry and my weary soul would have surrendered to the struggle.

I thank my family for respecting my writing time and cheering for me as I finished the novel. To my husband, for his encouragement. To my son, for his input and willingness to read the story from a man's point of view. To my daughter, whose undaunted spirit continues to feed mine.

People who deserve individual credit and without whom there would be many gaps in the story include:

- Harney County Sheriff David Glerup, now retired, who willingly answered my questions about the workings of the sheriff's department in eastern Oregon, the challenges they face patrolling the largest county in the state, and the kinds of situations into which they are called. From his descriptions I created the position of Deputy Lissa Frye. For the purpose of story, I gave Lissa a specialized job that doesn't exist in the everyday routine of the department, but whose responsibilities fall to each member of the sheriff's team.

- Sandra Longton and Heidi Gaul, who shared their personal journeys with cancer.

- Amy Rodman and Barbara Hutchins, from whom I gained

an insider's view of Children's Protective Services and how the agency works in the state of Oregon.

- ETC (EXW/ESWS) Troy L. Latham USNR Ret who helped me figure out the details of Lissa's naval career.
- E-4 Corporal Kurt von der Ehe, former USMC special operations, who shared his knowledge of weaponry and war from his experiences in Afghanistan.
- *Buck Brogoitti Animal Rescue* in Pendleton, Oregon, whose operations appeared in an article in the *Oregonian* and inspired the setting for the story's horse rescue center.
- *Crystal Peaks Youth Center,* whose newsletters and books by founder Kim Meeder, lent insights into the healing that can take place when rescued horses meet hurting kids. I read two of Kim's books in preparation for this novel. She and her husband Troy run the youth ranch in Central Oregon.
- *Burns Time Herald* for their article on the finer points of organized sage rat hunting.

Without the input of these individuals, the story would not have the personal touch it needed. Any mistakes in the facts are mine alone.

Thanks go to my critique partners— Mary Ellen Spink, Rebecca DeMarino, Heidi Gaul, Tammy Bowers, and Karen Barnett—for their professional insights as we finished the story together. Each of these women brought their unique abilities to the polishing of the manuscript. You ladies rock!

To my editors—Rebecca DeMarino and Jenny Gould Gibbs Mertes—who tirelessly made suggestions to improve the story, my publicist Nikki Wright, and my publisher Miralee Ferrell of Mountain Brook Ink I say thank you for making this book another dream come true.

CHAPTER ONE

LISSA FRYE JOLTED UPRIGHT, LISTENING FOR the strange noise that had broken the stillness. She squinted into the darkness as dawn's approach grayed the black interior of the room. The dresser and nightstand took shape, but still no clue to the sound's origin surfaced.

What was it?

A sharp claw, attached to a softer paw, touched her arm and she jumped. Sorrel's rough tongue licked her chin, the swish of a wagging tail a sign the noise had baffled the dog, too.

"Did you hear that?" At her question, Sorrel yipped. The dog panted, pushing her nose into Lissa's lap.

She stroked the dog's curly ears and petted her head. "Lie down, girl. It isn't time to go." The dog whined and retreated to her rug, the rustling of her tail as she settled the only sign the animal existed in the shadows.

The room again fell silent. The hush lingered like a menacing spirit, a ghostlike apparition that made Lissa uncomfortable. She'd regained her land legs since returning from the Navy three months ago, but the missing hum of the ship's engines and the ever-present roll of the vessel as it sailed had not been replaced. The quiet in the room roared louder than any ship ever had. Fifteen years of living with that reality would take time to fade. If ever.

Lissa stood and stumbled toward the dresser, stubbing her toe on the travel bag she'd left on the floor last night. The luggage, packed and ready to load in the Suburban for her trip over the mountain today, waited to be stowed after she signaled Sorrel into the passenger seat later. Hopping on one foot as she massaged her injured toe, she reached for the lamp. As she did, a light flashed to the left of its base, the strange buzz rattling the water glass beside it.

Her cell phone. On vibrate.

Oh, no. Not at six-thirty in the morning. She moaned as she read the time. Nothing good could come of a call this early. Unless it was Dad. Or Eily. Or Kurt? No, that was too much to hope.

She picked up the phone and checked the readout. Sheriff Matthew Briggs. Her boss. On a Saturday, no less. She'd worked the last three, all filled with emergencies her new job required her to handle.

What was it this time? A herd of cows that had pushed over their rotting fence and blocked traffic as they trotted along Highway 20? A raptor shot by some inexperienced hunter? A ram who'd led his flock into a ravine and couldn't get out?

She gritted her teeth. Whatever crisis awaited her meant she wouldn't be driving home anytime soon. Her trip would be postponed, maybe all weekend. She punched the screen to answer the call. Might as well get this over with.

"Don't you believe in sleep?" Lissa stifled a yawn as she waited for Matthew to respond. "This must be some emergency."

"I was afraid you'd leave for your folks' place before I reached you." His words, laced with warmth, made her smile. Matthew deserved her respect. She could picture him in his uniform, broad shoulders packed into his neat tan shirt. From beneath a massive crop of brown hair, grey eyes pierced the edges of her soul. Ever the gentleman, Matthew had treated her like an equal, accepted her into the sheriff's department without hesitation, and made her feel welcomed in an office of six other men. Too bad he was happily married. "You're not on the road yet, are you?"

"No. I planned to leave around nine." She waited for the other shoe to drop. "What's up?"

"Missing person report from a concerned storekeeper. Might be animals involved. Do you have time before you head out?"

Lissa knew what she'd have to say. Animal welfare pervaded

her job description and, though the trip she'd planned today to her father's home in McKenzie Bridge had waited too long, she had to respond to Matthew's request. Fifteen years in the Navy had kept her from Dad and his new wife, Eily, and now that Lissa lived closer, they expected her to visit as often as her new job allowed. This renewed connection to her father, after so much time apart, warmed her. But Matthew wouldn't ask if the case wasn't urgent. He knew how much she needed to reconnect with her family.

"How long do you think this will take?" Lissa worked to keep the impatience out of her voice. "I've got a four-hour drive ahead of me. Can we check this out before noon?"

"That depends on what we find. But I doubt it will take more than an hour." Matthew must have read her mind. "Bring your file on ranchers available to foster animals. We may need it."

"Got it." Lissa kept the file in her rig. "I'll meet you at headquarters at eight."

"That's fine. Wear your tall boots."

Clicking off her phone, she went to her closet and retrieved the last clean uniform she'd hoped to save for her return to work next Tuesday. If this call went well, she could replace the uniform in her closet when she finished. She grabbed a towel on her way to the shower. Duty called.

Mueller Ranch, Harney County, Oregon

Rain pelted the filly's bony back like gravel thrown from the roadway shoulder. The shower's chill burrowed into her hide. Beyond the fence, spring precipitation had greened the barren hillside, begging shoots of grass from the frozen soil. In the paddock where she stood, the downpour only added to the mud and manure, rendering the sludge sticky and deep. In the corner, a layer of green floated on the surface of the water trough.

As the filly stepped through the muck, her legs ached from the cold, her hooves heavy with packed manure. Though her coat shimmered with a cinnamon glow in the summer, the filth of the pen had dulled it to a dirty brown. Her skin itched, and the shedding hair clung like ticks on a coyote. The soupy ground beneath her offered no place to lie down and roll.

She longed for the growing forage beyond the fence, her stomach a tight knot of hunger. One blade had popped up near the fence post, but the meager shoot did little to satisfy the growling inside her belly.

Her mother wobbled on shaky legs beside her—coughing, wheezing, the gulps of air staccato and shallow. Mucous dribbled from the mare's nostrils. Her lungs whistled with every breath, similar in pitch to the fierce wind blowing in from the canyon adjacent to the ranch—the canyon where her mother had watched her prance last summer.

The filly's ears twitched, pointing toward the ranch house not a hundred yards away. The old man's decrepit machine, which bellowed loud enough to scare a rattlesnake, sat like a piece of ornamentation in the drive. Where was he?

The man had fancied her last July, a foal learning to run, gamboling on newborn legs. He'd allowed her freedom to roam, to frolic along the creek basin, never out of sight of her watchful mother cropping grass and weeds. The tough, tasteless fodder couldn't compare to her mother's sweet milk. As the summer progressed, however, the mare's supply of nourishment dried up, like the meadow under the summer sun, and she was forced to eat what her mother did.

The old man had provided hay all winter while snow covered

the ground. On occasion, she'd snatched the sweetened grain he rationed out for her mother. The molasses, corn, and oats made a welcome treat on a frosty day. But then he'd disappeared. No hay, no grain, no anything. Starvation became a reality.

She missed the man's chuckle. The way he scratched in all the right places behind her ears and between her eyes. She could still hear him boasting to his friends.

"Ain't she a beauty? Cinnamon like her mama. Tail and mane like her daddy. I saw him. Wild Kiger stallion snuck in right beneath my nose and got the mare pregnant. Didn't think ol' Bets could carry a foal to term. But, by gum, I'm glad she did. Ain't never seen a more beautiful filly. See the stripe down her back and on her legs? She's worth a mint, if you ask me."

Why didn't the man come? If nothing else, he could tether her mother against the hillside as he had last summer. The mare had grazed in the dried pastureland, nibbling at milkweed and snipping off thistle tops. The winter snowmelt had left the grasslands ripe for growing. Recent rains encouraged the meadow to soak up all the sky could muster. The new green shoots called to her. She and her mother could forage to satisfy their appetites once they escaped the paddock. If only he would come and open the gate—let them beyond their prison, into the spreading carpet of green.

Her mother groaned, shuddered, and bent her knees, sinking into the mud. Her breathing rasped now, loud and grating, like the file of the farrier who trimmed her hooves. Her head sank lower, her muzzle drifting into the mire. The filly nickered and nudged her mother, trying to get her to stand. She inched closer, the mud sucking at her legs. Hovering over the mare's back, she nuzzled her mother's neck, massaging the length of it with her chin.

A noise caught her attention. The filly raised her head, ears forward, nostrils flared as she tested the scent. At the top of the hill an engine rumbled. She tried to nicker, but no sound came.

The little horse bumped her mother with her muzzle. Help might be coming.

Lying down, the mare already sounded better. Even the wheezing had stopped.

Unable to sleep, Jayden Clarke counted the bumps in the popcorn ceiling, anxious for this day to break. Fingers of grey dawn crept in through the windows like burglars seeking a score. The sound of rain pattered against the glass.

He bolted to the window and lifted the blind. A fine mist fell, covering the driveway. Rain? On the first day of summer? Puddles occupied the spot where his mother's car should be. No! She'd promised to drop him at Bennie Mueller's ranch today. Why did she leave without him? He looked around his room and spied her note on his dresser.

Jayden, I left early for groceries. Have some toast and juice. I'll take you to Mr. Mueller's when I return, or you can ride your bike. George is sleeping. Let him. Mom

He put the note back. Riding his bicycle to Bennie's would take forever in the rain. Jayden cringed. This couldn't be happening.

With school out, he'd barely slept last night, excited to reunite with his old friend. He hadn't seen the elderly rancher since last September. Bennie suffered from arthritis and, even though Jayden was only ten last summer, Bennie had needed his help with the extra ranch chores warm weather brought.

Jayden couldn't wait to hug Duke, the black and white collie, or send the dog chasing the Frisbee after chores were done. He probably wouldn't recognize the yearling foal. He'd played peek-a-boo with her last summer, burying a carrot chunk deep in the hay. She would snort her way to the bottom to find the crunchy reward. He'd cleaned stalls and pitched hay until exhaustion claimed him. The three of them—he, the filly, and Duke—had been inseparable all summer. Nine months of school and a grueling winter left him eager to return. The ranch, the man, and the animals filled a void inside Jayden nothing else could satisfy.

His new stepfather, George Barnes, might be the reason his mother had left earlier than planned. The long-haul truck driver had arrived home last night after completing a cross-country delivery ahead of schedule, surprising Mom and upsetting Jayden. Off work until Monday, George had stopped by the bar en route and walked into the house edgy, irritable, and unstable. Jayden's heart sank, remembering the way his stepfather's speech slurred after a few beers. If George had started downing the booze again this morning as he often did on his weekends off, he could be anywhere—bedroom, sofa, kitchen table—drunk and mean. Jayden needed to be on his guard.

George's abusive temper made life at home a powder keg. When drunk, the man raged at any little infraction. Last night Jayden had made the mistake of asking his mother a question before she served George's dinner and received a slap to his arm. The blow lingered like a nasty bruise. The act had surprised Jayden because his stepfather had never been physically abusive. Next time he might break something. Jayden wouldn't wait around.

He tiptoed to the kitchen and fixed a light breakfast. Still in his pajamas, he wandered into the living room. He barely cleared the door when an empty Jim Beam bottle zinged by him, missing his shoulder by mere inches and landing on the couch. He whirled around, the buttered toast and orange juice shaking in his hands.

"Where is she?" George glowered at him from the recliner, bulbous nose puffed red and cheeks splotched with pink. At his feet lay another empty bottle next to an opened pretzel box.

Breakfast. "You deaf, boy?"

"She said we needed groceries." Being alone with this man in his drunken state made Jayden tremble. "Mom left before you woke up?"

"Melanie's not here, is she?" The words rode on George's tongue like a hissing snake, ready to coil and strike at the slightest provocation. "So I guess she's gone, stupid."

Jayden couldn't believe Mom had left him like this. She hadn't before—especially when George had been drinking. If his stepfather had slept in as his mother had written, she didn't see George this way before she left for grocery shopping. He probably didn't take a swig until she left—his mother had confronted George about his weekend drinking before. His penchant for liquor had fueled several fights in the eighteen months they'd been married. Since she knew Jayden would visit Bennie this morning, she must have trusted he would be safe—not facing a mean and nasty drunk. The vacant house echoed like a cave in the hills, the missing woman torching George's anger. The blame fell to Jayden.

"If you weren't such a wimpy, sniveling kid, your mother wouldn't need to shop so often." George's sneer, combined with the smell of booze on his breath, made Jayden's stomach churn. "She's always buying this shirt for you, or those shoes, saying, 'Wouldn't Jayden like that jacket?' My money, your gifts." He snorted. "I married her, and who do I get stuck with? A measly eleven-year-old who sucks all her affection away from me." George slammed his fist on the edge of the recliner. "Where is she anyway?" He tipped a third Jim Beam toward the ceiling, tossing the bottle to the floor when it emptied.

"Getting groceries."

George growled, kicked the pretzel box and the bottles away from his feet, and swiveled the recliner toward the window.

Jayden edged closer to the wall, waiting for a chance to slip out to his bedroom. He didn't know how soon his mother would return. She had her own money, resources she kept secret from George. Jayden's real dad's life insurance funded her shopping expeditions, paid for the clothes her son needed, and left a little for splurges. Jayden suspected Mom grew weary of the verbal abuse and, like him, found reasons to be gone.

When George sobered up, he'd morph into a different person, the sweet and generous guy she thought she married after Dad died. The trucker would hit the road again for another cross-country haul and leave Jayden and Mom alone for a week or two. But waiting from Friday to Monday when the man was home for him to recover his sobriety seemed like an eternity to Jayden. After last night's encounter, why hadn't she waited a little longer to take Jayden with her today? He didn't understand.

Snores interrupted his thoughts. George had passed out. He would sleep like this for hours, the effects of the booze crippling his ability to function while the alcohol laced his system. When he awoke, he'd hold his head, seeking sympathy for the hangover he claimed pounded him like a prizefighter. If Mom was doing a big shop, she might not return for two or three hours. By then George would have slept the booze off, sobered up, and taken meds for his headache. Jayden would stay away as long as possible.

During the winter months, classes and homework kept Jayden busy. He stayed out of George's way whenever they were both home. School offered a barrier of protection since his stepfather was well aware of the watchful scrutiny teachers kept over their charges. He worked longer hours in the winter, sometimes staying away for a month at a time. Worsened driving conditions kept him from returning home, even when the hauling slacked off around the first of the year—a welcome respite to Jayden. He and Mom enjoyed each other's company without the threat of George.

Now school was out. No homework. No classes. More George.

The snores grew in intensity. Seizing the opportunity, Jayden sneaked out of the living room with his breakfast, closing the bedroom door with a soft click. He sat on the edge of his mattress, trying to swallow the toast over the lump in his throat. Sunlight poked through the blinds, begging him to come outside.

He downed the orange juice, slipped into his clothes, and wrote a note to his mother. Leaving the paper folded on his bed with a prayer she'd find it, he grabbed his denim jacket and tiptoed into the hallway leading to the garage. He passed through the kitchen and checked the refrigerator for more to eat, but found nothing. Cereal would rattle in the bowl, waking George, and without milk, the dry flakes would be tasteless. Satisfied he could last until dinner, he slunk to the back door. He twisted the knob, hurried down the steps, and donned work boots. His bicycle beneath him, Jayden pedaled out through the open garage door like he'd been set on fire. He couldn't wait to see Bennie. If he never saw George again, it would be too soon.

Two miles of straight stretch burned beneath his tires, and soon he faced the rising elevation leading to Bennie Mueller's ranch. He peered over his shoulder to make sure he hadn't been followed, relieved when the empty road trailed like an asphalt ribbon behind him. Summer vacation awaited. Boy, horse, dog.

He stashed his bike in a roadside thicket rather than push it up the slope, the eight-mile ride from home leaving him winded. He wiped his rain-spattered face, and hoofed it the rest of the distance. Panting as he arrived at the top of the hill, he frowned at the scene below. Things at the ranch had changed. Bennie's pickup sat crooked in the driveway, exposed to the elements instead of protected by the overhang of the barn like the rancher preferred.

Not seeing the horses where they should be—grazing in the pasture—Jayden focused nearer the barn. Coat muddied and head down, an animal stood alone in the rain, mired to its knees in the muddy round pen. Was this the foal he'd played with? The creature raised its head. No welcoming whinny. Bennie would never have left an animal like this. Never.

When Duke didn't barrel up the hill barking like a windup toy on steroids, Jayden considered turning back. He sensed trouble. Should he go home and get his mother? That meant facing George again. No, if Bennie's truck sat in the driveway, the rancher couldn't be far away.

He summoned his courage and scrambled down the hill. He checked every tree and shrub while calling for Duke. No sign of the dog. He hurried faster to discover the reason. As he neared the ranch buildings, an engine sounded out on the empty highway he'd left twenty minutes before. The vehicle slowed, and Jayden's pulse soared. He didn't want to be discovered snooping around when Bennie appeared to be gone. He had to hide.

Lissa checked her uniform, grabbed her tote, and led Sorrel to the kennel run behind the house. "Sorry, girl. You'll have to wait until later. Emergency." After locking the gate, she stroked one of Sorrel's front paws as the dog stood on her hind legs, begging through the fence. "I'll be back soon. Promise." She returned to the Suburban, her tall boots waiting on the seat beside her, praying she'd spoken the truth.

Lissa closed the door of the SUV and did a final visual check to see if she'd left anything undone. The rented house she now called home waited in the quiet, shutters closed, drapes drawn. The small yard, green from spring rains and receding snow, sported dainty iris blooms popping up near the juniper tree. Nestled beside a rock outcropping, the last daffodil blossoms hung in weary silence, ready to sleep until next year.

A buzz at her side vibrated in her pocket. Anticipation fueled her fingers as she pulled out her cell phone. Might it be Kurt? Every ring of the phone nourished her hope he'd contact her. They'd met at a family Thanksgiving dinner two years before and had spent their week of leave visiting the ocean, shopping in Portland, and sharing a meal and a movie. He had promised he'd keep in touch when he left. He kissed her goodbye at the airport, sent her a handful of e-mails, and disappeared. His last contact was a year ago. He hadn't kept his word. She wanted to know why.

She checked the screen. Matthew again. "Change your mind?"

Matthew chuckled into the phone. "I'll be five minutes late. Don't shoot me."

"I should, after rousting me out before my morning coffee. Slave driver."

"Guilty as charged."

CHAPTER TWO

AN HOUR LATER, THE PATROL TRUCK bouncing beneath her, Lissa gripped her seat as Matthew maneuvered the vehicle down a winding gravel road. The ranch house, barn, and outbuildings hovered in the draw below like barracks in a concentration camp, weathered and battered under the grey of the intermittent rain. No lights burned in the home, and the barn appeared old enough to have been abandoned years before. The peeling, cracked siding stood in stark contrast to the lovely, open range extending for miles beyond the property.

No doubt this ranch, like so many in the area, butted up against land maintained by the Bureau of Land Management. Livestock wandered in and out of the government terrain. The ranchers sometimes accessed the expansive acreage beyond their property lines, and no one said anything. Keeping livestock off the free range could become a problem. Nobody had figured out a way to tell the animals they trespassed. Or the herd of Kiger mustangs living at the government's expense. Protected by the BLM, the herd wandered free, the stallion occasionally making house calls on domestic mares.

While they'd driven here, Matthew had filled her in on the details. The call had come early this morning. The frantic merchant in Hines reported Bennie Mueller hadn't picked up his monthly order of animal feed, nor had he requested his mail in that time. A neighbor had passed by the place on his way into Hines today and confirmed what the merchant feared—the ranch appeared deserted. It wasn't like Bennie, the proprietor said, not when the rancher's habits could dictate a calendar. Matthew knew Bennie and agreed with the store owner's assessment.

Lissa observed the contrasts of the abandoned property to its surrounds. Why would a man need animal feed when she couldn't see a live *anything* for miles?

"I wonder where Bennie's dog is?" Matthew's frown made his eyebrows meet in the middle. The talkative sheriff had grown quiet, his gregarious nature suddenly silenced as if suspicion gripped his tongue. His gaze met hers before it swept over the grounds, his right hand on the butt of his pistol as he slowed in the drive. "Usually Duke is the first one out to greet and the last one to quiet."

"My dad had a dog like that. He called him Blarney because he was full of himself."

Matthew chuckled at the image she'd described. "That sounds like Duke. Has to tell all he knows. Twice."

"Do you suspect foul play?" Lissa paused and prayed for protection.

"You never know out here." Matthew braked to a stop in front of the ranch house and leaned on the steering wheel. "But something isn't right."

Lissa appreciated the view. If not for the rain, the landscape would be breathtaking. When she finished her last tour of duty and resigned her commission to join the reserves, she'd sought a job where scenery flavored her work and allowed her occasional visits home. Here in the heart of Central Oregon's high desert, with Malheur National Forest nearby and Crater Lake to the south, all the countryside she could possibly visit awaited exploration. But with the isolation came opportunities for those with ulterior motives. "How do you want to proceed?"

"I'll go check the house." Matthew thumbed toward the darkened structure. "You snoop around and see what you can find near the barn. Check the round pen, too."

"The round pen?"

"The solid fence enclosure near the back of the barn. People around here use them to train horses. Bennie wrangled his share once upon a time."

A bobby pin had wriggled its way out of her hair during the rough truck ride and, as she opened the door of the cab, the pin dangled at the end of a loose strand below her ear. Her curly locks defied taming, but strict military dress code had dictated her hair be neat. Navy habits wouldn't die. Besides, she didn't know what else to do with it. She could let her hair hang down again, she supposed, the way she'd worn the massive cap of curls when she was younger. During the brief week she and Kurt spent together between deployments, he'd loved it when she let her hair hang to her shoulders. The tendrils around her face softened the chiseled cheekbones she'd inherited from her father—or so Kurt had mentioned when he kissed her—and enhanced her dark brown eyes.

She gathered the loose strand then poked the prongs back into the neat bun she wore at the nape of her neck and scrutinized her work in the rearview mirror. Satisfied, she pulled on her tall boots, descended from the truck, and glanced around. The open terrain reminded her of a vast prairie—the high desert's dusting of green sufficient to be interesting. Yet the barren land's surplus of brown seemed desolate enough to equal Kurt's descriptions of Afghanistan the last time he wrote her. Why did everything remind her of him?

Shaking away the loneliness and squashing down the nagging reminder she was thirty-three and single, she stepped away from the pickup, her boots sinking into the morass lining the gravel driveway. She tromped nearer the barn, stopping to listen to a faint snuffling sound followed by a low, animal-like rumble coming from the other side.

She edged around the building to the back. The pen Matthew had described came into view—only it wasn't solid. Many boards were either missing or hanging at precarious angles. The openings offered a view of the interior. What she saw through the hole made her heart bang against her rib cage.

A young horse, no more than a year old, hovered over another lying on the ground, nibbling as it worked its muzzle along the downed horse's neck. Head low and legs mired to the knees in sludge, the yearling wavered, its protruding ribs countable, its dirty hide covered in matted hair someone should have brushed weeks ago. The wads of fur hung like clusters of cotton—ragged, muddy balls of debris dangling from the skin.

Lissa's eyes pooled. She'd seen pictures of men battered after battle, their gaping wounds wrapped by medics as they waited transport to a military hospital. She acknowledged those atrocities as expected outcomes of war. But this scene sickened her. Through no fault of their own, these horses suffered from sheer neglect. How could one abandon dependent creatures like these?

She opened the barn door to check if other animals waited inside. The interior loomed in darkness, fragrant with baled hay. Headstalls and other tack were lined up along one wall, each hanging from its own hook in neat order. Two garbage cans stood side by side near the first stall. She lifted one lid and found a scoop and pail inside, sitting on top of grain smelling of molasses. The other can held oats.

Lissa scooped a mixture from the two containers into the pail, barely covering the bottom of the bucket, grabbed a flake of hay, and returned to the pen outside. The stench coming from the ramshackle corral offended her nose after the sweet aroma of the barn hay. Inhaling a deep breath for courage, she carried the bucket with the hay toward the gate, clucking to the young horse. She entered the pen, closed the gate behind her, and waited.

Eyes wide and nostrils flared, the yearling kept its distance, distrust written in its stance. Lissa shook the container. The young horse regarded the feed, snorting, the sound like a warning. But despite its obvious interest, the yearling didn't budge, as though getting unstuck from the mud required too much effort.

Avoiding the murky middle, Lissa measured her stride, stepping from one hard spot on the ground to the next. She inched her way around the edge of the pen toward the two horses.

The horse on the ground, positioned between her and the yearling, didn't stir when Lissa approached. Bending down, she touched the emaciated back and inspected the belly. The mare had probably been the yearling's mother. Cold hide met her fingers. No breath steamed from the nostrils. The animal didn't appear bloated, nor did flies hover, suggesting it died as recently as today. To her surprise, the mare's ears twitched. The horse lifted her head Lissa's way, rheumy eyes studying her, nostrils dripping mucous. Lissa shuddered. This animal needed immediate attention.

Lissa glanced up from where she knelt by the mare to find the young horse watching her, and from this angle she determined the animal to be a filly. The filly trembled as she reached out her nose toward the bucket, sniffing the feed. Lissa stood and stepped a foot closer, waiting for acceptance of her offering. She spoke in low tones, daring to take another step. "It's okay, girl. We're going to help you. Don't be afraid."

The filly snorted, head up and ears forward again. Lissa had seen other horses blow air when they wanted to bolt and run, but this one only stood there assessing her visitor, the gap between trust and fear closing as hunger forced her decision. Finally, near enough to offer the feed, Lissa lifted the pail, holding her breath. The filly examined the edge of the container, brushing Lissa's fingers with a moist muzzle.

After another minute passed, Lissa's patience waned. If the filly wouldn't trust her enough to eat, she'd have to try a different tack. Lissa's feet tingled from the cold, but as she started to leave, the filly thrust her muzzle into the bucket and scooped up a bite with eager lips. For several minutes Lissa and the young horse stood eyeing one another. Nickering sounds, mixed with the noise of crunching grain, came from the filly as she devoured the feed, the sweet aroma of molasses tingeing the air as she gobbled. She thrust her head into the bucket one last time and pushed forward, knocking Lissa off balance and sending her backward into the mud. The bucket flew out of her hands and landed at the filly's feet.

"Thanks." Lissa reached around, hoping to find something to help her regain her footing. "You got me into this—you plan to help me out?" Her hands were covered with mud, and the slimy, wet sludge seeped through her trousers. She rolled toward the fence and grabbed a rail, a damp manure pile adhering to the side of her pant leg. Lissa pulled herself upright and gagged as the smell threatened to dislodge her breakfast. "I do hope you're happy."

The filly, intent on licking up every smidgeon of grain, ignored Lissa's plight. Apparently satisfied the bucket was empty, the yearling pulled one slender leg out of the sludge, then another, and plodded toward the watering trough, flinging muddy water on Lissa as she went. The filly slurped from the algae-green film floating on top of the water, raised her head, and angled her face toward Lissa.

"I'll bet you want more, but I'm not sure I want to pay the price to get it." Lissa waited to see what she would do next. To her surprise, a nicker sounded—the low rumbling she had first heard when she left the truck. Lissa's resolve melted. "I'll get you hay, but not much. You can't overdo this first time. And I can't get any dirtier than I am now."

Another nicker sounded, louder this time as the filly ambled along the fence to where Lissa waited.

"Looks like you made a friend." Matthew stepped through the broken rails from the other side. He eyed her pant legs and pressed his lips together, a low chuckle permeating the silence. "Did you two have a fight?"

"She's starving." She ignored his banter and showed him the bucket. "This only held a handful when she started. She was so hungry she knocked me down. There's plenty of feed in the barn." She cocked her head toward the sheriff, seeking answers. "Why would anyone leave these animals like this? Especially when there's hay and grain available?"

"Bennie didn't intend to neglect them. I found his body in the bedroom. He's been dead a while."

Lissa's skin crawled—whether from the cold seeping into her legs or the thought of a villain on the loose, she didn't know. "Foul play?"

"No." Matthew's jaw tensed, his eyes intent on the countryside beyond. "I suspect Bennie died in his sleep. I called the coroner."

Lissa sighed. "It's probably a good thing he didn't see the animals, then. The mare's in bad shape and needs a vet. Her age is working against her. I know how my father would grieve over an animal in her condition."

"Bennie would have done the same."

"So what do we do now?" Lissa hadn't been down this path before. "Besides get cleaned up."

"Try to locate next of kin." Matthew glanced around. "And find his dog."

"What about the horses?"

"I'll call the vet, then drive to the next property and see if the neighbor can help. Around here we use a process called community caretaking, which gives us the authority to get help for the animals. I suspect the vet will remove the mare to his clinic as soon as possible. She needs medical attention. The filly is in better shape and old enough to be homed. Since Bennie has grain and hay, we only need someone nearby to feed this little girl. Speaking of which, do you have the list of ranchers willing to foster an animal?"

"In the truck. Why?"

"I'd like to start searching for a place she can stay."

Lissa crawled through the fence, hurried to the cab, and retrieved her file. As the new trainee for the sheriff's department, she hadn't yet learned all the ropes of her responsibilities, and much of the terminology still stymied her. Animal welfare came with her title, but it could encompass many different scenarios. Neglect and abuse topped the list. Keeping track of a herd of horses or rescuing a dog in a sewer also found their way into her job description. Dogs and cats she knew. The larger animals tested her limited experience.

The sheriff's office responded to calls about missing persons and foul play. When animals were at risk, the task fell to Lissa to investigate and act accordingly. She thumped a folder containing names of area ranchers who acted as hosts for homeless animals, reassuring herself she could find temporary holding stations while she sought permanent homes. She tucked the packet under her arm.

Matthew was rubbing the filly's forehead when she returned. She held up the file. "I have the roster."

"I called the vet's clinic." He exited the pen. "His assistant is on duty and will be here soon." Together they walked to a bench outside the barn. Sitting beside her, Matthew pored over the list, studying each name. "Ah, the Herrick Valley Rescue Center." He tapped the phone number. "Peggy Blake runs it. She would be a great person to send the filly to. She and her son Foster ran the rescue center before he entered the service. After he was killed last year in Afghanistan, she kept the place open. She says the rescue center helps her cope."

"The name sure sounds familiar." Lissa wracked her brain. Where had she heard of Foster Blake? Many soldiers' names passed through her intel while she served in the Navy, but most became a blur in her mind. Foster Blake stirred her memory.

"Can you send her a picture with your phone?"

"No problem." Lissa paused, weighing her options. "This is a three-day weekend for most. Do you think the filly's transport can happen on Tuesday?"

"It'll be up to the veterinarian." Matthew watched the filly circle the pen. "Might have to use a sling to help her stand in the trailer."

"I'll be right back with the photos."

Matthew strode toward the truck while she hurried to the pen. When she had several different shots, she returned to where Matthew leaned against the hood. "I found Peggy Blake already in my database, and I sent her a set of pictures."

"Be sure to mention the grain and hay when she responds. I know she'll use it."

"Is she short on funds?"

"She's taken in a couple of horses in recent months. The extra feed will help." Matthew walked around to the driver's side of the truck.

"Can't anyone take the filly home?" Lissa couldn't imagine leaving the distressed animal in the muddy pen another minute.

"We'll need a court order to remove her."

"How long will it take?"

"We can get one Tuesday, after the holiday. I'm betting there's a neighbor close enough to feed her." Matthew jingled his keys. "I'll check out the adjacent property. You try to lead the filly into a stall. Do you have Dr. DeLorme's phone number?"

"Who's he?"

"The veterinarian I tried to call."

Lissa flipped through her contact list. "I don't see his name listed here. It's probably in the file I left inside."

"Here, copy mine." Matthew held out his phone for her. "You'll be on a first-name basis with Dr. DeLorme soon."

"What do you mean?" Lissa entered the number in her contacts.

"He's the one vet who will always respond for a stranded or neglected animal. He's also on the board of directors for the Herrick Valley Rescue Center." Matthew pointed to the house. "I'm going to check for Duke one more time, then I'll drive down the road. It bothers me the dog's not around somewhere." His boots crunched on the gravel as he walked away.

Lissa texted the information Matthew had given her to the veterinarian. Bringing up the filly's picture, she pressed the send button to Dr. DeLorme. *Done.* She pocketed the phone. *We'll see what he says.*

CHAPTER THREE

KURT MCKINTRICK RESTED HIS LIGHTWEIGHT .22-CALIBER rifle over the side of the mobile platform he stood on, steadying himself as the wheels moved forward. Twenty other men occupied the bed of the oversized wagon, all eyes aimed at the middle of the alfalfa field ahead. Arid, flat terrain surrounded the immediate carpet of green, a reminder of what the land could be, if not for the cultivated field.

Growing up on the western side of the Cascades, where trees, hills, and lush vegetation embellished the landscape, he viewed the desert-like panorama of eastern Oregon with surprise. Having returned a month earlier from military duty in Afghanistan, where endless sand and jagged hillsides swallowed a man, along with his soul, Kurt considered this side of Oregon, near Crane, beautiful by comparison.

Veterinarian Damon DeLorme knelt beside him on the trailer, anticipation written on his face as Kurt readied himself for his first sage rat hunt. "Think you can hit one of these critters?" Damon's eagerness sprang from his words, his dimples making tiny crescents in his cheeks.

"Probably." As Damon's guest, Kurt had accepted the invitation to the hunt, but with reservations. He didn't understand the sport of shooting rodents, but he could handle a gun and Damon knew it. The veterinarian's description of the weekend, complete with resort-like accommodations and wonderful meals, had convinced Kurt to attend. "Can't be much different than sniper hunting in Kabul." Though he tried to make it sound lighthearted, Kurt's responsibilities as a sniper for the Marines haunted him. He'd been good. He'd done his duty. "Except for the range of the rifle."

"I don't know about that." Damon goaded him. "These pests sit up begging for mercy, tiny whiskers twitching, tails quivering, beady eyes focused on you."

Kurt didn't take the bait. "Let me guess. When you've changed your mind about shooting, they dart down their hole, pop up in another one, and have a good belly laugh."

"Hey, I thought you'd never hunted rodents."

"Like I said, not much different than the terrorists in the mountains of Afghanistan. Only smaller." *But no less intent on seeing you fail.*

He skirted the horizon with his eyes, the beauty of Steens Mountain in the distance rising above the level topography. Neighboring residents boasted of the mountain's magnificence— acres of protected land lay within the perimeter. Wildlife like bighorn sheep and Rocky Mountain elk roamed the ravines. The threatened redband trout swam in its lakes. Flowers grew along its boundaries, native species like the Steens paintbrush and Cusick's buckwheat. According to his boss at the horse rescue center, even a herd of Spanish mustangs, the last descendants of a famed stallion brought here by the Conquistadors, lived within the sheltered domain. What other secrets did the mountain hold?

"Keep count of your hits." Damon's tone suggested he was still teasing. "If you lose, you eat sage rat stew for dinner."

"I've eaten worse." Kurt stretched his long legs as he sat on the platform's bench and scanned the field. Other men on the platform chatted among themselves, pointing across the expanse. In every direction, green shoots colored the foreground. "Is the alfalfa a big money crop?"

"Yep. But losses to the vermin are huge." Damon pulled his coat collar around his neck, shivering in the early morning air. "According to a report I read from Oregon State University, each rat can eat fourteen pounds of alfalfa in three months' time."

"How do they know?" Kurt raised an eyebrow. "Did they weigh

them before and after dinner?"

"I don't know." Damon chuckled. "OSU prides itself on research. They must have calculated scientifically." He leaned back against the side of the platform. "I do know there can be close to ten thousand of these creatures in a two-hundred-acre field. What they don't eat, they cover up with dirt and destroy roots. And they carry disease."

"How many does one shooter get in a day?"

Damon cast him a crooked grin. "Depends on what kind of shot he is. It's why I invited you to join this hunt, ex-sniper and all. You ought to earn your keep."

"I think I'd do better down on the ground crawling on my belly." Kurt gawked at the green carpet below him. When the veterinarian first invited him to this hunt, Kurt had balked. Shooting from a raised flatbed on wheels sounded strange when new sprouts of alfalfa below beckoned him to lie on them. "Why the platform wagons?"

"Safety." Damon rested the rifle against his thigh. "Sage rat hunting got a little out of hand for a while. People would come in to hunt and they'd hit irrigation pipes and anything else imaginable, trying to get the critters."

"It's a wonder they didn't shoot each other."

"It's the other reason our hunt guide went to platforms. Up here we all shoot away from the others." Damon pointed to a row of pipes off to the edge of the field. "The rancher leases his land to our guide for the day and moves his irrigation pipes out of our range. The hunt organizer takes responsibility for damage that way."

"Smart man."

"You think?" Damon's eyebrows shot upward. "One rancher reported twenty-one holes in his irrigation lines after a few hunters went through his field."

Kurt snorted. "You mean they didn't improve his watering system?"

"No, unless you like geysers going off in the middle of the oasis."

Kurt laughed at the image. The poor rancher watching as water rocketed skyward while his seedling alfalfa waited, thirsty for groundwater to wet its roots. All because a pesky rodent ran from a hunter's rifle. He stiffened at a memory. *Like the guy who got away from me.*

He laid his weapon down and zipped his hooded sweatshirt. The breeze coming off Steens Mountain riddled him with cold. He shucked his military jacket over his shoulders and slid his arms through the sleeves, shivering. "I thought spring arrived."

"No one told the mountain."

"Like Afghanistan." Kurt rolled his head backward, trying to capture warmth along his neck. "Days could be warm, but nights were frigid. Hard on my trigger finger."

Damon sighted his rifle. "What kind of firepower did you carry?"

"The Remington 700 most often. It was a bolt action .308." Kurt flipped the barrel of the .22 in his hands. "We could hit a target at eight hundred to a thousand feet."

"Out in the open?"

"Yeah. We carried an MI 10 for urban detail." Kurt clenched his jaw. "You never knew what would be lurking around the corner or in the next dwelling."

"Is that where the IED was?" Damon's eyes narrowed, as if studying his reaction.

"No, we were patrolling the hills. I was carrying a Barrett E8 .50 caliber semi-automatic." He wrestled with the memory. He liked Damon, but his questions dredged up images he would rather forget. *Lord, will I ever forget?* Nor was he willing to be much more than a passing acquaintance with the man—not when Kurt's close friends all wound up dead. Damon would have to accept the distance Kurt put between them. "It's shot from the shoulder. Those big boys could shoot twenty-five hundred feet away."

"I've heard they could break a truck in two."

"Not a bad idea." Kurt had wanted to bomb the entire area outside Kabul when Taliban sneaked in and set an improvised explosive device. The ammunition cache his buddy Foster Blake found had been booby-trapped. A terrorist with a cell phone waited for a Marine to come snooping. Foster never knew what hit him. Kurt shuddered, the darkness of that night torturing his dreams. *God, please forgive me.*

The trailer stopped. Damon rested his gun on the side of the platform. "Okay, sniper man, let's see which of us can hit the most rats." Damon closed one eye and aimed at a patch of green nearby. Other men popped off shots beside him. A few cheers went up as shooters nailed their targets.

Kurt didn't see anything for a minute, but sure enough, when the alfalfa stopped moving Damon had hit a small brown critter right through the head. "Good shooting, man."

"Your turn. It'll take time to spot them because they love to camouflage in the grass and the dirt."

"I'm used to camouflage. It's the size that's going to get me."

"Relax and take your time. Soon you'll be seeing rats everywhere."

Kurt didn't respond. *I already do.*

An hour later, Kurt sat on the platform floor, reloading his firearm when Damon groaned and pulled his phone from his pocket. He read the message and sighed.

"Not your wife, I take it?" Kurt sighted the scope, laying the gun across his knees.

"No. It's a text from the new deputy sheriff. Neglect case."

"Animal troubles?"

"Yes. A horse needs to be rescued from her pen and brought into the clinic for evaluation." Damon texted an answer on his phone. "If my assistant can't transport her, I may have to leave early."

"Hey, no way am I eating scoundrel stew by myself." Kurt flashed a grin at the good doctor. "Are you sure this isn't a ploy to get out of dinner at the ranch headquarters?"

"Aw, you're onto me." Damon grew serious. "No, actually this is legitimate. Besides, I like the get-togethers when we're through here—like one great big party."

"You have to leave then?"

Damon blew out an exasperated puff of air. "Probably."

Designed for a man's appetite, the dinners provided with the hunt were supposed to be sumptuous. Kurt knew Damon wouldn't leave before the meal unless the situation demanded the sacrifice. "Abuse?"

"No, not this time. The owner died at home alone. Apparently a while ago. His two horses had to wait until somebody found them."

"At least they're alive."

"Yes. The mare is old, though, and the neglect didn't do her any favors." Damon checked his phone, waiting. "I knew the man. He cared for his animals. This would never have happened if he'd lived."

"One of the hazards of living in a remote area?"

"'Fraid so." Damon's phone buzzed, and he stopped to read the incoming text. "This will have a happy ending."

"Oh?" He waited, the twinkle in the veterinarian's eye suggesting Kurt would somehow be involved in the happily-ever-after.

"Herrick Valley Rescue Center has agreed to take the younger horse. I think you know that place?" He held up his phone so Kurt could read the incoming message.

"Oh boy, do I." Kurt shook his head at the screen. "I've gotten up close and personal with the center in the last four weeks. Real grimy work."

"My assistant has already hitched the trailer to his truck and will pick up the mare in an hour." Damon flashed a picture on the screen. "Isn't she a cutie?"

"I can't believe Peggy agreed to another horse." Kurt scrutinized the image on Damon's phone: a muddy animal standing in muck deeper than its fetlocks. Kurt didn't see anything cute about her, only a lot of work. No sooner had he learned the routine at the rescue center than his boss Peggy Blake brought in another animal with a different set of requirements. Not that he minded. Working with the animals gave him focus, their individual needs helping to meet a void within himself he hadn't yet identified. *God, help me find myself again.* "We have one stall left."

"One stall is all this filly will need. Once the mare is steady on her feet, if she lives, I'll place her somewhere else." Damon clicked off his phone. "For Peggy, the injured and neglected animals are therapy. I'm glad you volunteered to help her out."

"Foster said the rescue center was her life after his father died." Kurt's heart hurt, remembering the way Foster talked for hours about his mother's mission to care for neglected animals and unloved children. "He couldn't wait to get home and help her."

"So you came in his place."

"I promised him." Kurt blinked away the images, recalling

Foster's favorite verse:

The Lord preserves the strangers;
He relieves the fatherless and widow;
But the way of the wicked He turns upside down.

Foster hadn't planned to abandon his mother. He'd become a casualty of war. "Peggy welcomed my help."

"Foster was a great kid." Damon shoved the phone in his pocket and picked up his gun. "I understand he was a medaled Marine."

"He shouldn't have died." Kurt gripped the rifle in his hands, the memory seizing him. The familiar urge to seek vengeance pecked at the edges of his brain. He breathed in, then exhaled, calming himself. Though one less terrorist might be a boon for the world, revenge wouldn't bring Foster back.

"When we finish here Sunday, you and I will have work to do."

"You mean you don't have to leave?"

"The sheriff hopes to locate a neighbor to feed the filly through the weekend." Damon picked up his rifle. "If he finds one, I can stay here and eat sage rat stew. You and I will accept the horse's care on Tuesday."

"Whatever it takes. I'm ready to help." Kurt pressed the image of his dying friend from his mind. *I promised Foster I would.*

Damon lifted his gun to his shoulder and took aim. "What's the last count you had?"

"One hundred forty-two."

"Aw, they've got you feeling sorry for them." Damon pulled the trigger. "One forty-four and counting." He flashed a teasing grin. "Don't let their quivering chins and teary eyes hold you back now."

Kurt raised his rifle. "You're on." He squeezed the trigger. "Forty-three." He fired again. "Forty-four." He aimed once more.

"Forty-five." He beamed, making sure his mouth appeared smug. "Now who's eating stew?"

CHAPTER FOUR

"COME ON, GIRL." LISSA TUGGED AT the filly, trying to get her to move out of the pen and into the barn, but she resisted. Her mother still lay in the mud, only the twitch of her ears telling Lissa she lived. "You're not going to make this easy, are you?" Lissa petted the velvety ears and scratched the whiskery chin, hoping the nurturing would build trust. "I do know what I'm doing."

Round brown eyes considered her, unblinking, one ear pricked forward, the other tuned to another sound in a different direction.

Lissa yanked on the lead rope again. The filly balked, taking a step backward. The halter, designed for a larger horse, slipped over her ears.

"Oh, bother."

With a flip of her tail, the filly snorted and ambled to the water trough.

Lissa needed to find a smaller halter. She started for the barn, stopping when she heard Matthew's truck. Voices beyond the structure and the sound of footsteps on the gravel driveway made her turn. Matthew and a man she didn't recognize walked toward her from the house, deep in discussion.

"Lissa, this is Bennie's neighbor." Beside Matthew, the older man held out his hand.

"Sorry, I'm a bit horsey." Lissa rubbed her hands on her pants and returned the handshake while Matthew explained his news.

"He's available to check on the yearling tonight and tomorrow. He suggested keeping her inside where she'll be dry and warmer."

"If we can get her to go." Lissa restrained her frustration. "She's not cooperating. I don't think she wants to leave her mother behind."

"I'll get a rope around her rear end, and we'll adjust the halter on her head." Matthew ambled toward the barn. He spoke over his shoulder. "Did you try shaking a little grain?"

Lissa shrugged. "Didn't think she'd fall for the same trick since she'd already eaten."

"I'll see what I can find."

Lissa stood near the pen while the two men approached the barn, Matthew stopping to retrieve the bucket Lissa had left by the gate. The neighbor moseyed alongside Matthew, offering advice about where to find the necessary tack. Their voices trailed off when they disappeared through the huge double doors. A minute later they returned, the neighbor shoving the doors closed behind Matthew, who carried a smaller headstall, a loop of rope over his arm, and a flake of hay in his hand.

"Hey, little princess. See what I have." Matthew entered the pen and held out a flake of hay, shaking it so flakes fell to the ground. At the sound, the filly lifted her head and took a tentative step in the sheriff's direction. The mare turned her head as well, stretching her neck toward the hay, but she didn't try to stand. The neighbor knelt down and handfed the mare, lifting her head off the ground. When she quit eating, he lowered her head gently to the ground. "I'll get her some water."

"The grain scoop might make it easier to get the water to her mouth." Matthew pointed to the barn. "I left the bucket inside." As the neighbor took his cue, Matthew turned back to the filly. She'd taken another step his direction, ears pricked forward as if she assessed his offerings.

Lissa folded her arms across her chest, sulking. "Beginner's luck."

The filly stopped, nostrils flared as she sniffed the air, appearing to size up the sheriff. She edged closer.

"Nothing like a little bribery." Matthew inched toward the animal, talking in soothing tones and holding out his hand. The filly stood watchful, ears at attention and muzzle extended, as if to catch a whiff of the hay he carried.

Matthew winked at Lissa. When he drew close enough to touch the filly, he waited while she examined him with her muzzle, laughing when she stole a mouthful of hay from the flake he held. While the filly munched, Matthew rubbed her ears and neck and, with a single sweep of his fingers, slipped the smaller halter over her head. Lissa had never seen a smoother move.

The filly jerked, but Matthew gripped the headpiece, fastening the buckle to keep it secure. Clipping the lead to the ring at the bottom of her chinstrap and circling the hindquarters with another rope, he urged her toward the gate. With faltering steps, the filly followed, tempted by the hay Matthew held out to her. When at last Matthew lured the filly through the opening, he let her take a full mouthful.

"You've obviously done this before." Lissa dropped her arms to her sides, hands fisted, annoyed she couldn't get the filly to leave her mother. She had to give Matthew credit. "And you didn't even get dirty."

Grinning like an inebriated monkey, Matthew handed her the rope. "You can take her into the barn. Put a flake of hay in the manger at most." He gestured toward the pen. "I'll try to get the mare on her feet."

"Why no grain?" Lissa hadn't thought a starving creature could get too much to eat.

"If she's as hungry as I believe she is, grain could founder her or bring on a bout of colic." Matthew appeared to be lost in a bad memory, his face stern. Perhaps he'd lost another animal that way. "We don't want to lose her before we've finished a rescue."

"I'll see to it she gets fed and watered this weekend." The neighbor held his hat in his fingers. "I'd have been happy to take her if I'd known. Bennie thought he'd pulled a fast one when his old mare gave birth. He couldn't believe his eyes."

"Oh?" Lissa frowned. "Why?"

"Her daddy's a stallion from the Kiger mustang herd running on Steens Mountain. They're supposedly descended from runaway Spanish mounts when Coronado came looking for gold back in the 1500s. These Kigers are all related to one lone stallion."

"Runaways?"

"Yeah. The animals were cavalry stock for the Roman Empire originally, bred for their endurance."

"And this filly is one of them?" Lissa raised her eyebrows. The skinny creature didn't seem as if she were capable of enduring anything right now.

The old man continued. "In the early seventies, a wild horse specialist named Harding from the Bureau of Land Management discovered a cluster of duns living in a herd on Steens Mountain."

"I'm not following." She gave the man her full attention, a question forming on her lips. "Is the dun color unusual?"

"Not by itself." The man spread his hands in front of him, raising his palms. "But Harding was suspicious. He gathered a DNA sample and took it to the University of Kentucky for testing. Sure enough, the results showed a high level of markers for the original Spanish mustangs."

"Spanish mustangs?"

"They're different from the wild mustangs of the West. These can be traced back to Coronado's second voyage." The neighbor pointed. "See the stripe down her back?"

Lissa squinted at the horse's filthy coat. An almost imperceptible black line ran along her spine.

"And the stripes on her legs?" The man drew Lissa's gaze down the filly's fetlock. "Those markings are their trademark."

"Amazing."

The old man laughed. "And when she's cleaned up, she'll be a cinnamon dun. They all have different shades, from grey to red, with the dark manes and tails and the stripe down their spines. I think I remember her being cinnamon."

"How far away is this herd?" One more thing to add to her list of sightseeing destinations.

"They roam on Steens Mountain." He pointed to a large rise on the horizon. "Because they are thought to be the last of their kind, they're protected by the government. But the stallion doesn't care. If he sees a mare he likes, he comes a callin'."

"So this filly is something special?"

"She will be. Her new owner will get a nice animal."

Taking the bucket of grain from Matthew, Lissa watched as the filly's attention followed the exchange between them, her nostrils flaring as she sniffed the sweet hay. Lissa tugged on the halter, soliciting two steps before the animal balked. Progress.

"You've got her under control." Matthew dusted off his hands. "I'll work on getting the mare to stand while I'm waiting on the coroner. Will this make your trip today too late?"

"If I leave by one o'clock, I'll arrive home in time for dinner."

"Great. I'm sure we'll be out of here by then." Matthew joined the neighbor as he walked back toward the house.

Lissa started for the barn again, the filly in tow. Halfway across the gravel drive a sharp jerk on the rope threatened to pull her off her feet. She twisted around to find the horse bending her knees to lie down and roll.

The filly wiggled against the gravel on one side of her body before rolling over to the other, repeating the writhing gyrations Lissa had witnessed on the first roll. Stretching her knobby front legs, the yearling stood and shook the loosened debris from her hide, the material her coat picked up from the driveway flying in all directions. Chunks of gravel and bits of hairballs bombarded Lissa as a cloud of dust surrounded the filly.

"You are determined to get me dirtier, aren't you?" Lissa gritted her teeth. The little horse moved closer. Resolved to reach the barn, Lissa grabbed the halter and held on while she walked at the filly's side. She let go of the halter, the lead rope in her hand, and stopped to slide the door open on its track. She peered into the structure, allowing her eyes to adjust to the darkened interior. A cold, wet nose nuzzled the back of her neck. She jumped and found herself staring into a pair of surprised eyes. The filly snorted, baptizing her with what remained of the recent drink from the nearby water trough.

"Great. First the pants and now the shirt. If nothing else, you're thorough." She wiped her forehead and cheeks with the back of her hand. The filly nickered the low, rumbling greeting Lissa had come to know.

"If I understood whinny better, I'd say you were laughing at me." She stroked the filly's face, scratching along the wide, white blaze barely visible under the layer of dirt. "Or are you glad I now smell as bad as you?"

She led the filly into the nearby stall. Forking a couple of flakes of hay into the manger, she filled the bucket hanging in the corner with water. Slipping out, she secured the gate, snapping the lead rope off the halter, her memory playing in panoramic widescreen. When she'd lived on her girlfriend's family farm those last two years of high school before she enlisted, every morning began with barn duty. She'd loved the early morning routine—grooming, feeding, and lunging the horses in the paddock before turning them out to graze. Without that experience, she might not have qualified for this position.

The filly dropped to her knees again and rolled in the straw lining the floor. Returning to her feet, she shook off the dust, shedding bits of the hanging winter coat along with the dirt, but the scraggly remnants of balled horse hair still dangled in too many places.

"You're a mess, kid." Lissa jumped when the gate shook as the filly rubbed her shoulder against the rail, like a bear seeking a tree to scratch itself. "You're really itching, aren't you?"

When the horse rubbed her rump against the stall wall, Lissa wrestled with her need to drive home through the mountains today or to help the suffering animal. If she used this time to do an in-depth curry job, she would need a shower afterward—her second for the day—and her trip over the Cascades would be further delayed. She already had to do a load of laundry—she might as well be thorough.

When she'd helped her friend in high school, Lissa had been kicked once too often by entering a stall from behind and startling a horse. She picked up a curry comb and entered the pen from the adjacent stall, climbing on bales of hay. With the filly's attention fully on her, she dropped into the stall. Her trip home would have to wait. This little four-legged creature needed a beauty treatment, the grooming detail falling to the only human able to provide one—Lissa.

An hour later she still stood attending to her grooming detail when the barn door creaked open and Matthew entered. She patted the smooth hair on the withers, satisfied when only a smidgeon of dust popped up. The mane and tail had been combed out and most of the shedding hair had been loosened from the muddy hide. Her hands and arms were covered in dirt up to the elbows, her blouse a shade of grey, and her pants as furry as the horse's skin.

"Wow. She looks a lot better." Matthew leaned his arms on the top rail of the stall. "Can't say the same for you." He ducked when Lissa tossed the curry brush at him. "When she gets a little meat on her, she might even be pretty."

"I heard back from Dr. DeLorme." Lissa held up her phone.

"Is he coming soon?"

"No, he's out on a professional hunt and won't be available until Sunday afternoon. His assistant will provide emergency transport for the mare. He should be here in an hour. Dr. DeLorme will check the filly when he returns." Lissa cocked her head. "Will that be soon enough?"

"Yes. We don't have to wait for the vet's helper to get here. He has the authority to remove an endangered animal to medical care, and with this long Memorial Day weekend, we can't get a court order to move the filly until Tuesday anyway." He eyed Lissa's shirt and trousers, a crooked grin appearing at the side of his mouth. "I appreciate you getting into your work, but how were you planning to get home?"

"Can I sit on a feed sack?" She opened the stall door and slipped out.

"Only if you open a window and let air filter into the cab." Matthew snorted.

She raised an eyebrow at him. "Next time let me meet with the coroner."

"Sorry, not in your job description." Matthew gripped the stall gate and shook it, testing the latch. "This should hold her tonight and tomorrow."

Carrying the curry comb and brush to the wooden box where they had been stored, she picked up a rag near the workbench to wipe her arms and hands. "I'll stop by the hose outside and wash off as much as I can. Won't do much for the smell, but at least the dust will disappear." At Matthew's amused smirk, she rolled her eyes. "Or smear."

"As soon as you feel clean enough, let's look over the list." Matthew gestured for her to precede him out of the barn.

Outside, she splashed cold water from the hose attached to the barn on her hands and arms, then rinsed. She lifted a palm full of water to her face and rubbed at the splatters she could feel. "Is this any better?"

Matthew's mouth twitched. "Wait here." He jogged to his truck and returned a minute later, a washrag and a bar of soap in his hand. "I keep this with me for emergencies." He handed her the items. "And you, my dear, are an emergency."

"That bad, eh?" She dampened the rag using the hose nearest the barn and rubbed it against her cheek. The black spot clinging to the terrycloth when she withdrew it made her gasp. She rinsed the cloth out and, using the soap first, washed her face again. After three attempts the cloth came away from her skin clean. "I think this is as good as I'm going to get until I hit the shower at home."

"Definitely an improvement."

"My face feels like an ice cube, so this will have to do. I can't take any more hose water."

"You're fine." Matthew touched his nose. "Except for a spot right on the tip."

She rubbed where he pointed. At his nod, she returned the soap and cloth to him. "Thanks."

She was following Matthew to the truck when her phone pinged, signaling an incoming text. She scanned it. "Peggy Blake will take the filly."

"Great. She's got help at the rescue center now, a Marine who knew her son. He can load the grain and pack up the hay." Matthew stuck the keys in the ignition. "He'll probably help with the transport, too."

Lissa gasped. Now she knew why the name Foster Blake sounded so familiar. Kurt had considered Foster not only a hero, but his best friend. In the few emails she'd received, Kurt always told stories about his fellow Marine and the adventures they shared.

Eily had mentioned to Lissa that Kurt had returned to help out at the center not long after she'd come home. He'd become one of the inactive ready reserve, she said, a status that allowed him to work at the center like a civilian, but living with the knowledge he could be called up at any time.

Lissa couldn't imagine city-boy Kurt working at a horse rescue facility—mucking stalls and stacking hay. His experience with farm animals could be bundled in a shell casing. But maybe he'd needed a change from military life in the sandbox of Afghanistan as much as she'd needed solid ground under her feet after the Navy.

What would Kurt think when he discovered she'd sent him a dirty little filly? Or when she stood waiting by the barn as he drove up? If there was a more original way to get reacquainted, she didn't know what it might be. She couldn't wait for Tuesday.

CHAPTER FIVE

KURT'S STOMACH GROWLED. HE HADN'T EATEN since the noon meal, and now, with the sun sinking lower in the sky, the platform wagon had retreated across the field, ending their day of hunting. He and the others departed, eager to get to their lodging and grab some grub.

"You should have snagged a bigger lunch, man." Damon landed a playful punch to his shoulder. "I can hear your stomach complaining from over here."

"I forget I can eat. Patrolling in Kabul meant we carried a lot of MREs. They were nourishing, but for obvious reasons didn't overfill us." He made a face. "We'd trade items between guys, so we never ate the recommended daily requirement." He resisted rolling his eyes. "Dieticians designed those things so we'd have enough calories and balanced nutrition, but they forgot guys are guys."

"Then I'd say a home-cooked meal is going to taste mighty good tonight." Damon patted him on the back. "This guide's wife can cook."

"Great. I'm ready to eat." He opened the cab of his pickup and mounted the rifle on the gun rack, taking Damon's weapon and placing it on the second rung. "Those cabins they bunked us in were mighty inviting."

"Wait until you get there. The hot springs offers five-star accommodations." Damon climbed in the passenger side. "They serve refreshments in our rooms. We can snack and relax until dinner."

"My kind of vacation." Kurt slid into the driver's seat and started the engine. "All the amenities of a resort plus the chance to work off a little pent-up frustration killing vermin." A memory stopped him. "The pests in Afghanistan shot back, and nobody brought me hors d'oeuvres."

"Well, it's about time you learned to live, buddy." Damon adjusted his seat belt. "You've dodged enough bullets to last a lifetime."

Kurt threw the truck in gear. *If you only knew.*

Laughter reverberated from the rafters as Kurt walked through the buffet line behind Damon, scooping up spoonfuls of a pungent rice dish smelling of peppers, onions, and garlic. Beside it waited a platter of fried chicken and glazed carrots. Kurt's mouth watered.

"Told you the food would be good, didn't I?" Damon helped himself to the potato salad, piling a mound on his plate. "The hard part is deciding which of the salads to choose."

"I'm going to sample all three." Kurt spooned equal portions of the macaroni, potato, and three-bean salads around the edge of his plate. He landed a couple of chicken breasts in the middle, taking care not to knock the rice or the carrots over the side. "Those carrots remind me of a dish my mother made while I was growing up." He glanced up to find the hostess smiling at him.

"Your mother and I must share the same cookbook," she said.

Kurt appreciated her warmth. "Last time I ate these, I was home on an emergency leave for Thanksgiving." His commanding officer had sent him to recuperate from a nightmarish ordeal in the mountains of Afghanistan.

The woman frowned. "Did a member of your family get hurt?"

"Yeah, me." At her gasp, he continued. "My unit took fire from an ambush by Taliban soldiers."

"What happened?"

Kurt didn't mind retelling the story since she'd asked. His family had pried his experience out of him so many times he'd grown comfortable sharing it. "Two in my unit died, and I was listed as missing in action, presumed shot and wounded, and maybe dead. I holed up in a cave outside Kabul for nearly two weeks before I managed to escape one night and return to my unit."

"Oh, your poor family. Weren't they worried?"

"Mom was beside herself—she thought I might be dead." He'd called his mother from the hospital, letting her know he'd been rescued. At his CO's insistence, he'd hopped aboard the next freighter flying out of the region and arrived the night before the holiday, surprising her. "I showed up on Thanksgiving without telling them and shocked everyone." The meal together with his sisters, their spouses, and their children had proven to be what Kurt's aching soul needed. To them, their hero had returned alive.

The hostess grew quiet, the impact of his words dropping her jaw and widening her eyes. Moisture pooled along the edges of her eyelashes. "I'll bet that homecoming is a treasured memory."

Kurt couldn't have agreed more. "Mighty fine food, ma'am." He hefted his plate in thanks. "I appreciate all the work you put into this meal."

"My pleasure." She picked up an empty basket, checked the table with a cursory glance, and smiled at Kurt. "I'll be back with more rolls in a minute."

"I think I'll wait, then." Kurt stepped to the side so the man behind him could pass through, Damon with him. "Nothing I like better than fresh, homemade rolls."

The smell of baking bread sent his thoughts back to the Thanksgiving he'd come home. His mother had made a double batch of everything, having invited her widowed neighbor, Marshall, to join them. She'd spent the last seven years as a widow herself and believed the man would spend the holiday alone after a nasty fall and broken leg. Much to his mother's astonishment and Kurt's delight, Marshall's daughter, Lissa, came home on family leave to help her father cope.

Kurt smiled. He and Lissa Frye were immediately attracted to each other. Whether it was the military uniform, combat loneliness, or Lissa's natural good looks, he didn't know. But he'd spent every day of his leave after the holiday with her. They'd texted and emailed each other for more than a year before Kurt had been transferred to an isolated post. The seclusion played havoc with his ability to communicate. No doubt Lissa wondered what happened to him. He owed her an explanation.

In an odd turn of events, that Thanksgiving evolved into a romantic interlude for his mother and Marshall as well. The couple had married, making Lissa and Kurt stepbrother and stepsister. He'd learned through his mother that Lissa had resigned her commission when her tour ended. She'd returned three months ago seeking employment and apparently found a good position in a government training program. The hours were long, and she hadn't been to see them since she started. Mom had been sketchy about Lissa's whereabouts, but he believed she was on this side of the Cascades. Though he'd only been to his mother's new home once since returning from his tour of duty last month, he and Lissa were bound to cross paths sooner or later. He hadn't wanted to pry any details out of Mom for fear of appearing too eager. Still, Kurt wondered where Lissa had landed.

When the hostess returned, she offered the rolls to Kurt first. "I understand you hunters shot more than a thousand sage rats today."

"The number seems low." Damon frowned. "Kurt and I shot four hundred between us."

The woman smiled. "Not everyone is a good shot."

Kurt winked at her. "Aim is everything."

Something bad had happened.

Scrunched as far down as he could go behind the front seat of Bennie's old pickup, Jayden listened to the sounds of the sheriff's deputies moving around the yard. The man entered the house, the woman remained at the barn. Bennie didn't join them.

Jayden couldn't figure out where the rancher might have gone. After he'd descended the hill that morning, he'd scarcely made it to the barn when a vehicle appeared at the top of the drive. Peering from behind the tractor, he watched a man step out of the car and glance around. He stayed there for a few minutes surveying the scene, then climbed back in the driver's seat and left.

Relieved, Jayden had hollered for his friend. A knock at Bennie's door didn't get any response. He rushed out to the pasture and checked all the stalls in the barn. The man had to be here—his truck sat in the drive, the driver's side door open as if he'd been in a hurry to get out. Jayden couldn't figure out what happened. Where was he?

Not certain what he should do, he visited the filly, surprised at how awful she looked. Why hadn't Bennie brushed her? He whistled one more time for Duke, then climbed into the loft to check for Bennie. Up there, he heard another vehicle and dashed to the barn window. A green county truck pulled into the drive.

The *sheriff* had arrived?

Knees knocking and throat raspy, knowing he'd snuck away from his home this morning, Jayden hurried down the loft ladder, tiptoed to Bennie's pickup, and jumped behind the driver's seat to hide, pulling the door closed behind him. How had his simple plan for the first day of summer vacation turned upside down?

The cramped crew cab smelled like Bennie's tools, grease and gasoline melding together in a sort of mechanic-scented soup. Jayden took care not to bump anything that would set off a clang and signal he was in here. A tool on the seat poked at his back, and his ankle was sock deep in tire chains. Jayden stayed hunkered down, keeping low behind the driver's seat. He listened to the activity beyond the pickup, taking his mind off his confinement.

Outside the cab, boots crunched on the gravel. Jayden waited, anxious to spring should the sounds draw nearer. A door slammed, the sheriff's truck started up, and the pickup sputtered toward the main road. Jayden peeked through the back window of the cab as the truck disappeared. Only one person drove away.

He sat straighter, stretching his aching legs, and squinted around the yard to the barn. The other deputy tried to lead the filly out of the round pen. Jayden snorted as the little horse balked. She'd never liked halters or being led anywhere. Bennie had planned to train her during the winter, but Jayden doubted the filly had abandoned her stubbornness. This summer he would have worked with her, too. Now, though, his plans appeared cancelled.

The noise of approaching engines sent Jayden cowering to the rear floor of the cab. First one door, then a second, slammed. Footsteps on the gravel passed his hiding place. Once the sounds grew faint, he peered up over the seat. Two trucks sat in the driveway. The sheriff and another man Jayden recognized stood talking with the woman. The sheriff bribed the filly out of the pen and all of them disappeared. Jayden ached to escape the cramped quarters, but the squeak of the hinge as the pickup's door opened, or a sudden blast of wind slamming it closed, would give him away. He curled into a ball again, resigned to wait until they left.

The sound of another vehicle in the drive aroused Jayden's curiosity enough for him to raise his head and peer out the side window of the cab. A black van with the word *coroner* on the side pulled to a stop. A man stepped from the driver's side and met the sheriff at the door to Bennie's house. A second attendant moved to the rear of the van and pulled a gurney from the interior. Wheeling it over the gravel drive, the man followed the sheriff and the coroner into the dwelling.

Bennie Mueller was dead?

Jayden blinked at his tears, his summer plans spiraling downward like the trickle wetting his face. He brushed his moist cheeks and watched through the cab window. Within minutes the gurney appeared, this time with a black bag on top. Jayden cringed. Bennie really was dead. The attendant loaded the gurney into the van. Both he and the coroner shook hands with the sheriff, climbed into their vehicle, and left. Jayden sank down behind the seat, head in his hands. He'd have to go home. Nothing remained for him here.

Voices outside caught his attention. The neighbor—the man Jayden recognized as a frequent visitor to the ranch—and the sheriff approached. Jayden inched as close as he dared to the open window.

"I'll see that she's fed all weekend, Sheriff." The neighbor popped his hat on his head and reached for the door of his truck.

"Thanks. The vet said he'd do an examination late Sunday night or early Monday. If he gives the okay, Deputy Frye and the rescue center people will be here on Tuesday to transport her to their facility." The sheriff shifted position, his back to Bennie's truck.

"Sure a shame about Bennie." The neighbor shook his head. "Will they do an autopsy?"

"Have to. In cases of unattended death, the coroner always checks for cause."

"Good." The neighbor climbed into his cab and pulled the door closed. "Looks like Bennie left his windows down."

Jayden scrunched lower, making himself as small as he could against the floor. The door of the pickup squeaked open, and the sound of the sheriff rolling up the window screeched too close for comfort. He held his breath. If the sheriff glanced over the top of the seat, he'd see him. The pickup door slammed closed and he exhaled, holding his queasy stomach. The second window remained open.

"See you around, Sheriff." The neighbor started his engine. "Bennie wasn't a young man, but he always seemed healthy. His death surprises me."

"We never know when our time is up, that's for sure."

"But he was ready." The neighbor shifted gears. "He knew he was heaven-bound."

"I know. He used to teach me about Jesus in Sunday school." The sheriff chuckled, and Jayden's attention perked up. "Now you know I'm a young whippersnapper, don't you?"

"Never had any doubts." The truck engine whined. "I'll be here to meet the vet on Sunday."

Jayden listened, a plan developing in his head. When the sheriff and the lady left, he could go home and check on his mother. Maybe George would leave for another haul. If he didn't, Jayden could come back here and wait in the barn. No one would know where he was and he'd be safe. Alone. Hungry. But safe.

CHAPTER SIX

THREE HOURS, A LOAD OF LAUNDRY and a hot shower later, Lissa called Sorrel to the Suburban and drove west over the mountains to McKenzie Bridge. A mental image of the filly filled her thoughts, the curried coat, clean hooves, and shining mane a vast improvement over the sorry little horse she'd first seen. Left in the capable care of Bennie Mueller's neighbor, with Dr. DeLorme confirmed for a checkup tomorrow, the filly had whinnied at her when she left. Thanks enough for Lissa.

After the exhaustive morning coupled with the lengthy drive still ahead of her, Lissa yearned for a quick nap, but the satisfaction of knowing the filly no longer itched or suffered from hunger infused her weary body with new energy. The hot shower lessened her aches, and a short stop at a coffee kiosk for an espresso masked her fatigue. When she returned Tuesday morning, she could only hope the filly would give her a grateful hello. Not to mention Kurt. Wouldn't he be surprised?

The family ranch house stood in the shadows of twilight when Lissa pulled into her dad's driveway. Hunger needling her like a sliver under her thumbnail, she hoped she'd arrived in time for supper. A large, golden retriever-mix dog came bounding from the back of the house, barking like a sentry, announcing her arrival. Sorrel emitted a muffled woof beside her, ears forward and tail wagging on high speed in the passenger seat.

"Looks like you might have a friend waiting." Lissa parked the SUV and reached over to pat Sorrel on the head, attaching her leash. "This dog is called Goobers, and he thinks the place is his. So be on your best manners, okay?"

Sorrell whined, anxious to leave the vehicle, while Goobers circled like a sentry on patrol. Lissa heard a voice and glanced up at the tall silhouette of a man walking out from the shadows. He waved and called Goobers to him.

"Dad." Lissa had missed him. Though she and her father had dueled for many years, the sight of him now made her want to leap from the SUV and run into his arms. Lissa unfastened her seat belt and stepped from the cab. Sorrel followed, her exuberance tugging on the leash in Lissa's hand.

Her father hurried toward her, his gait brisk and determined. "How's my girl?" Marshall Frye wrapped his arms around her, grabbing her in a bear hug. After kissing her cheek, he held her at arm's length to study her face, warmth emanating from his smile. "Eily and I were beginning to think you weren't coming today."

"Almost didn't." Lissa tugged on Sorrel's leash and brought her to a sit. "Had a serious situation to attend to. Didn't check your texts, did you?"

"New-fangled technology gets me every time." He grinned. "Come inside and tell us the story." Her father gestured toward the house. "Eily's got supper on."

"I hope I didn't make you wait." Lissa followed him up onto the porch.

"No, she fixed a slow cooker of homemade stew. When she heard the SUV in the drive a minute ago, she put the biscuits in the oven. By the time we anchor your dog and wash, they'll be done."

"Sorrel can stay on the back porch with Goobers."

"Good. Let's go find Eily."

They walked through the living room, the familiarity of its furnishings haunting her like a museum. The pictures of Lissa and her sister Delaney still adorned the wall beside the portrait of their mother, Gina, in the same space they'd shared since Mom had died nearly twenty years before.

On the adjacent wall Eily had hung portraits of her four children and late husband, Kenny. The blend of families warmed Lissa.

Eily's respect for the lives she and Marshall lived before they found each other affirmed the love the woman carried within her.

Lissa looked over the array of smaller pictures hung around the portraits—photos of Eily's children's spouses and her grandchildren. A similar set of photos surrounded her sister Delaney's portrait. Her husband David and their twins, Lenna and Liam, smiled into the camera, the Pacific Ocean in the background.

She lingered on Kurt's picture. He stood for the camera, dressed in his Marine uniform, assuming the official military pose at attention. His blue eyes sparkled from the photo, his sandy hair almost colorless in the severe military cut he wore under his cover.

She still remembered the way Kurt noticed her when she'd first walked into Eily's living room that Thanksgiving so long ago. She'd been sent home on family emergency leave by her commanding officer to help her dad, who'd broken his leg. When she arrived, Dad had been invited to join the neighbors for dinner. Kurt also showed up on leave. The day evolved into a week of wonderful memories—a trip to the Oregon zoo in Portland, an excursion to the beach, and romantic dinners every night. How strange that he was now her stepbrother.

Lissa shook her head. Too weird.

"Welcome!" Eily dashed in from the kitchen, arms opened wide, catching her in a warm embrace. "I had hoped you'd be able to make it today. How's the new job working out?"

"I'm still training, but I think I'm going to like it." She smiled into Eily's loving face. "But I haven't escaped all the death and injury I witnessed in the Navy. We were called to a scene where an old man died alone in his bed. He's why I'm late."

"How awful." A timer dinged from the kitchen, and Eily held up one finger. "You're right on time for biscuits and stew. Come into the kitchen and we'll get dinner served."

"Sounds wonderful. I haven't eaten since breakfast."

"You must be starved." Eily handed her two oven mitts and pointed to the slow cooker. "You want to carry this to the table while I toss the biscuits into a basket?"

"Sure." Lissa lifted the steaming container and set it in the middle of the table. Three place settings waited at the edge, woven rectangles of yellow. Each bore a white plate and bowl, a rim of tiny, purple violas circling the dinnerware. Lissa suspected the dishes were new to Eily. She admired the woman for choosing plates in colors matching the flowers her father painted on the soffits above the cupboards. The purple and green morning glory vine decorating the ceiling's perimeter still amazed her. "I see you're still painting."

"I am." Her father brought glasses from the cupboard and added them to the place settings, his eyes narrowed in a tease. "You still drink well water, or are you wanting a stronger remedy for your thirst?"

"Water sounds wonderful, Dad." Her dry throat squeaked its approval.

"Pitcher on the top shelf."

Lissa opened the refrigerator and grabbed the graceful glass container, a bittersweet sting of memories waking her subconscious. Images of happy holidays blurred with more painful ones, formed in the wake of her mother's lingering illness, when the grip of cancer threatened the family's existence. How many times had she filled this decanter, hoping whatever it contained at the moment might ease the pain in her mother's eyes? Might wash away the bitter taste of the medicines the illness required? In the end only the glass pitcher remained, a poignant reminder of the family shattered under its care.

"Here we go." Eily's cheerful smile radiated in her face as she carried the hot biscuits to the table. Their aroma flooded the room, heightening Lissa's hunger.

"Wow. Eily, you're a wonder." Lissa set the water on the table, taking the chair her father offered her. "All I could think about while driving here was I'd be too late for supper."

"You arrived right on time." Eily's eyes glimmered. "Whenever a guest is coming here from a great distance, I try to plan foods that can simmer all day and then come together at the last minute. Like these biscuits. I turned on the oven about fifteen minutes ago, and I was only waiting for the sound of your car in the drive."

"Care to teach me your secret?" Lissa glanced across the table to where her father pulled out a chair for Eily. "I have trouble making a sandwich in time to eat with my soup."

"Practice is all you need." Eily smiled her thanks to her husband. "Of course, raising four kids might have helped, too."

Marshall laughed. "I'm sure it made a big difference." He sat between them and reached for each of their hands. "Father, for this food we give you thanks and for Lissa's safe arrival, we praise you. Amen."

Lissa glanced up as her father squeezed her fingers. "Thanks, Dad."

Reaching for their bowls, Eily ladled the stew into each one. "Did you know Delaney is coming tomorrow?"

"She's driving down this weekend?" Lissa stared, words lodged on her tongue. "It will be great to see her." Her sister worked as an accountant and rarely escaped her busy schedule filled with job, twin teenagers, and husband. "I hope she's not sacrificing family time to be here with me."

"No, David and the twins are coming, too." Though her dad didn't break his smile, Lissa sensed another emotion working behind his words. "She hasn't seen you since you arrived home from the Navy and left for your training program."

"I miss her." Lissa's throat closed, the tightness gripping her windpipe like a vice. "I'm touched she would sacrifice one of her days out of her long weekend to come visit me."

"I think she has matters to discuss with you." Her dad's sober face spoke volumes. He passed the container of biscuits to her. "She called it one-on-one sister time, I believe."

Lissa handed the basket to Eily and buttered the biscuit on her plate. Delaney wanted to talk. When her sister phrased her intent this way, she always had an ulterior motive. Years of experience sharing secrets with her older sibling made Lissa wonder what lay ahead. By the look on her father's face, the news wouldn't be welcomed.

Jayden stashed his bike and hid in the shadows of the trees as he approached his family's home. A paramedic truck sat in the driveway, a handful of men moving in and out of the entry. He hunkered down near a snowberry bush and watched through the white blossoms. Within minutes a gurney like he'd seen at Bennie's house rolled out, someone strapped on the bed. He strained to see in the growing darkness. Who were they taking away? Mom? His stomach roiled.

He gasped and stood, then stooped again, waiting to see what would happen. He fought tears, scrunching his eyes so he wouldn't sob. *If that man hit her. . .*

"Please find Jayden." His mother's voice sounded raspy, and a bandage covered her left eye. "He was supposed to go to the Mueller ranch today."

Jayden's fright kept him from running to his mother's side, but as he summoned his courage, George appeared in the doorway, handcuffs on his wrists, two sheriff's officers on either side. Jayden slunk back. If his mother was in the hospital and George in jail, he'd wind up in foster care. He'd heard other kids' stories at school. He stepped back into the protection the snowberry offered and waited.

The paramedic leaned over Jayden's mother and said something to her in a low voice. Another attendant joined the first and loaded the gurney into the waiting ambulance. With a slam of the doors, the men climbed into the cab and the vehicle pulled out of the driveway.

The two officers escorted George to their patrol car. His stepfather staggered, his hands fixed behind him, probably as smashed as he had been this morning. A string of nasty curses escaped the drunk's mouth when the larger policeman opened the patrol car's door and gestured for George to climb in.

"Nothing has happened to the no-good kid," George yelled. "He wanders off without permission. Probably snuck off to the horse ranch he loves. When he's hungry he'll come home." George shouted over his shoulder at the house. "He's probably in there right now stealing himself a sandwich. He's fine, I tell you. Fine!"

"We'll see about that." One of the officers pushed George's head down and into the patrol car, and a minute later, the officers left with Jayden's stepfather.

Jayden waited a few minutes to see if anyone else might be in the house. All seemed quiet, so he sneaked around to the back of the garage and crawled through a window. He made his way through the shadows of the dim interior, feeling the walls to the steps leading into the kitchen.

He turned the knob and the door opened. No one had thought to lock it. Jayden exhaled a sigh. At least he could find food here, making George's curses accurate. He wandered into the kitchen, stumbling over a couple of bottles on the floor. Flipping on the range hood's lowest light and peering around, he couldn't believe the scene before him. Bits of broken glass lay strewn across the counter, larger pieces shattered on the floor. A bowl of soup had overturned, its contents dripping over the edge of the sink. A box of crackers lay smashed against the backsplash. He gripped the edge of the counter and felt something wet and sticky. He drew back his hand and looked at the dark, thick liquid on his fingers. Jayden's mouth went dry. Blood.

Jayden couldn't stop his fears. He sank to the floor and let his horror convulse within him. What happened here? Had George and his mother fought over him? Was his mother seriously hurt? Could she die? He hiccupped, his breath labored. *I deserve to be locked up. Throw away the key. If I hadn't gone to the ranch, George wouldn't have hurt Mom.* If his mother couldn't be here, he didn't want to be here either.

A noise outside in the yard caught his attention. Jayden stood and snapped off the light over the range. He waited in the darkness, listening for the sound to come again. The eerie silence sent goose bumps over his arms. He didn't move. Couldn't breathe. An eternity passed while he lingered alone in the kitchen.

The noise came again—a muffled whimper on the back porch. Jayden stepped through the darkness like a tiger on the prowl, inching toward the side door. The whine sounded once more. Louder this time. Jayden peered through the door's window. A shadow lay slumped on the porch, two alert ears pointed toward him. A tail slapped against the timbers of the deck floor, the thump loud in the stillness.

"Duke?" Jayden had agonized over where Bennie's dog could be. But here he sat, wagging his tail and yipping. Jayden opened the door and the dog barked, his excitement in seeing Jayden contagious. Jayden knelt down and wrapped his arms around Duke, felt the bones of the dog's ribcage under the skin. Duke smelled different, like prairie grass and juniper, as if he'd been wandering a while. Bennie must have been dead a long time for

Duke to be so thin. "Did you follow me here, boy? Come in and we'll find food for both of us."

The dog trailed Jayden back into the kitchen, his front legs prancing in little half-steps.

"Stay."

The dog lay down, his head on his paws.

Jayden couldn't risk turning on an overhead light for fear of alerting a neighbor. He grabbed the push broom his mother used on the deck and shoved the broken glass and debris into a corner. He found the dust pan and cleaned up the pile he'd collected. He didn't want his mother to come home to the mess. Confident Duke wouldn't hurt himself now on glass shards, Jayden called the dog to him.

Opening the fridge, he stared inside. Milk and lunchmeat sat on the middle shelf. He spotted a carton of strawberries tucked in the vegetable drawer. Mom had been out shopping as she'd written in her note.

Hunger drove him as he grabbed the bread, meat, and cheese. Moonlight streamed in through the window, giving him enough light to see. He handed Duke a couple slices of bologna before he made his sandwich. He filled a glass with milk. An opened can of cat food caught his attention, and he dumped it on a plate for Duke. The dog slurped it up in one gulp.

A few minutes later, after eating a second sandwich, he remembered the berries and retrieved them. He held each berry by its stem, tipping his head back and nibbling at it like a man he'd seen in a history book his mom had shared with him. His mother would laugh at his antics if she were here. She wouldn't approve of him feeding Duke at the table, though. He shuddered. The image of his mother on the gurney shook him to his core.

Still hungry, he went to the pantry to see what else he could find. His mother's shopping trip yielded more treasures. She must've stocked the shelves before George unleashed his fury. Canned soup, crackers, and his favorite chips—sour cream and onion.

How much time had passed before Jayden came home to the grisly scene in the driveway? His absence must have fueled their fight. The weight of his actions settled on his heart like a blanket, and he trembled. Mom took the blame for his disappearance. How would he find out if she was okay? The nearest hospital was in Hines, thirty miles away. He had to find a hiding place until he could get there.

He opened a grocery bag and loaded up the chips, a box of crackers, and more cat food. He carried the bag to the fridge and dumped in a brick of cheese and several apples. With the bag in one hand and the milk carton in the other, he returned to where Duke lay waiting. Duke whined, his tail thumping in wild rhythm on the kitchen floor.

"You and I are going back to Bennie's house," Jayden whispered, though he didn't know why. "It's not safe here. If they release George, he'll come home angrier than ever, and I don't want to be around."

Jayden could depend on Bennie's house staying empty this weekend, but he couldn't assure his own home would remain secure with George out there. On Tuesday, the sheriff would return to collect the horse. Maybe things at home would simmer down by then. If not, he and Duke would find another place to hang out.

With that thought, Jayden stuffed the food and a flashlight in his backpack. He opened the door to the porch, calling for Duke, and slipped into the night, making his way back to the bike waiting in the snowberry bush. Full for the first time today, his stomach would be quiet. If he could put aside his fears, he might sleep, though his mother's absence reinforced his guilt. He knew the direction he needed to go. He'd escaped there many times before.

The filly nickered a welcome when Jayden entered the barn with Duke. The trip had taken longer in the dark, but with Duke at his side and a full moon in the sky, Jayden had felt safe. The dog yipped outside the stall while Jayden climbed on the gate and scratched the horse's ears. She nuzzled his hand, and he sighed. "Sorry, girl. No carrots tonight. Maybe I can find a few tomorrow."

He hopped off his perch and called for Duke to follow him. When Jayden reached the ladder to the loft, he frowned. The rungs, spaced a foot apart, went straight up the wall. A dog couldn't climb them. He searched for a tool he could use—nothing. If he left Duke down here, the dog would whine and bark, giving away his hiding place. But remaining on the main floor, he ran the risk of being discovered.

Jayden peered inside the stall at the end of the barn, where several bales of hay sat in a stack, creating a ready supply when Bennie had needed fodder in a hurry. Loose hay filled one corner at the back, where wayward strands had escaped the opened bundle. Jayden grabbed the knife Bennie kept hanging on a hook and snapped the twine off the top bale. After dropping two flakes to the floor of the stall, he opened the gate and called Duke to join him. He shook the hay loose, making it appear as if the bale had already been opened.

Jayden shoved the dried grass around and soon had a comfortable bed on which to lie. A horse blanket he found in the tack room would keep them warm, though it smelled of animal sweat. Jayden re-entered the stall, closed the gate, and slipped into the layer of hay with Duke. Within minutes he and Duke were toasty, and they wouldn't be discovered behind the solid stack of baled hay across the width of the enclosure.

His mother's condition hung like an anchor on Jayden's mind, but the events of the day had taken their toll. The last sounds Jayden remembered hearing before his eyes closed were the barn owls flapping their wings in the rafters.

CHAPTER SEVEN

LISSA DROPPED HER TRAVELING BAG ON the floor and marveled at the lavender walls and the colorful floral bedspread. When she was ten she'd insisted her bedroom be purple, and her tolerant father had painted the daring color on three of the walls. The fourth was a pale lime green, a suggestion made by her mother. Lissa had loved how the vibrant colors enhanced the bedspread design and made a nice place to hang pictures. The unchanged room surprised her, and she smiled when Eily knocked. "Fresh paint? Same colors?"

"Your dad repainted when you told us you left the Navy." Eily carried fragrant towels into the adjacent bathroom before stopping in the doorway. "You're most likely to be the one who visits us. I found the bedspread. It's different than the one you had before, but—"

"Not nearly as faded." Lissa laughed. "I gave my bedroom a workout when I lived here."

"I'm so glad you're home." Eily's eyes glimmered. "You've no idea how much your father missed you."

"Thanks to you, I think I do." Lissa remembered the Thanksgiving she'd met Eily. The woman's heartfelt advice led to the reconciliation she and her dad needed after years of mistrust and hurt. "I can never repay you for helping me connect with my dad again and for making me see we both needed to forgive."

"Heartache makes people do things they wouldn't if circumstances were different." Eily put her arm around Lissa's shoulders and gave her a squeeze. "Good night. Marshall and I go to bed early. Spring is here and the garden calls."

"I'll see you in the morning." Lissa hefted her luggage onto the bed. "Oh, Eily?"

Her stepmother popped into the doorway, a question on her

face.

"Will Delaney and her family stay the night?"

"Yes. We converted her old room into a guest room. Kurt uses it when he visits. And the kids like to sleep in the den."

Lissa couldn't resist the opportunity to confirm what she suspected. "Where did Kurt land when he came stateside? You mentioned he came home to help his friend's mother?"

"He did. I haven't seen you to tell you, have I? In fact, he's probably not far from where you are. The place is called the Herrick Valley Rescue Center outside Buchanan. Ever heard of it?"

Lissa unzipped her bag before answering. "I believe I have."

"See you tomorrow, then."

The sound of the tractor growling its protest in the garden roused Lissa's curiosity as she lounged in her covers a little longer than she normally would on a Sunday. She rose up on an elbow and peeked through the mini-blinds. Daybreak colored the horizon, the early morning hues golden, as the sun climbed above the foggy shroud veiling the hills.

Her dad's tall frame sat on the tiny seat, hunched over the wheel of the machine, its engine droning as he tilled the wintered clods into fine, fertile soil. After years of conditioning, adding manure and other fertilizers, this garden yielded to the man who worked it, every seed coerced from its slumber. Few resisted the touch of the experienced gardener.

Lissa peeked at her clock, shaped like a yellow sunflower with a smiling face and green leaves for hands—another reminder of her early life here with her family. The clock's curly tendrils pointed to the six and the twelve. Groaning, she fell back against the pillow and pulled the blanket over her face. She'd thought she left the Navy disciplines behind her. Dad never let daylight grow between him and his need to nurture.

She lay there, letting an hour drift by as she dozed, listening to the tractor do its duty. Suddenly the engine cut and the silence woke her. She sat up, stretched, and grabbed her robe, tiptoeing to the shower.

Once dressed, she brushed her hair, the mane of curls exploding around her face as it dried. The smell of coffee wafted from the kitchen and the scent of cinnamon trailed in with it, telling her breakfast would be soon. She decided to leave the unruly tendrils free today. The back porch screen slammed and a dog barked. Sorrel's excited yip echoed as Lissa hurried downstairs.

"Morning, Lissa." Eily's smile warmed her face. "I've made sticky buns for breakfast."

"Sounds wonderful." Lissa glanced around for signs of Sorrel. "Let me take my pooch out for a morning run and I'll be right there."

"Your dad already let her out to run with Goobers in the garden." Eily nibbled her lower lip. "I hope it's all right with you. I'm afraid Sorrel got a little dirty."

"A lot dirty, you mean." Dad appeared at the kitchen doorway. "She loves her new companion, and Goobers did his best to entertain his company."

"Let me guess." Lissa narrowed her eyes. "Took her to the manure pile?"

"'Fraid so." Her father shrugged. "She'll need a bath later today."

"Where is she now?"

"Running in the yard with Goobers."

Lissa groaned and shook her head. "She won't want to go

home."

"Fine by me." Dad stepped up to the kitchen sink and washed his hands. "As long as it keeps you here, too."

"Nice try." Lissa walked to where he stood and landed a light punch on his shoulder. "But I have responsibilities I promised to fulfill."

"Try telling that to Goobers." Her dad gestured toward the table, where Eily had set a pan of rolls. "He hasn't had this much fun since he chased Eily's cat under the house."

"Now there's another story." Eily brought the coffee pot and sat at the table. "Let's eat these before they get cold and hard."

An hour later Lissa was placing the last plate in the dish drainer when she heard tires crunch on the gravel driveway. Voices and squeals blended with the excited barks of the two dogs. Car doors opened and banged closed. "Sounds like the brood has arrived."

"We finished in perfect time." Eily rinsed her sponge under the faucet and set it on the sink's edge to dry. "Thanks for your help with the dishes."

"My pleasure. Thanks for a wonderful breakfast."

"Grandma?" A young girl's voice called from the living room, followed by the sound of rapid steps heading their way. "Grandma, we're here." A girl about Lissa's height bounced through the doorway.

Lissa gasped. When had her little niece transformed into a long-legged teen? "Lenna?"

The twin's bright smile greeted her, a tumble of golden curls falling around her shoulders almost to her waist. No longer the skinny kid with braces, Lenna had a figure with graceful curves and a tiny waistline. "Aunt Lissa! You're here, too." The teen wasted no time crossing the kitchen to wrap Lissa, and then Eily, in delightful bear hugs. "Grandma Eily!"

Behind her, David and Delaney appeared. A young man Lissa

guessed to be Liam walked in with her father. Her nephew stood shoulder to shoulder with her dad, his curly, blond hair darkened to a shade of golden brown.

"Liam." Her nephew gave her a quick hug, and Lissa stood in stunned disbelief. What a difference two years had made.

She searched David's face, puzzled by the deep lines furrowing his brow, his expression a storm of worry. She'd witnessed the same visage in her father last evening when he spoke of Delaney and her reason for a visit.

Delaney opened her arms and caught Lissa in a warm embrace. Her blonde hair, full and thick like their mother's had been, fell in delicate curls around her face. Her eyes glimmered as she met Lissa's gaze. "It's been too long. I'm so glad you're close enough for a visit now and then."

"Me too." Lissa gestured toward the twins. "But who are these kids, and what have you done with my niece and nephew?"

"They've grown up." Delaney smiled at her children. "They entered high school this year."

"Unbelievable." Lissa shook her head. "I hardly recognized them."

"We haven't changed, Aunt Lissa." Lenna's mischievous smile spread across her face. "We're still the ornery kids who teased you when we were little."

Lissa pointed at her niece. "Now I know who you are."

She focused on her sister. Delaney appeared relaxed, no hint of anything amiss in her demeanor. The stress of working long hours and raising a set of twins hadn't left a mark. If anything, her sister's beauty had only deepened with the passage of time.

Lissa darted another glance at David. His pensive expression remained unchanged—a smile without warmth and eyes without their twinkle. Lissa shoved her fears aside and prayed the reason for this visit didn't bring with it troubling news.

Eily broke the tension. "Do you have luggage? Delaney, you and David can have your old bedroom. Kids, Grandpa will help you unfold the hide-a-beds tonight, so why don't you put your things in the den?"

Liam and Lenna scrambled past each other, heading to the door outside. David followed them, a quick gaze over his shoulder at Delaney catching Lissa's eye. A silent message passed between the couple, but Delaney remained all smiles, blowing her husband a kiss as he disappeared.

"It's so good to see you." Delaney grabbed Lissa's hand and pulled her to the living room. She gestured to a recliner, but Lissa waved her off, content to perch on the ottoman so she could remain closer to her sister. Delaney sat instead. "I wanted to come down when you first returned home, but work and the family wouldn't let us get away." She clasped her hands in her lap. "You'd think I'd have found one weekend in three months to get here."

"You're here now. That's what's important." Lissa placed her hands over Delaney's. "Thank you for wanting to see me. I felt like a castaway on an uncharted island when I came back. Fifteen years in the Navy transformed me into a stranger in my own country."

"I'm sure things have changed a lot." Delaney leaned back in the chair.

David returned, carrying a valise and an overnight bag. "I'll put these in the bedroom, honey, and then the kids and I are going to have a look at your dad's garden."

"Is anything up?" Delaney asked her husband. "Surely nothing's above ground?"

Lissa lifted her hands and made a space of three inches between them, as if plants grew there. "The dirt's up. All five acres of it. Before I had even climbed out of bed, Dad was plowing the top soil into furrows."

David rolled his lips inward, fighting a grin. "And your dog and

Goobers are having a grand time running all over it, digging and rolling in the mud."

"Yuck! How will I get her home tomorrow?" Lissa winced at the thought of all the work needed to get Sorrel clean enough to ride in the Suburban. "She's usually such a little lady."

"Not anymore." David winked at his wife. "Cinderella has turned into a field mouse."

Lissa made a face at her brother-in-law. He shrugged, an amused grin on his face, and left the room. A few minutes later, Lissa heard David and the children outside, their voices mingled with her father's laughter as he whistled for the dogs.

Lissa focused on Delaney. "Nothing like adventures at Grandpa's farm."

"The kids don't get to see him nearly as much as they'd like. Even though they're teenagers, they still adore Dad. All those summers when he took them to the fair—he always made time for their activities." Delaney's voice went soft, her face melancholy. "Mom missed so much by dying young."

Lissa sensed the change in Delaney's mood. "It'll never make sense, what happened." The same persistent dread poked at her, wondering what news Delaney brought to share. She didn't want to imagine trouble, so she pressed forward to a happier topic. "You haven't changed a bit. Tell me about the kids and all they're doing."

For an hour, Delaney related events of the time they'd been apart, catching Lissa up on all the Mathews family had accomplished—the children's ice skating trophies, the Hawaiian vacation, the changes in Delaney and David's jobs. When she finished, she offered Lissa a wistful smile. "We've certainly led a busy life."

Lissa nodded, waiting on edge, certain there was more. "Lots of great family memories."

"But all of this could change."

"Why?" Lissa's pulse quickened, the throbbing in her ears persistent. This was it. Delaney had news she'd waited to share, news that could change everything. "You and David seem very happy. Is one of the twins sick?"

"Not the twins." Delaney wrung her hands, shoulders slumped, head down. "Me."

Lissa scooted to the edge of the ottoman, drawing closer to her sister. "Delaney, what's wrong? Tell me, please."

"I had a cyst on my ovary." Delaney raised her gaze to meet Lissa's. "With Mom's history, the doctor pressed me for a genetic screening and a blood test—a CA-125."

"What's the testing supposed to show?" Lissa's throat tightened, Delaney's words taking on black storm clouds and menacing thunderbolts in her mind.

"It identifies women at risk for ovarian cancer."

Lissa's stomach dropped. She hesitated before posing her next question. "What were the results?"

"I'm a carrier for the gene. The doctor performed a laparoscopy and found no evidence of lingering material after the cyst healed."

"This is good, isn't it?" Lissa's pounding heart slowed.

"Yes and no. The cyst and Mom's history mean the doctor will insist on a blood test every six months. David and I decided I should have my ovaries removed, since we're not having any more children."

"Sounds radical."

"Not when you weigh the risk factors." Delaney closed her eyes as if the thought pained her. "I remember how Mom died. I don't want Liam and Lenna to endure the same trauma, if I can avoid it."

Lissa flinched. Painful memories surfaced like the pods of humpback whales that had played havoc with her Navy vessel, threatening to drive the ship off course. Nothing would bring back her mother, but in the aftermath of her death, even fifteen years later, Lissa struggled to remain on track, haunted by those final days of her mother's life. When the humpbacks withdrew, her ship sailed on. Would Lissa ever find placid waters on which to live her life? Delaney and David had made the right choice. Liam and Lenna deserved a better future than the past their mother, along with Lissa, had endured.

"When will you have the procedure?"

"Probably after the kids are out of school. They're both good to help at home, and I'll need assistance for a while."

"I can come." Lissa glanced around for her purse. "Let me get my calendar."

"Not necessary, but thanks." Delaney's smile faded. "But you need to see a doctor, too."

"Why?" Lissa hadn't known her heart could fit in her throat, but there it throbbed anyway.

"Unmarried women with the gene can be at higher risk than those of us who have borne children. The hormones of pregnancy somehow reduce the risk of developing the disease. As do oral contraceptives." Delaney grew more sober. "As my single sister, and our mother's second daughter, that's you."

This couldn't be happening. Lissa had left the Navy with a list of unfulfilled dreams, resigning her commission and joining the reserves. She'd intended to begin the next segment of her life— wishing for a mate and planning for a family. God heard her prayers for months before she made the move. A test for ovarian cancer never made her list. The wrong results could detour all she'd come home to find.

In her mind, she heard the fragments of her future shattering like bits of glass. Hadn't God listened? "Are you sure?"

"Of what? Your need to be tested?" Delaney nodded. "Yes. But you have so much of Dad in you, from your hair color to the set of your jaw. Maybe these genes bypassed you completely." Delaney touched her shoulder. "And you haven't had any problems, have you?"

"None."

"Then there's no rush. But a sudden onset of pain in your side or menstrual problems should send you to a doctor as soon as you can arrange it." Lissa sat up straighter, her body tense. "Not exactly what I expected to hear from you. But thanks for warning me."

"Think about it. Okay? You're important to me." Lissa couldn't respond. She loved Delaney. Appreciated her concern. But the thought of being tested for a disease that still gave her night terrors snatched away the words she wanted to say.

"Thank you for telling me. I only wish I was more ready to hear it." Lissa stood and hugged her sister. Over Delaney's shoulder, Lissa eyed Kurt's picture on the wall. A passerby had bumped the frame, causing the photo to list to the right, as out of kilter as her dreams.

CHAPTER EIGHT

DUST MOTES DANCED IN THE CROSSBEAMS of sunlight probing the shadows of the loft above Jayden, their erratic dips and darts creating a fairylike wonder as he sat in the hay munching an apple. The increasing intensity of the rays suggested morning had broken hours earlier, but he and Duke had slept through it, the peace of the barn wrapping him like a welcomed hug. His belly growled, and he opened the bag of food beside him, searching for more to fill him. Cheese and crackers sounded good.

Beside him, Duke whined and wagged his tail.

"Gotta go, buddy?" Jayden rose with caution, peering around the barn's interior. No sounds met his ears, except for the occasional bump of the filly in her stall at the other end of the building. He crawled beneath the rail and called Duke to follow him.

At the back of the barn, he pushed open the trap door Bennie had once kept for his chickens. The open range beyond the ranch's borders harbored too many critters seeking a free dinner and over time the varmints had claimed the unsuspecting hens from their roosts. Bennie had believed replacing the flock was futile.

Duke burst into the sunshine and zeroed in on a nearby tree, taking care of business. Not ready to give up his freedom, he meandered along the back pasture, nose to the ground, sniffing as he went.

Jayden shuffled to the house, circled around to the open-air back porch, and after climbing the steps, found the hidden key for Bennie's door. He shivered in the cold interior, whether from knowing the house's owner had died or from the lack of heat, he wasn't sure. A lingering odor filled the rooms. Jayden wanted to hurl.

He used the bathroom not far from the rancher's bedroom, telling himself Bennie wouldn't begrudge him a flush or the use of soap and a towel. The nearer he drew to the bedroom, the stronger the odor became—the smell of death. Goose bumps on his arms, he hurried to the kitchen. Duke barked outside on the porch, and Jayden let him in.

He opened the pantry, searching for dog food. Bennie always kept a supply on hand for Duke, but now its location remained a mystery. In his search Jayden found lots of Bennie's favorites, but nothing for the dog. The cat food Jayden fed him yesterday might not be best for the dog long term.

Jayden wandered out of the kitchen back to the porch, ignoring Duke, who sat there, looking expectant. He fought the tears besieging him as he walked past Bennie's old rocking chair. Here he and the old man had sat for hours, the open range beyond the ranch offering a host of wildlife to watch on hot afternoons. They drank root beer Bennie made, sometimes needing to consume more than one when the caps popped off in the heat. Bennie's homemade brew tasted better than any drink Jayden had ever had from a store.

Jayden had listened when Bennie read his Bible out loud. Told him what a fine man Jayden's father had been. "Men come in two varieties—the good and the bad. Your dad was one of the good guys. He wanted you to be one of the same. Always remember, Jayden, who you are is a choice you make. Don't blame others for your problems. Fix them."

Jayden wiped the tears from his cheeks and continued his search, Duke's whine a reminder of why he'd come.

Rummaging through the shelves of garden tools and plumbing supplies, Jayden found nothing edible. At the end of the enclosure he spied a closet and opened the door. Duke barked, his tail wagging in excitement, the message clear. A shelf lined with canned dog food sat at eye level, and a garbage can full of kibble waited on the floor.

"This will taste better than cat food." Jayden filled the dog's bowl, and Duke plunged his nose into the crunchy mixture and ate in earnest. Jayden picked up the other bowl and carried it to the kitchen for water.

When he passed the window, a glint of sun on steel caught his eye. A pickup chugged down the driveway. He left the water dish, slipped back to the porch, and locked the door he'd come through. He needed a place to hide—quick. A washer and dryer sat at the other end of the porch, and Jayden hid between the dryer and the wall.

Duke barked at the sound of tires on gravel, bounded down the steps, and raced around to the front of the house. Whoever had arrived wouldn't suspect anyone else was here with the dog outside. Duke always greeted visitors. Showing up today only meant he'd been chasing jackrabbits yesterday.

Jayden waited, his hideaway within hearing range of the visitor.

"Hey, Duke." The neighbor's voice reached Jayden's ears. "Where you been?"

Loud, excited howls answered the man.

The neighbor laughed. "Are you hungry, fella?"

Jayden scrunched back into the corner, pulling a clothes hamper in front of himself. One of Bennie's jackets hung above. Jayden yanked it down, letting the heap look as if it'd fallen over the hamper.

Footsteps creaked on the porch. Jayden listened as the neighbor moved tools and clinked flower pots. "I don't see anything here for you to eat."

Duke barked again, his feet scratching along the linoleum as he raced up and down the narrow aisle. His excitement threatened the safety of Jayden's hiding spot.

"You want to go home with me, Duke?" The neighbor sounded close.

Jayden froze. *No. Don't take the dog. Please.* He held his breath—he couldn't jump up and call Duke back. *Run away, Duke. Don't go with him.*

"I got to go feed the filly, and then we'll see about taking you home." The pad of footfalls grew fainter as the neighbor left the porch.

Duke came trotting back to the dryer, sniffing his way down the aisle. When Jayden peeked out from under the jacket, Duke sat by the hamper, his tongue hanging out in a doggy grin.

"Good boy." Jayden patted the dog's head before giving the command Duke always understood, one that would send him on a wild chase across the field. "Horse, Duke, horse! Herd!"

The dog hesitated for a moment before racing away. Certain Duke was tearing across Bennie's pasture as he had watched him do a thousand times before, Jayden relaxed, the barking growing faint. Jayden waited, a smile on his face. As the dog hunted for horses to move and with no animals to pester, Duke would be gone a while.

A few minutes later, footsteps sounded again. "Hey, Duke!" The neighbor called and whistled. No answering bark. "Confounded dog."

A pickup door squeaked open and banged closed. The engine started, and Jayden heard the tires roll on the gravel. He stayed quiet for several minutes until he heard Duke barking again. Jayden smiled. He wasn't alone.

He eased himself out of the hideaway, hunger gnawing at him as he walked back into Bennie's kitchen. He filled Duke's water dish and carried it to the porch. Duke had returned and lay on the cracked porch linoleum, panting from his run, his huge brown eyes fastened on Jayden.

"You want the canned stuff, don't you?" Jayden grabbed a can and spooned a large glob into Duke's dish. "You can have the rest of this later, boy."

Jayden returned to the kitchen to wash his hands in the sink and spotted a brown paper bag on the counter. *Save for Jayden* was written on the outside. Peeking in, Jayden found his favorite cookies, snack packets of cheese and crackers, and a jar of peanut butter. Bennie had anticipated the boy's return when school was out and evidently had bought the snacks they always shared. Jayden's lip quivered at the man's thoughtfulness.

At the ranch last summer, he'd finish his work at the end of each day and bid the rancher good night. Jayden insisted on biking home, even though Bennie offered him a ride. The last thing Jayden needed was to show up at his parents' house in a stranger's truck—not when his stepfather hunkered down in the living room, finishing off bottles of booze like they were cartons of orange juice. Each evening Bennie offered him another sandwich or a piece of leftover chicken, and Jayden refused, citing the dinner waiting for him. At the last minute he'd give in with a huge sigh. Always a sigh, as if he couldn't eat another bite, but he couldn't refuse Bennie either. He acted as though he made the sacrifice to make the old man happy.

Thanking him for the food and promising to return soon, Jayden would head out as if going home. He'd circle back to the barn, climb to the loft, and snuggle into the hay. The family of barn owls busied themselves in the top rafter, keeping watch, while the peaceful, shuffling lullaby of the two horses feeding below soothed Jayden to sleep, his belly full of Bennie's food. He drifted into dreamland, and the hay cuddled him through the night.

When dawn broke, Jayden would climb down the ladder and work his way around the back side of the barn to the nearby field. After a few minutes of skirting the hillside, pushing his bike, he would arrive at the top of the driveway, refreshed after his night of sleep, and ride down. To the passerby he appeared to be visiting. Not an early riser, Bennie always greeted him with a warm smile, asking Jayden to join him for a muffin before putting the boy back to work.

Jayden's mother often commented how generous Bennie was to open his home to a youngster and that she was glad Jayden had such a wonderful place to spend his summer hours. She never questioned his absence. He spent the summer happy, enjoying great times. Whenever he came home, though, his stepfather berated him for his absence, his face set in a perpetual frown, as if he didn't approve of Jayden's freedom.

Shaking off the memories and biting back the tears, Jayden reached into the paper bag. He'd have the cheese and crackers now and carry the rest of the items to his hiding place. He sat at the kitchen table and enjoyed the feast, thinking of all the times Bennie had fed him. Jayden's heart ached for his friend, no longer here to help him. This small token of Bennie's affection made the loss harder to bear.

George always needled Jayden for crying, but here no one witnessed his tears. And he needed to cry. To talk to a friend who understood his pain. His mother's condition remained unknown— her whereabouts as well. Bennie was dead. Only Duke provided a link between last summer and this one.

He wiped his eyes with the back of his hand, picked up the bag, and hustled to the barn. Tomorrow the veterinarian would stop by and examine the filly, so Jayden needed to find a better place to hide than the stall. What would he do about Duke? The dog loved to greet anyone who came by. If the neighbor dropped in again, he'd wonder who'd fed the dog.

Jayden climbed the ladder to the loft and positioned himself in a corner where he could watch everything below, but not be seen.

Duke whined at the bottom of the ladder, circling like a buzzard—a dead giveaway if anyone was watching.

Jayden crossed the loft floor, sidestepping the holes that allow hay to drop to the feeders in the stalls below. He paused above the filly's stall, watching her munch on the feed the neighbor left her. He dodged bales until he was over the stall where he and Duke had slept last night. He lowered himself through the opening and landed on the top bale, then slid off the back to the nest he had left behind. The stacked hay made a perfect place for a secondary escape out of the loft if needed.

Duke barked and crawled under the stall door, dancing in little circles now that Jayden stood back on the ground. He smiled at the dog. "Let's go outside for a while, boy."

He led the way to the end of the barn where the filly waited. She nickered at him, thrusting her head over the stall rail. Jayden stopped to scratch her ears. Her muzzle, inches from his face, stretched the short distance and gave him a wet kiss, her whiskery chin tickling him. Giggling, he wiped the moisture away, then headed out the barn door and picked up a stick lying near the entrance. He threw it as far as he could into the field and Duke raced after it, barking. The dog paused long enough to retrieve the stick before hurrying back with the prize in his mouth.

Glad for an activity to pass the time, Jayden tossed the stick across the pasture again and again, while Duke kept up the pace, never tiring of the game.

The sun stood high in the sky when Jayden heard a vehicle rumbling down the drive. He called Duke and together they hurried to safety behind the barn. Jayden peered around the corner, trying to glimpse the car or its driver.

The pickup rolled to a stop beyond the round pen, the words *Harney County Sheriff* painted on the side. Hatless, the deputy climbed out, his hand cupped over his forehead as he surveyed the property.

Jayden crept to the chicken door he and Duke had used that morning and slipped into the dimness of the barn. Duke's tongue lolled as he stayed on Jayden's heels, following him instead of racing out to greet the visitor. Jayden petted the dog, holding his jaw to keep him from barking. Together they waited in the chicken pen, listening for the deputy's footsteps.

The front barn door creaked open, the filly's whinny greeting the man. Duke wiggled in Jayden's grasp, but he wrapped an arm around the dog and held him close. Footsteps echoed the length of the building, the beam of a flashlight peeking into stalls and trailing along the ceiling. Soon the visitor's footfalls retreated, the door of the barn sliding closed on rusty hinges. The engine sounded, and Jayden relaxed as the motor purred away from the barn, the gravel drive giving telltale assurance the deputy had left. Jayden released his grip on Duke.

"I'm going to sleep upstairs tonight, boy. I'm taking our food with me. I'll be down to feed you in the morning. Okay?" Jayden held the dog's head in his hands, loving the way Duke stared back at him, his chocolate brown eyes trained on Jayden's face. "You can lie down here and keep watch."

He picked up the food sack and climbed the bales to the hole in the ceiling, eager to disappear from sight. He slid through and put the sack on the loft floor when Duke leaped through the opening, wagging his tail and wearing a doggy grin.

"Duke, you did it!" Jayden wrapped his arms around the excited dog, rolling with him on the loft floor. Then Jayden rose and poked his way to the far corner, where the cold air was blocked by two structural walls and a ten-foot blockade of baled hay. Gathering loose silage from around the loft, he carried mound after mound to the corner and made a soft nest for the two of them. Stashing the food sack along the wall, he reached in and grabbed an apple.

Duke sniffed along the floorboards, exploring the new level. After circling the expanse three times, he appeared at the end of the bales, surveyed the area, and with a sigh plunked down on the bed of hay.

Satisfied he and the dog were safe, Jayden lay down beside Duke. Darkness would soon creep in. Jayden wanted to be rested and ready when daybreak hit, awake before any visitors might surprise him again.

Lissa pulled into her driveway Monday night, the sky darkening as the sun made its final descent into the western horizon.

Sorrel barked, tail wagging at high speed, exuberant at being home again. Her burnished copper coat shone, the mud and manure she'd picked up at Dad's farm washed out of her fur and the burrs brushed out of her tail. No longer dirty, the sorrel color once again matched her name.

Lissa fingered the dog's feathery ears, soft after the bath. "You had a good time at Dad's, didn't you?"

Sorrel whined, her tongue dipping in and out of her mouth as she waited on Lissa, paws beating out a rhythm on the front seat.

Lissa laughed. "Okay, go do your thing, girl." She opened the door and hopped to the ground, the dog on her heels.

As if she'd been set free from prison, Sorrel barked and disappeared around the house.

Lissa grabbed her bag from the Suburban and hauled it to the front door. Once she stepped inside, the quiet of the empty house echoed like a tomb after the busy, laughter-filled warmth of her father's home, the noises of the teens and the adults mingling together in her honor. The special Memorial Day service with family had uplifted her—the moving mix of praise songs and expository preaching notably missing in her life. Lissa needed to find a church in Hines. Too many weekend emergency calls for work had kept her from attending services.

Delaney's sobering news haunted her the entire journey as she drove over the mountains. The reality of a repeat performance of their mother's illness chilled her, as if the disease licked at the heels of the two daughters Gina left behind. Lissa thought she'd buried the images of her mother's death, but the woman's grey pallor and pain-filled eyes troubled Lissa once more. Scenes from the hospital where her mother lay dying jumped into the horrors of her mind. As if it were yesterday, the nasal tube once again helped her mother breathe and the pulse oximeter on her index finger checked her pulse. In the blink of a memory Lissa returned to sixteen—holding her mother's withered fingers, screaming at her father not to withdraw the life support, and running from the hospital once her mother slipped away. The reality had threatened to knock her feet from under her.

At least Delaney's family supported her. If the illness struck, her sister was already on top of the treatment needed, prepared to fight the disease with David and the kids at her side. But other than her father and Eily, Lissa lacked anyone to support her. A diagnosis of ovarian cancer in her life would shatter a bright and promising future. She refused to move forward in a relationship if the disease caught up with her. She vowed she'd never put a man through the sorrow she'd watched her dad endure.

What could be the shards of her broken dreams poked the edges of her heart. *Lord, will this be one of those things that work together for good as you promise in your Word?*

She heard Sorrel outside and returned to the front door, grabbing a towel from the closet where she kept emergency supplies. Opening the door, Lissa bent down and grabbed Sorrel's collar. "Sit."

The dog obeyed, lifting each paw as Lissa wiped away the dirt and debris. Satisfied the dog was clean enough to enter, she let Sorrel in and picked up her phone. Two missed messages. Flipping on the light above the sink, Lissa pressed the voicemail playback.

"Matthew here. Hope your weekend home refreshed you. Peggy Blake and her helper will meet you at the Mueller ranch tomorrow about ten. Stop by the office before you go. I'll have the court orders ready for you so the horse can be legally removed from the property. Call me on my cell if you run into any problems."

She paused. *No problems, Matthew.* Except for the first time in two years she'd face a man with whom she once dreamed of sharing a relationship. A future now clouded with the possibility of a life-threatening disease. She stared out the kitchen window. *Nothing short of awkward. But hey, it's all part of the job, right?*

Lissa didn't like her thoughts, but after hearing Delaney's news Saturday, she no longer counted on tomorrow or the reunion that would take place. She wouldn't seek more than friendship with Kurt when she faced decisions that could drastically alter her future. What man found a woman attractive whose ability to bear children remained uncertain? She lowered her head and pressed her lips together, her eyes filling.

But Kurt might not want anything to do with her. After all, he'd silenced his contacts without warning. Another love interest, perhaps? She would never have believed Kurt to be the type to love and leave, but experience sang a different tune. Maybe marriage to Kurt, or anyone, might not be God's plan for her life. Her jaw clenched. *Traitor.*

"Get a grip, woman." Her words fizzled in the empty kitchen. She'd always had a flair for the dramatic and, in the face of devastation, the tendency brought out her worst. She pushed the play button again. A second message followed.

"Hi, this is Peggy Blake. My assistant, Kurt, and I are looking forward to meeting you in the morning. Kurt's got the horse trailer ready to load. We'll bring a sling with us. Dr. DeLorme thought it best. Oh, and he said to tell you the mare is showing signs of recovering. Thanks."

Lissa stared at the phone as it finished playing, the message confirming what she already knew. Wasn't this just dandy?

CHAPTER NINE

TUESDAY MORNING KURT CHECKED THE HITCH on the horse trailer. The Mueller ranch where he and Peggy were driving this morning occupied two-hundred-acre parcel five miles south of Crane on the Steens highway. The acreage bordered a large stretch of BLM land. Unfamiliar with the area, Kurt had consulted a map to find the road. His phone couldn't seem to find a satellite to help him.

"Did you load the sling?" Peggy stepped from the tack compartment on the front of the trailer, her red plaid shirt tucked neatly into her jeans, a colorful scarf tied under her thick, black hair streaked with grey.

Kurt had been with her son, Foster, when he purchased the scarf at an open-air stall in Kabul. As Marines, their weaponry and camouflage gear stood in stark contrast with the strange *burqas* covering the Afghan women from head to toe and the *parahan tunban* the men wore. Despite the stares of the villagers, Foster was determined to gift his mother with an ethnic souvenir, but the opportunity to send it never happened. The scarf arrived with his personal effects, wrapped in newspaper, a note from Kurt attached. Peggy had mentioned many times how she cherished this last, tangible connection to her son.

She closed the front of the trailer and locked it. "The deputy told me the filly walked on shaky legs."

"The sling is here." Kurt reached into the bed of the truck and lifted a strap. "You want it in with the tack?"

"No, it's heavy enough to ride there." Peggy inspected the sky. "Lots of cumulus clouds today. Our trip shouldn't run into foul weather."

"What time do we meet the deputy?" This horse made Kurt's third pick up since he'd returned home and joined Peggy on her ranch. Loading horses and cleaning up after them made for a full-time job. Work kept him busy, leaving little time to think, which was good. Thinking always got him into trouble. The past seemed to find a way to haunt his thoughts.

"Ten." Peggy glanced at her watch. "We'd better get on the road. Traveling with a trailer will eat up our time."

Kurt nodded and climbed into the cab. Peggy adjusted her seat belt while he started the engine. Putting the rig in low gear, he eased out of the driveway, the tug of the trailer jerking the half-ton pickup as the tires slipped in and out of the graveled ruts. Roads like Afghanistan—only those rough stretches hid explosives in the sand while sneering enemies waited for a chance to snuff travelers. As he reached the paved highway, Kurt shifted into drive, and the weight of the trailer evened out behind him. "Let's hope there's a lot of pavement between here and the ranch." He patted the steering wheel. "It'll be a lot easier keeping this on the road."

"Don't get too comfortable." Peggy rolled down her window and adjusted the side mirror. "This ranch is rather remote, and I'm willing to bet the driveway will be full of chuck holes."

"Like other roads we can think of." Kurt hoped to learn the ropes of this often-wild countryside. "Hope I don't have to move horses each time."

"No IEDs to haunt us." Peggy bit her lip and glanced at him, misty-eyed, before she broke into a smile. "Sorry. Foster fills my thoughts at the oddest times."

"It's okay, Peggy." Kurt reached a hand to her shoulder. "Foster was too fine a man to forget."

Peggy glanced out the passenger window, an almost imperceptible shake vibrating across her shoulders. Kurt had seen her cry more than once—the raw wound of losing her only child gaped like a bleeding slash. After Kurt's father died, his mother wept when she thought no one was watching, hiding her sobs in the kitchen, busying herself at the sink while she cried in silence. Kurt had already joined the Marines by then, but his home leaves always brought out Eily's tears, the ache for her late husband linked with fear for her son's safety.

"What do we need to know about this filly we're picking up?" He kept his eyes on the road, waiting for Peggy to collect herself and join him again. "Will she need special care? Or time?"

"Dr. DeLorme checked her yesterday afternoon." Peggy crooked a finger into the wrinkles framing her left eye, and followed through to the other, wiping away the moisture streaking her mascara. She sniffed. "The owner died in his sleep, and the vet thinks the filly and her mother were left without care for at least two weeks, maybe a month."

"There are two horses to rescue?" Kurt rolled his head on his shoulders as tension crept up his jaw. "This old trailer might not hold two horses, skinny or not."

Peggy shook her head. "No, only one. The mother was transported to DeLorme's clinic on Saturday."

"Did she survive?" Kurt closed his eyes. He'd seen enough of suffering in the remote villages of Afghanistan. In many areas, people seldom had enough to eat. The military envoys were welcomed when they brought supplies, even though terrorists lurked in the crowds waiting for their opportunity to kill the very troops bringing help. He and Foster always carried chocolate. Children would wait in clusters for the military personnel, knowing they'd be fed, not caring that they had to lick the melted candy off the wrappers. He shook the images away. The American forces performed good deeds in the region, but they weren't always appreciated.

"So far. It's too bad what happened." Peggy's voice startled him from his musings. "According to the sheriff's deputy we're meeting, there's plenty of grain and hay in the barn. She told me to take the grain for the filly's care, and we can load all the bales we can carry as well."

"She?" Kurt frowned and glanced toward his companion. "The sheriff's deputy is a woman?"

"Yes. Apparently, she acts as a sort of liaison between BLM and the sheriff's department and responds to all reports of animal abuse and neglect." Peggy chuckled. "What? Don't you think a woman can handle this kind of thing?"

"I'm surprised, that's all." Kurt tapped the steering wheel, a nervous sensation creeping along his middle. What if this deputy turned out to be Lissa? He knew she'd trained for a special job but wasn't sure what the position entailed. Feeling Peggy's eyes on him, he skirted more discussion on the subject. "Did you get a picture of the horse? Dr. DeLorme got one on his phone while we hunted sage rats."

"I'm sure I received the same photo. The horse looked dirty and scrawny, but she's adorable. I've already named her Kiger Lady."

"Kiger?" Kurt inclined his head toward her. "Can't say I've ever heard of a horse named Kiger."

"It's why I like it. The deputy sent the picture via phone, or through the air, across the Kiger ridge. Almost called her Skype in honor of the technology, because I liked that as well.

Kurt resisted rolling his eyes. Skype had been the one thing he'd promised Lissa while they were deployed. He'd cut off contact with his home world after Foster's death, and that included Lissa. He'd earned the title of jerk. Now a horse might have borne a similar name? Nothing like picking at a wound already infected.

"If you say so." Kurt came to a fork in the road. "Better check the map."

"We need to keep following the Steens highway. We'll find a road called Saddle Butte that will take us to the ranch."

"Okay, so left."

Peggy reached out and punched his arm. "Sorry. I forget you aren't from around here."

"As long as we don't get lost. Never know what's in them there hills." Kurt cast her a grin, framing his humor to lighten her earlier grief.

"Horses and deer and bears." Peggy mimicked the line from *The Wizard of Oz,* making a face.

Kurt raised an eyebrow. "Oh, my!"

And perhaps an angry stepsister thrown in the mix.

Thirty minutes later, Kurt blinked at the steep, sloped graveled driveway Peggy indicated. Would the horsepower under the hood be enough to pull the horse in the trailer, along with the feed, back up the long hill when they were loaded? He shifted into low and inched the pickup forward, his foot tight on the brake to hold the trailer in place behind him. The drive twisted at several intervals, slowing the descent to the ranch below. A sheriff's service vehicle waited by the barn, the building's doors open. Kurt inhaled, bracing himself for the driver to appear.

"They put the filly in a stall for the weekend." Peggy pointed. "Probably best to pull ahead of the doors, so the trailer is even with the barn."

Kurt did as instructed, stopping the pickup so the hood pointed away from the property. A tall, lithe form popped out from the big barn doors, the image caught in his side mirror. Kurt's pulse raced.

Every bit as professional and alluring as she'd been in her Navy uniform the day he'd met her, Lissa stood waiting, hands on her hips. She wore a brown shirt and green pants denoting her current position, the trim uniform accentuating every curve. Her hair dangled in wispy curls about her face, the mass of brown she only let down in private, with friends—with him—still captured in a neat bun. He gave thanks she hadn't worn her hair down today or his resolve would have flown out the window, along with the shreds of his heart.

He licked his lips, lifted his baseball cap, and ran a hand through his hair. Glad he'd taken time to shave this morning, he followed Peggy's lead as she stepped from the cab. He watched Lissa's face, waiting for recognition to appear in her eyes. His heart thumped like the foot of an animated rabbit.

"Morning, Deputy." Kurt drawled out the title, grinning at her and touching the brim of his hat. "Imagine finding you here in the middle of nowhere."

Lissa stepped forward. "It's been a while."

"Yes, it has. I left the military for greater adventures. I'm now a member of the inactive ready reserve." Kurt struggled with his thoughts. Lissa's nearness made him want to take her in his arms and kiss her hello the way they'd kissed goodbye before she left for San Diego two years earlier. "It means I'm free until they jerk my chain."

Before he could shake Lissa's hand, Peggy came around the side of the trailer and stopped, her glance traveling between him and Lissa. The expression on her face said she'd done the math, her lips straight-lined as if she'd caught them necking. Feeling the heat rise above his Adam's apple, he hastened to introduce her. "Peggy Blake, this is Deputy Lissa Frye, formerly Intelligence Specialist Frye of the United States Navy. And an old friend."

"Hey, easy on the *old* there." Lissa offered her hand to Peggy, taking the woman's outstretched palm between both of hers. "I'm Lissa. Very pleased to meet you. I'm sorry to learn of your loss. Kurt mentioned Foster several times in the sporadic letters he sent me. I know what a fine Marine your son was."

"Thank you." Peggy glanced from Kurt to Lissa and back. "I didn't realize this was going to be a reunion of sorts. How nice you two know each other."

Peggy's face reflected surprise, as well as something else Kurt couldn't put his finger on. His high school band had played Mendelssohn's bridal theme once, and he suspected the musical work now reverberated in Peggy's head, complete with surround sound. Women. All the same. Well, not this time. Not ever. Not after Afghanistan. He'd promised Foster he'd help Peggy if anything happened. He wouldn't renege on his pledge.

He inhaled to bolster his courage. "Yes. Lissa and I are related." At Peggy's questioning frown, Kurt chuckled. "Her father married my mother about two years ago. I served as the best man. Lissa was out floating her boat."

Lissa reddened. "I couldn't get additional leave or I would have joined you. I'd already taken more family leave than normal."

"I know. But tying the knot between our parents made us stepsister and stepbrother." Kurt angled his face Peggy's way to gauge her reaction. "So to answer your first assessment, yes, we know each other."

"I had no idea. What a lovely coincidence." Peggy's beaming smile, coupled with her sweet, loving nature, told him she had plowed through assumptions he'd have to correct over time.

"As siblings, we should work together well." Kurt nodded at Lissa, knowing his pinched grin appeared condescending at best. "Right, Sis?"

Lissa's smile disappeared, a stony expression set in its place. "Shall we go meet the filly?" She gestured through the barn doors behind her. "She looks a little better than she did in the first picture I sent you, Peggy. I groomed her on Friday, and the neighbor who's been feeding her over the weekend gave her more tender loving care since." Lissa led them through the doors, pausing to let

Peggy join her before walking into the interior. "The neighbor says she's an offspring of the Kiger mustangs."

"Really?" Peggy's voice sounded animated. "They're protected here."

"Yes, I know." Lissa led the way to a stall at the end. "And the filly's markings showed up when we groomed her."

"I decided to call her Kiger Lady." Peggy glanced about the empty barn. I considered Skype, but her heritage seemed more important."

"Clever name." Lissa glanced over her shoulder, skewering Kurt with her gaze. "Skype's a great way for people to keep in touch long distance."

He winced and followed the two women, listening to the conversation from which Lissa no doubt excluded him. Her back rigid, shoulders squared, she'd returned to the no-nonsense business stance she'd perfected in the Navy. He didn't blame her— not when they'd parted on such friendly terms.

Now he felt nothing but emptiness. Life had changed him, the war had left its mark, and his promise to Foster had taken precedence over his own desires. He had to find the man he'd been before anything else could happen. Too many people close to him wound up dead. That could be years in the future.

No, Lissa Frye could have no place in his future. Not now. Maybe not ever. His heart couldn't risk losing her. A second time.

But why did she have to be so beautiful?

CHAPTER TEN

LISSA GRITTED HER TEETH, TRYING TO cap the gathering storm inside her head. Kurt's brief dismissal of their relationship as mere siblings hurt. Was that all they'd had together? She didn't remember it that way. But maybe the lack of correspondence, coupled with his reluctance to use Skype, had been his way of telling her they had no future. *Coward.* He should have told her outright, not sent smoke signals.

Kurt had changed. Taller and thinner than she remembered, but still handsome and built like a man of steel, he lacked the self-confident air he'd carried before. His sapphire eyes, like patches of evening sky, now spoke of brokenness, as if their light had dimmed in the darkness he'd faced.

When they reached the filly's stall, Lissa unfastened the latch and stepped inside, confident the filly wouldn't bolt, now that her mother had been taken to the vet's clinic. The filly nickered a greeting, coming to where Lissa stood. "She's quite affectionate. I think Mr. Mueller must have spent a lot of time with her."

Peggy reached out her hand and the filly nuzzled it, shoving her nose near the woman's belt loop. "What's she looking for?"

"A treat." Lissa reached into her trouser pocket and pulled out a piece of carrot, flattening her palm so the filly could slurp up the tidbit. Her satisfied crunching echoed in the barn. "She's a little spoiled."

"I think she's perfect." Peggy patted the filly's neck and ran her fingers through the mane. "Aren't you the little lady?"

Grooming the filly, with special attention to her mane and tail, may have stolen an hour of Lissa's time and a heap of her dignity—oodles of tangles, burrs, and mud balls—but today the brushed coat, devoid of the debris and filth, reflected the markings of the horse's heritage. The cinnamon color of her flanks contrasted with the dark stripe between her withers and extending down her back, from her black mane to her black tail. Lissa basked in her accomplishment.

Peggy glanced her way. "I'll see to it she has a good home."

The filly's head lifted, and her nostrils flared, attention fixed on Kurt as he entered the stall. He scratched her forehead and ears and had reached her neck when the filly stepped back a stride and snorted, spewing the remnants of the carrot down his arm. Brushing off the gooey deposit, he frowned.

"I think she likes you." Lissa suppressed a wry chuckle.

"Odd way of showing it." Kurt reached for a bandanna in his back pocket. He wiped off the drool and shook the fabric, letting the handkerchief dangle between his fingers. "She could use a few table manners."

Ears pricked forward, the filly stretched her neck toward Kurt's hand, her head angled to the side. Snatching the colorful bandanna between her teeth, she raised it in the air, shaking it like a flag above Kurt's head.

"Hey! Be nice." Kurt grabbed at the handkerchief.

The filly shook her head, tongue wiggling to detach the object stuck in her lower lip. When the bandanna finally dropped to the ground, she curled her lips back, revealing a full smile of teeth. She pointed her muzzle toward the ceiling, widened lips wiggling as if she couldn't get the feel of the dry rag out of her mouth. To the ordinary onlooker, she appeared to be amused, bobbing her head like a water pump crank.

Kurt gave a snort of his own. "Lady is not what *I'd* call her."

Lissa dared a glance at the older woman, and they both burst out laughing.

A frown creased Kurt's forehead. "Now I know what it's like to be outnumbered three to one. Got any more tricks up your sleeve?"

Lissa averted her eyes, enjoying his predicament. "I'm sure she'll keep you guessing her next move."

"Speaking of move, we should get her loaded." Kurt spoke to Peggy. "Do you want me to stash the feed first?"

At Peggy's nod, Lissa closed the stall gate and gestured for Kurt to follow her. "The grain is in the two aluminum garbage cans near the barn entrance." She stopped and pointed up a ladder. "The hay's in the loft. Probably a truckload."

"I doubt we can get all the bales today. The pickup is only a half-ton. Adding the horse's weight to the trailer, the rig might not be able to pull everything." Kurt craned his neck, studying the opening above. He climbed the ladder's rungs and stuck his head into the loft. "We can haul our fair share, though. We can fill the second stall in the trailer to the top of the divider."

"I brought the county pickup." Lissa pointed out the door. "Load bales in the bed. I have tarps to protect the hay from the weather."

"And what? You'll follow us home?"

Kurt's scowl made Lissa shudder. Didn't he want her close? She remembered his hugs, his kisses, his tender goodbye. What happened? His rejection weighed like an anvil on her heart. She squared her shoulders. "Part of my job description."

"The rescue center is twenty miles from here." Peggy raised her palms in front of her. "Are you sure you want to make the trip?"

"I'll need to evaluate Lady's progress. Getting familiar with your location will make my to-do list." Lissa faced Kurt and rested her hands on her hips, claiming the upper hand. "Like you, I'm new to this area, too."

Kurt grew silent, seeming to study the clouds above. Her victory seemed shallow in light of his indifference. She lifted her chin, mustering her resolve to see the task through to the end.

Peggy glanced at her watch. "We'd better get started. It will soon be time for lunch."

"Let's load my pickup first." Lissa jingled the keys in her hand. "I'll back up to the opening, and we can drop the hay into the bed. What won't fit we'll stack in the trailer. We'll load Lady last."

She stomped to her pickup, not bothering to glance backward. Let him pout. She didn't care.

Jayden watched through a knothole in the loft floor as the three talked about moving the horse. Beside him, Duke sat on wiggling haunches, his jaw cupped in Jayden's hand to hush the barks. Jayden had awakened at dawn, thankful for Duke's prompting. He and the dog had eaten breakfast on Bennie's back porch—Duke his kibble, Jayden another apple and cheese.

Tempted by the emptiness of the house, he'd slipped in and opened Bennie's refrigerator. The smell of rotting food gagged him. Amazing what time did to raw meat, even refrigerated. He'd slammed the door and waved his hand in the air, trying to clear the odors. The freezer contained a bag of ice and little else.

Yesterday Jayden had waited above the stall while the veterinarian inspected the filly and phoned his approval to move her. After the vet left, the neighbor arrived, fed the horse, and called for Duke. Holding the dog close, Jayden hid in a corner of the loft, away from prying eyes until the neighbor gave up and left.

No one, that he knew of, had come looking for him. An empty ache lodged behind his breastbone. What if no one ever came?

The trio talking below started Jayden thinking. He had to leave, too. With them, if possible. He didn't want to go home. He didn't have enough food to stay here. But how could he do it? The younger woman's words about dropping the hay onto the truck sent a shiver down Jayden's spine.

He tiptoed toward the stall piled with hay. A pickup engine sounded outside, the grind of gears growing closer to the loft opening at the barn's other end. Jayden slipped down through the hole, Duke on his heels, and crawled through the rails toward the chicken door at the back. Outside, he shooed Duke away. The dog barked and raced around to the front. The distraction worked—the trio paused to inspect what they believed to be a missing animal.

Jayden searched for a safe place to hide while they loaded the hay. The house sat too far away to make a run for it, and nothing but open fields and pasture waited beyond. Jayden crouched down, pondering what to do next. The people out front discussed Duke's fate, the animated murmur of their voices drifting to where he waited. The dog's diversion would give him time to make his move. Knowing they'd load the hay from the front of the barn where the large loft opening allowed access, Jayden sat on a bucket near the tractor, thinking, while he spied on the action.

He didn't want to return home, not when he had no idea what awaited him there. Staying here was an option, except he was down to a couple of apples, a bag of chips, and a quarter brick of cheese. He hadn't had much extra to eat, but he'd never been without anything either. Mom made sure he always had food.

Duke came back twice, sniffing the ground and wagging his tail. But both times someone from the party out front called, and Duke disappeared around the corner. Jayden stuck his head in through the chicken door, listening for clues. Laughter came from the direction of the filly's stall. Before he knew it, the horse would be loaded, and he would be left behind.

Jayden crept around the outside of the barn, careful to watch for the three strangers hefting the hay bales. When he reached the front corner, the man stacked what seemed to be the last bale in the two-horse trailer, filling up one entire side. Jayden waited while the visitors discussed loading the filly.

"I'll load the grain. You get the horse." The man thumbed toward the barn, striding for the doors.

The women followed him inside. A minute later the man exited the barn and walked to the trailer's tack compartment, a garbage can balanced on his shoulder. Setting the garbage can down, he turned back to the barn and emerged a minute later with the other can of grain riding high.

Jayden gasped at the man's strength. He and Bennie had filled those garbage cans with scoops after Bennie wheeled the grain into the barn on a hand truck. Neither of them could budge the cans after they were full. This man picked them up and carried them across the drive like they were laundry baskets? Jayden could think of only one man he'd ever known this strong—his dad. He scrunched up his eyes, fighting the pain the memory brought. A squeak drew his attention back to the activity in the drive.

The man shoved the cans in from each side of the front gates, wedging them close to each other, their weight centered over the tongue. Through the opening, a shaft of light appeared behind the cans—a space big enough for him. Closing both entries, the man returned to where the women waited inside.

Jayden saw his chance. Hurrying to the trailer, he climbed inside, squeezing into the space made by the side-by-side garbage cans against the feed trough. The wooden trough built into the front of the stall made a natural cover. Hidden down here, he wouldn't be seen or suspected.

He scooted further under the manger, pulling down more loose hay from the rack above. His shoulders ached, and his knees cramped from being stooped over, but he scrunched tighter into the space. He couldn't risk being discovered.

Outside Duke whined, circling and barking. Jayden held his breath, fearing the dog would give him away. He wished he could open the door and let the dog in—plenty of room, but a surefire way to expose his hiding spot. Within minutes, Duke settled down, the sound of him crawling beneath the tongue disturbing the gravel. Convinced the people in the barn wouldn't leave a helpless creature behind, Jayden relaxed. They'd find a way to bring Duke with them. He could be reunited with the dog once he'd ridden with the filly to her new quarters. Where they were taking the horse, he didn't know, but anything would be better than going home to George.

Lissa snapped the lead rope onto the halter and opened the gate. Clicking her tongue, she led the filly out of the barn. Lady gave a snort, eyes wide and ears forward, as she approached the trailer's ramp.

Kurt checked the stack of hay bales in the second stall and came around to where Lissa stood. "Think she's going to do this?"

"I'm letting her examine the space a little." The filly nuzzled the back gate, sniffing her way along the top edge. Lissa let the rope slack as the curious horse stuck her head in and investigated the empty stall, whinnying as if she'd met an old friend. She snatched a bite of hay from the bales inside. "Peggy said she brought a sling?"

"We didn't know if she'd be strong enough to stand while riding." Peggy reached in the back of the truck bed and held up the straps of the contraption. "What do you think?"

"Let's see how she loads. She's a lot perkier than when I saw her Friday." Lissa rubbed the filly's head. "Amazing what tender, loving care and food can do."

Kurt lifted a small can. "I thought she might need coaxing. I reserved a little grain before I closed the garbage cans."

"She's got you wrapped around her tail." The filly's attention had shifted to the man, her neck stretching in his direction. "You're on her radar. Why don't you put the grain in the feed trough?"

"Anything I can do?" Peggy stood a few feet away, giving them room to work.

"Be ready to move in case she puts up a fight." Shaking the can, Kurt called to the filly. "Look, girl." He waited while Lady sniffed before proceeding into the trailer. "She sure likes this stuff."

With Kurt out of reach and the smell of molasses tempting her, Lady leaned forward as far as she could, placing a hoof on the ramp. The hollow sound of the steel floor echoed and the filly spooked, backing up and snorting.

Kurt called to her. "Come on, girl. It's all right." He shook the can again, poured the grain into the waiting manger, and walked to where Lissa stood. "Give me her rope and tie another one to the corner of the trailer."

She hurried to comply, holding the end of the tether, her fingers brushing his as she transferred the lead to him. She trembled as Kurt, like a knight in shining armor, took charge. Only instead of riding up on his gallant steed and whisking her away, he was loading the horse and putting Lissa out to pasture. She clenched her teeth, stemming the heat rising in her middle and willing herself to shake those thoughts from her mind. She tied another line to the corner.

"I'm going to pull on her halter and encourage her to step up." Kurt spoke in low tones, as though soothing a child. "If she gets stubborn, come around her rump with your rope and tighten it. When I say pull, we'll apply pressure together."

Lissa waited, holding her breath.

Kurt held the filly's halter and gently encouraged her to take a step. Lady raised her head, a snort leaving her nostrils. She resisted the tug he gave on her halter. At his nod, Lissa walked the rope around the horse's hindquarters and slipped the end through an opening in the trailer's divider. He tugged again on the halter, and Lissa tightened the rope across her rump. The filly strained against them for a moment, then with a wobbly step climbed into the trailer.

"I'll tie her off up here," Kurt called from inside. "Shut the gate."

Lissa stared into the darkened space. "How do you plan to get out?"

"I'll crawl out through the window if need be. But I'm going to try to slide past Lady to the back, see how steady she is on her feet. Then we can decide to use the sling." He shoved against the filly's side, edging her over as he eased past her shoulder. "Keep the gate closed until I get there."

"Got it." Lissa pressed her lips inward as Kurt turned sideways in the narrow stall, pushing Lady as far over as she would go. Next to him, the filly moved like a featherweight.

He inched past, clearing the horse in two steps. Reaching the gate, he dusted off his hands, mouth curled in a twisted grin. "She's a lightweight."

Lissa opened the gate to let him out, but the squeak of the hinge startled Lady. She sent a well-aimed hoof straight at Kurt's backside. Kicked off balance, the big Marine fell forward from the step, landing face down in the gravel.

"Kurt!" Lissa snapped the gate shut and clicked the lock before bending beside him. "You okay?"

He spat twice. "Sure, if you like a little horse mixed with rocks for brunch." Kurt pushed himself up and stood, brushing his shirt and jeans free of embedded dirt and rubbing his hands together. "Yuck." He ran the back of his hand across his mouth and spit again. A trickle of blood spotted his lip.

"Are you hurt?" Peggy came to his side. "Lady sure landed a wallop."

"Wouldn't think an animal this small could exert such power." Kurt rescued his baseball cap from the ground and plopped it back on his head. "I'm glad I'm tall enough she didn't hit anything vital."

"Other than your pride." Lissa suppressed a giggle, her nerves rerouting the seriousness of the moment into humor. *Don't laugh. He's hurt. He deserves respect, if nothing else.*

Kurt rewarded her with a grin.

Peggy climbed on the wheel well and took a quick look inside the trailer. "I guess this answers the question of whether or not she needs a sling."

Kurt rubbed his backside where the filly had landed her knock down kick. "She's stronger than she looks."

Lissa bit her lip, but Kurt caught her gaze, narrowed his eyes, and smirked. His silly grin undid her, and they both broke into a belly laugh. "I wish I'd had my phone out."

"If you posted that picture, I'd have you court-martialed."

"Sorry, honorably discharged civilians can't be court-martialed."

"I would've figured something out." Kurt raised an eyebrow, teasing in his glare.

"Wouldn't want your macho Marine friends to see you face down in the dirt, eating horse manure." Lissa arched an eyebrow. "Think of the damage to your delicate ego."

"You put it in such appealing terms."

"What are *sisters* for?" Hands on hips, Lissa cocked her head. If he could dish it out, she could return it. Only the banter sounded more like the relationship they'd shared before. Not what she'd intended. Would Kurt notice?

"Touché."

"You think Duke will ride with me?" Lissa scouted the field for the busy dog. "We can't leave him here."

"Do we need permission to remove him, too?" Peggy whistled to see if the dog would come running. "I'd love to have him at the rescue center."

"I didn't ask about Duke because he only showed up this morning." Lissa pulled her phone from her pocket. "If I can get service out here, I'll text Matthew and see what he says." A few seconds later Lissa's phone warbled. "Matthew says the dog can come too, if you want him."

"Let's take him, Kurt." Peggy glanced around. "If we can find him. He'll make a good watch dog."

Kurt shrugged. "I don't have room for any more feed. If Mueller had food for him, we can't take it."

"We don't have a key to the house." Lissa shuddered, remembering what Matthew had found inside. The structure now stood empty across the drive. "If there's dog food inside, we have no access."

"It's okay. With all this horse feed, I can easily spare a few dollars to buy Duke a bag of kibble." Peggy glanced at her watch. "Let's get on the road, shall we?"

"We can't leave without him. Where do you suppose he went?" Lissa raised two fingers to her mouth and whistled. Duke whined and crawled out from under the tongue of the trailer, his tail sagging. "What were you doing under the trailer, boy?"

The dog crept toward her, ears drooping and tongue lolling. He looked over his shoulder at the front of the trailer before sitting on his haunches in front of Lissa.

"He can ride with me." Lissa bent down to stroke his head. "I have room in the cab for him." She walked to the county truck's passenger side and patted her thigh. Duke trotted over to where she stood, but as she reached for his collar to pull him into the truck, he wrestled out of her hands and returned to the trailer. He sat, tail wagging in the gravel, as if waiting for her to open the trailer door. "Looks like he wants to ride with Lady."

"There's a little room left in the tack compartment." Kurt strode to the front, opening the gate. "Let's see if he'll load in there."

Duke barked, his excitement bubbling out of his dancing feet, and jumped through the opening. Once inside he peered out of the hole before collapsing beside the garbage cans as if he'd found the perfect spot to ride.

Kurt slammed the door shut and secured the lock. "Settles it."

CHAPTER ELEVEN

THE ENTIRE TRIP BACK TO THE rescue center Kurt brooded about what he could say to Lissa to make her understand. Beside him, Peggy rode in silence, for which he was grateful. The long, arduous journey became as grueling as the burden of his personal thoughts—the weight of the grain and hay, coupled with the horse in the trailer, tested the pickup's endurance.

What explanation could he give Lissa for his aloof behavior since his return stateside? Her badgering back at the ranch rang with hurt. He owed her an apology.

Checking his rearview mirror every few minutes, he could see Lissa following him, her creamy skin and dark hair easy to spot in the dim interior of the county truck. Once he'd thought a relationship with her might be the best future he could imagine. Infatuated since the fateful Thanksgiving when she'd entered the room dressed in her casual Navy uniform, he still remembered touching his hat brim, her Navy rank at the time a notch above his Marine standing. When he'd saluted, she'd blushed at his attention, but she'd remained the professional, spitting out the words, "At ease."

What had happened to the promises he'd made during their one-week romance? He'd started out faithful—texting her whenever he could. They'd stayed close for a year. But Foster's death changed him. Losing someone so close to him made him afraid. And Lissa paid the price. After his reassignment, he never texted her, hadn't bothered with Skype or writing a letter, which required too much effort. The war had stolen his hopes and dreams, leaving him an empty shell. Foster's accident haunted his thoughts, defining his days. He couldn't be close to Lissa, or anyone. Not anymore. People close to him wound up dead. Until he could escape the grip of those memories, his future with Lissa would have to wait. Maybe forever.

He flipped the left turn signal, slowing to turn into Herrick Valley Rescue Center, and braced himself for these final moments with Lissa. He had no explanation for her. He maneuvered the rig up the driveway and stopped beside the barn. A herald of whinnies trumpeted through the air as Peggy's two other horses greeted the newcomer. Lady returned the equine welcome, her call higher in pitch, the squeal of a younger animal.

Easing her pickup to a stop beside him, Lissa looked over at him. He nodded at her through the closed window, wishing he could smile. Wide-eyed, her face brightened as her eyebrows lifted, the barest trace of a smile on her lips. She killed the engine, stepped from the truck, and waited.

"Good trip. But long." Peggy released a weary sigh and shoved the squeaky passenger door open. "Is the stall ready for Lady?"

"I filled it before we left. I figured you'd want to isolate her for the first few days."

"Yes, until we can get her stabilized and eating well."

Kurt and Peggy walked to the trailer. When Kurt caught Lissa's gaze, he thumbed toward the back. She nodded, meeting him and Peggy there. Another shrill whinny sounded. Kurt grabbed the trailer gate. "She's glad to be here."

"Think you can sneak in the way you snuck out, cowboy?" Lissa raised an eyebrow as if she doubted his ability. "Or do you plan on taking a hoof to the chest this time?"

"Funny lady." Kurt jumped up on the wheel well and reached for the rope holding Lady's halter. "Open the gate, Lissa, and I'll try to let her back out."

Lissa lowered the ramp and opened the left gate. The barrier creaked as it swung free.

Kurt leaned through the trailer's open-air window, untying the lead rope and shoving on the horse's chest. Lady backed up a step, then another, then stopped when she heard the hollow sound of her hooves echoing on the floor. She bolted forward, ramming the manger.

Kurt shook his head and let out a frustrated whistle. "Lissa, come hold her in place while I crawl in beside her."

"You sure?"

"No choice." He handed her the lead rope, and she climbed up on the wheel well as he had and waited. He moved to the rear, talking in low tones, and reached up and patted the filly's rump. She quivered at the touch of his fingers, hooves moving in short little steps beneath her, but didn't kick.

Kurt stepped forward and with one swift movement leaned into the filly, shoving her over in the stall. He inched past her side. Taking the rope from Lissa, he moved close to the horse's head. "Come on, little girl. We can do this. Back up slowly. I've got you. No need to fear. One step after another."

Caught between the sides of the trailer stall and his overpowering strength at her head, the filly backed, each furtive step calculated. When she reached the end of the trailer, he shoved against her, forcing her to step down the ramp. She tried to bolt, but he held tight, pressuring her to move away from him. "You can do this. Two more steps and you're out of here."

The filly backed away from him, hind legs reaching the ground and front legs at the joint where the ramp met the trailer. She stepped to the middle of the ramp with her right leg, dragging the other hoof down the incline, bringing it to rest on the driveway. He stepped from the trailer and rewarded the filly with a pat. "I knew you could do it." He reached into his pocket for a reward and offered it to her. "I think we're home free."

"Good." Lissa's gaze vacillated between Kurt and Peggy. "Where do you want the hay?"

Peggy pointed to the small, oddly shaped space resembling a roof on the side of the barn. "In the lean-to."

Lissa frowned at Kurt. "Will this hold it all?"

"Should." He handed the lead rope to Peggy. "Get Lady into her stall. I'll angle the rig closer to the lean-to."

"You want me to move my truck?" Lissa reached in a pocket, pulling out keys. Lady nuzzled the key ring, her lips twisting along the top of Lissa's fingers. "You learn fast, don't you girl?" She shoved her other hand into an opposite pocket and produced a chunk of carrot. Palming it, she held the treat out to the horse. Crunching followed, along with drool, which Lady happily shared in a snort. "Yuck. Peggy will have to work on your manners."

"A horse with etiquette?" Kurt chuckled. "Drive your rig around the end of the barn. We'll empty your load near the stalls."

Lissa drove around the barn and parked, returning to join Peggy. Lady nibbled at her fingers. "Ready for your new home, girl?"

"I think Dr. DeLorme needs to examine her teeth." Peggy stroked the filly's head and muzzle. "She drools a lot for a horse so young."

"Congenital problem?"

"It happens." Peggy gestured toward the barn and they fell into step together. "The back teeth might need floating."

Lissa tugged on the lead rope and Lady trailed behind. "Could neglect cause it?"

"It's a possibility." Peggy strode forward and unlocked a gate. The roomy stall beckoned, straw and sawdust both on the dirt floor.

Lissa led Lady into the new quarters and released her. She patted the filly's shoulder. "This will be a good place for you to get better. You'll make new friends."

Jayden held his breath as the filly backed out of the trailer. Duke whined and barked, drawing attention to the front of the transport. The side door of the tack compartment opened and the man, Kurt, called the dog to him. Duke jumped out and the front gate swung closed.

Voices outside sounded too near for Jayden to escape his hideaway. He hadn't expected the journey to be so long or so bumpy. Every bounce of the trailer had jarred him, making his head bang on the manger, throwing his shoulders against the garbage cans. How far had he come? Would he ever find his mother? His stomach rumbled—he hadn't eaten since early this morning. He'd have to be careful when he stood. Lightheadedness might leave him dizzy.

The roar of a nearby engine and the crunch of tires rolling on gravel suggested the other truck was being moved. Duke continued to yip and race, circling the trailer and the people. The guy they called Kurt spoke to the dog, trying to quiet him, but Duke persisted, enjoying his newfound freedom. Footsteps faded away. A second engine sounded, and the trailer moved forward a few feet. The driver exited the cab, the slam of the door reverberating through the metal chamber. Jayden's heart hammered in his ears, waiting in fear of discovery, but the steps of the second driver grew faint. Duke's barking quieted.

Jayden's time to escape had come. He chose the opposite door from where Duke had exited, hoping the hinge wouldn't creak and alert the dog. He had to hurry, not knowing what he would find when he crawled out. His knees burned from being cramped under the manger and his muscles ached as he stood. Pausing long enough to get steady on his feet, he peered through the horse trailer's windows, trying to get a grip on his bearings, but all he could see was the barn. The door to a lean-to on the end of the building stood open, and Jayden decided the opening offered his best chance to hide. He slid through the trailer's side door and grabbed his food sack, which had torn during the journey. Checking to make sure nothing had escaped, he crumpled the sack in his arm and raced across the short span into the lean-to.

Waiting for his eyes to adjust to the dim interior, he heard the women's voices through the wall. Behind him what sounded like a tailgate dropping caught his attention. He waited, listening for movement. A ladder against the wall led to a hole opening to the top of the barn. He grinned as he stepped on the bottom rung and scrambled upward. This routine he understood.

Kurt had already unloaded several bales when Peggy and Lissa emerged from the other side of the barn where they'd housed Lady. Lissa watched him, a question on her face. He'd yet to find an opportunity to speak with her, and time grew short.

"Need help?" Lissa lifted a hay hook off the wall. "I can slide the bales out while you stack them."

"Sounds like a plan." Kurt wiped his forehead with his sleeve. "We'll unload the grain and hay from the trailer into the lean-to after we empty your bed."

Lissa glanced around. "This place is bigger than I thought."

"And most likely, older." Peggy knocked on a nearby rail, as if testing its sturdiness. "One of our neighbors helped us expand the old barn before Foster left for Afghanistan. The stalls are on one half of the building, and the tack and storage are on this side."

"Great floor plan."

"If a stall gets left open, the horses can only go outside, not over to this part of the barn where they can get into grain and founder." They walked to the end of the truck. "The lean-to acts as an entrance lobby to both sides." Peggy grabbed a bale. "And we can unload feed without getting out in the weather or slipping in the mud."

"Even better." Lissa pulled bales while Kurt stacked them. Within minutes the load of hay stood waiting, Lissa's truck swept clean.

Kurt led the way to the lean-to. "Want to switch jobs? I'll carry the bales inside. You and Peggy can stack them on the pallets."

Together Peggy and Lissa stacked the bales three high and two deep while Kurt busied himself emptying first the trailer stall, then the bed of the rescue center's truck. He reached into the tack compartment to retrieve the garbage cans filled with grain. As he pulled the second one out, a can of cat food rolled out with it.

"Looks like Duke is bringing his own food with him." Kurt held up the can. "I guess he doesn't trust us to feed him."

"How did it get in there?" Peggy took the can and rotated it in her fingers. "It's not dog food, Kurt. This is for a cat."

"Duke must have brought a friend along." Kurt chuckled at his joke, and the women grinned.

"We could use a cat around here. Keep the mice population down." Peggy set the can on a nearby rail.

Kurt nodded, but the incident didn't set right with him. If he were still in Afghanistan, he'd be aiming his gun. However the cat food got inside, he intended to investigate until he was satisfied.

Duke returned to the trailer and circled it twice, whining as he passed the doors to the tack compartment. Nose to the ground, the dog sniffed his way to the lean-to, barking as he raced inside, tail wagging in excitement.

Thanks to his military background in surveillance, Kurt's senses soared to high alert. Perhaps he'd spent too much time in Afghanistan, but the dog's behavior made Kurt suspicious. Could a cat have ridden in the trailer? Would Duke get this excited about it? Kurt wanted to shrug off the feeling, but common sense told him no animal could have loaded the can of cat food.

He hefted the first grain can to his shoulder and carried it inside, wary as he watched for evidence of an intruder. His sniper training had taught him eyes could be stalking him from any angle. He glanced up at the loft, which waited half full, leaving lots of tidy spaces to hide. His gaze lowered to the row of stalls, three of the four claimed by animals, and scrutinized the empty one for signs of movement. Seeing none, he decided to return later for a closer inspection. Let the intruder make his move. Kurt would be ready.

He stepped back outside for the second garbage can to discover Lissa and Peggy deep in discussion and exchanging business cards. "You leaving, Lissa?"

She glanced at her watch. "Yes, I have other responsibilities today." She opened the cab door and rolled down her window. "I'll be back to check on Lady, but if you need anything, don't hesitate to call."

If it were only that easy. He clenched his fists, hating the knot tightening his throat, strangling the words he longed to say. Instead, he nodded, unable to speak his heart. "See you around, Sis."

A sheen moistened her eyes, but she blinked it away, a furrow forming between her brows. Her smile sagged. "Yeah."

Lissa's eyes held unshed tears as she drove back to the sheriff's office. She slammed the steering wheel with her fist, tripping the horn. Alone on the road, she considered hitting the thing again, her fury needing a release. Kurt's cold dismissal burrowed to the soft places of her heart, searing the affection she'd held for him since they'd parted two years ago. What had changed him so much? Did he have another girlfriend? She'd known the reunion would be awkward, but she hadn't expected him to be unapproachable. She couldn't think of anything she'd done to cause his reaction.

She swiped at the wetness threatening to smear her mascara and pulled a tissue from the box riding on the dashboard. Grinding the gears, she shifted into third and sped down the highway, trying to find the professional demeanor that had landed her this job. If her heart wouldn't cooperate, her mind would.

After ten miles, her rationale kicked in. Kurt owed her nothing. She staked no claim on him. She'd merely found a good home for an abandoned animal, and Kurt happened to be part of the rescue. She'd done her job. Her report would reflect her efficiency. Kurt served as interference, nothing more. All things considered, it was better this way.

She pressed a smile into her frown and drove the remaining miles to headquarters. None of this mattered. She had tests to complete and a doctor to see. The last thing she needed was an arrogant man in her way. Now if only she could convince the ache in her heart.

CHAPTER TWELVE

JAYDEN CHOMPED ON HIS LAST APPLE, savoring each bite. Nothing remained in his sack. He'd finished off the brick of cheese, licked the crumbs off the inside of the potato chip bag, and saved the apple for his late afternoon snack. A bag of his mother's cookies would taste good right now. She always kept a dozen or so frozen for emergencies. Why hadn't he grabbed a few? Leaning into the bale of hay and missing his mother, Jayden pondered his next meal.

The people who'd transported the filly had gone inside the house, Duke with them. Probably enjoying a big fat sandwich and a fancy dessert for dinner. Thinking about the food made Jayden's mouth water. He still had two cans of cat food he'd pilfered from his mother's pantry, but he couldn't imagine eating it. Horse feed would taste better.

He needed to get his bearings in this barn. Built sturdier and newer than Bennie's, the floorboards of the loft still had little spaces between them where he could peek through the cracks. The loft spaces to drop hay were further apart and each hole served two stalls instead of one. Below him the filly munched on hay. The smell of molasses wafted up from her manger and the sweet aroma made Jayden's belly growl. What was in horse feed that could hurt him? He'd seen the oats and corn coated with the molasses. He'd eaten oatmeal and grits for breakfast—how would it taste raw? The molasses coating might make it taste good. He decided to wait until dark and sneak a handful out of the grain can for himself.

"Hey girl." The voice below startled Jayden, the pace of his pulse tripling as if he were a cat whose tail had been stomped. When did this guy arrive? Had he heard Jayden exploring the loft? The barn door hadn't creaked, nor had Duke barked.

Jayden flattened against the boards. If he knocked hay or loose seeds down through the cracks in the loft floor, he might as well sound a gong. Below, the man brushed the filly, taking extra time to comb out her mane and tail. "You'll like your new home. Peggy will take good care of you."

Duke pattered into the barn, nose to the ground, hustling up and down the aisle in front of the horses. He whined outside the filly's stall and the man leaned over the gate. "What do you need, boy? Looking for your missing cat friend?"

Missing cat friend? Jayden froze, frowning at the remark.

"I'm keeping the can of cat food ready for him or her. Peggy wants a mouser, though, so your buddy needs to earn his keep."

Jayden searched his memory. Can of cat food? Two cans remained in the sack. Had there been three? He pressed himself against the loft floor, nose tucked inside his shirt to silence his breathing. Moving meant certain discovery. Perspiration beaded his forehead. His brain ached staying so still, jaw clamped closed.

Below him, the man exited the filly's stall, carrying a water bucket. Duke followed him outside. Jayden popped upright, skittering across the loft to his hiding place. Panting from the possibility of being discovered, Jayden scrunched into the hole he'd made between two bales of hay and the back wall. He wished he knew where his mother had been taken. He'd be safe with her. If he were found here, who knew what might happen? Foster care? Or worse, home to George? Neither option suited him. Staying clear of both meant safety, even if it included eating horse feed. His stomach growled. His hunger hurt.

The filly nickered. Faint murmuring drifted to where Jayden waited as the man soothed the horse. The sound of tin against wood rattled the barn. He heard the click of the stall gate latching and footsteps growing faint. The barn door slid closed, a muffled bang as it stopped. All became still again.

Jayden waited, listening for what seemed like an eon before venturing toward the ladder. Except for the movements of the three horses below, no other sounds ruptured the peace. He took care to lower himself to the ground, inching his way to where the grain cans stood. A thread of moonlight streamed from the loft opening. He lifted a lid and scooped a handful of the fragrant molasses feed into his mouth. The oats and corn were chewy, but the molasses tasted like his mother's gingerbread. A wave of homesickness washed over him. He lowered the lid in place and took a step toward the loft's ladder.

"Think you're going to like eating horse feed?"

Jayden jumped, his heart leaping into his throat. Twisting to the sound of the voice, he squinted into the dim interior. The man appeared out of the shadows, his towering frame and muscled bulk ominous in the barn's diminishing light. Jayden coiled, ready to spring, unsure of himself. The barn door was closed, the giant form between him and where the loft ladder hung. Neither option would provide escape. His shoulders went limp; the truth bubbled from his lips. "I was hungry."

"And cat food didn't appeal, right?"

Jayden waited as the guy drew closer, stepping into the light of the moon. Face placid and mouth set, the twinkle in his eyes gave Jayden hope. "No, sir."

"I'm Kurt." He extended his hand. "And you are?"

He returned the handshake. "Jayden."

"You the reason Duke keeps circling the barn and whining?"

"Probably." Jayden peeked up. He remembered how tall his father had stood, but this fellow dwarfed him by several inches, and the width of their shoulders was similar. Both would have made George look like a wimp. "Duke protects me."

"Why don't you come in the house and tell me your story? Peggy made fried chicken for dinner and there's a piece or two left over. Think you could help her finish it?

Jayden gulped, staring at Kurt to see if he was serious. When Kurt raised his eyebrows, cocked his head, and pointed in the direction of the house, Jayden nodded. "Yes, sir. I'd be glad to help out."

Kurt smiled. "I thought you might."

If only today were Friday. Lissa needed the weekend to sleep. After the long morning moving the filly to her new home, she'd returned to the office to write up her report and discovered Matthew and the other deputies deep in discussion over a map of the area.

"What's up?" Lissa hadn't expected an explosion of voices to respond to her simple question, but all the men spoke at once. Matthew held up his hand for silence.

"We arrested a man Friday night during a domestic dispute that sent his wife to the hospital." Matthew pointed at the map. "And her son went missing around that time. We've been searching for him since."

"Runaway?"

"It's what the man would have us believe, but judging from the bruise on his wife's face, we're concerned the child suffered the same, only more serious."

Her stomach wrangled itself in a knot. "How old is the boy?"

"Eleven."

"Why do men beat up little kids?" She shuddered. "My dad saw lots of things while he worked as a school principal. He said none of it ever made any sense."

"This boy is a stepson."

"Do you want to expand the search?"

Matthew scratched his head. "That's our dilemma. According to the mother, her son came home from school Friday after early dismissal for summer break." He tapped the calendar. "The mother left to buy groceries Saturday morning and the boy was headed to a friend's house. When she returned, the son hadn't, and she got into an argument with her husband about the child running all over the county." Matthew held up a local map. "If we're looking for a runaway, a boy his age could cover a lot of territory. But if we're searching for a body, we need to confine our investigation closer to home."

"Did the mother say who the friend was?" She posed her question to the half circle of men.

"Bennie Mueller." Matthew's gaze pierced hers. "You didn't see a kid out there, did you?"

"No." She wracked her brain, thinking back over the morning they'd spent investigating the neglected horses and the discovery of the dead man's body. "You were in the house and I was at the barn. If he were hiding, there were lots of places we didn't go."

"You're right." Matthew sank into a nearby swivel chair. "But if he saw us, why did he hide?"

"He might have thought he was in trouble. Or maybe he saw the coroner's van and got scared." She didn't remember much about being eleven, but she did recall being frightened. "I know I would have been afraid if the sheriff and the coroner showed up someplace where I'd gone to see a friend."

"I'll call the hospital and see what Mrs. Barnes says." He picked up the phone, but before he dialed he glanced at her. "Better yet, why don't I send you over there? The mom might be more willing to talk with you."

"I'd be happy to talk to her." She looped her tote strap over her shoulder. "Women tell other women things they'd never discuss with a man."

"You're on." Matthew nodded dismissal to the other men. "We'll wait for your report."

An hour later, Lissa entered the hospital. Following a nurse's directions, she found the room and arrived in time to see a woman tucking a wad of papers in her purse, one hand on a wheelchair. "Melanie Barnes?"

"Yes?" Melanie straightened, wincing as she did, catching her shoulder like an ancient with arthritis. The bruise above her left eye sported eerie shades of purple.

"I'm Deputy Sheriff Lissa Frye. Would you have time for a few questions before you leave?"

Melanie's eyes pooled, the pupils as dark as a piece of onyx. She sank into the wheelchair. "Have you found Jayden?"

"I need to discuss his disappearance with you." Lissa pulled up a chair beside the woman and sat down. "When did you last see your son?"

"Friday evening." Melanie slumped lower in the chair, lines gathering around her mouth and crinkling her eyes. "I never leave Jayden home when George—he's my husband—has been drinking. But Saturday I needed to buy groceries since George came home earlier than expected from his long-haul truck trip. He was still sleeping when I left. Jayden told me Friday he wanted to go visit a friend that day. I thought he'd be safe."

"Do you know who the friend was?"

Melanie visibly relaxed as she mentioned the name. "Bennie Mueller. He's a rancher who lives about eight miles south of us. He lets Jayden care for his horses in the summer. Jayden was excited to be out of school so he could pick up where he left off last September."

At the confirmation of what she'd been told, Lissa worked to mask her reaction. Suspicion had written its name all over this investigation. A missing boy and a dead man—the combination couldn't be coincidental. Maybe Matthew had been wrong in his assumptions about the rancher.

"Did you feel comfortable with Jayden visiting Mr. Mueller?"

"Yes, Bennie was so good to Jayden. I know he let him stay overnight many times last summer." Melanie wrapped her arms about her waist. "Jayden never stopped talking about Bennie."

"Who else might Jayden have visited?" At her silence, Lissa prodded. "A close school friend?"

"Jayden's best friend moved to Hines at Christmas." Melanie frowned. "They rarely get together anymore."

"Do you think your husband could have harmed Jayden?" Lissa watched the woman's mouth and eyes. "He hurt you. Could he have done the same to your son?"

Melanie's cheeks glistened in the wash of her tears. "I don't think so. George wasn't angry until I asked him if he'd seen Jayden in the afternoon. He accused me of letting my son wander all over the countryside when he should be home doing chores."

"He was drunk when he said this?"

Melanie shook her head. "No, he'd run out of liquor in the morning and slept it off. I had to pick up more for him. I hadn't restocked while he was gone on a haul. He was just irritated."

"Is he away from home a lot?"

Melanie nodded. "He's a truck driver. We rarely see him during the winter because he's gone so much." She sniffed. "It's how we manage."

"I'll be in touch." Lissa rose. "I'll relay this to Sheriff Briggs and let him proceed with the investigation."

"Please find Jayden." Melanie grabbed her arm. "I don't know what I'd do if I lost him too. He's all I have left of my marriage to his father."

Lissa stepped back from the wheelchair. "Are you going

home?"

"No, my sister is taking me to her place." She sniffed. "I had a restraining order placed on George because I don't feel safe with him around right now. I told the deputy I want to press charges."

"I understand." Lissa retrieved a pad of paper from her purse. "Why don't you give me the address where you'll be and a phone number, so we can reach you when we find Jayden?"

Melanie scribbled on the pad of paper then handed it to Lissa. "Call me as soon as you know anything. Please?"

"Of course." Lissa stood, tucking the notepad in her tote.

A woman whose facial features resembled those of Mrs. Barnes appeared at the door, a frown across her face. "Ready to go, Melanie?"

"This is my sister, Keri."

Nodding at the woman, Lissa took her leave. Behind her, the sister said what Lissa had already thought. "I don't know why you've stayed with George this long. I told you he wasn't any good."

Lissa hurried out of the hospital and to her truck. Lessons often had to be learned the hard way. She started the engine while she prayed Melanie wouldn't learn hers by losing the most precious person in her life. Lissa shuddered. She'd been there.

Kurt grinned as Peggy bustled about the kitchen, warming food for the hungry boy. She heaped Jayden's plate with leftover chicken, dinner rolls, and creamed corn. When he'd cleaned his plate, Peggy spooned three scoops of ice cream into a bowl and laid fresh chocolate chip cookies on a napkin, setting both beside him. Kurt shook his head in amusement—Peggy and his mother were two of a kind. A starving kid meant a need for food, and lots of it.

Jayden ate with care, laying his utensils down, keeping his mouth closed, using a napkin. His hair smacked of a professional cut. The young man displayed a good upbringing—someone cared about him—yet he was alone and hungry. His eyes, like dark stones beneath a bubbling creek, captured everything around him. Duke lay at his feet, the dog's gaze one of an animal who'd found his best friend and wouldn't be moved.

For Kurt, the situation suggested missing information. Terrible circumstances must have driven Jayden away from those who loved him. He guessed the boy had smuggled himself aboard the trailer, though he couldn't figure out how. The tack compartment had been full, no space for anything in there. The second stall next to Lady had been loaded with hay. "Where in the trailer did you find room to ride here?"

Jayden's eyes went wide, worry lines furrowing themselves between his eyebrows. He stopped chewing, his mouth frozen in place.

"You can keep eating, Jayden." He touched the boy's shoulder. "I'm only curious."

The boy nodded, chewing his food and swallowing. He drank his milk and wiped his mouth with a napkin before speaking. "I scrunched up under the manger on the other side of the garbage cans."

"You fit in there?" Kurt's voice signaled his surprise. "Weren't you uncomfortable?"

"Yeah. I thought I was going to turn into a pretzel."

Kurt couldn't contain his laughter. "If we'd lost the trailer on one of those twists and turns, you would have. Riding in a trailer with a live animal is very dangerous."

"I know." Jayden's rueful smile revealed dimples in both cheeks. "But I couldn't exactly ask for a spot on the front seat, could I?"

Kurt sobered, his next question certain to be misconstrued. "What were you doing at Bennie Mueller's place?"

"Bennie's my friend." Jayden's face contorted. "Or he was."

"Why did you hide from us?" Kurt watched the boy's face. "Did you think you were in trouble being there?"

"I didn't know what to think. Bennie's place didn't look right." The boy's eyes searched his.

"What do you mean?" Kurt spun a chair around and sat, his years as a Marine in special ops fueling his curiosity. "Had things changed since you were last there?"

"Yeah. The mare and her foal were out in the rain in the old round pen." Jayden scowled. "Bennie treated his horses like royalty. They either went to the pasture or he stuck them in the barn. He'd never have left them out in the mud."

"Really?"

Jayden nodded. "And Bennie always parked and locked his truck under the overhang of the barn. I found it crossways in the drive with the door open." He shook his head. "Something terrible must have happened for Bennie to leave things undone." The boy gazed up at him, his mouth quivering, tears gathering at the corners of his eyes. "How did he die?"

"I don't know." Kurt sensed the boy's pain. "The sheriff will conduct an investigation."

Jayden nodded, gaze fixed on the floor. "Bennie let me help him around the ranch last summer. I groomed his horses, fed them, and moved them from the corral to the pasture."

"Which is when Duke got attached to you." Kurt stood and refilled Jayden's glass.

"Me and Duke are best buds." At his name, the dog sat up on his haunches, resting his chin in Jayden's lap. "I was afraid he was going to give me away in the trailer. He kept whining and circling like a buzzard."

"I thought it strange he wanted to ride with the filly." Kurt tucked his hands into his pockets and leaned against the counter. "I never suspected anything human could squeeze into such a small space."

"Me either." Jayden squirmed, quiet as if he didn't know what to say. He peeked at Kurt. "You gonna send me home?"

"Where's home?" Kurt waited while the boy slid backward into the chair and propped his elbows on the table. Only then did Kurt notice the huge black and blue mark on the kid's forearm.

Peggy picked up Jayden's plate, her narrowed eyes sending a signal to Kurt. She smiled at the kid. "Is home a safe place?"

Jayden caught their exchange and dropped his arms to his sides, sitting up straighter. He glanced about the room, refusing to make eye contact.

Kurt reached across the table and rested his hand on the boy's shoulder. "Jayden?"

Fidgeting in his chair, he lowered his chin, gaze on the floor. "Home *was* safe. Before George Barnes moved in and married my mom."

Peggy offered him another round of cookies. "Is he the one who bruised your arm?"

Jayden nodded. "The day before the sheriff came to Bennie's house." He sniffed and turned worried eyes in Kurt's direction. "My arm hurt so bad I had to get out. I can't go back if George is still there. I won't."

Kurt doubled his fists. Afghanistan had been bad enough—the hungry children, the men who treated their wives like chattel—but to return home and find similar conditions made him want to throw a grenade. Old instincts wouldn't die. His training ran too deep. He stumbled over his words, labored breathing interfering with his speech. Feeling his anger brewing, he spat out his resolve. "You aren't going back to the same situation. I'll see to it myself."

Jayden sniffled as a single tear escaped down his cheek. He swiped at the sudden intrusion and conjured up a stoic face. "Thank you." The rasp in his voice belied his tough exterior. "My mom and I get along fine."

Kurt squeezed Jayden's good shoulder. "Give this time, son. Things have a way of working themselves out."

Jayden nodded, finishing off the last cookie. "I hope so."

"But right now, you're safe. Peggy will see you have food, and I'll make sure you and Duke spend time together. We'll check on all the legal stuff in the morning. Okay?"

"Okay."

Kurt stood and gestured for Jayden to follow Peggy. As the boy plodded down the hall, Kurt opened and closed his fingers. He breathed in and out, fighting for control. The injustice triggered memories he tried to suppress. He hadn't felt this rattled since the night the explosion claimed Foster. All he'd wanted to do was run screaming into the night. To get away from the terrors of the scene before him.

The chaplain had shared a passage from Isaiah in an attempt to help him cope with the burden of guilt he carried. "For they fled from the swords, from the drawn sword, from the bent bow, and from the grievousness of war." Nothing, the chaplain assured him, could have prevented the attack. And certainly not him.

The room spun around Kurt, and he headed outside. *Lord, I need assurance now.* Maybe a little fresh air would help before he tried to sleep—if he could. *God, help me.*

CHAPTER THIRTEEN

KURT RE-ENTERED THE HOUSE A FEW minutes later. The fresh air helped calm him, his breathing slow and steady. He followed the sound of voices to the den, stopping at the doorway.

Peggy had tossed pillows aside and was tugging on the sleeper sofa. Kurt strode into the room and gave the cranky bulk a jerk, extending the mattress. He took the sheets from Peggy and tossed them at Jayden. "Think you can give up your hay bale for a real bed?"

Jayden yawned through his grin. "Yeah."

Peggy opened a hall closet, returning with one of Foster's old t-shirts and a pair of sweats. She handed the garments to Jayden. "You can shower and change in the bathroom." The boy left, and Peggy finished making the bed.

The smell of coffee beckoned Kurt down the hall. "I'll wait in the kitchen."

Half an hour later Peggy joined him. "He's already asleep. Duke's on the floor in front of the sofa." She pointed to the carafe sitting on the warmer. "Want another cup?"

"No, I'll never drift off if I drink any more tonight." Kurt pulled up a kitchen chair while Peggy poured her mug full. "Did you see the bruise?"

Peggy's gaze dropped to the table, her smile sagging. She shook her head. "He's only a kid."

"That man needs to pay. Big time. No excuses." Kurt didn't know what the procedure might be to protect the child, but he was determined to find out. The only drawback would be possibly crossing paths with Lissa. As a sheriff's deputy, she'd point him to the authorities needed to protect Jayden. But working alongside her, knowing how he had disappointed her, would make them both uncomfortable. He wouldn't blame her if she didn't cooperate. Perhaps another alternative existed.

"You probably don't know this, but I'm a licensed foster mother." Peggy's eyes twinkled, the cyan blue of her irises vivid, like a reflection of a lake beneath an azure sky. "Haven't had a child here since Foster left for Afghanistan. He used to call the kids we sheltered Foster's fosters. He was licensed, too."

"Really?" Kurt sat up straighter, surprised his answer to prayer sat before him. "You'd take Jayden, then?"

"In a heartbeat."

"Apparently his mother is not to blame." Kurt stared at the kitchen wall, unseeing. "Jayden told me his stepfather is the one who hit him. He said the man hasn't physically hurt them before. Only bellows a lot."

"His behavior is escalating?"

"Appears to be." Kurt pulled a hand across his chin. "Why does a woman stay with such a man?"

"She may be too afraid to leave." Peggy sighed, shoulders slumping. "I've seen it before—women who blame themselves for the abuse. They think they'll fix things by being a better wife, or keeping the house cleaner, or whatever. The behavior continues to deteriorate."

"And their children suffer with them."

"Women don't see the problem when they're tangled in the middle of the abusive web." Peggy carried her cup to the sink and rinsed it out. "But their children are recording the behavior, one ugly scene after another."

"How do I report this?" Kurt's chair scraped the floor as he stood and scooted the legs under the table. "We can't keep Jayden, can we?"

"No." Peggy stepped to the table beneath an antique wall phone. She lifted what appeared to be an address book from the drawer at the top. Flipping through pages, she came to a stop, her finger pausing midway down the fourth page. "I have a number for Children's Services of Oregon. I'll call the caseworker I used to work with and tell her the scenario." She grinned. "Remember the form I had you complete when you moved in?"

He nodded. "You said you had to check me out."

Peggy laid the open directory beneath the phone. "I wanted to be ready, in case I decided to take in foster kids again."

"Did I pass?"

"Not yet." Peggy shook her head. "But I'm glad we're ahead of the game, for Jayden's sake."

"Will the state take Jayden away from here?"

"His mother will have to be contacted. An investigation will follow. But I imagine Jayden can remain here while all this happens. Placement comes last and I can request him, since he's already here."

"Sounds great." Kurt rolled his shoulders, the tension of the evening, coupled with the workload today, taking its toll. "I'm heading for bed. Thanks for wanting Jayden."

"Horses aren't the only things we rescue around here." Peggy pinned him with her gaze. "Giants hit the ground hard when they fall."

"I know." Kurt's eyes narrowed. "You've picked me up more than once, if I remember right."

"War and abuse are the devil's tools."

The roar of rocket propelled grenades lit up the night sky, casting an eerie glow over the endless sand. His body burrowed alongside a rock outcropping, Kurt spotted enemy invaders sneaking closer to where his unit waited outside a remote Afghan village. Through his night goggles, he surveyed the area to the right of the last dwelling. A pile of debris, layered on top to look like a mound of rubble, remained untouched. He and Foster had discovered it this morning, the arsenal of ammunition beneath holding enough fire power to raze the village. Clever—the disguise had almost gone unnoticed. Almost. Foster noticed a glint in the sun about the same time Kurt found the ends of the buried rockets. The hovel beside the mound contained more.

Kurt spied a shadowy form skulking along the base of an outbuilding, inching closer to the arsenal. As he sighted the marauder through his scope, Kurt's heart ricocheted in his protective armor like a machine gun on overload. His palms grew damp, his breathing labored. One well-aimed shot was all Kurt would need. "Looking for trouble, vermin?" Kurt raised his Barrett semi-automatic, waiting for the terrorist to show himself. "I'm ready for you."

Another grenade pierced the darkness, sending the enemy sprawling for cover. The man he'd been tracking disappeared into the shadows. Kurt scanned the area, moving his scope inch by inch over the darkened landscape. Nothing.

"McKintrick. You there?" Foster's voice in his headphones.

"Ready and able."

"I'm going to check the hovel next to the cache of ammo we found." Foster's voice over the radio broke up, raspy and erratic. "Captain says to stand down."

"No! Let me do it." Kurt spoke with more force than he'd meant to, his arms like dead weights at his sides. "Saw enemy moving."

"Guard's still on duty," Foster replied. "Captain's orders."

"Not yet." Kurt aimed his rifle in the direction of the cache, but the butt wouldn't settle on the wall's edge. No figures appeared in his vision, except one. Foster. "Stop. It could be a trap."

"Cover me." Voice fading, his buddy trekked toward the protected hideaway, gun at the ready, and approached the door of the hovel. He pulled it open and peered inside. A second later, an explosion loud enough to rock the ground beneath Kurt's hideaway shot flames in every direction. Debris colored the sky like Fourth of July fireworks gone awry. Fire and smoke rolled from the shattered building. Kurt squinted, trying to see through the haze. Ten feet from the doorway, a body lay unmoving.

"Foster? No!" Kurt burst from his hiding spot, fighting the sand beneath his feet. He paused to orient himself, trying to figure out which way to run. He stared into the darkness, nothing but spinning walls surrounding him. Sweat poured down his face, his body drenched in perspiration. His breathing rattled like a body in death throes, legs wobbling beneath him and arms caught in webbing around his middle.

A knock sounded at the door. "Kurt?" Peggy's voice. "You okay?"

The full moon outside the window wakened his senses as confusion crept from the recesses of his mind. He bumped his head on the headboard and fought the bed covers twisted about his shoulders like shackles. He slammed his fist into the pillow. His body shuddered, first hot, then cold, while his heart fibrillated, and dizziness threatened to topple him. Another firefight lost. Another menacing dream. Another reminder of his failure.

He unwound himself from the bedding and staggered to the door, easing it open a crack. "Sorry to wake you. Flashback."

"Foster?"

He nodded.

Her voice caught. "Praying."

"Thanks."

The next morning Lissa entered the office, the disappearance of the boy on her mind and Kurt's icy welcome on her heart. Why had seeing the man unnerved her? The erratic fluttering he'd caused in her abdomen wormed its way to her lungs, leaving her panting, only fueling her fury this morning. Kurt's response when she'd greeted him still grated on her, rubbing her emotions raw. His behavior bordered on the peculiar.

"Good morning." Sheriff Briggs wiggled a finger, signaling Lissa to approach his desk.

Curious, she wandered around the rows of desks to where he sat hunched over a message pad. "Sheriff?"

"The Herrick Valley Rescue Center reported a stowaway in the trailer yesterday."

"Stowaway?" Lissa frowned. "A horse and a dog, if I remember correctly. No room for anything else."

"Peggy Blake called here this morning and said Jayden Clarke rode in the trailer with the filly to her new home."

"Jayden's been found?" Lissa's mouth dropped open, drawing in a slight gasp. "Is he a runaway?"

"No, he's being taken into protective custody. Did you get Mrs. Barnes' temporary address?"

"Yes. She's at her sister's place." Lissa pulled her phone from her pocket. "The address as well as the number to call is here."

"Good." Matthew copied the number. "She'll have to be told."

"What's the reason?" Lissa hated to put the mother through any more suffering. "Can't Jayden simply go home? George is in jail."

"Peggy reported bruising on the kid's forearm. Jayden claimed his stepfather hit him."

Matthew's words spun in her head. "Melanie told me she has a restraining order against her husband. That's not enough to reunite mother and son?"

"No. The boy was injured in the home she shared with the stepfather. Jayden's not safe in her care, as long as George is in the picture. There's quite a process for her to reclaim her child."

"How long does this take?"

"Depends. The state likes to get kids back with their folks. But George is not Jayden's biological father, so uncovering the man's need to abuse his stepson might take time."

"Where will Jayden go?"

"The judge placed him in a temporary home for now. Peggy is a licensed foster parent and as soon as her helper is checked out, he will be added to the list of people caring for Jayden."

"You mean Kurt?" Lissa gritted her teeth. Did this require another encounter with the man?

"You know anything about him?"

"Once upon a time." Lissa shrugged. A lifetime ago. The flicker of hope still burning from those yesterdays spluttered in her mind. One good poof and the flame would die. Only the memory would remain.

On Friday Jayden rode beside his court-appointed advocate to the state-supervised meeting with his parents in Burns. The woman assured him, that even though both parents were required to attend, she would speak up for him if things went bad at the meeting. The turmoil in his belly could be from car sickness or nerves—Jayden didn't know. If he could skip this altogether, he would. He'd do anything to avoid an encounter with George. He doubted the woman could do much to control the man.

This past week blurred in his memory—moving from one place to another once he'd been discovered in the Blake barn. He'd spent the last two days at a temporary shelter, and now he would meet his mother and George in a closed session with a children's services official. All he wanted to do was get back to the rescue center and Duke. Facing George after last Saturday frightened him. The man couldn't be trusted to hold his tongue or his temper.

At last they arrived at the official-looking building, and he followed his advocate down the hall. Entering the meeting room with her, Jayden gulped air, trying to find his courage. His mother and stepfather sat talking with someone he didn't know—a young woman in a dark blue suit. The room grew quiet when he approached and sat where the advocate placed him: across the table from them.

"I'm Molly, your caseworker." The young woman stood and held out her hand. "It's nice to meet you."

Jayden acknowledged her greeting and shook her hand.

"We're here today to determine if you should go home." Molly tapped her pencil. "When someone your age runs away, we need to know why."

"I didn't run away." Jayden peeked up at the caseworker. "I came home Saturday night and the ambulance guys were wheeling Mom out of the house." He pointed at George. "And he was staggering drunk and yelling."

Mom gasped. "You were there?"

"I told you he was in the house hiding." George sneered. "Causing trouble."

Jayden shook his head. "I wasn't in the house. Not until the police left. I went in through the garage door and cleaned up the mess in the kitchen."

"Mess?" Molly raised her eyebrows. "What do you mean?"

"Broken whiskey and beer bottles." Jayden spoke into his

trembling hands. "Spilled food. Scared me."

"And then you left again?" Molly sank back into her chair.

"I was afraid George would come home later." Jayden gulped. "So I went back to Mr. Mueller's place."

"Peggy Blake said you had bruises." Molly leaned toward him. "May I please see your arm?"

He held his arm out for inspection, exposing the fading bruise.

"Do you remember how this happened?"

"George slapped my arm when I interrupted his dinner." Jayden breathed in deep.

"Has he done this before?"

Jayden shook his head. "This was the first time he hit me. He usually just yells."

George's face reddened as he studied Jayden, eyes narrowed to slits.

"Can you think of any time you might have hurt yourself?" The woman sounded as if she were on George's side. "Did you fall on the school playground? Or play too hard with a friend?"

"Only Duke."

"Duke?"

"Yeah, he's Bennie's dog." Jayden chewed on his lip. "He likes to chase sticks and I like to throw 'em."

"See?" George blurted out. "He's off running around, not even home when he should be. Those bruises could have come from any number of places." The man wagged his finger in Jayden's face. "Tell the truth."

"Mr. Barnes." Molly's tone held a warning.

"I don't like being accused by a mealy-mouthed kid as if I'm a criminal. I drive long hours to bring home good money, and the kid shares in the bounty."

"I'm sure you do. But Jayden's safety is important here."

"He's safe enough. He eats three meals a day, has a bed to sleep in, and a roof over his head. He's provided for, more so than many." The volume of the man's voice rose as he spoke, his face reddening to crimson. "I took him in when I married Melanie."

His mother sat in stoic silence. Stitches over one eye lined up along her eyebrow. Her eyes held unshed tears, lower lip caught in her teeth, and hands clasped tight enough to turn the knuckles white. Jayden ached to hug her, to tell her he loved her, but with George in the room such an action would only fuel the man's temper.

Molly's gaze travelled from his mother to George to Jayden. "I've made a decision." She laid her pen down. "Considering the fact that you, Melanie, have filed for a restraining order against your husband, and in light of these few moments together, I agree with the judge. Jayden needs to stay in protective custody for the time being."

The room went silent. George crossed his arms across his chest, the sound of him grinding his teeth turning Jayden's stomach.

Molly continued. "When the two of you have sought counseling and worked through your issues, you can appear before the judge and seek custody of Jayden."

Mom sagged in her chair, gave George a quick, nervous look, and burst into tears. "I can't lose my son."

George snarled. "You'd rather lose me?"

"We'll schedule supervised weekly visits during his time in state care." The woman's tone grew more serious. "But until we're certain Jayden is in a safe environment, he will remain in the custody of the state children's services. Do you both understand?"

"Yeah, I understand." George stood and spat his words at Jayden. "As far as I'm concerned, he can rot there." He hitched his pants up over his beer belly and stomped out, a security guard on his heels.

Molly closed her briefcase. "I assure you, Mrs. Barnes, this is for the best."

Her lips pressed into a straight line, his mother stood, holding her arms out for a hug. "I'm so sorry, honey."

Jayden hurried toward her, feeling her arms wrap around him as she wept quiet tears into his neck. He slipped his hands behind her back and held on tight.

"So sorry." A sob escaped her lips.

"Me, too, Mom." Jayden hugged her again and took a step back. "But I knew we had trouble when I got up the morning you went shopping." Jayden let go and gazed into his mother's eyes. "George wishes I wasn't there."

"I'll get this sorted out as soon as I can, okay?" She framed his face in her hands, stroking his temples with her thumbs. "Your dad would never have allowed this to happen."

"I know. Dad was a hero." Jayden pulled away from her grasp, his voice hollow in the empty room. "But he's not here."

CHAPTER FOURTEEN

TWO DAYS LATER, PEGGY STOOD WAITING when Kurt returned from his trip to the Hines Feed Store. The pickup bed held fifty pounds of dog food for Duke, several bags of grain for the horses, and two sacks of groceries Peggy had asked him to buy.

"What's up?" Kurt slid from the cab and reached over the side of the bed to hand her the smaller sack nestled in the corner. He lifted the heavier one and walked beside her to the house. "You look like you have news."

"I do." Peggy beamed. "Children's services rushed your background check, and Jayden will return tomorrow."

"Thank goodness." Kurt rolled his head backward and massaged his neck. "I didn't think I could take another day of playing with Duke to keep him happy. I've never seen a dog so enamored with a kid before."

"Remember, the dog lost his first master not much over a month ago. And then Jayden. It's a wonder Duke functions at all."

"Function is not a term I would use for Duke. He spends all day with his head on his paws, stretched out by the door of the barn, staring down the driveway." Kurt set the bag of groceries on the kitchen counter. "Maybe with Jayden back, we'll get our work done around here."

With a knowing laugh, Peggy reached into the grocery bag and lifted out cans of tuna and a box of macaroni. "You aren't fooling me. You're as attached to the boy as Duke is."

Kurt took the empty bag and folded it before answering Peggy. "He reminds me of kids I saw in Afghanistan. Dark brown eyes filled with vacant stares, chilling me to the bone." Images of the child soldiers the Taliban had recruited flitted across his memory—including six-year-olds sent out as suicide bombers.

"One afternoon, after a particularly troubling morning, I came across a verse in Psalms that made me think." Spotting his Bible on a chair in the corner, he picked it up, flipped to the middle, and read: "You are the helper of the fatherless. Break the arm of the wicked and the evil man." He tapped the page where he'd read. "I vowed when I returned home I wouldn't let any child suffer the way I saw those children suffering. I intend to keep my promise."

"Foster said the same thing." Peggy's eyes glimmered in memory. "He shared every ounce of chocolate I sent him." She busied herself tucking the boxes of cereal into a corner cupboard.

"The kids loved him." Kurt smiled at the image the mention of chocolate resurrected. Clusters of children had swarmed around Foster, playing ball with him before he dug out the candy—testing them and watching. Not all children could be trusted. "But some of them were plotting, even as they accepted the chocolate."

"How sad that kids are drawn into this deceit." Peggy shook her head, gaze on the floor as if caught in the image he'd described. "But you still ministered to them with the candy, not passing judgment."

"Speaking of chocolate, do you have enough junk food stashed?" Jayden's appetite knew no bounds. "I don't want to catch the boy eating horse feed again."

"When he arrives tomorrow, you can make a store run and stock up."

"Don't complain about what we buy." Kurt lifted his chin in a defensive move. "We guys tend to satisfy our cravings before we think about eating healthy."

"Like chocolate instead of carrots?" Peggy opened the refrigerator's veggie drawer and filled the space with the carrots, broccoli, and cauliflower she'd requested. She winked.

"Just sayin'."

Peggy shoved the drawer closed, laughing. "Boys are always

boys, even when they outgrow their boy duds."

"I plan to put him to work when he gets here." Kurt pulled out a chair, plopping on the seat. "Bennie Mueller let him help around the ranch last summer."

"He needs to keep busy." Peggy agreed with a nod. "He's in love with that filly. But I want him to have a fun summer, too."

"Wonder if he hikes?" Kurt lifted an apple from the fruit bowl. Rubbing it with the heel of his hand, he sank his teeth into the shiny green peel and snapped out a chunk. "Malheur National Park isn't far down the highway."

"Neither is Steens Mountain." Peggy folded the rest of the grocery sacks and stuck them in the broom closet. "You might see the herd of Kiger mustangs."

"Jayden would like that. Lady's sire is supposed to be a Kiger." Juice threatened the corners of his mouth, so he swiped his cheek with his knuckle.

Peggy popped open a package of napkins, handed him one, and filled the napkin holder next to the fruit bowl. "Doesn't surprise me, as close to the area as Bennie's spread lay."

"Am I always going to be your extra kid?" Kurt chuckled and wiped his mouth, wadded up the napkin, and tossed it at her.

Catching it mid-air, Peggy grinned. "I'm a mom. Old habits never die."

Kurt nodded. "My mother would say the same thing. No wonder Foster and I were friends." He got to his feet and stretched. "I better get started on those stalls. I'm sure the horses have left plenty for me to sift out of the shavings."

"Tomorrow is supposed to be sunnier. We can turn them out for a while. Lady needs to run off pent-up energy."

"You know she'll roll in the mud. Jayden will have his hands full grooming her."

Peggy's eyes twinkled, a mischievous grin on her face. "I'll call

Lissa. She can give Jayden pointers on getting the filly clean, don't you think?"

Kurt schooled his face to remain impassive. "No need. Jayden said he's been grooming the filly since she foaled. He'll get the job done." He pulled on his baseball cap and aimed for the door. "I've got stalls to clean."

"You two work well together." Peggy's chuckle slapped at his back. "And don't tell me you didn't notice."

"Jayden's a good kid."

"Nice dodge, Kurt McKintrick."

Kurt resisted slamming the door as he exited. Peggy didn't understand the situation with Lissa. But then, he wasn't sure he did either.

Kurt stacked two bales of hay near the loft's feeding area while Jayden worked beside him, pitching loose silage to the three horses waiting in their stalls below. Duke whined, pacing back and forth between the loft ladder and the barn door. Though Jayden had only settled in two days ago, he'd proven how much he'd learned from Mr. Mueller. Kurt admired his determination to help.

"Lady! Get out of the way." Jayden banged the pitchfork on the edge of the loft and stomped his foot.

"What's she doing?" Kurt strolled to the rim of the feed hole and peered down.

Lady stood staring up at them, ears cocked forward. Her nostrils flared as if she'd not smelled Kurt before. Or was she hoping to steal another handkerchief? Bits of hay clung to her mane and dusted her back.

"She stepped under the hay the second before I let it fly."

Jayden mumbled under his breath. "Now I'll have to curry her all over again."

"She likes having you around."

Jayden's expression softened, a slow grin working its way across his face. "You think so?'

Kurt nodded. "Both Duke and Lady seem mighty attached to you. You must have given them excellent care last summer."

As if on cue, Duke barked, sitting on his haunches outside Lady's stall. His front feet danced in little excited pats on the concrete as he bounced from one foot to the other.

"He wants to play." Jayden whistled at the dog. "He likes to be outside and run."

"He's a herder." Kurt stuck his pitchfork in an unopened bale and grabbed the top of the ladder, stepping down on the first rung. "Instinct tells him to move things from one place to the next."

"It's what he used to do at Bennie's place." Jayden followed Kurt down the ladder. "All I had to do was shout 'herd' at him and he'd race across the field and bunch up Bennie's cattle or torment the horses." Reaching the barn floor, he called Duke to him. "He got antsy after Bennie sold the cattle at auction."

"He's a good dog." Kurt extended a hand and patted Duke's head. "He'll keep intruders away."

"He kept me company when I hid in Bennie's barn." Jayden's eyes clouded, as if his mind was caught remembering the incident, his gaze distant and brooding. "I didn't know what I was going to do. But Duke laid next to me and kept me warm."

"Considering he had to eat cat food, that's loyalty." Kurt grinned.

Jayden giggled, the young boy inside him bubbling to the surface. "Nah, the cat food was for me. I found kibble for Duke. I'd never insult him with kitty chow."

Kurt laughed, glad to see Jayden's sense of humor surfacing.

He'd only been here two days since the state cleared his placement, but with Peggy's need to feed and Kurt's companionship, the boy had blossomed. The bruise on his arm had faded to a sickly yellow in the time he'd been away, but no permanent damage to his physical well-being remained. Kurt worried about the emotional damage waiting to explode without warning. He'd seen enough of it in traumatized military personnel in Afghanistan. Time would provide distance for Jayden, and youthfulness would play a role. Kurt silently vowed to make a difference in this kid's life. Maybe then he could atone for the things he couldn't prevent during the war.

"Hey, you guys." Peggy stood in the barn door. "Breakfast is on the table. Have you worked up an appetite yet?"

"We'll be right there. We need to grain the horses."

"Okay. Five minutes max." The sound of Peggy's footsteps faded as she walked toward the house. She stopped and called over her shoulder. "Cinnamon rolls."

Jayden measured the grain into the buckets like Kurt had shown him and carried the feed to the waiting animals. Lady whinnied, her nose poking up over the stall gate. Jayden reached up and caught her muzzle with his right hand, left hand scratching along the filly's cheekbone.

Kurt filled the water troughs and shut off the hose, coming to stand next to Jayden. "I guess we're ready for breakfast."

"Race you to the cinnamon rolls."

"You're on, slowpoke." Kurt jerked Jayden's baseball cap down over his eyes and jogged to the back door of the house, passing Peggy, who had reached the door. Stopping to open the screen for Peggy, Kurt grinned at the boy behind him.

Jayden came running, face bright pink with the exertion. Kurt slipped in behind Peggy and let the screen door slam shut. He slipped the hook into the eye to secure the door and watched

Jayden's jaw drop. "I'll save you one if you're good."

"Hey, no fair." Jayden tugged on the screen, but Kurt held the handle closed. "You can't eat all of those."

"Wanna bet?"

Jayden's mouth puckered, and his eyes narrowed. "But I'm a skinny little kid who went without food for days. I kept a can of cat food handy in case my dog got hungry. Surely you can show me a little mercy, can't you?" He flattened his hands against the screen and pressed his face into the wire mesh. "Please, mister, can you spare me a cinnamon roll?"

"You ought to be on Broadway." He unhooked the screen door and popped it open. "You've been smooching with the horse, so go wash before you sit down. Understood?"

Jayden disappeared down the hall with lightning speed, returned like a rabbit, and plunked himself into his chair at the same time Kurt sat in his.

"Did you use soap?"

"A squirt of suds and a quick rinse." Jayden wiggled his fingers. "You want to smell the flowery scent?"

"No, let's pray before these get cold." Kurt offered the blessing, noticing, as he glanced up, Jayden watching him, a question across his eyes. Perhaps the boy had never prayed before. Kurt made a mental note to begin a dialogue with Jayden about spiritual matters. He handed the plate of rolls to Peggy and then to Jayden. "Dig in."

After breakfast, Kurt and Jayden carried their dishes to the kitchen sink. Kurt handed Jayden a towel. "Whoever cooks, relaxes. Whoever eats, cleans. I'll wash, you dry."

Jayden frowned at the mention of work but didn't move away. Kurt washed plates and the baking dish while Jayden dried the dishware. He stacked it on the counter beside him.

Peggy smiled and patted the boy on his shoulder. "You and

Duke can let the horses into the north pasture. Don't forget to activate the electric fence."

"Thanks, Mrs. Blake."

"Please call me Peggy."

"Uh, okay, Peggy. Mom insists I call adults mister and missus. I forget."

"Call me Mrs. Peggy, if that makes you more comfortable, but here on the ranch I think Peggy is fine."

"Okay, Peggy." Jayden scurried to the door and whistled. Duke appeared on the porch, his excited yips filling the outdoors. "See you all later."

Peggy appeared wistful as Jayden and Duke disappeared from view. "The boy has such nice manners. Makes you wonder why his mother would marry a man mean enough to hurt her child."

Kurt leaned against the counter. "She might not have known the man long enough before she said yes." He shifted his weight from his right hip to his left, crossing his arms. "Or the guy's a chameleon. Charming and attentive one minute. Demeaning and ugly the next."

"I suspect alcohol plays a role in all of this." Peggy untied the apron around her waist and hung it on a hook near the stove. "Many men can be monsters when they're drunk."

Kurt lifted the stacked dishes into the cupboard. "Saw it in the military. Guys on leave would drown their tensions in a bottle." He closed the cabinet door, making a note to oil the hinge. The squeak had gotten louder.

"Speaking of leave." Peggy pointed to the calendar. "Father's Day is a week from Sunday. You want to spend it with your family?"

"My father is dead, Peggy." Kurt straightened, assuming a no-nonsense tone. "My mother remarried two years ago, but her new husband has adult children, so they'll probably celebrate with them."

"You mean your stepsister, Lissa?" Peggy's smile tipped at the corners of her mouth. "You can't avoid her forever."

"Not trying to." Kurt stood straighter, his eyes intent on the sun filtering in through the window. "Our paths don't cross much."

"I know what I saw, Kurt McKintrick. You two have a past, and from what I could tell, it was a good one." Peggy poked him in the breastbone. "What aren't you telling me?"

"The war changed me." Kurt shuffled his feet, allowing the incidents of battle to replay in his mind for a moment, the darkness of those encounters wreaking havoc with his sanity. "After Foster's accident, I asked for reassignment to an outpost more remote. Lissa and I lost track of each other. I don't think I can pick up where I left off."

"Foster wouldn't want you blaming yourself for his death." Peggy slid the chairs into place around the table. "I know you promised him you'd help me with the rescue center. I'm grateful. But I won't let you waste your life here."

"I'm not wasting my life." Kurt pierced the woman with a determined look. "Coming here, I'm finding it again."

"Okay. But promise me you'll try to find time with Lissa too." Peggy's eyes shone warm and caring. "If nothing else, to give her closure. I don't think you have."

"I'll think about it." Kurt ambled toward the door. "It's all I can promise."

Peggy crossed the room and clutched his arm, then hugged him. "Start by going home and seeing your family. Father's Day would be a good time for a visit."

"Why don't I go next week instead?" Kurt smiled at the persistent woman. "The visit would allow me to test the temperature of the waters. See how deep it is where I need to swim."

Peggy nodded. "A good place to start."

He pushed the screen open and walked into the sunshine, Peggy's words haunting him. Closure? No, if he were truthful, the need to spend *more* time with Lissa festered in a pocket beneath his heart. His desire to return to the relationship they'd shared before Afghanistan had vaporized into wishful thinking. The man he'd been and the man he'd become were two different people. Lissa might not like the new version. He certainly didn't.

CHAPTER FIFTEEN

LISSA FINISHED BUTTONING HER UNIFORM AND donned a jacket before stashing her pistol in its holster. Sorrel barked from the kennel outside, where Lissa had taken the dog earlier so she could dress. She had fifteen minutes until she'd leave for work—enough time to clean up the kitchen. She'd rinsed a cereal bowl when the phone chimed on the counter beside her. Pushing the device to speaker, she grabbed a spoon and fork to wash while she greeted the caller. "Hello?"

"Lissa?" Delaney's voice wobbled in the empty room. "You there?"

"Right here, Sis." Lissa stacked a cup on the drainer mat. "How are you?"

"Good." The phone went silent, save for the sniffs coming from the other end.

Lissa stopped cold, hands dripping water into the sink. "Why are you crying?"

"I'm going in for surgery next Monday." Delaney stopped and blew her nose. "I'm sorry. I didn't think I'd get emotional. It's not like I didn't know this was coming."

Lissa's heart banged beneath her breastbone. "What kind of surgery are we talking about?"

"I have another cyst. Like the one I mentioned before. The doctor biopsied the tissue and said I shouldn't wait any longer. Especially with Mom's history of ovarian cancer. The kids are out of school next week, so Eily and Dad will keep them."

"Delaney, I'm so sorry. What can I do?"

"There's nothing much to do. I know you've barely started your job. I'm sure you can't get away, can you?" Delaney's voice grew hoarser as she continued. "But I wondered if you could come."

Leave it to Delaney to avoid being a burden. Of course she would be there. Delaney was her sister, after all. "Family emergencies take precedence over a job. Any time." Perspiration beaded across her brow. "If you want me, I'll ask this morning."

"David will be here with me. But he can only get one day off, maybe two. More time off would require a leave of absence. Eily can care for me at Dad's place, but the problem is getting there."

"Say no more. I'll make it happen." She mentally calculated how much she could get done before Friday. Matthew had called her in on three of the last four weekends. She'd earned a little payback time.

"Thank you for trying." Delaney's uneven breathing vacillated between stifled sobs and hiccups. "I'll understand if you can't."

"I'll call you tonight and let you know." With their goodbyes said, Lissa clicked off the speaker phone and grabbed her keys. She'd planned to go home for Father's Day the weekend after next. An early visit wouldn't be out of the question—better chance of avoiding a certain Marine. All of his sisters would remember the attraction between Kurt and her while they were on leave two years before and if they showed up, would ask questions. She couldn't risk the embarrassment. Or the scrutiny.

Sliding into the driver's seat, she slumped, Delaney's condition raking at her conscience. She'd promised her sister she'd see a doctor and get tested for the cancer gene. Gripping her middle, she rocked, bracing against the paralyzing dread nibbling her dwindling self-confidence. A negative blood test alongside a positive diagnosis could destroy all the plans she had made, fade her dreams, and diminish her happiness. Like a snake slithering in the grass, ovarian cancer lurked in her past, haunted her present, and threatened her future. If the tests proved true, she might as well have stayed in the Navy. "Please, Lord, I know this is selfish. But keep me from Mom's illness."

As she drove to the office, past images of her mother fed her worries. She couldn't be stupid and not have the tests done. Early detection could save her life. But what kind of life would it be without the hope of a husband and children? The desire for a husband had prompted her resignation from the Navy. Dreams of a family had fueled her journey home. She'd been attracted to Kurt because he loved kids and grew up in a larger family. Could she find a man to whom a family could be children they adopted? Most of all, would that satisfy her need to nurture? Her age didn't leave her a lot of time, and fighting an illness like this would steal years she didn't have. All her dreams would shrivel like a balloon leaking air.

Pulling into the parking lot, Lissa killed the engine and calmed herself. Right now, she had to help Delaney. Her sister had symptoms, had taken steps to avoid their mother's illness, and needed support. This much she could do. Perhaps in the reality of the situation Lissa would find the courage to protect her own life and seek medical attention. She could rethink her plans after she knew the truth. Kurt's nearness only made matters worse. She'd do well to stay clear of him, whatever it took.

Lissa spotted Matthew on the phone when she entered the department cubicles. He motioned for her to come to his desk. Hanging up the phone, he smiled. "Good news. Jayden Clarke is going to stay at the Herrick Valley Rescue Center along with the filly you saved. I'm putting you at the heart of the case so you can follow up on the domestic dispute between George and Melanie Barnes. I also want you to keep track of the investigation into Bennie Mueller's death. Think you're up for it?"

"Follow the paper trail, right?" Lissa would have a lot of work to do before she left on Friday. She'd wait until later to mention the leave of absence.

"Pretty much. Kurt McKintrick will be your point man. He lives there and can report on the filly's progress as well as apprise you of Jayden's proceedings. He should be easy to work with. He's ex-military like you."

Lissa nodded. Kurt McKintrick represented a lot of ex-everything. She ought to know.

Later in the afternoon, Lissa steeled herself for the discussion she needed to have with her boss. She had spent the morning touching base with Jayden's case manager and had read the coroner's report. Nothing conclusive had shown up on Bennie Mueller's autopsy, though the medical examiner found a couple of unusual things. Bennie's brain scan revealed a subdural hematoma, and his right shoulder had been dislocated. Both injuries were consistent with ranch-related accidents, and neither appeared to have caused his death. Yet the coroner marked them as anomalies to be noted, should more details emerge.

She showed the report to Matthew. He frowned as he read the document. "I'm thinking we should have an investigator scour the place." He glanced up at her. "Dust for fingerprints. Look for blood splatter." His lips pressed against each other as he thought. "Once the place is released for disposal, all evidence could be destroyed."

"You think we might uncover proof we missed?" Living in a drama made for television had not been Lissa's plan when she came home.

"Nothing about this case has been normal." Matt shook his head. "As fine a man as Bennie was, I owe it to him to be sure his death was natural."

Matt returned to his desk and Lissa resumed her paperwork, still waiting for an opening to broach the subject of leave with him. She opened the files on the Barnes case. Melanie had agreed to attend a state-funded parenting class in Bend, two hours away. Upon his release from jail, George had skipped town, leaving on a cross-country haul for his company. Melanie didn't know if he'd return, saying her husband accused her of siding with her son. The woman agonized over every day that passed without Jayden. But until completion of the class by both parents, along with additional counseling or a legal separation, neither George nor Melanie would see Jayden. The wait would free Lissa to go home. The opening she needed.

"Matt?" She approached his desk, waiting for him to cradle his phone. "I need to take a leave of absence."

"Really? You've barely gotten started here." Matthew's brow furrowed. "Everything okay?"

"My sister's having surgery next Monday, and I'd like to be there for her." Her voice caught, the struggle for composure a battle. "I'd be gone a week."

"Should work." Matthew studied his desk calendar. "I put the wheels in motion on the Mueller death investigation. An examiner will begin work tomorrow or the next day. We won't have anything conclusive for several days." He sighed. "I'll pray we don't have any more animal rescues until you get back."

"Thanks. I appreciate you understanding."

"Family is important."

"Ours has been through a lot together." She forced a smile even though her heart frowned. "I know Delaney would do the same for me."

"Get as much done on those cases as you can before you leave on Friday." Matthew leaned back in his chair. "May I contact you if something surfaces and I need information?"

"After Monday. Delaney will be in recovery, and I'll be freer to talk."

"Tuesday, it is."

Lissa prayed as she drove to Portland the following Sunday. She'd stopped by her dad's home in McKenzie Bridge to drop off Sorrel before steeling herself for the two-hour commute to see her sister. The tedium wouldn't end there. Delaney's surgery, scheduled at dawn tomorrow, promised a long wait in the hospital lounge.

David and the twins would visit Delaney before she went into the operating room. As the procedure progressed, David would take the kids to school and return.

Lissa would keep vigil, a responsibility for which her sister depended on her. According to Delaney, offering moral support to David would be Lissa's most important role. The man loved her sister with a protective tenderness Lissa envied. Delaney had married young—her choice a good one. But in case David proved stronger than Delaney believed him to be, Lissa brought a book to read and snacks to share. Neither of them would need to leave the surgery waiting area for long.

Lissa glanced at her watch. Delaney would be readying for bed soon, her early morning check-in time at the hospital requiring David to get her there. Lissa had hoped to see her sister before she went to bed, but maybe it would be better to wait until morning. If she were still awake, Delaney would no doubt drill her about the doctor's appointment Lissa promised to schedule, a phone call she'd all but ignored. Why she dragged her feet, Lissa didn't know, but deep inside the possibilities of illness stifled her resolve to the point she couldn't move forward. Seeing Delaney and hearing her doctor's prognosis might be the kick in the pants Lissa needed to act.

The lights remained on in the house as she drove into the driveway. Lissa grabbed her overnight bag and walked to the door, anticipating her stay in the Mathews' guest room.

David opened the entry and extended his hand, taking her bag. "Glad you're here."

"Is she asleep?"

"No. She waited for you." He escorted her to their bedroom.

Delaney sat up, leaning against her pillow. "You made it." Delaney's smile from the bed lit up the room.

Lenna and Liam rose from their chairs to give her hugs. "Aunt Lissa," they said in unison.

"Okay, kids." David motioned toward the door. "Let's give your mother and Lissa time to talk. Tomorrow will come early."

Lenna stopped and hugged her mother, her eyes squinting as if she fought tears. "I'll see you in the morning, Mom."

Her brother offered a hand to his mother, bending down to kiss her cheek. "My high school group prayed for you at Sunday School this morning." Liam cleared his throat. "You're in good hands."

Delaney kissed her son. "Thanks, honey."

Liam's attempt to control the emotion Lissa saw threatening his composure warmed her heart.

David bent over his wife, sliding his palm down the side of her cheek. "I'll be back in a few minutes."

With the family out of the room, Lissa pulled a chair closer to the bed. "You have great kids. I'm angry at myself for missing so much of their growing up years."

"You kept in touch." Delaney reached out a hand, patting Lissa's shoulder. "They talked about their aunt in show-and-tell at school. Nobody else knew an intelligence officer who worked aboard a Navy vessel. You made them unique."

"Show-and-tell, eh?" Lissa chuckled. "Makes me sound like a specimen."

"To them, you're a hero." Delaney's smile faltered. "Have you made your appointment?"

"Nothing like being abrupt." She leaned back into the chair and shook her head. "Not yet. The ramifications still overwhelm me."

"You mean the possibility of cancer?"

"Yes, and how a diagnosis could alter all the dreams I've made for my life." She dropped her arms, hands resting in her lap. "Part of me doesn't want to know."

"I understand. If it hadn't been for the cysts, I would have preferred to ignore the possibility myself." Delaney squeezed Lissa's hand. "But living with different dreams is better than not living at all."

She gazed into her sister's eyes. Delaney had everything Lissa wanted—husband, children, career. Her sister couldn't know or realize life without those elements because they were part of her existence. Lissa, though, feared the loneliness a diagnosis could trigger. No man wanting her. No children of her own. She'd lived with her personal isolation the past fifteen years. To survive in the future she wanted, Lissa might be forced to make choices she'd never anticipated. Compel her to carve out a different path from what she'd imagined. Making her dreams happen grew more remote by the day. Delaney would never understand how frightened she was.

Lissa waited in the recovery lounge the following morning. Delaney's surgery had ended a few minutes after nine, and the nurse appeared soon after, telling David his wife had been moved to recovery and he could see her when she awakened.

Noon came and went; Lissa's hunger came and stayed. She snacked on a package of nuts and offered a second pack to David, but he shook his head.

"Why don't I visit the cafeteria and grab us both a sandwich?" She fumbled through her handbag, retrieving a twenty from her wallet. "Turkey, ham, or roast beef?"

"Should I go with you?"

"No. Stay here in case Delaney wakes up. If you're not in the lounge when I get back, I'll find you." She stood and slung her bag over her arm and tapped her brother-in-law's shoulder. "You want to tell me what kind of sandwich, or shall I surprise you?"

"Turkey and Swiss, if they have it."

"See you in a few." Lissa headed down the hospital corridor, catching the elevator to the main floor and the Food Court. Her mood lifted. Like a mole digging his way to the earth's surface to discover sunlight, Lissa's escape from the monotony of waiting did wonders for her mental outlook.

Fifteen minutes later, she returned to the sixth-floor waiting room carrying a tray laden with water bottles, two sandwiches, and a bag of chips for David. Her brother-in-law had disappeared. She approached the nurse's desk. "I'm here to see Delaney Mathews. Is she out of recovery?"

"Room 623." The nurse gestured to her right. "Follow the corridor and make a right."

"Thanks."

David and Delaney were speaking in whispers and secret smiles when she peeked into the room. David cradled his wife's fingers in his right hand, the knuckles of his left caressing her temple and touching her hair.

Delaney's eyelids fluttered, the movement of her head an almost imperceptible shift as she spoke. "Lissa."

"I brought your husband a sandwich. Thought maybe he'd stop pacing if I did." She set the tray on the bedside table and moved to the other side of the bed, clasping Delaney's hand in hers. "Nice to have you back with us."

Delaney blinked. "Not sure I am. They've got me dopey on powerful drugs."

David spoke to Lissa. "Her doctor came and left. They didn't find any obvious cancer."

Lissa exhaled, not aware she'd been holding her breath. "Wonderful news."

"She's not to lift anything and is restricted to limited activity for two weeks until they remove the staples." David gave his wife a wink. "I know Eily will have great fun taking care of you."

"As will Dad." Lissa squeezed Delaney's fingers. "I don't think he's forgiven either of us for moving out and leaving him."

Delaney closed her eyes, eyebrows creasing as if pain flitted across her forehead. "But he understood. He knew how hard it would be to stay in our home without Mom. I still can't wrap my mind around how he stayed there alone for fifteen years."

"The house held memories for him. Mom lived on in her kitchen, in the décor, and in the life they shared." Lissa's words wobbled. The memories had so threatened to choke her, she'd refused to stay in the house for nearly fifteen years after her mother died. "You and David won't have to face that kind of future."

"Amen." David picked up one of the sandwiches. "Which one of these is mine?"

"The triangular one. Turkey and Swiss."

"I guess the hoagie is for you, honey." David winked again at his wife. "After the Jell-O and chicken broth."

"Nice try, big boy." Lissa frowned. "The triple-meat gut-buster is for me, and I'm not sharing." Her stomach growled. "My tummy seconds the motion."

Delaney chuckled, mouth contorting. "Don't make me laugh. It hurts."

"Oops, sorry." David handed Lissa the hoagie. "I think Lissa and I are suffering from post-op battle fatigue. Keeping watch for four hours is mind-numbing."

"I'm sure it is." Delaney tipped her head back and rolled her shoulders inward, stretching her neck. "Lying on my back is also tiring."

The door popped open, and a nurse appeared. "I need to check your bandages." She aimed a pointed look at David and Lissa. "It will take only a few minutes."

"Sure." Lissa grabbed her sandwich, gesturing for David to follow her with the tray. "We'll be outside wolfing down our food if you need us."

In the hallway, Lissa pressed David for answers. "Is that all the doctor said? No lifting or pressure on the abdomen?"

"She has to wear a wide band of netting, like a girdle, around her middle for about four weeks. The muscles have to heal as well as the sutures."

"When can she go back to work?" Lissa unwrapped her sandwich.

"It will depend on the final pathology report."

"The pathology report?" She glanced up, the bite of sandwich suddenly tasting like sand. She forced herself to chew. "I thought there was no cancer."

"No *obvious* cancer." David rubbed the toe of his shoe against a spot on the floor, as if avoiding Lissa's statement. "They found a small mass on the right ovary. They removed it without rupturing it, which is good, but if there are cancerous cells inside, they may order chemotherapy."

"They took the ovary or the mass?"

"Only the mass. We had elected to have the ovaries removed,

but Delaney is a young woman. They've found removing the ovaries early in a woman's life can lead to other health problems like heart disease. But if the mass ruptured, they may go back and remove that ovary." David shook his head. "We won't know until Wednesday."

"Can't come soon enough for me." Would she ever see daylight again?

CHAPTER SIXTEEN

KURT PULLED INTO THE DRIVE AT his mother and stepfather's home the following Wednesday, noting the extra vehicle sitting alongside his stepfather's pickup. The rig seemed familiar, though he couldn't think why.

He hadn't called his mother since he'd visited on Mother's Day, having made a promise to return for a reunion with his sisters around the third weekend in June. Sneaking in ahead of schedule meant he could connect with two of his sisters and their families and share a few meals with his mother. His idea allowed him to leave before Marshall's girls arrived to spend Father's Day with their dad. He'd miss one sister by being early, but all things considered, perhaps this would be best. Having a new stepfather with two grown daughters, one of whom he'd dated, complicated his life. Visiting any or all of them required strategic measures. He remained confident the genius of his plan knew no bounds—perfect to its core.

Facing Lissa petrified him. He'd withstood Taliban terrorists without breaking a sweat, yet the idea of explaining to this woman why he hadn't communicated in more than a year parched his throat. He bore the blame. He hadn't kept his end of their promise to stay connected, allowing the budding beginning of a great relationship to wither and die. But until he could come to terms with the images Foster's death imprinted on his mind and what they'd done to his soul, a relationship with Lissa remained only a distant possibility. How could he explain how he felt? Would she understand if he did?

Goobers came flying around the end of the house, another dog the color of polished copper at his heels. The two circled Kurt's pickup, barking in excited harmony, their tails wagging as fast as their jaws flapped. He'd thought Duke was noisy.

Stepping from the cab, he heard a shout and the dogs raced away. The tall frame of his stepfather lumbered into view. Kurt raised his hand in greeting as Marshall drew near, a pair of work gloves in his palm. The older man adjusted the canvas cap on his head, sweeping errant strands of grey beneath the brim. Approaching the truck, he extended his hand.

Kurt returned the handshake. "Hey, Marshall. How's it going?"

"Glad you've come for a visit. How's life on the other side of the mountains?"

"Busy. The rescue center is a full-time operation."

Marshall's eyes twinkled. "Yeah, I heard you got a branding from one of the newer tenants there." He inclined his head as if he empathized with Kurt. "Probably damaged your pride more than your back, right?"

"I can only imagine the version you heard."

"I doubt it." Marshall's attention drifted beyond his shoulder, the sound of footsteps on the gravel, accompanied by giggles, approaching from the roadway behind.

Kurt's gaze followed Marshall's, and as he turned in the direction of the noise he stood nose to nose with a surprised Lissa, her niece and nephew at her side. Curly locks tumbled about her shoulders, wispy tendrils teasing her cheekbones. He groaned in silence. Why was she here? And looking like an actress from a romantic movie. Her untamed beauty threatened to melt his resolve like ice cream in the summer sun. He resisted the urge to wrap his arms about her waist and lift her off the ground. "Lissa?"

"Well, imagine finding you here. My long-lost stepbrother in human form." Lissa's eyes narrowed, the smile usually adorning her face missing, a pout in its place. "How did you find your way home, *bro?*"

Kurt's tongue caught on the roof of his mouth, words stuck like peanut butter in his throat. Though seeing Lissa again played havoc with his senses, the storm in her eyes suggested she didn't share his pleasure. He inhaled, waiting for the tempest to follow.

"Need any liniment for your backside?" She cuffed his shoulder. "Or have your aches and pains faded along with the hoof prints?" Tucking her hands into her jeans pockets, she stuck her right hip out and rocked on her left heel. The silence made his cheeks grow warm.

Marshall cleared his throat. "Lenna, Liam, let's go see if Eily has any lemonade ready. Lissa, Kurt, you can catch up with us anytime."

The twins joined their grandfather and headed for the house. Marshall glanced over his shoulder at Kurt, the look one of warning.

"Thanks, Dad. I won't be long, I'm sure." Lissa returned her scowl to Kurt. "We caught up on news earlier this week." She arched a brow. "*Didn't* we?"

"I'm surprised to see you here." Kurt frowned, his mind racing to figure out what event on the calendar he might have forgotten. "Father's Day isn't until next Sunday." That much he had checked. Leave it to her to complicate his plans. "Do the twins have a birthday?"

"No." Lissa clenched her teeth and huffed. "So why are *you* here?"

"Peggy thought I needed time away from the ranch." Kurt's words failed him again, his reason to be there abandoning him for the moment. What had happened to the discipline he'd learned in the military? Always ready with an answer. "Jayden has settled in. It was a good time to get away."

Lissa's brow furrowed, causing a crease in her forehead. "I see."

Judging from the look in her eyes and the rigor of her stance,

Lissa felt more hurt than angry. The intensity of her gaze said the source of the pain stood before her. He inhaled for courage, all his broken promises lining up in his mind like unopened packages awaiting delivery. He should have acted sooner. "I came to see my mother this week so I wouldn't invade any Father's Day celebration you and Delaney might have planned for your dad." He lifted his baseball cap, shook it, and replaced it on his head. "I didn't think you'd start this soon."

"Didn't call, either, did you?" Lissa placed her hands on her hips. "No surprise there."

"Why don't you fill me in?" Kurt feigned his sweetest smile. "I've got nothing but time."

"And I'm fresh out." Lissa spun on her heel and marched away from him, calling over her shoulder. "You may have to sleep in the garden shed." She stopped at the steps and glared. "But it can't be much different than Afghanistan, can it?"

Kurt followed her at a distance. Whatever trouble had stuck a burr under her saddle, he didn't understand. He didn't believe he'd caused *this* reaction. Had he? If it were true, he'd find a way to fix the problem—staying through the weekend or World War III, whichever came first. He wasn't sure which battle he preferred.

Lissa stomped all the way to the house, clenching her teeth and squeezing her eyes to keep the tears at bay. Kurt didn't deserve the mean jabs she'd given him, didn't deserve bearing the brunt of her emotional state. She swallowed her shame—he had been an easy target, her aim perfect.

She couldn't erase from her mind this morning's scene with the doctor. Delaney's surgeon shared her sister's good news. No need for follow-up chemo. A blood test every six months for the next three years is the only procedure necessary. Delaney and David's smiles glowed from their happy hearts.

But the doctor didn't end there. She'd focused on Lissa. "As Delaney's sibling and a patient genetically linked to this disease, may I recommend you see a specialist soon? Delaney told me you're only a couple of years younger than she is and unmarried. I don't want to alarm you, but testing is important to your health too."

She didn't want to alarm her? The doctor might as well have purchased billboard space. By the time Lissa left with Delaney in her car, the doctor had arranged for a blood test at the hospital, taken down her medical history, and scheduled a follow-up appointment with a physician who practiced in Hines. If nothing else, Delaney's specialist redefined thorough. Returning home after this weekend, Lissa would be given the results of the rest of her life. If she had one.

"Lissa?"

Kurt's voice stopped her at the top of the porch steps. She swiped at the tears that had escaped, doubling up her cold fists and pressing them against her burning cheeks. She couldn't smile, opting instead for raised eyebrows and pressed lips. She faced the man.

"Can we talk?"

She shook her head. "Not now."

"Later this week, then?"

"Maybe." She pulled the door open. "I'm not making any promises." Stepping into the darkened porch, she let the screen door slam behind her. Kurt's reflection in the kitchen window mocked her as she hurried to the entry, his gaze following her retreat. *I can't encourage him now. Not until I know more. I should let him go. It's best for both of us.*

Kurt sighed, stepped off the porch, and wandered toward the garden. Straight rows of young shoots lifted their tendrils toward the sun, the green of their bodies bold against the rich, black soil. Though only half of June had passed, many of the plants appeared close to harvest. Onion and carrot tops sprang from bulging roots. Tomatoes, small and green, already hung from sturdy stems. Everywhere he looked life flourished.

His stepfather possessed a green thumb, if ever such a thing existed, but Kurt's thumb appeared to grow nothing but melancholy and bitterness. War had stripped him of feeling—the aftermath of losing a friend hurt too much. Yet right now he yearned to sprout a little affection in Lissa. But she was keeping her distance. He could only blame himself. Had he ruined everything between them? Were there no seeds of their former relationship still sleeping in her heart, waiting for the right conditions to encourage them to grow? Was he the man to tend them?

"Kurt?"

He jerked around, startled.

His mother stood behind him, holding a glass of lemonade. She extended it to him. "Welcome home."

He closed the gap between them and wrapped her in a hug. "It's so good to see you, Mom." He stepped back and took the glass. "How did you know I was thirsty?"

"Lucky guess. I know your trip over the mountains is as long as Lissa's." She aimed a knowing look his way. "And you never take time to stop."

"Right on both counts." He drained the glass and handed it back. "But I think my timing is a little off." He rubbed the back of his neck, his nerves threatening to bunch up his muscles there. "I was trying to beat the Father's Day rush and ran smack dab into it."

"I wondered why you were here in the middle of the week."

"Peggy said I needed a break and suggested I go home." He dug the toe of his boot in the dirt. "I figured Lissa and her sister would show up for Father's Day, so I opted for an early visit to give them space." He queried his mother. "I understand there's no room in the inn?"

"I already called your sister and asked if you could have one of the upstairs rooms in her house." His mother placed a hand on his shoulder. "Zoe said you could have your old room if you don't use the window as a fire escape."

"She's not sneaking in through the window anymore?" Kurt laughed. "Dad was so mad when he found out."

"You two were pills, for sure." A breeze rose up from the field, and his mother pulled her sweater tighter around herself. "Staying at Zoe's will be noisy. Erin has an upstairs room all to herself, and so does Sean. Zoe hasn't moved her twins upstairs yet. Your old room is now Zoe's guest room."

"Sounds good to me. I didn't get to see the house the last time I was here because they were away visiting Colin's mother. I'd enjoy seeing how they fixed it up after the fire." His mother shivered, and Kurt drew her closer. "Is it nice?"

"Beautiful." She leaned into him. "I still have nightmares when I think about that night."

Kurt kissed her temple, remembering the phone call two years before that stilled his heart. His sister, Kathryn, had sobbed into the phone. "Mom's in intensive care. The Christmas tree caught fire. Marshall's quick thinking saved her and Zoe's kids, but Mom's in serious condition. Please come home." He rested his chin on his mother's head.

"Thank God the ladder you and Zoe used for your capers lay in the grass."

"Thank God is right." Kurt kissed her on the cheek. "Will Zoe feed me or do I have to fend for myself?"

"You can eat here." She looked over her shoulder toward the house where Marshall approached. "I'm making casseroles because Laney's twins are staying as well as their mother. At fifteen, Liam eats like there's no tomorrow."

"Reminds you of me at that age, I'll bet."

"I don't remember you consuming as much." She turned and studied him. "But considering your size, maybe I do." She patted his shoulder. "Anyway, you're welcome at our table."

Kurt hesitated. "I don't know, Mom. Lissa's not happy to see me. I may opt for a trip to Newport to see Rudy Taylor. I need a good dive in the ocean to clear my head."

"Have you seen him since you returned from Afghanistan?"

"Only once." Kurt shook his head at the memory. "Catching up with Rudy might be easier than irritating Lissa with my presence. I don't want to strain dinner conversation."

"She's upset about Delaney."

"Delaney?" Kurt scuffed his heel against a misplaced thistle growing in the row.

"She had surgery on Monday. Lissa brought her here to recuperate."

"Serious?" Kurt sucked in a gulp of air, the information punching him like a kick in the gut. Lissa's reaction now made sense.

"It could have been, but she's all right. The surgery resurrected too many unpleasant memories of their mother." She smiled at Marshall as he stopped beside them. "Am I right?"

Marshall nodded. "My first wife's illness impacted all of us. Lissa doesn't want a repeat performance."

"Is Delaney in danger?" Kurt's pulse raced. "Please tell me she doesn't have the disease."

Marshall clasped him on the shoulder. "They received the pathology report this morning. The small mass they biopsied remained intact, and they believe Delaney's out of danger. Which relieves all of us."

Kurt relaxed. "No wonder Lissa is strung tighter than a bass drum."

His mother reached for Marshall's hand. "Tense doesn't even come close to describing what everyone's feeling."

"I can understand why." Kurt admired his former family home across the fence, now fully restored after the fire. "I *will* take Zoe up on her offer. If I have to, I'll drive into town and eat there. I wouldn't want everyone to wind up with indigestion because Lissa is glaring at me."

His mother hugged him. "A trip to see Rudy would be good for you too."

"I might have time for both."

Marshall's eyes narrowed. "No food fights at my house, young man. Understood?"

"No, sir. Wouldn't think of it." He saluted and sized up the house his mother and stepfather now occupied. Which window might be Lissa's room? As a trained sniper, he could land a bullet in a soup can at five hundred yards. Here he'd have to try a shot less deadly and more annoying. A well-placed wad of mashed potatoes at dinner might make her smile. He'd definitely have her attention.

CHAPTER SEVENTEEN

HOME. THOUGH LISSA HAD ONLY PROVIDED transport south for Delaney's convalescence at Dad's while David went back to work, she had to admit the rest and relaxation nurtured her soul as well. The sounds of giggles and barking dogs outside her window drew her there. The twins were tossing a stick for Goobers near the garden. Sorrel stood on the side, tongue lolling, waiting her turn. Lissa smiled at the scene, resurrecting memories of playing with Delaney and one of Dad's many rescued mutts.

Her attention drifted to the back of the garden and into the neighboring yard beyond the fence. As a child, she'd not known the family who first owned that home. The house faced another road, and the occupants' children were high schoolers when she entered third grade. The McKintrick family moved in after Lissa's mother died, and Lissa had run away to live with her best friend's family. If she hadn't disappeared, she and Kurt could have finished school together. Who knew? They might have been high school sweethearts if she'd stuck around.

As if he heard her thoughts, Kurt appeared at the back porch, skipped down the steps, and leapt over the rail dividing the properties. His broad shoulders rippled under the t-shirt he wore, his long, lean body tanned and trim as if he'd just returned from hours of patrol in Afghanistan. He covered the garden distance in a dozen strides. His sandy locks peeked out from beneath the baseball cap he wore backwards, so different from his short, almost non-existent Marine cut. As if he sensed her watching, he zeroed in on her window, a smile on his face.

Lissa ducked back into the room, pulled the curtains closed, and gathered her things for a shower. Breakfast aromas wafted from the kitchen, as they always did when Eily prepared food for company. Lissa's stomach growled. She wouldn't pass up one of Eily's breakfasts, even if it meant sitting across the table from Kurt. She'd perfect her glare while she showered. Who was she kidding? That would never work. If she were truthful, she still wanted to reconnect. She wouldn't make it easy for him, though, falling at his feet and begging him to remember what they had. Maybe by the time she left on Saturday, the disappointment of having Kurt so near, yet emotionally distant, would work its way free. He'd become one more man in an ocean of them. She could survive two more days. Couldn't she?

Half an hour later, she entered the kitchen and smiled at her stepmother. She finger-combed her damp hair, shaking the curls away from her face. "Morning, Eily. Smells good."

"Good morning." Eily set a plate of biscuits on the table. "Can you grab the pitchers of juice and milk for me?"

"Sure." Lissa produced the containers and set them in place.

Eily stepped to the porch and hollered. "Breakfast!"

The buzz of several voices sounded from the porch as family members clambered up the steps. Lenna and Liam appeared through the door first. Her dad followed, sharing a laugh with Kurt. Lissa braced herself for the awkward silence she expected.

"Morning, Lissa." Kurt found his chair next to her father and sat, scooting over so Liam could squeeze in next to him. "Sleep well?"

Before she could respond, her niece grasped Lissa's elbow and pulled her to a place beside Eily. "We can fix a plate for Mom."

Lissa plopped into her seat, nodding an answer at Kurt. She didn't know what to make of his subtle grin, but his face had all the nuances of a person plotting mischief. She'd have to be on her guard.

Marshall extended his hands to his right and left, grasping Kurt's and Eily's fingers as he led in prayer. "For this food we thank you. We ask you grant Delaney a speedy recovery. Thank you for the good pathology report yesterday. Amen."

Ignoring Kurt's eyes on her, Lissa filled a plate for Delaney and handed it to Lenna. "You want to take this to your mother?"

"Okay." Lenna balanced the plate of food in one hand while she poured coffee into a cup with the other. Lifting the steaming brew, she stepped away from the table. "Be right back."

"How is Delaney today?" Kurt's gaze landed on Lissa once again. "Is she still drugged?"

"She's sitting up." Eily passed the eggs to him. "But her incisions are uncomfortable, and the bandages pull, so she'll be lying back down as soon as she eats."

"Her recovery is expected to take about a month." Lissa took care not to return his stare. "They cut through muscle tissue when they removed the mass."

"Are you here that long?" Kurt stabbed a sausage and held it aloft, waiting as she answered.

"No, I'm going home Saturday." To think of leaving upset her. Despite the painful memories home held for her, Lissa sensed her need to heal, not of physical ailments like Delaney, but from an ache in her soul still lingering after her mother's death. Kurt's presence added to the memories, but those were happy ones she could reflect upon, even though he seemed to have forgotten what they once meant to each other. The tension between them at the Mueller ranch had stretched like a taut rubber band ready to snap. He'd hurt her, but after coming here she so wanted to forgive him. She ordered her heart to return to her chest and bit into her biscuit.

"That's a shame. Zoe and Colin have invited me to dinner with Kathryn and her brood Saturday night. You haven't seen my crazy sisters and their husbands yet, have you?"

"Not since we met at Thanksgiving two years ago."

Kurt's eyes widened. "I'd forgotten they were there."

"Your sisters are delightful." Lissa smiled at Eily. "Must take after their mother."

Kurt lifted an eyebrow and studied her for a moment. Without another word he forked a sizeable mound of eggs into his mouth. He leaned back in his chair and chewed, that unreadable grin back on his face.

Lissa focused on the breakfast, tongue caught between her teeth while she avoided Kurt's penetrating stare. His boyish good looks and muscular build distracted her from her resolve to act disinterested. She needed more from him than he'd given her since his return home. She wanted to revisit the week they'd dated while on leave two years ago and pick up where the pieces had frayed. She and Kurt had clicked—spending days at the ocean, the zoo, and the mountains—burning up I-5 like they owned it.

If only this disease, like an unwelcomed visitor, hadn't invited itself into her life. If only her future weren't hanging in the balance. She had no answers—yet. If the tests revealed problems, she didn't think she could find the courage to tell him. If Kurt tried to rekindle their relationship, her kindest act would be to release him. Doing so would be easier on her, though that would be the furthest thing from her desires. Her heart ached, the pieces of broken promises picking at her sense of duty like a scab over a wound.

Lenna rejoined the group at the table, carrying an empty plate. "Mom asked if you could come see her when you've finished breakfast."

Lissa smiled at her niece, grateful for a reprieve from the eyes of the Marine sitting across the table. "Sure. Does she want any more to eat?"

"Another biscuit."

Lissa carried her plate to the sink and rinsed it. "Eily, I'll be back to help with the dishes as soon as I talk to Laney." She grabbed a biscuit, plopped it on Delaney's plate, and headed toward the bedroom.

Delaney's smile greeted Lissa as she sat at the edge of the bed. "Heard you could use another helping?" She held out the plate to her sister.

Delaney shook her head. "I needed a ploy to get you in here so we could talk."

"About what? As long as it's not about my blood tests or the Marine in the kitchen."

Her sister frowned. "Then I guess we don't have anything to talk about."

"Delaney." She huffed, the short blast of air lifting tendrils around her face. "Let me guess. You want to advise me about my love interest?"

"He's awfully cute." Delaney giggled, then caught her side in a moan. "And I have it on good authority he's crazy about you."

"Ha! Men who kiss and run are not crazy about their girlfriends. He didn't contact me in almost two years. We met by chance at the scene of a horse rescue. And then he had the nerve to call me sis. Sorry, Delaney. He's not crazy about me."

"Would you put away the pity party for a minute and listen?" Delaney's brown eyes flashed, a signal Lissa understood well. "There's more to this story than you're seeing."

Lissa picked at a loose thread on the bedspread, eyes narrowed as she waited for her sister to speak. "All right. I'm listening. Please make it quick—I've got dishes to do."

"Kurt experienced tragic losses in Afghanistan. Eily says he's still suffering." Delaney reached out to squeeze Lissa's shoulder. "He might need a listening ear, another soul to be there for him."

"Being there for someone is a two-way street, and he hasn't been there for me." Lissa stood and reached for the plate. "I'll think about it. I've got my own challenges."

"He's not the kind of guy to intentionally hurt you."

Lissa paused, staring at the ceiling. How she wanted to believe Delaney's words. Admitting she agreed would only add fuel to her sister's fire. "If he acts interested in rekindling our relationship—and that's a long shot—how can I encourage him, knowing what I may be facing in my future? I haven't forgotten how Mom died. I promised myself I would never knowingly put a man through the hell Dad experienced with her." She faced her sister. "This isn't the scenario I had planned for my return to civilian living."

"You can be friends." Delaney leaned back into the pillows. "You would have Kurt's support, at least."

"No, I'd probably have his pity." Lissa would never settle for that. "I'd rather not."

"Promise me you'll make an effort."

Lissa gritted her teeth, fighting the war raging within her chest. "For you, I will." She swallowed the lump blocking her throat. "And he'd better appreciate the effort."

Delaney nodded, blinking as she dozed off.

Lissa tiptoed to the door and left. If she received anything different than a clean bill of health, Kurt would never know.

When Lissa returned to the kitchen, Kurt stood at the sink, an apron tied about his waist, hands immersed in the suds. He smiled and tossed a towel at her. "Since you volunteered for this, I thought I'd make myself useful."

Lissa stepped up to the drainer and lifted a plate. "This bears all the earmarks of a setup, you know."

"You think?" Kurt grinned, edging next to her and whispering under his breath. "Remember, I'm the cunning Marine sniper. I've got all the angles covered."

"Are you flirting with me, Kurt McKintrick?" Lissa's guard rose as she took a step back. "You're about two years too late."

He leaned against her shoulder and nudged. "Better late than never, don't you think?"

"I'm not convinced. You have a lot of explaining to do."

"Will you listen?" Kurt's nearness made her heart pound. "Your shoulder has been rather cold."

"Lots of time on the ocean." The smile she'd kept at bay forced itself across her mouth. "Nice apron, by the way."

"You like the frilly lace trim?" He pirouetted like a clumsy hippo, holding the apron out for a curtsy.

She couldn't help but laugh. "You have my undivided attention."

"Finally!" Kurt handed her a handful of silverware. "These are hot."

"Thanks for the warning." Lissa gazed into the sapphire eyes, remembering the tenderness of Kurt's kiss when he'd left her at the airport. So much promise in that kiss. Both of them had headed back to their units—Lissa to the *USS Ronald Reagan,* which carried her across the Pacific, Kurt to Afghanistan by way of San Diego.

"I'm sorry about Delaney's surgery." Kurt set three more plates on the drainer. He swished through the dishwater and retrieved a cup and two forks. "Mom told me your mother's history when we moved here." He drained the sink and dried his hands on his apron, untying it as he did. He laid the apron on the counter. "This has to be scary."

"Terrifying, actually." Lissa finished the last plate and draped the towel over the glasses. "Let's go outside. These can finish air-drying."

When they reached the porch steps, Lissa stopped, hovering

inside the screened porch while Kurt moved on through. She put her hands on her hips. "Why are you here?"

Kurt stopped at the bottom of the porch, one foot on the second step, his hand on his knee as he leaned toward her. "I already told you. Peggy thought I needed a break and sent me home. I came early to avoid crashing any Father's Day party you girls planned."

"We didn't plan a party, though I'm sure you've realized that by now." Lissa worked to keep her voice calm and demeanor gentle. "I brought Delaney here to recover because David couldn't get enough time off." Lissa's composure threatened to crumble. "Your mother volunteered to care for Delaney while she's off work."

Kurt nodded. "Sounds like my mother. Always busy nurturing." He straightened. "She snagged your father by cooking, you know."

Lissa smiled at the memory. "He was putty in her pot roast."

Kurt laughed, then sobered as he studied her. "How are you doing in all of this?"

Lissa clenched her teeth. She couldn't tell him. Not yet. She shrugged her shoulders. "I feel like we missed a bullet."

"Always a plus. Especially in my profession." The silence widened between them. Kurt surveyed the yard, his fingers tapping his jeans pockets. "I can't wait to bring Jayden here."

"He seems like a special kid."

"I hope to make a difference in his life." Kurt shifted his weight from one foot to the other. "Can we talk about us?"

"Us, Kurt?" Lissa fought the urge to scream. "I haven't heard from you in more than a year, and the year before that was sketchy at best. There is no us."

Kurt studied the ground. "I know. And I'm sorry."

Lissa blinked back the nuisance of tears that threatened to interfere. "I thought we were friends when we parted."

"We were. Are." Kurt straightened. "At least I want to be."

"Friends don't stop writing cold turkey. No e-mails, no letters, no Skype." The fury in her voice surprised her. "No anything."

"May I explain?" He extended his hand. "Let's walk out to the garden."

Lissa hesitated. The request seemed so innocuous, yet spending time with the man tugged at the wounds burning inside. She needed this as much as he did.

"Please, Lissa?" Kurt's eyes pleaded with her, his lips a thin line. "You don't have all the facts."

Remembering Delaney's plea and her promise, Lissa nodded and followed him down the steps. This better be good.

CHAPTER EIGHTEEN

Lissa, determined to stand her ground, didn't take Kurt's outstretched hand. The discussion ahead promised to be painful, Kurt's nervousness obvious as he shrugged and tucked his hands into his jeans pockets. He fell into step beside her. They walked in stark silence to the garden shed, skirting the budding rows of vegetables her father managed to plant every spring. In another month Lissa could explore the area without unseen eyes watching from the house. Today, though, the exposure probed like a microscope, she and Kurt the specimens under glass.

"Foster Blake and I were like brothers." Kurt stared out across the field, as if seeing a scene she couldn't. "We trained together, patrolled together—we were inseparable."

"I remember you mentioning him in one of your letters." Lissa peeked at Kurt, his stance one of a Marine on duty. "I'm sorry he was killed."

Kurt's shoulders sagged. "Me, too."

"Were you there?"

Kurt raked his hand through his hair, shuffling the toe of his boot in the loose garden soil. His eyes closed, jaw clamped, muscles beneath the skin rippling as he gritted his teeth. Kurt exhaled what sounded like silent rage. "I got him killed."

Lissa stopped, searching for words, her mind racing in a thousand directions. This couldn't be true. An infusion of heat crept up her neck. Kurt leaned both hands against the wall of the garden shed, head face down in his biceps, and she looked away to give him privacy.

A breeze flitted across the green corn tops. Cucumber foliage crept from mounds at the garden's perimeter, tiny yellow blossoms peeking from beneath the leaves. The promise of life surrounded

Kurt and her here, even while talk of death lingered on their lips. She refocused on Kurt. "What happened?"

He straightened and cleared his throat. "I'd seen a guy slinking around a weapons cache we'd discovered. I couldn't get him in my sights without risking a civilian."

"But you didn't find him?" Aboard ship, Lissa had only heard bits of battle. Her intel always named the place and time and sometimes, news of the wounded, but the details Kurt would know never reached her.

"No." Kurt faced her, his countenance dark. "Kids were playing. People were going about their business. No sign of anything amiss. The man eluded me." Kurt lifted one shoulder, then the other, as though the tension threatened to paralyze him. "I stayed on watch through the night." Lines etched his brow, sapphire eyes empty and distant.

"All night long?" Folding her hands into fists, Lissa fought the urge to touch him. If only she could.

"Our commanding officer had me stand down the next morning. Foster and I rejoined our unit on patrol." A rattling breath escaped his lips. Though his eyes met hers, he was caught in memory. "When we came back through the area later that night, we encountered enemy fire. I waited on a ridge while my guys scouted the village. I wanted to inspect the building one more time but never got the chance. Instead, Foster crept up to the hovel like a cat. I covered him while he walked through the door. Everything exploded. He never knew what hit him."

Lissa shuddered, thinking of all this man had witnessed. How could Kurt think it was his fault? "But that does not make you his killer."

"I didn't get the guy earlier, the one who set the bomb." Kurt stared at the sky. "If I'd done my job, Foster would be alive."

Lissa exhaled. "Or you would have entered the building

instead."

Kurt turned his attention to the garden, and nodded. Lissa didn't know what to say. "Why didn't you write and tell me?"

"I asked for reassignment." He seemed locked in the memory, again unseeing. "Got sent to a remote outpost where communications were rare." Kurt's expression turned to chiseled stone. "I hoped to never return."

"Maybe so, but you did." Lissa folded her arms across her chest, trying to balance the gritting of her teeth with the pattering of her heart. Why did she want to smack this man upside the head one minute and in the next yearn to wrap her arms around him and never let go? She searched for the right thing to say, wanting to relieve Kurt's pain without making it sound like she was hitting on him. "God let you live. Don't disgrace Foster's sacrifice by refusing the gift of life you've been given. Otherwise he died in vain."

"How can I enjoy life knowing he lost his?" Kurt's words punctuated the air. "I don't know how to do that." He raised his hands, then dropped them, as if chopping at an unseen enemy. "His death haunts me every night, and my days are wracked with memories I'd rather forget." His voice deepened in tone, as if while trying to convince her, he wanted to persuade himself. "Foster was my best friend. I'm afraid to care about anyone else. Knowing me, they die. I can't move forward. I can't go back. I'm stuck in a hell I can't escape."

Lissa pressed her lips together. She'd only thought of her disappointment, dashed hopes, and hurt feelings. Kurt sounded broken and confused. In his present state of mind, he might be a long way from wanting a future with anyone, let alone her. Maybe he never would. Her heart went out to him—she wanted to help. "You've taken the right step. You came home and found purpose."

"No, I came home to keep a promise to Foster." Kurt spat out the words, his face red. "I told him I'd help his mother run the rescue center." He crammed his hands into his hip pockets. "But every day is a reminder he's gone and I'm the stand-in." Kurt faced her, his chin quivering. "I can feel him everywhere. It's as if his spirit returned to the ranch. I'm the imposter."

"Did he share your faith?"

"Yes. It's the one thing I did right." For an instant, a smile flitted across his face, disappearing almost as soon as it appeared. "Foster had never given God much time, even though he grew up attending church and Peggy is a believer. But he saw me reading my Bible one night and asked me about it. One thing led to another and soon we were studying the scriptures every chance we could." Kurt beamed, hope in his eyes. "One week before he was killed, he surrendered his life to Christ." He twisted away from her, hands doubled into fists. "Only one week. That's all he got."

"Amazing." Lissa reached out and touched Kurt's shoulder, fighting the tears her heart wanted to give him. Maybe she could help. "Don't you see? Foster didn't get only one week, he gained eternity." Lissa moved around to study his face, and placed her palms against his cheeks. "God put you in a place where you could share your faith with him. God knew ahead of time Foster would die, but because of your presence in his life, Foster is enjoying heaven."

"I know, but still. . ." He stepped back, jaw clenched and brow furrowed. He wouldn't look at her.

"No buts about it." Lissa punched his shoulder with her fist before giving him a side hug, squeezing him with all the tenderness she could work into her fingers. "God put you there. Planned for Foster to meet you." Sharing this moment with Kurt, Lissa didn't know whether to laugh or cry. How amazing that they'd found common ground.

"You think so?" For the first time since she'd seen him here at home, a glint of hope appeared in his expression. He inhaled, then blew the air out. Reaching in his pocket, he retrieved a handkerchief, dabbing at the wetness she hadn't noticed on her face. "I should have talked with you sooner."

"You're right." Lissa kept her voice soft, warmed by the tenderness of his touch. "Give this time to heal. What you suffered is not a surface wound. You've been stabbed in the heart."

"And it hurts." Kurt's voice broke with emotion. "I blocked everything and everyone out when Foster died." Kurt stuck the handkerchief back in his pocket. "I never meant to hurt you."

She met his gaze, blushing when he looked at her, the sallow circles beneath his eyes a telltale reminder of his anguish. She had to protect him from more pain by maintaining her distance. At least for now. Maybe she'd have better information in a week or two.

She chose her words with care. "I understand how his death affected you. It couldn't have been easy, going through this like you did." She turned from him. "But not hearing from you, not knowing if you were alive or dead, and wondering what I'd done wrong, wasn't easy either."

"I'm sorry." Kurt paused. "I only hope you can forgive me."

"Now that I understand, I do." Keeping her answer short knifed into her determination, when her heart screamed *I love you.*

"It's all I can expect, after the way I've treated you." Kurt's ragged breath sounded like it came from his toes. "I'll be at the ranch for the foreseeable future. We'll be close."

Lissa ignored what he implied, reminding herself she had to wait for answers. "Peggy appeared to enjoy your company. I know loading feed and hay is way too much for her to handle." Lissa cocked her head. "Do you find the work challenging?"

"Since Jayden has joined our merry group, I have renewed purpose. So does Peggy. She's carrying on Foster's legacy. Jayden will help her move on." Kurt searched her eyes. "She's hurting, too. She and Foster were very close."

"How are you doing with Jayden?" She could imagine him with the child. Big, tough. A hero in the kid's eyes.

"He's a great kid. Polite. Willing to work." Kurt paused. "He needs a good role model. Reminds me of the children I saw in Afghanistan, haunted by events they couldn't control. I see an opportunity for me to make a difference—not something I could do over there."

"Perhaps you and Peggy can find new meaning in your lives by ministering to Jayden's needs." She studied him. "He might help you both heal."

"And we'll help him. Jayden's got a long road ahead." His face, filled with hope, turned toward her. "I'd still like to include you."

"That's good, because you are stuck with me until this case is closed. Matthew assigned me to oversee the investigation at the Mueller ranch and to keep an eye on the parenting progress with Melanie and George Barnes."

"I couldn't be happier." Kurt reached for her hands. "But I'd like to revisit our relationship as well."

Lissa bit her lip, eyes closing as she fought the truth she needed to share with this man. "I'm not sure I can go there again." She couldn't involve him in her life until she had test results. He'd already lost a close friend. Her future might not be the happily-ever-after she sensed he sought. She lifted her chin and summoned her resolve. "All I can say is, I'll think about it."

She had to get out of here before he said something to make her melt. Lissa double-timed her path across the garden, not stopping until she reached the porch. Kurt stood watching her, a lone pillar in a sea of green. The image matched one she held in memory of her father after her mother died. Right before she decided to run away. Blocking out the remembrance, she slammed through the back door and went to find her sister—running—the way she'd always done before. Would history never stop repeating itself?

Kurt pulled up at his sister Zoe's house Saturday night, excited to see his nieces and nephews again before he headed home. He'd traveled to Newport, a three-hour drive from McKenzie Bridge, to see his friend Rudy yesterday. A day on the Oregon coast and a short swim in the Pacific with his buddy had sweetened his trip over the mountains. Now a family dinner would complete it.

His older sister, Kathryn, and her husband, Connor, had already arrived and were chatting with Zoe in the kitchen. Their three teenage sons—Peter, Paul, and Patrick—sat on the sofa, each with an electronic tablet in his lap.

"What are you playing?" Kurt leaned over the back of the sofa and peered down at the small screens in his nephews' laps.

"We've got a three-person game going." Peter, now a muscular eighteen-year-old, raised his tablet closer to Kurt. "I'm about to expand my kingdom."

"Looks like fun." Kurt watched the three brothers moving their men across the screens. "A lot like football."

Colin brought Kurt a glass of lemonade. "Glad you could stay another day. Is Lissa coming later?"

"She went home this afternoon." Kurt sipped the drink, bracing himself for the inevitable questions. Though Lissa made sure she avoided him Friday, today he'd hugged her good-bye before she headed over the mountains. The scent of her hair lingered in his memory. "Mom and Marshall have their hands full, caring for Lissa's sister and her twins."

Zoe emerged from the kitchen, holding the hands of two toddlers who'd been born while he was in Afghanistan. "Speaking of twins, this pair is missing their Uncle Kurt." Zoe crossed the room, children in tow. "Which one do you want first? Nikki or Nate?"

Kurt set his glass down, knelt, and lifted Nate. "This little guy will play football when he's older."

Zoe laughed. "He's a chunk, that's for sure." She searched the room. "Where's Lissa?"

Colin picked up Nikki. "She's not coming. Kurt scared her off."

Zoe's mouth popped open. "Are you two fighting?"

Kurt resisted rolling his eyes. "Until a week ago Tuesday, when we both showed up at the same ranch to rescue a horse, we hadn't seen each other since we said goodbye at the airport two years ago." He gulped his lemonade. "In fact, when I arrived here Wednesday, I surprised her. It's why I'm your house guest. I didn't know she and Delaney would be here."

Zoe cuffed him on the shoulder. "Get with the program, brother. What's the matter with you?" Zoe crossed her arms. "I saw you two in the garden the other day. Lissa's not a woman you should let get away."

Kurt shook his head. "She's the one running, Sis."

"Well, chase after her!" Zoe huffed, heading for the kitchen. "Dinner's about ready." She speared Kurt with a devilish smirk. "Even for Mr. Clueless."

"Ouch." Colin sidled up beside him. "You know Zoe. Never without an idea how to make things better."

"Trust me, I remember." Kurt rescued his empty glass from the table where he'd left it and followed Colin into the dining room, Nate in his arms. Kathryn and Connor came from the kitchen, signaling their boys to the table. Kurt set his glass down. "You should have seen her face when Dad caught her coming in after curfew. She'd switched ladders, thinking the taller ladder would make sneaking in late easier."

Colin listened, amusement on his face. "And?"

"The ladder was aluminum instead of wood. She might as well have rung a bell banging up those steps outside Dad's window." He chuckled. "Boy, did *she* get in trouble." Kurt settled the child in his high chair. Peter, Paul, and Patrick sat to his left, Peter intent on teasing the baby. Kathryn folded her arms, raised an eyebrow, and gave her boys a motherly stare. Connor winked.

"At least I tried." Zoe's eyes narrowed. She tucked a bib around Nate's neck, waving off the three teens. "You're letting Lissa go."

"What can I do?" Kurt stepped back from the high chair.

"Think." Zoe shook her head and handed Colin a bib for Nikki. "You dated her. You connected. You probably even kissed." Her eyes narrowed. "I'm right, aren't I?"

"We spent a week together. I might have caught a kiss or two. So what?"

"I *knew* it." Zoe rested her hands on her hips. "I'm willing to bet you discovered many traits unique to her during those times together. Figure it out and build on your information. Women are usually easy to please."

Colin laughed. "You've got to be joking."

Kurt smiled. "Maybe I should buy her a new ladder?"

Zoe aimed her face skyward and rolled her eyes. "It's no wonder she's running."

CHAPTER NINETEEN

JAYDEN LIFTED A PITCHFORK OF MANURE and tossed the waste into a nearby wheelbarrow. Kurt had been gone all weekend, but today he and Kurt were traveling to Steens Mountain. Camping gear waited in the pickup and Peggy had risen early this morning to pack a cooler. Jayden had promised to get the horse stalls cleaned before they left. One mare had fresh shavings and had been turned into the paddock. Lady made number two. The third mare, Dolly, waited, her head over the stall door, ears pricked forward.

Tethered in the open aisle, Lady watched him work. She nickered, head secure in the double leads he'd snapped to either side of the alleyway. He reached into his pocket and pulled out the last chunk of carrot he'd brought for her. Palm up, he offered the morsel to the filly, feeling her blow air across his fingers as she nuzzled his hand.

Stroking her neck, Jayden spoke in low tones. "You're pretty spoiled, you know that?"

The horse ignored him, content to chomp on the crisp vegetable. She lowered her head when Jayden reached her ears, stretching her muzzle forward and leaning on his shoulder while he scratched in all the right places.

Feeling dampness on his sleeve, he checked the spot. "Did you have to drool on me?"

The filly snorted, wide-eyed, sending a spray of moisture that connected with his neck.

"Great. Carrot juice and snot. You're a nuisance." Jayden grabbed the handkerchief Kurt had insisted he carry with him, wiped horse dew from his skin, and dabbed at his sleeve. "Peggy will kill me."

"I doubt that."

Jayden jumped, his eyes locked on the feeding chute above the stall. "How do you keep so quiet?"

"Stealth training." Kurt grinned at him from the loft. "How are you coming on those stalls?"

"Lady only needs shavings, but Dolly still needs mucking." Jayden patted Lady and pivoted to the wheelbarrow. "I should be done in about thirty minutes."

"Good. I want to leave as soon as we can." Kurt dropped hay into the mangers. "I'll put down enough feed for tonight and tomorrow so Peggy will only have to grain them."

"Should I fill the water buckets?"

"Good idea." Kurt disappeared, his boots clomping on the loft floor. Soon he shimmied down the ladder and came to where Jayden stood, pushing the larger wheelbarrow. "Let me pitch while you take Lady to the paddock." Kurt reached for Jayden's pitchfork and thumbed toward his load of manure. "Bring a load of shavings back with you after you dump that, will you?"

Jayden nodded. He unsnapped Lady from her tether and led her outside into the waiting sunshine. He swung the gate wide enough to allow the horse to pass, removing the lead rope from the ring in her halter. He stepped back after giving her a solid whack across her rump. The filly snorted and bounced away. He laughed as she cavorted along the fence.

Lady bucked, throwing her hind feet in the air like a little kid released for recess. Shaking her head and prancing in a playful run, the filly stopped near a dry patch of sod, bent her knees, and sank onto the bare ground. The horse grunted as she rolled, wiggling like a stranded tortoise upside down on its shell. When she'd managed to coat her back with dirt, Lady stood and shook.

"Hope you got all the itches out." Jayden latched the gate and returned to the barn. Grabbing the wheelbarrow handles, he steadied the load as he pushed the weighted cart to the manure dump behind the barn's lean-to. He grabbed a shovel by the door, scooped up shavings, and filled the wheelbarrow.

When Jayden finished dumping the shavings into Lady's stall, Kurt returned with a load for Dolly.

"You've already finished?" Jayden stared at the clean stall and moaned. "Wish I could work that fast."

"One day you will." Kurt pulled off his cap and wiped his forehead. "You won't always be eleven and skinny."

Jayden laughed. "You mean I'll be thirty-three and fat?"

"Okay, that's it." Kurt grabbed Jayden around the waist, his chuckle ignoring the boy's protest. "You've earned your first official horse trough seminar."

"What if I don't want it?" Jayden squirmed in Kurt's grip, his laughter making it difficult to resist the man's strength. "Won't Peggy be mad at us?" His real dad had often wrestled him over his shoulder, and Jayden remembered how good it felt to be held by strong arms. He kicked his feet and flailed his hands, but the effort proved futile. He was no match for this powerful man.

"She'll understand." Kurt plopped Jayden over his shoulder like a sack of grain and headed outside. "Everybody needs an initiation now and then."

When they reached the water trough, Jayden kicked and shouted between giggles. "No, no, I'm sorry. I didn't mean it." He pushed himself up from the man's shoulders, but Kurt proved too much for him.

Without fanfare, Kurt dropped him, fully clothed, into the murky water.

Jayden sputtered, trying to stand in the slick-sided tank. Finally upright, he wiped the water from his eyes and snorted to clear his nose. When he opened his eyes, Peggy stood beside Kurt, towel in hand, laughing with the Marine. Jayden grinned. "That was fun. Can we do it again?"

"No, you need to shower off and get into dry clothes." Kurt glanced at his watch. "We leave soon."

"Drop your wet clothes in the mudroom before you go on into the house." Peggy handed him the towel. "And don't forget to put on your hiking boots."

"Got it." Jayden jogged to the house, unbuttoning his shirt as he ran. Stopping on the porch, he left his barn clothes on the floor by the washing machine and hurried to the bathroom. Being here with Kurt and Peggy, his life had come alive. And now a camping trip with Kurt waited—he couldn't be more pumped.

Hearing the door slam, Kurt grinned at Peggy. "I wonder if he's ever gone camping before."

"He told me he went with his dad and mom when he was little." Peggy looked to the door where Jayden had disappeared. "Paul and I did the same with Foster when he was small."

"I'm sure having Jayden here brings back a lot of memories." Kurt touched her shoulder. "I know he keeps reminding me of those kids I saw in the war."

"I'm sure he does." Peggy returned his smile. "But memories are good things. I don't mind remembering the great times we shared as a family."

"You could make new memories with Jayden, you know." Kurt nudged her with his elbow as they started toward the house. "We have plenty of room in the tent."

"Thanks, but the ground is probably as hard as I remember." Peggy shot him a no-nonsense glare. "The cooler is packed. Did you load the tripod for the campfire?"

"Yes, ma'am." Kurt matched his stride with hers. "Did you

remember the marshmallows and candy bars?"

Peggy arched an eyebrow. "Jayden's not the only one excited about this trip."

"Can't blame me, can you?" Kurt opened the screen door and allowed her to pass. "At least here, I don't need to sleep with one eye open and my hand on a semi-automatic."

"Never know. Page Springs Campground is pretty remote. Lots of wild things out there in the brush besides the mustangs who live in Kiger Pass."

"Antelope, rattlesnakes, and cougars, oh my."

"Duke wants to go." Peggy glanced around for the dog. "Room for him in the tent?"

"No, you need him here." Kurt spied the dog sniffing near the barn. "He'll alert you if there are any uninvited visitors nearby." Kurt focused on Peggy. "I could take my gun, if you're worried."

Peggy's mouth twisted into a grin, her eyes sparkling. "No. If the need arises, you can contact the local sheriff." She chuckled. "I understand a pretty deputy patrols the area these days."

"Nice try." Kurt feigned a frown. "But there's very limited phone service where we're going."

"Then I'll call her if I need you." Peggy's puckered grin teased the corners of her mouth. "Fair enough?"

"She'll send someone else." Kurt narrowed his eyes. "That charming little number was prepared to send me packing last time I saw her, until I slipped in a hug."

"See, you two still have common ground. She's only testing your determination."

"Don't count on it."

Two hours later, Kurt crossed the Donner und Blitzen River and maneuvered the pickup into Page Springs Campground, stopping to check his reservation. He found the campsite, a secluded spot encompassed by trees, and parked in the drive.

Beside him, Jayden stared out the windshield as if mesmerized by the scenery. If he hadn't locked his seatbelt in place, Jayden would have ridden the entire seventy miles to Steens Mountain on the edge of his seat. A grassy meadow, green like a well-manicured golf course, extended ahead of them, with hilly slopes circling the perimeter. In the distance the Malheur National Wildlife Refuge waited. Jayden's excitement bubbled from him. "Oh, look, we got a table!"

Kurt nodded. He checked his gas gauge and relaxed when he read three-quarters of a tank on the dial. At four thousand feet the climb up the mountain had been arduous. Advisories to those visiting the Steens Mountain Cooperative Management and Protection Area insisted that campers come with plenty of fuel, water, and emergency supplies.

In this remote area no convenience stores or mom-and-pop franchises waited around the next bend. The unincorporated community of Frenchglen three miles away boasted its own historic hotel, but with a population of twelve, they wouldn't have much to offer in the way of provisions. Kurt liked how remote the area was—less chance for unwelcome visitors. At least this campground came with running water and working bathrooms. He'd hike the Blitzen River Trail with Jayden this afternoon if it wasn't too hot. He'd brought binoculars so they could visit the Kiger Mustang Viewing Area tomorrow.

"Let's get our tent set up and then we can break out sandwiches and fruit." Kurt parked the truck and smiled at Jayden. "You hungry?"

Jayden curled his lips into a pout. "What do you think?"

"I could probably rustle up horse feed if you're starving."

"You're never going to let me live that down, are you?"

"Maybe in thirty years." Kurt opened his door and slid off the seat. "Think you can wait that long?"

Laughing, Jayden joined him at the back of the truck. Kurt hefted the tent stakes into the boy's waiting arms and grabbed the canvas cover for himself. He found a level area off to the side of the fire pit, sheltered by the trees, and pounded stakes into the ground. Within minutes the tent stood erect. Jayden's fascination with the zippered door that doubled as a weather guard on the front filled the air with the buzz of the closure as he slid the fastener up and down its track.

"Good job." Kurt walked back to the pickup and lifted the cooler from the bed. He grabbed the sleeping bags and tossed them, one at a time, at the unsuspecting boy. "Take care of these. Peggy may want them back. She's had them a while."

"Hey, no fair." Jayden managed to catch one, but the other one cuffed his shoulder and sent him sprawling into the dirt. "What is this, boot camp?"

Kurt chuckled. "Not exactly. Stick those inside the tent. You can roll them out if you want. Less to do later."

"Why are they so heavy?" Jayden unzipped the tent door and shoved the sleeping bags through one at a time. "They feel like they weigh a ton."

"They're designed for cold weather, and Peggy stuck an extra wool blanket inside each one." Kurt carried the cooler to the table. "Tonight you'll be glad she did."

"But it's summer." Jayden raised his hands in the air, eyes squeezed closed in the sun. "It's not cold."

"We're on the mountain," Kurt reminded him with a sweep of his hand. "Freezing temperatures at night are not uncommon here." Kurt opened the cooler and lifted out the wrapped sandwiches, a bag of chips, and a container of fruit Peggy had sent with them. He tugged on two plastic plates wedged tight behind the carton of milk and set them on the top of the cooler. "Here you go." Kurt smacked his lips. "A corn, molasses, and oats sandwich with a side of hay for you."

"Very funny." Jayden took the plate and sat on a log beside him. "Actually, the molasses wasn't that bad."

Kurt reached for Jayden's hand. "Let's pray." Kurt bowed his head, peeking to make sure Jayden did the same. "For this food and for this beautiful country, Lord, we give you thanks. Amen."

"Amen." Jayden lifted one of the triangular halves of the sandwich and inspected it before pulling out a slice of tomato. "Why do you pray?"

"God tells me to pray." Kurt licked mustard from the edge of his sandwich. "The Bible says we have not because we ask not."

"You get everything you pray for?" Jayden's eyes grew round.

"No." Kurt swallowed the bite he'd snatched before he continued. "But prayer keeps me in a thankful mood. It reminds me of who is in control. God wants to be part of my life. He even says, in the book of Jeremiah, He has a plan for me."

"I don't think God knows who I am." Jayden stuck a fork in a piece of watermelon. "He left me with George as a stepfather. Doesn't sound like planning to me."

"I can understand why you feel that way." Kurt paused, thinking about what to say. "You've lived through rough times at home. But Mr. Mueller protected you. And Peggy took you in. How do you know God didn't plan for those people to take care of you?"

Jayden sat silent for a moment. "I never thought about it. I've always depended on my mom."

"I prayed a lot in Afghanistan." *Lord, give me the right words to say to this child.* "God was there with me, even though not all my prayers were answered the way I wanted them to be."

"What did you pray for?" Jayden took a bite of sandwich.

"For safety. For my friends. For a chance to go home."

"Not everybody got to come home." Jayden's words were a whisper. He peeked out from lidded eyes. "Did they?"

Kurt sighed. "No. I lost my best friend, Peggy's son, in a fire fight. But one week before he died, he asked Jesus to be his Savior. He'd had opportunities earlier in his life, but he resisted taking that step. God knew he would be killed, and I believe God made sure Foster had one more chance to know him before he died. I will see Foster again in heaven."

Jayden shrugged, scraped the remaining fruit off his plate, and set it down. "Peggy sure makes good lunches."

"Did you get enough?" The subtle sidestepping of the conversation didn't escape Kurt. He took his cue to change the subject and popped open a container of cookies. "Peanut butter?"

Jayden bit into the soft brown texture. "Tastes like the ones my mom made." The boy's face sagged.

Kurt nudged him. "You missing your mother a lot?"

Jayden nodded, chewing the cookie in slow motion, his eyes squeezed shut.

"When she gets things worked out with your stepfather, you'll probably get to return home." Kurt rubbed the boy's neck and patted him on the shoulder.

Jayden shook his head. "I don't want to go home. Not if it means living with George again." He bit off another piece of sandwich. "And I don't want to leave Duke and Lady behind."

"Lady could get adopted when she recovers." Kurt stuck a plastic fork in his fruit and retrieved a strawberry. "Duke could also be claimed by Bennie Mueller's brother."

"Brother?" Jayden gaped at Kurt. "You mean, there's a relative out there?"

Kurt nodded. "We got the call this morning before we left. Apparently, Bennie and Bertram weren't close. But they always remembered birthdays. When Bennie didn't send a card to Bertram on his birthday last month, the brother got worried. He called, and of course no one answered. He arrived late last week and found the house deserted. Then he called the sheriff."

"He might take Duke?" Jayden's shocked expression and the paleness of his skin suggested this news sidelined him like a club to the head. "That's terrible."

"I wouldn't worry about it too much. Duke's a cattle dog and Bertram lives in Portland. Neither would be happy if Duke moved in with Bertram."

"I wouldn't be happy either." Jayden picked at his fruit. "When I go home, Duke can't come with me."

"Well, until everything is settled, Duke's staying at Peggy's with you." Kurt reached over and tousled Jayden's hair. "You need a haircut."

Jayden shuddered. "Not until school starts."

Half an hour later, after stashing the cooler inside the tent, Kurt studied the map of the park, pointing out landmarks to Jayden. The Blitzen River Trail took off from the southern tip of the campground at the base of Steens Mountain. "You up for a hike?" Kurt pointed across the grassy meadow. "Steens Mountain is the big rise you see. Could be a lot of rocky slopes and hilly climbs."

"Where does the trail go?" Jayden squinted, as if trying to see the end from the beginning.

"It follows the Donner und Blitzen River upstream to where it joins with Fish Creek. About eight miles."

"Eight miles isn't so far." Jayden pumped his fist. "I had to walk eight miles to Bennie's place whenever my bike tire was flat."

"Then I'd say you're up for this." Kurt grinned. "Keep your

eyes open, though. Rattlesnakes are known to lie in wait around here, as well as cougars."

Jayden's mouth hung open, giving Kurt his rapt attention. "Are you serious?"

"It's what the trail map says." Kurt held up the proof. "Just sayin'."

"Are there fish in the river?"

"Yep. Redband trout. But we can't keep them if we catch them." Kurt pretended to toss a fish away. "The advisory says catch and release."

"That stinks." Jayden shuffled the toe of his boot in the dirt. "I'd hoped for fresh mountain trout for dinner, along with wild berries."

Kurt stashed the map into his shirt pocket. "Where did you get that idea?"

"A book I used to read, about a family of bears and a vacation they took."

"I remember a similar book I read as a kid. It's still around?"

Jayden nodded. "Even made it into a cartoon clip."

"Don't use Papa Bear as your guide. He didn't know anything about camping." Kurt tossed Jayden a water bottle. "Tuck this into your jacket. You'll need it before we're through."

They followed the dusty path quite a distance before Kurt stopped and pointed. Handing Jayden the binoculars, he gestured to the left. "See the white speck out there in the flat land?"

Jayden squinted into the binoculars, his head weaving slowly right to left. "Wow!" He stared up at Kurt. "What is it?"

"Antelope." Kurt waited while Jayden drank in the scene through the binoculars. When the boy returned the glasses to him, he perused the landscape again. "I wouldn't be surprised if we see a herd of deer."

The path twisted right and left and soon they found themselves climbing a rocky slope. Kurt led the way, checking for snakes sunning themselves on the warm rocks nearby. As they entered the trees again, Kurt pointed upward. "Cougars like to wait on tree branches. Don't get separated from me."

Jayden stopped dead still. "You mean I could *become* cat food?"

"Yell loud and stay close. And whatever you do, don't run."

The trail wound back around. Before much more time passed they found the spot where the Donner und Blitzen river joined Fish Creek. Mule deer jumped from the brush and leaped away into the rim rock.

"They're amazing." Jayden's face didn't turn, his focus on the retreating herd. "Are they hunted?"

"This is part of the Malheur Wildlife Refuge," Kurt said. "They're protected here."

The sun hovered low, the crimson and purple rays of its descent coloring the sky. Kurt guessed they had another hour or so before they'd be immersed in darkness. "We better head back to the tent. How are your feet holding up?"

"I'm okay." Jayden rubbed his stomach. "But I hope there's more food when we get there."

"Peggy sent burgers to cook over our fire. And potato salad."

"Let's go." Jayden scrambled down the trail, light-footed as a deer, leaving Kurt scurrying to catch up.

"Don't get too far ahead. Remember?"

Jayden giggled and scooted up the rocky slope like the deer he'd seen minutes before. He disappeared around a curve, and Kurt's pulse climbed. With the boy out of sight, Kurt's sense of danger spun into military mode. He climbed the slope and rounded the bend to find Jayden standing dead still in front of him.

"Jayden?" Kurt caught up to where the boy had stopped. Ahead of him a great horned owl sat on a low branch of a tree, staring, eyes widened like two miniature moons in a sea of feathers.

"He's so beautiful." Jayden's words, not above a whisper, spoke of awe and wonder. "Wish I had a camera."

Kurt gripped the boy's shoulder, handing him his cell phone. "Push that button."

Jayden held the device up, pressing the button as Kurt had instructed. With a whoosh the owl flew upward, landing higher in the tree. "He got away."

"Let me see." Kurt searched the images and found Jayden's picture. "Not completely." He held up the phone. "You've got him forever."

Jayden smiled, the width of his grin bright enough to light up the entire refuge.

"Let's go get our grub." Kurt pulled a flashlight from his pocket and handed it to the boy. "We may need this, if we don't hurry."

CHAPTER TWENTY

THE CAMPGROUND GLOWED LIKE A CAKE with birthday candles when Kurt reached the parking lot, sparks shooting from the fire pits along the drive. The hum of quiet voices drifted out from each campsite as they passed, several campers gathered around the open flames roasting marshmallows. The occasional clink of a metal pan sounded against the grate. He led Jayden to their tent, handing him the other flashlight when they neared the picnic spot. "Hold this, and I'll get a fire going."

"Will that be enough light?" Even in the growing shadows, Jayden appeared skeptical.

"You're right." Kurt dug out his keys. "You know how to turn on the pickup so we can use the headlights?"

Jayden shook his head. "Mr. Mueller showed me how to start the tractor once."

"Come on. I'll teach you." Kurt led the way to the cab. "Climb in."

Jayden hopped up on the seat, the dome light casting a dim pall over the interior. "I can't reach the pedals." His defeated smile made Kurt chuckle. "The tractor ones were closer."

"The tractor probably had three speeds and three pedals." At Jayden's nod, he continued. "The pickup is automatic. To start it, you put it in park or neutral before turning the key."

Kurt pointed to the dash indicators. "If you turn the key off while the truck is in gear, the engine will automatically stop and you can't restart it until you take it out of gear. But that's dangerous at high speeds. If the engine cuts out and you take it out of drive to restart it, the action could send you into a spin. The power steering and the brakes stop when the engine does." Kurt handed him the key. "The truck's in neutral. Try it."

Jayden inserted the key and the engine purred.

"Find the headlight switch and pull them on." Kurt grinned as Jayden flicked on the lights. "Now we can set up our supper."

From the back of the pickup Kurt retrieved the kindling, along with the matches. Firewood stacked by the pit had been left by a previous camper. He handed Jayden a stack of newsprint. "Here, make a ball out of this and stick it at the bottom."

"Like that?" Jayden peered up at him, tufts of paper sticking here and there around the stacked kindling.

Kurt opened the box of matches. "Take one and strike it against the side of the grate and touch the paper."

Within seconds the kindling crackled. A breeze drifted through the camp, adding momentum to the flames. Jayden stood and watched the blaze build, the wonder on his face like that of a newborn fawn. Bringing the kid had been the right thing to do. The trauma of the past few weeks must still haunt him. "Go turn off the lights and kill the engine. Don't forget the key."

Jayden strode to the pickup.

Kurt imagined Lissa at his side, sharing the moment with him. He shrugged the thought away. As the wood combusted and the warmth rose, he pivoted to the tent to retrieve their cooler. He set it on the ground beside Jayden, who had returned and handed him the key. "Good job." Jayden's smile spoke volumes, rewarding Kurt with memories from his childhood. Nothing like a kid and a car. "Dig into the side of the cooler and see if you can find the burgers. I think they're wrapped in foil."

Kurt spent a few minutes coaching the boy on cooking the meat over hot coals. Jayden took his responsibility seriously, maintaining a close watch on the patties until they were thoroughly browned. Kurt made a final check with the tip of his knife. "Yep. I'd say those are cooked through. Another good job."

"Thanks. I'm hungry enough to eat all of them." Jayden's

stomach growled. "Told you."

A truck wandered down the campground drive as he helped Jayden fix his hamburger. The vehicle stopped when it reached their site. *Harney County Sheriff* stood out on the side along with the county logo. He hadn't expected anyone to look for them. The door opened.

"What are you doing here?" Kurt stared, amazed, as Lissa stepped from the vehicle and snapped a leash on her dog.

Dressed in uniform, she filled out the curves of the tan shirt and green trousers like a model on a fashion show runway. A leather belt accented her slender waist. Finger curls dangled like deserters at her forehead and along her cheekbones, no doubt victims of a long and trying day. The neat bun she wore at the base of her neck had lost its crispness, errant tresses declaring their freedom from the confining pins.

His heart picked up its pace, and he swallowed hard. He remembered the hug she'd allowed him when she left on Father's Day, the fresh flower scent of her hair and the citrus smell of her skin. He breathed in deep, bracing himself for this encounter.

"I came to find you. Official business." Lissa nodded to Jayden, who had bent down to pet her dog. Lissa tousled the boy's hair. "How you doing, big guy?"

"We're fixing hamburgers over the grill." The kid stood and pointed to a plate where his burger sat, ketchup oozing from its side. "Want one?"

"Thanks, but I've already eaten." Lissa focused on Kurt, her stance professional, but her eyes full of worry he didn't understand. "Can we talk for a minute?" She angled her head toward the truck. "Privately?"

Seeing the question on her face and the arch of her eyebrows, Kurt's stomach did a somersault, his attention to duty kicking in. "Jayden, can you watch the dog?"

"No, let him eat, Kurt. I'll tie Sorrel up to the table." She tied a slipknot around the table leg to secure the dog's leash. "Be good for Jayden."

Sorrel whined.

Lissa led Kurt to the passenger side of her truck. "What's wrong?"

"Jayden's stepfather has returned." Lissa's eyes flashed, her voice a whisper. "Apparently he didn't move away forever."

"I thought his disappearance sounded a little sketchy." He leaned against the truck's hood, remembering his need for air after discovering what the man had done to his wife and stepson. "Bad pennies always return, or so the saying goes."

Lissa nodded. "George found out where the boy's mother was staying and knocked her around pretty bad before she could call for help."

"What about the restraining order? Did she follow through and press charges?"

"Restraining orders on paper do little to stop an angry drunk. The department is looking for him, but he's eluded them." Lissa kept her voice low. "He escaped, but not without threatening the woman and her son." Lissa's eyes narrowed as if watching for his reaction. "He visited Peggy today after you left."

"How did he know about Peggy?" He straightened, pulse escalated, breath coming faster.

"I don't know. Unless he discovered Jayden's whereabouts at the first meeting with social services." Lissa stiffened. "Or he slapped the information out of Melanie."

"Is Peggy all right?" His fists clenched, fingernails pressing into his skin.

"Duke alerted her before the man got to the door, so Peggy went prepared. I guess she keeps a revolver on hand for emergencies." Lissa glanced over his shoulder. "He asked to see Jayden, and she told him the boy was gone for a few days." He followed her gaze to where Jayden sat helping himself to a couple of pickles. "Peggy called me because you don't have cell service out here. Melanie wanted you to know Barnes is looking for the kid and said he threatened Jayden in her presence."

"You think he's casing the rescue center, waiting?" His jaw tensed, thinking of the danger Peggy might be in. "Should I pack up and go home?"

"No way to be certain." Lissa peered over his shoulder, a smile creeping across her face. She refocused on him, mirth dancing in her eyes. "But when you head home, call in to our office, would you?" Her question puzzled him and, from her reaction, it showed. "I know you can take care of yourself, but this guy is unstable. He could cause a lot of trouble, and innocent people could get hurt. The department is already on the lookout for George, but we'll add additional personnel when you return." She directed his attention to the table. "Jayden could probably pelt him with marshmallows."

"What?" He turned and sputtered, catching Jayden tossing marshmallows into the air and grabbing them with his teeth as they fell. "Jayden, save a few marshmallows, would you? Remember, I've got the makings for s'mores."

"I forgot." Jayden's sheepish grin, cheeks bulging with marshmallows, and the fire enhancing the sparkle of his eyes, warmed Kurt's heart. What a delightful kid. "Better eat your hamburger, Kurt. It's getting cold."

"Be right there." He returned to Lissa. "Want to join us for s'mores? Peggy packed plenty."

"I'd love one." Lissa grinned. "It's been a long time since I've made those."

Kurt followed Lissa to the campsite like a lovesick puppy, her neat uniform and professional stride holding his attention. He fought the impulses her nearness aroused. He longed to kiss her.

"Thanks for the heads up. Are you driving home in the dark?"

Lissa sighed. "'Fraid so." When they reached the table, she sat beside Jayden. "How's the camping trip going?"

"We hiked today. Saw deer, and owl, and antelope. So cool." Jayden chomped another bite of burger. "Made up for the long trip here." Jayden stood and walked to the fire. "Are we going to make s'mores now?" His eyes flashed with expectancy, and his mouth hung open, as if he feared the answer to his question. "I left a lot of marshmallows."

Lissa smiled at the boy before looking to Kurt for the answer. "You've thought of everything, haven't you?"

"Even the sticks." Kurt grabbed a handful of willowy sticks from the end of the table. Handing one to Lissa, he reached into the marshmallow bag and withdrew two of the fluffy, white puffballs. "Jayden, have you done this before?"

"Yeah. My dad and I made s'mores when I was little."

"Be sure the stick goes all the way through the marshmallow or you'll lose it in the fire." He dug through the cooler. "I'll set up the plates with your graham crackers and chocolate while you cook."

"You're too kind." Lissa pursed her lips, an unspoken retort written on her face. She approached the spot where Jayden crouched, warming his hands. "Can I share your fire?"

"Sure." Jayden's worried face shifted to Kurt. "Can I eat the s'more without the marshmallow, if I ate too many?"

Kurt held up the bag still almost two-thirds full. "I don't know. It'll be close." He winked at Lissa. "Do you think we should share?"

"I haven't had one of these in fifteen years. Not much call for marshmallows on the ocean. I'm overdue for my chocolate fix." She grinned at Kurt, offering a solemn face to Jayden. "There's only about twenty-five left. I suppose I could share one."

Jayden's smile sagged. "Only one?"

Kurt laughed. "She's teasing. There's more left than we have chocolate. So, yeah. You can make one."

"Thanks." Jayden's grin returned. He took two marshmallows and a stick from Kurt, pushing the soft, white lumps on the end. He positioned his stick over the fire, letting the marshmallows toast. With a spurt of blue, the marshmallows caught fire and plopped into the flames. Jayden's face blanched, his jaw dropping and eyes full of surprise. "My marshmallows!"

"It's okay. You got too close." Kurt replaced the burned goo with two more marshmallows on the end of Jayden's stick. "Hold them *above* the flame, not in it."

Lissa pulled hers from the fire and showed Jayden. "See how they turn golden brown? Now I'll lay this on top of the chocolate pieces and melt the candy. All that's left is to add the top and eat." Lissa squished the graham cracker down on the marshmallow and pulled the stick out. Lifting the s'more to her mouth, she bit into the gooey mixture. "Yum! It's been too long."

Kurt swiped her lip with his thumb. "If moustaches tell time, you haven't eaten a s'more in quite a while." His gaze lingered on her mouth. "Even a bit of a goatee."

Lissa rubbed her chin with the back of her hand. "Smart aleck."

Jayden stood, his stick bobbing over the table. "Where's my chocolate?"

Kurt winked at Lissa before handing Jayden a plate with a graham cracker square and a piece of candy. "Lay the hot marshmallow on the chocolate and cover with a cracker like Lissa did. Then pull the stick out gently."

Jayden, tongue caught in his teeth, did as he'd been told, and soon the s'more sat waiting to be eaten. He lifted the treat to his mouth and took a bite. "Man! This is better than cold marshmallows any day."

Lissa laughed. "Good job, kiddo." She ambled to where Kurt

stood. "Thanks for the food. I'd best be going. The road's not going to straighten out with me standing here." She untied Sorrel from the table leg where the dog had been napping, tousled Jayden's hair again, and walked into the night. Her footsteps echoed in the quieting campground. She reached her vehicle, the dome light outlining her silhouette before the door slammed closed. The ignition whirred, and the rig rolled backward out of the parking space and onto the pavement.

Kurt waved as the truck disappeared from view, fighting the urge to run after it. He walked to the cab of his pickup and retrieved the handgun from the glove box. Tonight's vigil over the campground would be his responsibility. He wouldn't fail again.

CHAPTER TWENTY-ONE

KURT SLIPPED OUT OF THE TENT the next morning and rummaged through the equipment, looking for the skillet. The night had passed without incident. Sun filled the sky above them, promising a great day. He thought of Lissa's warning and scanned the campground for evidence of an intruder. All remained quiet, the smell of coffee wafting through the air, low murmurs drifting from other campsites.

Inside the tent, Jayden stirred and pressed his face against the screened window. "Horses today, right?"

"Think you can eat a plate of pancakes first?"

"Pancakes?" The boy stretched and yawned, rubbing his eyes with his fists. His face registered disbelief. A scowl bracketed his forehead. "Out here?"

"Yep. Peggy made the batter and sent a frying pan." Kurt unzipped the tent. "Get dressed, and I'll stoke the fire."

When Jayden emerged a few minutes later, Kurt had the fire crackling. He set the frying pan over the heat and warmed it. He showed Jayden how to pour circles of batter in the bottom, the kid's mouth puckering as he concentrated. Kurt returned the pan to the heat. "Get a plate."

Jayden retrieved the plates and the bottle of syrup from the cooler.

Kurt stacked the cooked food on Jayden's plate. "I'll take it from here. You go eat your breakfast before it cools."

Jayden sat at the table, wolfing down the pancakes.

"Taste all right, then?" Kurt smiled at Jayden's nod.

"Can I have a glass of milk?"

"Sure. Check the corner of the cooler." As Jayden dug for the quart-sized carton, Kurt flipped the four pancakes he was cooking and transferred them to his plate. Adding syrup, he sat at the table and took a bite.

"Good, huh?" Jayden stood and stuck his plate in the washtub.

"Tastes better because we cooked them over an open fire." Kurt popped the last bite in his mouth. Thank goodness for Peggy's pre-mixed batters.

Breakfast over, Kurt set the utensils in a pan of soapy water over the campfire. Jayden dried the utensils as fast as Kurt washed, and soon they were ready for their day. "Let's go find Lady's family."

The cutoff to the Kiger Mustang Viewing Area snaked on for miles. Kurt was thankful he'd brought the four-wheel drive. The terrain around them kept repeating itself, the blip of the odometer the only proof they'd traveled another mile. Sagebrush, juniper, and stands of scrubby trees stretched to either side of them.

Jayden's excitement waned with each stretch of road. The terrain yawned flat as far as the eye could see, the open range covering thousands of acres. Finding the horses they'd come to discover proved more of an impossibility. Jayden's smile sagged a little more with each passing mile. Kurt turned off the main highway and drove parallel to a rock fence, one early settlers had built on the ridge more than a hundred years ago. Beyond the fence, patches of juniper trees blocked the view. Failing to find the elusive herd without trekking across the terrain on foot became a definite possibility.

Jayden perked up and pointed across a straight stretch. "Aren't those deer?"

Kurt slowed the truck, squinting where the boy indicated, catching a fluff of white leaping over a mound of brush as the black-tipped tails of the mule deer bounded away. "Good spotting."

"Their color makes them easy to see." Jayden leaned against the dash, straining his seat belt. Interest piqued, he scanned the hillside, head moving like a camcorder, left to right and back again. The truck bounced as it hit a hole in the road and Jayden's skull connected with the doorpost.

"Whoa, that was quite a lurch. You okay?" Kurt slowed the truck as the road became less navigable the farther they traveled. At Jayden's nod, he returned his gaze to the unending stretch of sage brush and juniper trees. Wildflowers dotted the landscape—blues, yellows, and oranges sprinkled like paint on a canvas of green.

"What's that?" Jayden pointed off to the left where a mass of caramel color moved through the brush, meandering at a snail's pace.

Kurt stopped the truck and withdrew the binoculars from beneath the seat, focusing on the wildlife spotting the landscape. He grinned and handed the field glasses to Jayden. "You have found your horses."

"Can we get out?" Jayden unhooked his seatbelt and reached for the latch.

Kurt grabbed the boy's elbow, slowing him. "Don't make any noise. Slip out and close the door without a click." Kurt raised his eyebrows to see if Jayden understood. At the boy's nod, he opened his own door and stood on the side of the road.

Jayden came around to the driver's side, binoculars still in hand. Eyes wide and grin stretching his cheeks taut, the boy crept to the edge of the road and hunkered down.

The horses continued to wander toward the perimeter of the area, drifting nearer as though they didn't see the two humans watching them.

Kurt motioned for Jayden to follow him. They skulked across the open terrain, placing their feet on grassy spaces. By avoiding the rocky ground where stones and larger aggregate crunched under their feet, they kept their intrusion quiet. Kurt led the boy to a row of juniper trees, crouching behind the trunks as they inched toward the animals now less than a hundred yards away.

The stallion's head shot up, ears forward and nostrils flared, a sure sign he sensed their presence. The other horses grazed at leisure, seemingly unaware of the people invading their territory.

Kurt knelt beside Jayden, his attention on alert. Knowing they could be challenged, Kurt didn't want to excite the unpredictable horse. He and Jayden were on the stallion's turf, threatening the security of his mares, and a viable enemy. The esteemed leader might run or stand his ground. Either way danger lingered nearby. Kurt signaled Jayden to curl up at the base of the tree where they hid and would wait the animal out.

Jayden watched, still as death, as the mares grazed in peaceful tranquility. Foals scampered around their mothers, tails flying like flags in the wind. A kick of their hind legs, coupled with a buck at the withers, raised the youngsters off the ground. They squealed and stopped, cavorting for the sheer joy of it, and turned to race off again.

Watching the young horses play, Jayden giggled. "They're like little kids."

Kurt nodded, unable to hide his grin. Freedom enabled these creatures to live without fear—grazing, sleeping, and playing under a canopy of blue sky. Freedom the many Afghani children didn't have. Images of those struggling to survive filled his mind—youngsters who through no fault of their own had forgotten how to play. Tyranny had claimed their innocence. Kurt shuddered, willing the memories to the back of his mind.

Jayden nudged him and pointed.

The stallion had stepped closer, the magnificent animal near enough for them to hear him blow and snort. His coat shone like grey velvet, the grullo color a mouse-colored silk against the striking contrast of his long, black mane and tail. He pawed the ground, arching his neck and shaking his head up and down. Eyes fixed on them, he stood at full alert, the delicate tips of his ears pointed in their direction. His head bobbed, as if nodding and telling them he'd discovered their cover.

Kurt waited for the animal to act, ready to grab Jayden and run should the stallion challenge them. A shrill whinny cut the air like a bolt of lightning, and within seconds the mares broke into a stampede, racing through the juniper and sage to higher ground. The stallion followed, stopping to turn and rear up on his hind legs, striking the air like a fighter in a ring. Falling forward on his front legs, he lifted his hindquarters out behind him, kicking at the wind before galloping up the hillside behind his mares.

"Awesome." Jayden stood and stared at the departing herd. "Did you see those colors?"

"Cinnamon, caramel, and that grey Grullo color—all with black manes and tails. The buckskin markings are a trait that defines them."

"Lady looked like that when she was born. Cinnamon with black fuzz on her neck."

"She will again." Kurt laid his hand on the back of Jayden's neck. "She only needs a summer to recover and a good hand to brush her to a shine."

"I know how to do that." Jayden beamed.

"Yes, you do." Kurt caught sight of something Jayden would love. "Look—the stallion has turned."

At the top of the ridge the stallion faced their direction and whinnied, the loud sound piercing the hills around them. With a final call, he spun around and followed his herd over the rise.

"I guess he told us, huh?" Kurt grinned at Jayden.

"Yeah, like leave my mares alone or else."

"It's the way God created him. To protect and defend his herd.

We men are here to do the same for our families."

Jayden's face crumpled. "My dad was like that. I never felt afraid when he was home."

Kurt hesitated. He hadn't wanted to pry, but since Jayden had brought it up, Kurt decided to ask. "What happened to your father?"

"He died when I was nine." Jayden stared at the hillside where the horses had retreated, not seeing. "Afghanistan."

"Your dad was in the service?" Kurt jerked to full attention.

"Marine." Jayden's voice wobbled, and he sniffled.

Why hadn't Kurt guessed this before? Jayden lived as another casualty of the war, a child who had lost his focus. Like the horses, he longed to be free of his pain, but like the children Kurt had seen living under the threat of the Taliban, Jayden lacked the experience to know where to begin. "Where was his unit?"

"Kabul." Jayden's eyes brimmed with tears, face stoic as he tried not to cry in front of Kurt. "Ambush."

Kurt stopped. Ambush in Kabul? Two years ago? About the time he went missing in action, spending more than a week hidden in a cave after his unit was ambushed. Kurt searched his memory, pulling up the names of the two men from his unit who took enemy fire and didn't survive. Carl Stephens and . . . Jordan Clarke. He stared at Jayden, his mouth dry like sun-baked crackers. "Are you Jordan Clarke's son?"

Jayden's eyes popped open, his mouth hanging at an angle. "How do you know my dad?"

"We served in the same unit and both dodged enemy fire in that ambush." Kurt wrapped an arm around Jayden. "Your dad called you Jay-jay, didn't he?"

Jayden nodded, the dam of water behind his eyes bursting through his wall of hurt. He leaned into Kurt and sobbed.

Kurt lifted his eyes to the sky, his aching heart pounding in his chest. He hadn't saved Foster, he hadn't rescued any kids, but he could protect Jayden. This child needed him. For the first time in two years, he'd found purpose.

Lissa entered the office behind schedule the next morning, the drive to and from delivering the message to Kurt making her arrive home well past her bedtime. She'd crawled under the covers at midnight and forgot to set the alarm. Sorrel's need to go outside woke her shortly after eight, an hour later than usual. She panicked at the tardiness of the hour and called her boss as soon as he arrived.

Matthew, though, had chuckled at her exasperated apology. "This is the biggest county in Oregon. Driving seventy miles to do our job is part of the routine. Come in at ten—you've already put in the other hours last night. We'll catch you up to speed in no time."

Now, with her late arrival needling her conscience, she glanced around the office. Four of the deputies were already gone.

Matthew sat at his desk, ear to the phone, scribbling on a tablet. He waved her over, finished the conversation, and hung up. "Glad you're here. Melanie Barnes has changed locations since George arrived in town."

"Is she hidden well enough to keep out of his radar?"

"No. She chose to go home."

"What?" Lissa's jaw dropped, her breathing shallow. "You can't be serious."

"I can't make her hide. Apparently, she's had enough and wants the marriage to end." Matthew tapped his pencil on the desk. "She decided to confront George while he's sober and able to comprehend what she wants." Matthew dropped the pencil and clasped his hands. "George is still at large, and we're trying to find him. Melanie thought she'd be the bait."

"Did she take a deputy as escort?" Lissa's palms felt sweaty, pulse kicking like an untamed horse. "Won't she be in danger?"

"Not according to her." Matthew leaned back in his chair. "She said George is a very nice guy when he's not drinking. Attentive, generous, and loving."

"Not according to what Jayden said. She's covering for him."

Matthew nodded. "Makes you wonder why she keeps him stocked in booze."

"Yeah. But I'd rather she bring home the stuff than have him drink and drive." Lissa moved toward her desk. "Anything new I need to take care of?"

"Keep tabs on the Barnes couple. Custody of Jayden could return to Melanie, once she's free of her husband. But for now, Jayden will remain a ward of the state." Matthew handed her a stack of papers. "Here's more on the Mueller case."

"Nothing suspicious turned up, I take it?"

Matthew shook his head. "Bennie's time was up and God called him home." He held up his hand. "Wait. You did get a personal call this morning. The message is here somewhere. The receptionist had to leave early." He shuffled the papers on his desk, retrieving a pink message pad. "Ah. Here it is." He held it out. "Your doctor called and wants you to come in tomorrow."

Lissa fingered the message like it contained poison, a noticeable tremor in her grip.

"Everything all right?" Matthew frowned as he searched her face. "You're not sick, are you?"

Lissa inhaled and shook her head. "Routine testing is all." She fought for composure lest she give away her fear. "Can I have the time off?"

"Always." The phone rang, and Matthew swiveled in his chair to answer it. "Sheriff Briggs here."

Lissa tried to act nonchalant as she returned to her desk. Routine testing? Who was she trying to kid?

CHAPTER TWENTY-TWO

LISSA ENTERED THE OFFICE OF THE women's clinic where she would meet with the gynecologist to whom she'd been referred. The thump of her heart throbbed at the back of her skull. She advanced to the counter, where a receptionist spoke into a phone. Holding up a finger to Lissa, the woman wrote on a pad of paper, nodding into the phone as if the caller could see her.

Lissa perused the office. Four doors lined the lobby area, decorated in potted plants and western-themed artwork. One other woman waited, legs crossed at the knees, a magazine flipped open on her lap. If she shook inside like Lissa did, she didn't show it.

The receptionist deposited the handset and glanced up. "May I help you?"

"Lissa Frye, appointment with Dr. James at nine."

Handing her a clipboard, the receptionist tapped the top page. "Fill out the first page with your insurance information, list your history on the second page, and sign the third." She smiled, the practiced response of a professional who had no idea what medical issues Lissa might be facing.

Lissa followed the questions down the page, checking the boxes pertaining to her medical history. She landed on the question asking about cancer in the family and shuddered. Writing *mother* in the blank, she closed her eyes and prayed. *Not again, not me, please.* She signed the form, returned the clipboard to the receptionist, and found her chair.

A nurse came out of door number three. "Lissa?"

Shaking off her fear, Lissa rose and followed the woman down a corridor to a scale and blood pressure cuff, then on to an office with a desk and a swivel chair. Directed to sit, Lissa gazed at the walls—certificates of professional achievements on one, family pictures of a man, woman, and three grinning boys on the other. She blinked back the moisture threatening to rain on her dignity and inhaled a slow cleansing breath. She'd be satisfied with only one child. Was that too much to ask?

The door opened and a woman her age entered, stuck out her hand, and smiled. "I'm Dr. James. Glad you came in today."

Lissa tracked the woman's movements to the desk, looking for a clue to the news this person would deliver. Dr. James opened a folder, sat in the swivel chair, and studied the documents before her. What seemed like an hour passed before the doctor looked up and met Lissa's gaze, even as the wall clock behind her read five minutes after nine. Lissa's skin crawled with goose bumps.

"How's Delaney?"

"Ready to move on." Lissa relaxed. "She's recovering at my dad's place. Her husband's back at work and her teens are with her."

"She's the one who insisted on your tests?" Dr. James leaned back into her chair, folding her arms across her middle.

"Yeah. Her diagnosis prompted worry, and she knew I wouldn't be tested without a fight."

Dr. James turned a page in the folder she'd opened. "Everyone should have a sister like Delaney. We all need someone to watch out for us. Even a tough Navy intelligence officer like you."

"Navy reserves now." Palms pressed together, Lissa fidgeted with her thumbs. "And I'm not so tough."

"Didn't think you were." Dr. James lifted the folder from the desk. "But, like your sister, the tests you had done in Portland came back with questions. The CA-125 shows no evidence of elevated levels of anything in your blood. The numbers are all normal, except for one."

The room tilted for a second while Lissa fought to catch her breath. Unstoppable tears wet her cheeks. "What does that mean?"

"We need to run the test again. Like an abnormal pap smear, we test again. Routine." Dr. James handed her a tissue. "But your blood pressure has been high. Are you experiencing a lot of stress in your life?"

"This medical uncertainty has weighed on me like a ton of concrete. I left the Navy hoping to start a new life—marriage, career change, children—and Delaney dumped the cancer information in my lap. I've lost sleep wondering what my future holds."

"Working as a sheriff's deputy would make anyone lose sleep." Dr. James pointed to the pictures on her wall where wild animals grazed and horsemen rode behind cattle herds. "Out here, we get the really good or the really bad."

Lissa understood what she meant. "Mostly I deal with good and bad cows, horses, chickens, you name it." She blew her nose. "A few weeks ago I rescued a horse and discovered a missing boy with his dog."

"Sounds as if you like your new job. Your health is good." Dr. James tucked Lissa's folder under her arm and stood. "Once you are re-tested, I'd say all those dreams you mentioned can certainly come true." The doctor cast her a mischievous grin. "I can't help you with the marriage part."

"Are you sure? I've got a candidate who needs a brain adjustment." Lissa stood, looping the strap of her handbag over her shoulder. "I haven't pursued him because of the ramifications all this testing might indicate. I didn't want to get involved if my future was murky."

"Assuming you've found the man of your dreams, I'd say your future is bright." Dr. James moved around the desk to where Lissa waited, and Lissa saw for the first time the bulge beneath her white coat.

Lissa gaped at the woman, caught off guard by the obvious. Dr.

James read her like a book. "Yep, I'm pregnant. Due first of the year. And when you start *your* family, come back and see me. The best part of my practice is delivering babies."

"I'm relieved to know the future I've dreamed of living is possible." Lissa extended her hand, warmed by the doctor's interest in her happiness. "I wasn't so sure when I walked through your door."

"Let's get that blood test re-scheduled." Dr. James tapped her file folder. "Don't wait too long to make it happen. At thirty-three, your biological clock is ticking. I don't want to give you fertility drugs, if I can avoid them."

"I'm working on it."

"Good." Dr. James pointed at the wall. "My husband and I had our first during my residency—a boy. Two more boys have followed." She patted her bulge. "We're hoping this next one is a girl. My husband wants a princess."

"You can't find out ahead of time?"

"Choose not to know." Dr. James adjusted her lab coat. "We like to be surprised."

"Congratulations."

"Get those tests done." Dr. James walked to the door and gestured for Lissa to precede her. "I'll call you as soon as we have the results. After that, you can proceed with your life plan."

"If I can capture the heart of a stubborn Marine, maybe I will."

"Those fish take a different kind of bait, but hooking them is worth the effort. I know. I'm married to one." Dr. James cast an admiring look at the picture of the man smiling into the camera. "Retired, of course."

Lissa didn't know whether to call Delaney immediately or wait until she received the results of the second blood test. She still couldn't tell Kurt anything, and she reaffirmed her resolve to not get involved with him until she could give him a good future with her. She opted for the call and dialed Delaney's cell phone number.

"Delaney?" Lissa listened to her sister's heavy breathing as she twisted the phone to her other ear. "Did I disturb your nap?"

"No, Lissa. Hi." Her sister's voice sounded wobbly, as if she had yet to fully wake up. "I've had shum pain medication problems and they deshided to give me a new one. It's a wollopaloozer."

"Makes your head spin, and your eyes roll?"

"Yeth, that's de one." Delaney giggled. "Am I talkin' thunny, too?"

"Yes. You sound totally out of it—more than usual."

"Shanks." Delaney yawned. "What's new?"

"I don't know if you remember, but I had to see the doctor in Hines about those tests you insisted on in Portland?" Lissa's grin stretched her mouth so wide it almost hurt. Though her tests were inconclusive, she still felt relieved to have the first round over. "I went today."

"That's right!" Delaney snapped to attention, her words racing like machine gun fire. "Wow! You're what I needed to clear my brain fog. What'd the doctor say? Z'it good news? Please tell me you have good news. Lissa, talk to me."

"I will when you calm down." Her sister could be so passionate and erratic, making her all the more loveable. "My tests were inconclusive."

"Does that mean you have to be retested?" Delaney sounded hesitant. "What are they looking for?"

"The doctor said my numbers were normal, except for one."

"And you said you'd do it right away?"

"Yes, Delaney. It's already scheduled."

"Good girl."

"I'll keep you posted. But the doctor was very reassuring." Lissa fought the sudden interference of tears. "I was so scared. I have watched my whole life dissolve before my eyes. Now I can dream again."

"Well, I hope those dreams include a Marine, a family, and happiness."

"Me, too." Lissa choked on the words. "More than you know."

"Thanks for sharing this with us." Delaney's voice wobbled again. "I think I'm drifting. This medicine's a real trip, let me tell you."

"Don't take any chances with it, Sis." A thread of fear pulsed up her spine. "If this keeps up, you should tell your doctor. Pronto."

"This coming from the one who fought me about those tests?" Sarcasm laced Delaney's speech. "Thanks, Lissa. Dad has already called. But it's nice to know you're on our team again."

"Never left, Laney." Lissa's voice deteriorated to a whisper. "Sidetracked, maybe. But never, ever, left."

Thursday afternoon Jayden rode in quiet contemplation on the drive home from Steens Mountain. Three nights at the campground and four hikes amid the beautiful scenery left him tired, but happier than he'd been since his dad died. He'd forgotten George, his situation in foster care, even his mother's problems. Life had been good for three days straight, and Jayden didn't want this time to end.

Kurt sat beside him, eyes on the road, fingers tapping the steering wheel in time to a country song playing on the radio. Jayden couldn't help but think of his father when he sat next to the big Marine. It was almost as if his dad were here next to him, the two men were so much alike. "Think Peggy has work for us to do?"

"Let's see. Three horses, one dog, and the threat of a rain storm coming. Make your best guess."

"I'd call that a yes." Jayden grinned, loving the way Kurt treated him like a friend, not a little kid, reminding him of those fun times he'd had with his dad. "Aren't I supposed to see my mother first thing tomorrow morning?" Jayden wanted to see his mother, but Kurt hadn't mentioned the meeting once since they'd left. The prospect of seeing George made him wary. "I think the caseworker said we had to go to Bend."

Kurt gripped the steering wheel tighter, eyes straight ahead, and didn't answer.

"Kurt?" Jayden's stomach flipped, a whole jar of butterflies escaping as it tipped over. "What's the matter?"

"Your visit had to be rescheduled." Kurt punched in another station on the radio as the frequency of the one they'd listened to earlier faded.

"Rescheduled? Did something happen?" The butterflies fluttered against his stomach wall, as if seeking an exit. Jayden swallowed his jitters. "What aren't you telling me?"

"Your stepfather ignored a restraining order and visited your mother, uninvited." Kurt clipped the words, the narrowing of his eyes and the set of his mouth defining the news he tried to hide. "I haven't heard if Mr. Barnes is still unaccounted for, or if your safety is compromised." Kurt had slipped into military speak. Jayden remembered how his dad phrased things.

"Is my mom okay?" The back of Jayden's throat was so dry he bit his tongue to moisten his mouth.

"She will be." Kurt opened his window a crack and cool air flooded the hot cab. "He slapped her around a bit."

Jayden doubled up his fists. His real father had never treated his mother this way. George's temper fueled Jayden's need for revenge. "You think he's looking for me?"

"He visited the rescue center Monday, not long after we pulled out." Kurt's voice grew quiet, as if he feared Jayden's reaction. "That's why the sheriff's deputy came to the campground."

"Now you're telling me stories." Jayden laughed. "Lissa came to see you."

Kurt took his eyes off the road ahead and gave Jayden a vigorous shake of his head. "No, she came because George threatened to find you."

Jayden's pulse raced to overdrive. He'd already tasted George's rage and didn't want a repeat performance. Sitting here next to Kurt, though, he felt safe. This man could make lunchmeat out of George. Jayden loved the cocoon of protection Kurt wrapped around him. As if he were a shield.

"Okay, I believe you. I'm glad he didn't find me." Jayden watched Kurt with a sideways glance. He remained serious, but Jayden couldn't resist teasing him. "Making s'mores wasn't part of the warning, was it?" Jayden smirked. "She seemed awfully happy to help."

"Are you trying to play matchmaker?"

Jayden leaned into the seat. "I don't need to. It's obvious you and Lissa like each other. Peggy and I talked about it."

"Oh, so Peggy put you onto me." Kurt reached over and tweaked his ear. "Your partner in crime."

"Hey, Lissa's a nice lady. What's not to like?"

Kurt aimed his attention out the window. "It's complicated."

"Haven't you ever asked a woman out before?" Jayden enjoyed the banter, and right now he'd rather do that than think about George hitting his mom. He shoved the threat away, choosing to dwell on Kurt's love life. A strong, great guy like Kurt could date any girl he wanted.

Jayden's mother had told him she couldn't resist his father's strength and deep brown eyes. Every time she hugged Jayden, she remembered his father. From the look on her face, the memory of his dad remained a good one. He'd never seen her look that way around George. Go figure. Jayden refocused on Kurt. "Getting a date with Lissa can't be that hard."

"I've dated Lissa." Kurt lifted his eyebrows and twisted his mouth into a pout. "And if you can keep a secret. . ."

"What? What secret? I can keep it. I promise." Jayden couldn't wait for the juicy morsel Kurt's remark promised. "Spill."

"You sure?" Kurt glanced his way. When he nodded, Kurt chuckled. "I've even kissed her."

"You've kissed Lissa?" Jayden blinked. "Which means you like her. Why aren't you dating her? Man, are you stupid?"

"Hey. Show a little respect."

Kurt hit the gas and the truck sped down the road at a faster clip. Whatever Jayden had said had touched a sore spot.

Jayden grew quiet. He understood the heartache caused by loving from afar. His mother and dad had cherished each other, even though his father's enlistment left each of them alone for long periods. When his dad came home in a coffin, his mother withdrew, spending long hours in her bedroom alone, as though her heart had ridden the casket into the ground. She hadn't grieved long before George swept in like an avenging angel, filling her head with promises of a bright future, assuring her of his faithful and steadfast love. Too heartbroken to resist, she'd fallen for George's clumsy claims. Now Jayden and his mother lived with the regret. "I'm only saying, if you liked her enough to kiss her once, she's probably wondering why you stopped."

"When did you get so wise and worldly?" Kurt's eyes twinkled, a sure sign a tease followed. "You're too young to have kissed a girl."

Jayden exhaled, relieved he hadn't caused hurt and feeling bold enough to speak his mind. "No, I haven't kissed anybody but my parents. But they loved each other so much that my mom fell apart when the chaplain showed up at our door." Jayden scrunched his eyes tighter to stem the tears threatening to fall. "George was no replacement for my dad. If you care about Lissa, don't let anyone else sneak in and take your place. She'll be miserable and so will you."

Kurt drove in silence. Whatever he thought, he wasn't sharing.

Jayden waited for a reply, but none came.

Finally, Kurt cleared his throat. "I'm sorry about your dad, Jayden. It's obvious his death matured you beyond your years. I saw what war did to the children in Afghanistan. I didn't expect it to affect children here as well. But it has." He reached over and touched Jayden's shoulder. "I lost my best friend in Kabul. I swore I'd never get involved with people again, because it seemed everyone who knew me died. I didn't want to risk involvement. But I'm promising you I will do whatever it takes to make your life better."

"And Lissa?"

"She will take time." Kurt appeared to want to laugh. "But I'll give your suggestions thought. Fair enough?"

"Peggy and I will be waiting." Jayden giggled. "Action figures are made of plastic, but you're the real deal. Peggy and I expect action."

Kurt laughed. "You're too much, you know that?"

"You're the one who sent me to the horse trough seminar. I learn quick."

CHAPTER TWENTY-THREE

AFTER HER DOCTOR'S APPOINTMENT, LISSA TRIED to think of an excuse to visit the Herrick Valley Rescue Center, but sitting in the office, drinking Sheriff Briggs's version of coffee, she couldn't come up with anything legitimate. Her stomach roiled as the bitter brew hit bottom, and she searched her tote for an antacid. Kurt had called in, as she'd requested, and should be arriving at the horse facility any time. If only she could see him, tell him her news, and explain the fear she'd hid behind.

In conversation on the phone for the last several minutes, Matthew slammed the handset into its cradle and stood, sending his chair rolling backward into the room. "We've got trouble."

She stood to attention. "What's up?"

"George Barnes has been spotted on Cow Creek Road, headed toward the rescue center."

"You don't think he'd show up in broad daylight, do you?" Lissa's pulse raced, thinking of all the ways this could indeed be trouble.

"According to the report we got, he's capable of brash and unpredictable behavior. Melanie's sister called in a few minutes ago to say Melanie isn't answering her phone. After George slapped his wife around last Sunday night, trying to get information on Jayden, I'm worried. The kid may be his target, though I haven't figured out why."

"I know the man living at the rescue center. He's the guy Peggy Blake sent her message to on Monday." Lissa calmed her voice. "He's an ex-Marine and can handle himself."

"And George is fueled by booze. Irrational and dangerous. With the weekend attempt a failure, George will probably try to find another way to get at Jayden."

"Why? Jayden's a boy." Lissa couldn't fathom someone deliberately harming a child.

"I have my own theory." Matthew swiped at his forehead before settling his hat in place. "George sees him as a roadblock in his relationship with Melanie. He as much as said the boy stole food from him and that Melanie spent too much of his money on his stepson. Why do women marry such losers?"

Lissa had no answer for her boss. She'd seen plenty of female sailors vying for the attention of unattached men in the Navy, starved for male companionship. Melanie had probably fallen into that same mindset, and George took advantage of her loneliness. "Perhaps Jayden reminds Melanie of her first husband, and George can't handle the scrutiny."

"You're right on target. Jayden's father was a medaled Marine, shot in an ambush by the Taliban in Kabul."

"Really?" Lissa stopped, surprised her assessment had come so close to the truth. A second husband standing in the shadow of a hero. The information explained a lot about his behavior. Male egos were often sensitive landmines waiting to be triggered. In her rise to Navy intelligence officer, she'd learned much about the male mindset, often bypassing men who thought they deserved the promotion.

Kurt had saluted when she first met him. Outranking him made her cheeks burn. Even now she chastised herself for the feeling. But she couldn't help it. Kurt was the most handsome man she'd ever seen. While she remained there tongue-tied, he stood at attention waiting for her dismissal. Kurt had pushed beyond the military barrier separating them and stolen her heart anyway. "The Marine living at the rescue center survived an ambush by the Taliban."

"Quite a coincidence." Matthew grabbed his jacket. "I'm driving out there to join our patrols. More official vehicles might chase George out of the brush."

"Need me to do anything?" Lissa bit her lip, willing her boss to send her out too. After the encounter at the campground, she'd give up leave to see Kurt again. Even the thought made her lightheaded. "Has anyone called Peggy?"

"Do that first, then head out there. Bernie Mueller, Bennie's brother, released his claim on the dog and the horse. Don't you need to check on the progress of the animals?" Matthew's smile curved upward, eyes twinkling as he studied her. "The filly may be up for adoption soon, I understand."

"Then I'd better see to it, hadn't I?" Lissa moistened her lips, sensing Matthew intended to say more. "What aren't you telling me?"

"Who, me?" Chuckling, Matthew pivoted to the door. "I'll work my way to the center after I spot George. I need to meet this medaled Marine."

Kurt pulled the truck around to the back of the barn as he and Jayden returned from the camping trip. He stepped from the vehicle, his movements deliberate and cautious. His gaze skirted the immediate surroundings for signs of trouble as Jayden climbed out the passenger door.

Jayden's revelation about his dad's death and the coincidence of Jordan Clarke being part of Kurt's unit in Kabul had shaken Kurt. He'd make it his duty to protect the boy. He and Jayden shared grief over two men they'd both loved and lost in a desolate place filled with sand and sorrow. Kurt's need to comfort and restore Jayden's broken heart trumped his bitterness over Foster's death. Though he still mourned the loss of his best friend, Kurt's mission had changed. This child, ravaged by the war Kurt hated, needed him, presenting a rare opportunity to make a difference, to avenge both deaths and rid his soul of its pain.

A bark sounded. Duke raced to the passenger side, pawing his way up Jayden's torso. Jayden wrapped his arms around the dog's neck, bending down and talking to Duke in gleeful murmurs. Kurt enjoyed the moment, boy and dog falling on one another, bubbling as if they'd each discovered a new playmate. Jayden giggled as the dog licked his cheek, and the dog's tail wagged at high speed.

Peggy appeared at the hood, a contented calm across her face, her eyes on the dog and boy. She turned her attention to Kurt, her eyebrows raised, and a knowing look in her eyes.

"How's everything?" Kurt studied Peggy's expression, watching for signs of trouble. "I heard through the sheriff you had a visitor after we left."

"Merely a drunk looking for a place to flop." Peggy touched her lips with her index finger. "I introduced him to Smith and Wesson, and he decided he'd find another place to stay."

"Remind me never to cross you on a dark and stormy night, Peggy."

"He's headed this way." Peggy's gaze darted to Jayden, then she refocused on Kurt.

"Seriously?" At her nod, Kurt clapped Jayden on the back in a rough but friendly big-brother gesture. "Jayden, help me unload the truck, then we've got chores to catch up on."

Jayden told Duke to stay, then noticed Peggy and grinned at her. "Did you miss us?" He caught the sleeping bags as Kurt tossed them down.

Peggy nodded. "Duke couldn't contain his restlessness with you gone."

"We had an awesome time." Jayden's words spilled out like candy from a ruptured bag. "Kurt and I climbed a hill and saw a stallion that could have been Lady's daddy and we hiked down a trail and saw an owl and an antelope through the binoculars and I got him all squared away on Lissa."

Peggy laughed. "All in one weekend? You'll make quite a counselor when you grow up, if you already solved Kurt's love life."

"Hey, you two. I resent being the victim of your plotting." Kurt feigned a frown as he finished unloading the truck. He handed the empty cooler chest to Peggy.

"That's what you get for slacking off in the mountains," she said over her shoulder. "There's lots of chores to do, so get busy, lover boy."

"Ma'am, yes ma'am!" He watched her disappear into the house, then gave Jayden a broad wink.

"Aren't we going to rest or something first?" The confused look on Jayden's face made Kurt laugh.

"Nope. We work, then we eat and rest. Besides, you rested in the truck all the way here. I heard you snore."

Kurt cleaned the stalls and directed Jayden to fill a wheelbarrow with shavings. Within an hour, they'd returned the horses from the pasture to the barn, fed and watered each one, and curried their coats to a fine sheen. Even Lady, whose hide made a slow recovery after her confinement in the round pen, shone with a glossy glow.

"She'll be a beauty here one of these days." Kurt nodded his approval to Jayden. "And she'll have you to thank."

Jayden beamed. "She likes when I scratch all her itches. Behind her ears and under her chin." The boy's face fell. "Mr. Mueller showed me how to make her happy."

"He'd be proud of you." Kurt roughed up the boy's hair. "You learned his lessons well."

A dark green Explorer rattled up the driveway, the county sheriff's logo visible on the side.

"I *wonder* who's here?" Jayden taunted him. "I think I'll go see if Peggy has any carrots. Give you a little privacy while you work on your game, *Romeo.*"

"Remind me to take you to the water trough for lesson two."

"Oh no, you don't." Jayden took off running. He turned and made smacking sounds. "Kissy, kissy!"

"Brat."

The SUV pulled to a stop in front of the barn. Lissa stepped from the cab, lifting her hand to her forehead, shading her eyes from the sun. Her trim figure in the neat uniform made Kurt's hands sweat.

"Kurt?"

"Back here by the stalls." Kurt gripped the pitchfork tighter, trying in vain to steady his breathing. "Driving a different rig?"

"All the others are out on patrol." She stepped inside the barn and peered over the gate at Lady. "Wow. She's looking better and better."

"Jayden can't get her off his mind." *Like I can't stop thinking about you.*

"How is he going to handle losing her when she moves to a permanent home?" Lissa stroked the filly's muzzle.

Kurt fingered the pitchfork handle. "I don't know. He may stay here for a while." Kurt patted the filly's neck. "Can't Lady stay, too?"

"If Peggy wants her to stay, she can. Mr. Mueller's brother signed the papers releasing his claim to both animals."

"I thought he might." Kurt leaned against the stall door. "Duke would have died living in an apartment in Portland."

"And an apartment is no place for a restless filly." Lissa grinned at her joke.

"You talking about the horse or a former intelligence specialist?" Kurt narrowed his eyes, waiting for her to react. "The

Navy officer I remember loved movies, hikes along the beach, and petting zoos."

"Not petting zoos." Lissa reddened. "I like the real thing with lions, tigers, and bears."

Kurt angled his head, studying her. "Not many zoos in Harney County. We have our own form of wildlife."

"I understand Malheur National Refuge has an abundance of wild critters. Did you and Jayden see anything else after I left?"

"Jayden thought he spotted Lady's daddy at the wild horse lookout." Kurt rested his pitchfork against the stall. "But no two-legged varmint came around making trouble."

"Actually, that's why I'm here. Sheriff Briggs is scouting Cow Creek Road. George was sighted out there in his truck." She paused. "And Melanie is unaccounted for."

"How close is the search to us?" Kurt's defense mechanism shifted into alert status. "Should I alert Peggy of the increasing danger and round up Jayden?"

"Keep tabs on them. We don't know what George is up to. But his threats against Jayden could be real and not the empty promises of a drunk."

"I saw the bruises, Lissa." Kurt's face froze in memory. "A man like that won't stop at slaps next time." He climbed out of the stall. "Melanie's disappearance is related?"

"We can't say for certain." Lissa walked beside him to the barn opening, stopping near the county vehicle. "But we have to assume so."

"She'll be in danger. George can't be trusted."

"You've certainly grown attached." Lissa turned her attention on him. "Will you be okay when Jayden's reunited with his mother?"

"Jayden needs someone to love him like his own son." Kurt's gaze skirted the nearby roadside and surrounding pasture, searching for signs of Jayden and Duke. Beyond the fenced paddock, Jayden threw a Frisbee for the dog to chase. "Hey Jayden—stay inside the fenced area where I can see you. Don't get sidetracked and drift onto the open range."

Jayden waved and tossed the Frisbee.

Kurt scanned the horizon for movement or activity other than the two playmates. Finding none, he focused on Lissa. "I found out his real dad was one of the men from my unit who died in the Taliban ambush two years ago."

"No kidding? When you were missing in action?" At his nod, Lissa's mouth hung open, surprised. "What a coincidence."

Kurt relaxed into the at-ease position without even thinking about it, hands clasped behind his back. "I know you're going to think this is sudden, but I believe God brought me here for a different reason than the one that first drove me." Kurt drew a labored breath. "I told you about the suffering I saw over there. Children whose lives were snuffed out or damaged because of the war. I wanted to make a difference." Kurt tucked his foot up behind him, catching his heel on the SUV running board, Jayden's revelation over the weekend still haunting him. "But when Foster was killed, I didn't want anything but revenge. I came home to help Peggy and to hide. I didn't believe I could change anything, because it seemed like everyone I touched died."

"I knew you'd withdrawn, though I didn't know why." Lissa leaned against the hood of the Explorer.

"Jayden has given me a new direction. Renewed purpose."

"Anything is better than hiding in the past."

"I disappointed you." Kurt studied the ground. "You weren't sure you could go back to where we were, and I don't blame you." Kurt searched her face, his mouth set in a firm line. "I've been thinking about a way to fix this, and I wondered if we could simply start over?"

Lissa closed her eyes, dreading what she had to say, wishing this moment hadn't come. "There's something I haven't told you."

"Sounds serious."

"It is." Lissa opened her eyes and drew a deep breath. "I've been looking for answers myself."

CHAPTER TWENTY-FOUR

JAYDEN TOSSED THE FRISBEE AS FAR as he could spin it across the pasture. The disc fluttered, wobbling in the light breeze. Duke raced beneath, tongue lolling as he waited for the disc to drop. Catching it in his teeth, he pranced back to Jayden, tail wagging like a high-flying pilot.

His antics delighted Jayden. "Good boy, Duke. You caught it." Duke dropped his prize at Jayden's feet, panting, eyes keen on the disc.

"You never get enough, do you?" Jayden laughed, picked up the Frisbee, and, with a flick of his wrist, launched the toy across the pasture once more. The dog gave chase, venturing into the open range Kurt had warned Jayden to stay away from. A flash of sunlight against metal blinded him momentarily, and he raised his hand over his eyes to see better.

His stepfather's pickup truck rolled to a stop along the side of the road leading away from the ranch, back where it wouldn't be seen behind the outbuildings. What was he doing here?

Jayden slowed his steps, ready to run the other way, Kurt's warning stuck at the back of his mind.

A woman in a light-yellow dress descended from the passenger side of the cab, the sunlight making her appear angelic. She took a few steps away from the pickup. "Jayden?"

"Mom?" Jayden burst into a run and covered the uphill slope of the pasture as fast as he could. What was his mother doing here? Had she come for him? Could they go home? Out of breath, he neared the roadside, reaching the fence one stride ahead of Duke. He tried to catch his breath, panting as hard as Duke. "Why are you here?"

"I—I've come for—for you." Face ashen, his mother

stammered as though she was nervous. She took a step backward and gripped the pickup's door. "I've missed you so much."

"I've missed you, too, Mom." He glanced at the empty truck. Something didn't seem right here. His mother wouldn't trick him, would she? "How did you get George to let you drive his pickup?" Jayden paused, scanning her face for signs of bruising. "I heard he hurt you again."

She thrust an arm in his direction, her hand trembling. "Let me give you a hug."

Jayden hesitated. Why was she so scared? He'd never seen her like this before. "Mom?"

"Please?" Her smile allayed his fears. She looked so pretty in her yellow dress, his real dad's favorite color. "You're my son, after all."

"Sure, Mom." Jayden grinned and crawled between the fence's wooden rails. His mother had come to see him. Kurt would understand. He had pulled his left leg through when he saw a figure come from behind the truck and stride toward him. Too late, Jayden glanced up and stared into George's reddened face. With no escape route, he stood his ground. "What are you doing here?"

"Doing your mother a favor." George grabbed the back of Jayden's shirt, encircling his waist with a brawny arm and heaving the boy over his shoulder. "She won't leave with me unless you come along too."

"No! I won't go with you." Jayden kicked and squirmed, but the man's grip around his middle tightened, making it difficult to move. "Help me, Mom!"

"Jayden, we're moving away from here." She clasped her hands beneath her chin. "George promised to take you with us if I cooperated."

"I don't want to go. Help!" He pounded on George's shoulders, landing a fist in the middle of his back. "Help!"

Duke leaped over the fence and charged George, snapping and growling at the man's legs. George kicked at the dog, landing a boot to Duke's belly. The dog yelped as he flew through the air, but as soon as his feet hit the ground, Duke charged again, barking as though he'd treed a skunk. George aimed another foot at the dog, but Jayden twisted as hard as he could in George's arms, throwing his stepfather off balance. George landed hard against the bed of the truck, spouting a stream of words that made Jayden wince. He dropped Jayden to the ground, pinning him against the pickup. "You stupid kid—I ought to kill you!"

"George, no!" his mother screamed. "You promised."

Another string of expletives left the man's mouth. He raised his arm and took aim at Jayden.

"Duke. Herd!" Jayden shouted at the dog, ducking as George's fist came flying at his face. "Duke. Herd!"

The dog hesitated a second, then cleared the fence and ran barking down the hill toward the barn.

Jayden screamed one more time. "Help!"

George clasped his hand over the boy's mouth, his odorous breath in Jayden's ear. "Shut up. You hear me? Shut up." Opening the pickup door, George shoved Jayden onto the bench seat, then grabbed his mother. "Get in, Melanie." He slammed the door and stomped around to the driver's side of the cab. Turning the key, George jerked the pickup into gear.

Jayden sank against the seat, winded and fighting tears. Here he sat, right back where he'd started, next to a bully who thought nothing of hurting him. Would he ever see Duke or Lady again? Peggy or Kurt? Nausea roiled in his stomach, the need to hurl mounting. Wouldn't that fix things?

He peeked at his mother sitting beside him, her trembling body scaring him. Tears streamed down her cheeks. She lifted her hands to her face. That's when Jayden noticed the bruises around her wrists. George would never stop.

Lissa swallowed the leathery taste in her mouth. What would Kurt say to her news? Would he be angry she hadn't told him? Or happy that the report was good? Her heart couldn't bear his rejection again.

"Kurt." Lissa shook her head. "I had to have lab tests done. . ."

The frantic barking of a dog interrupted her. Beyond the pasture near the roadway, Duke's frenzied howl sounded, the dog tearing down the hill like he was being chased by demons. Not seeing Jayden, she scanned the hillside from where the dog had come. A pickup parked by the road caught her gaze. A door slammed, and a burly man disappeared around to the driver's side. The engine roared to life, the pickup lurched forward, and the tires spun in the gravel. She grabbed Kurt's arm and pointed. "Look!"

"Where's Jayden?" Kurt ran to the gate, focusing on the oncoming dog. "He's gone!" Kurt tore out of the driveway, running toward the hill. He stopped when he reached the dog and slammed his fist into a fence rail.

"That has to be George." Lissa gasped as the departing vehicle kicked up dust in its getaway. "Kurt, get in and ride with me. I'll radio dispatch."

Lissa hustled into her service rig. "C111 reporting, Dispatch, patch me through to C100." With Kurt beside her, she gunned the engine and sped up the driveway toward the main road.

"C100 here. What's your twenty?"

"Leaving the rescue center." Lissa relaxed at the sound of Matthew's voice.

Kurt sat rigid beside her, eyes narrowed, focused on the hillside.

"There." He pointed to a cloud of dust disappearing around a bend to the east, where the fleeing pickup fishtailed on the dirt road.

Lissa spoke again into the mic. "We're in pursuit of a silver-toned pickup that left the rescue center and is heading eastbound on Highway 20. We believe George Barnes is driving the vehicle and Jayden Clarke is inside. Kurt McKintrick is riding with me."

"Melanie called her sister and said she and George were moving away." The calm in Matthew's voice lent confidence to Lissa. "She may be in the vehicle too."

Lissa spoke again. "We'll confirm when we get close enough to see."

"Ten-four. Suspect may be armed. Proceed with caution. I repeat, suspect may be armed. I'm five miles out, but I'm on my way. All units report. Code 3."

A straight stretch loomed before them. Kurt leaned forward in the seat. "Gun it. We've got to get within a hundred yards."

Lissa flipped on her lights and siren. Praying for protection of all involved, she floored the gas pedal, and the SUV roared in protest as they pursued the fleeing truck.

The straight stretch along Highway 20 gave way to a series of twists as the vehicle ahead of them slowed to maneuver the curves. With each slowdown, Lissa fought to bring the sheriff's rig closer to the target, but their speed made for treacherous driving. Her head hurt from the concentration, and her breathing grew shallow. Kurt sat perched on the edge of the seat, the handsome, loving guy transformed into a machine trained to perform under pressure.

Lissa reached under the seat and handed Kurt binoculars. "See if you recognize anyone in the cab."

Lifting the binoculars to his eyes, Kurt studied the truck ahead. "Jayden's in the middle. Another person is on the right, but I can't tell if it's a woman or a man."

"Melanie?"

"Could be." Kurt laid the binoculars beside him. "This highway is heading toward serious curves, and he'll have to slow down or risk overturning the vehicle. I wish I had my rifle."

"You couldn't shoot at this speed. You'd risk injuring Jayden."

Kurt banged the dash with his fist. "I'd still like to try."

"I have my revolver, but I don't want to use it." Lissa could only pray the speed of the Explorer would not claim its own victims.

Jayden clung to the edge of the bench seat as George raged beside him, shouting and cursing. His mother huddled by the passenger door, leaning against the headrest, arms wrapped tight around herself. With each bump in the road, the pickup bounced, careening around corners like an aerialist on a circus high wire—front wheels intact, back wheels lifting off the ground. Jayden squeezed his eyes shut, afraid the next curve would overwhelm the pickup and throw all of them through the windshield.

"George, please slow down." His mother sucked in a gasp of air. "You'll kill us."

"That shouldn't surprise anyone." George spat his words at her. "The entire county thinks I'm a mean, drunken bully, thanks to your bratty kid. If not for him, I'd be back on the road driving my rig, making money to share with my loving wife." He yelled out the open window, as if those following them might hear. "My traitorous, *loving* wife." He stomped the gas pedal to the floor as a straight stretch loomed. "Couldn't leave without her precious son."

"How could you expect me to abandon Jayden?" His mother's voice hovered above the engine noise, barely audible in the rattle of the cab. "You knew he was part of my life when you met me."

"And how convenient his dad is a medaled Marine. A hero. An all-around *swell* guy." George's sarcasm rankled as he yelled at Jayden's mother. "Everything you've made clear I'm not."

"I never said any of that." Mom gripped the dash, her arms locked as she struggled to stay upright.

"Didn't have to." George's eyes narrowed, glaring at Jayden in the rearview mirror. "All those nighttime stories about Jordan this, Jordan that. What a great father he was, how brave he was to go off to war, how much he loved his son. You make me sick."

"I wanted to keep Jordan's memory alive for Jayden. It was never a reflection on you—ever."

"Shut up, Melanie." George maneuvered around another corner and gunned the accelerator in the straight stretch. "It's too late for saying sorry. You and this kid are going with me—like it or lump it. And you'll get what money I say you can have—not one red cent more."

"Then let us go." Jayden's mom sat up straighter. "If you don't want a life with us, why are you taking us with you? I have Jordan's military pension to support us. Why not let us go?"

Without warning, George's arm flew out, striking Jayden, snapping his head against the cushion. The next thing he saw was George's hand squeezing into a fist and swinging at his mom. The force of his arm slammed her against the pickup door, the blow knocking her head against the window. Jayden held his sore cheek, eyes on the ignition. Kurt's words from the campout swam in his head. *If you turn the key off while the truck is in gear, the engine will automatically stop.*

He eyed the key again, his mind replaying Kurt's warning. *If the engine cuts out and you take it out of drive to restart it, the action could send you into a spin. The power steering and the brakes stop when the engine does.* He had to take the risk. If the truck stopped, he could jump and pull his mother with him.

Jayden gripped the dash and held on as George sped into another straight stretch. When the time was right, he'd do what he had to do. The ignition was his only hope.

CHAPTER TWENTY-FIVE

KURT GROUND HIS TEETH AS HE steadied himself against the side of the vehicle. This highway stretched on for miles, but at the slightest bend in the road, accelerating could cause a tire to spin out, especially if they slipped onto the shoulder taking the curves.

Images of children injured at the hands of the Taliban flashed across his memory, and he ground his teeth, remembering the suffering he'd witnessed, all in the name of Jihad. Vacant eyes created by empty stomachs gawked from behind low-hung roofs and crumbling doorposts. Now Jayden rode with a man whose mental outlook couldn't be any better than the terrorists Kurt and Foster had fought to stop.

Beside him Lissa clutched the steering wheel, mouth rigid, brow furrowed, a reflection of the military training she'd received—focus, plan, and execute. A woman intent on catching the vehicle ahead. A woman he still wanted to love.

He'd made a mistake withdrawing from the attraction he held for Lissa, shutting her out of his pain the last year he served and discarding the affection they'd shared. War had snared him, determined to twist a simple Marine—him—into a wounded victim if he let it. War would triumph if something didn't change, snuffing out all the good Kurt and Foster had planned for their futures. Kurt couldn't let the war win.

Lissa would be his starting point. But could she forgive him? The way her body tensed when near him and her lips flattened when she spoke covered her like battle garb.

"C111, come in please." The radio burbled from the dash. "C100 here."

Lissa grabbed the mic, steadying the wheel with her left hand. "Matt, 10-20?"

"We're behind you a good mile and a half. The community of Drewsey should be coming up soon. Watch for side roads. George might try to shake you." The sheriff's voice faded in and out. "He's a long-haul truck driver, so he knows this terrain better than you. Probably stopped for coffee and a donut a time or two."

"Visual on suspect." Lissa gripped the wheel for another long curve, the mic caught between her index finger and her thumb. "A lot of straight highway makes him hard to catch."

"We'll get him. Stay in pursuit. C100 out."

"C111 out." Lissa returned the dispatch mic to its place.

"You're doing a good job, Deputy Frye." The way she rolled her eyes at him and cast a crooked grin his way made him smile. "I've never ridden with a woman packing heat."

"I was hired to rescue dogs and cats." Lissa cleared her throat, never taking her eyes off the road. "Not perform high speed chases down empty highways after criminals."

"I hadn't seen you in action." Her resolve amazed Kurt. "You're one tough woman." A squeal captured his attention as the vehicle ahead took a curve too fast and spun in the middle of the road. Losing valuable time, the truck straightened and sped away, but not before Lissa closed the gap to five hundred feet between them.

"Way to go." Kurt waited for the moment when George would miscalculate and veer off the road. "Another curve like that last one, and we'll end this chase."

Lissa nodded, sitting up straighter in the seat as her fingers clamped the steering wheel tighter. She checked her rearview mirror. "Seems like we should have a visual on Matthew and the others behind us. We'll need them for an arrest."

"I know."

Ahead, the truck slowed again, a right-hand curve blocking visibility. Without warning, the vehicle turned onto Stinking Water

Creek, its rear end skidding in a dangerous left swerve as it performed the high-speed maneuver.

"I can't make the turn at this speed." Lissa braked, but passed the intersection. She reversed the Explorer and backed up.

Kurt braced himself, ready to jump as the brake lights of the fleeing truck flashed. The vehicle stopped dead in the road like a balloon losing all its air, the sound of the motor gone.

"Somebody turned off the ignition." Kurt gripped the door handle.

With a bellow the engine returned to life, the tires squealing as the vehicle tried to speed away, smoke rising from the asphalt. The pickup jolted forward in jackrabbit fashion, the force bouncing the cab into the sagebrush. Connecting with the gravel edge, the rear axle spun around so the truck's hood faced them, tailgate pointed toward the creek.

The passenger door popped open, swinging wide on its hinges, and a woman fell from the pickup, dangling by a seat belt. Behind her Jayden leapt out the door, hitting the ground and rolling, coming to a halt near a juniper. Steam poured from the hood.

Lissa pulled to the shoulder of the road. Another county rig appeared behind them, lights flashing as it turned at the intersection. The sheriff roared past and came to a stop in front of the truck. A second patrol car pulled alongside the first. Sheriff Briggs and a deputy Kurt didn't recognize emerged, guns drawn.

Briggs drew his weapon and shouted, "Get out of the truck and place your hands on the hood."

No one moved. The only sound came from the hissing radiator. After a minute, the sheriff shouted again. "You in the truck. Out now."

The driver's side door creaked open. Hands in the air, George Barnes climbed from the pickup, face reddened and legs wobbling as he stumbled to comply.

Kurt jumped from Lissa's truck, feet running when he hit the ground, racing to the side of the pickup where Jayden lay motionless. Melanie dangled from the seat belt, moaning, her face bloodied, one leg twisted under the other. Kurt stopped beside her and started to help when Lissa pushed in beside him.

"I've got the first aid kit. Go see to Jayden." She turned back to the woman. "Melanie? Can you hear me? It's Lissa Frye, the sheriff's deputy." Lissa touched the woman's shoulder. "I'm going to help you. Don't try to move."

Kurt feared what he would find when he knelt beside Jayden. The boy had tumbled out of the vehicle with such force, Kurt could only imagine what the kid might have injured. "Jayden? Hey, bud, it's me." He patted the boy's shoulder, getting no response. "Jay-jay. Wake up. Please."

The boy's eyes fluttered, mouth puckered as if he might cry. "He hurt my mom." Jayden gasped, his rattling breath interrupting his speech. "He hurt her. I turned off the key. When the truck slowed down, I opened the door and jumped out." Jayden's eyelids closed to slits as if he were in pain. "She's not dead, is she?"

Kurt brushed Jayden's hair out of his eyes, caressing his cheek. "Lissa's tending her. We'll get an ambulance here soon. Where do you hurt?"

"In my heart." Jayden choked back the words. "If my mom dies, my heart will break."

"Your quick thinking probably saved her." Kurt fought to speak above the knot lodged in his throat. "Lissa's working to make her better. Hang in there." Kurt rested his fingers on Jayden's neck. "Did you injure yourself when you fell out of the truck?"

"I don't think so." Jayden rubbed his shoulder and patted his leg. "My dad taught me how to duck and roll, like you guys do when you're under fire." The boy's eyes shone. "That's what heroes do."

Kurt leaned over and hugged the boy. "You're right. Heroes have to know how to act in danger, like you did." He touched Jayden's chin. "Your dad would be proud."

Jayden's smile could have lit up the rest of Harney County. "Thanks. Knowing you helps me remember my dad."

Kurt's eyes stung.

Lissa leaned over Melanie, checking her for cuts and broken bones. A red stripe crossed the woman's neck, caused by the seatbelt strap when she hung from the cab. Melanie's cheek sported a bruise, the purple impression growing deeper in color the longer Lissa watched. Probably where he had hit her—again. *Monster!*

Behind her, she heard the unmistakable sound of a suspect being handcuffed, and Matthew's voice saying, "Dispatch an ambulance from the Harney District Hospital in Burns."

Lissa touched Melanie, waiting for her to respond. "My boss wants to call an ambulance."

"Can't I ride in the patrol car?" Melanie, her voice weak, caught Lissa's hand. "I'm beat up, but I can walk."

"Let me ask." Lissa hurried to where Matthew and Deputy Lindstrom were assisting George into the back of the patrol car. "Melanie wants to transport in one of our vehicles."

"I can take her with me." Matthew nodded over his shoulder. "Lindstrom will take George to the jail." His eyes narrowed. "I need to get Melanie's statement, anyway. Kidnapping a child in state protection is a serious crime. She may be labeled an accessory, even if she is his mother."

Lissa couldn't hide her surprise. "That's all she needs." Lissa crossed her arms. "Isn't there another way?"

"Can't be helped. Until I get information otherwise, by being in the truck she appears to have assisted with the kidnapping."

"What about George's truck?" Lissa glanced over her shoulder. "The radiator is steaming and one front tire is blown out."

"Dispatch a tow truck. Drewsey might have one. They're a little way down the road."

Lindstrom chimed in. "Not much in Drewsey, Sheriff."

"Call Hines, then, if you can catch a signal. Or call dispatch." Matthew nodded toward Melanie. "I'll go talk to the mother."

Finding a tow truck took several calls to the county headquarters since Lissa wasn't familiar with that kind of follow-up work. *Nothing like on-the-job training.* She gritted her teeth as she ran her finger over the available apps on her phone.

After spending a few minutes in discussion with Kurt, Jayden, and his mother, Sheriff Briggs loaded Melanie into the patrol car.

Matthew walked to where Lissa waited. "You'll have to drive to Hines to get Jayden checked out in an emergency room. They'll need to document any injuries they find for the criminal charges against George. Escort Jayden back to his foster home. I'll see you in the office tomorrow." Matthew looked at Kurt. "Glad you rode along."

"I thought we were going to chase the man into Idaho." Kurt wrapped an arm around Jayden's shoulders. "He was carrying valuable cargo."

Matthew nodded. "He probably would've crashed before that—or run out of gas. Ontario's the next real town, and it's ninety miles away on a straight stretch."

"A man could get lost out here and starve to death, couldn't he?" Kurt's gaze shifted to the east.

"It's happened more times than I care to remember." Matthew jingled his keys. "Got to transport Mrs. Barnes back to town. Make sure Peggy keeps an eye on the kid. He may have suffered trauma he won't admit, or they may find other injuries at the hospital." He directed a question to Lissa. "You okay with gas?"

"I've got a can in the back. I can make it to Buchanan to drop off Jayden and Kurt."

"See you tomorrow then." Matthew slid into his patrol car and drove away.

Lissa's pulse quickened, watching the Marine and the child together. Kurt's gentle interaction with the boy warmed her heart, melting her resolve like ice in summer tea. Kurt moved beside him, talking in low tones. Jayden leaned into his muscular frame, head against his shoulder. Though toughened by his military training, Kurt had the heart of a teddy bear. If he ever focused his attention on her, she'd be reduced to silly putty. She moved to where the pair still stood talking. "You two want a ride or do you want to hoof it the forty miles back to Buchanan?"

"Wow. You're one demanding lady." Kurt winked, his hand on Jayden's neck as he walked him to the SUV. He opened the passenger side and helped Jayden climb into the middle.

Lissa fished in her pocket for her keys, ready to go to the other side.

"I can ride in the back seat." Jayden's eyes twinkled, searching Lissa's face.

"No need. Plenty of room up front." Lissa frowned. "Sheriff Briggs wants you home in one piece."

"But you and Kurt need to talk." Jayden sported a lop-sided grin. "No privacy with me here."

"We don't have anything private to discuss, Jayden." Lissa narrowed her eyes, guessing where this conversation was headed. "Right now your return to the safety of the foster home is our priority."

"Will you stay for supper?" Jayden's eyebrows rose, hopefulness on his face. "Peggy always makes plenty."

"My dog is locked up in her kennel at home." Lissa fought the urge to laugh. This kid survived a high-speed chase with a maniac, and he was inviting her to dinner. "She's not happy being left there too long."

"We'll get you home before dark, won't we, Kurt?"

Lissa's focus turned on Kurt's amused face. "Well, Kurt? Will I get home before dark?"

Kurt's smile deepened, eyes darkening to pools of silvery blue. "Not if I can help it."

"Way to go." Jayden's smile stretched across his cheeks. "It's about time you got with the moves, man."

Kurt leaned close to the boy "You ever heard three's a crowd?"

"I said I'd ride in the back."

"No, you'll ride up front like Lissa said. We have to concentrate on getting you checked out at the hospital." Kurt bopped Jayden on the shoulder. "And you'll keep quiet."

"Yes, sir." Jayden chuckled, scooting across to the middle. "And I'll keep all the lovey-dovey talk to myself."

"Anyone ever tell you that you have an overactive imagination?" Kurt slid in beside the boy and closed the door.

"Anyone ever tell you you're as slow as a snail in Montana snow?" At Jayden's comment Kurt's face reddened and he pursed his lips.

Lissa was losing her battle with the need to burst out laughing, struggling so hard she thought she'd hyperventilate. She turned away and walked around the front of the SUV. Biting back a snicker, she slid into the seat and stuck the key in the ignition.

Jayden sat beside her, his mouth wide like the proverbial cat who swallowed the canary.

Kurt narrowed his eyes, aiming a frown at both of them. "For a kid who has endured a horse trough seminar, you're either a glutton for punishment or you learn real slow."

"Education is the key to advancement." Jayden pumped his fist. "Bring on the lesson."

CHAPTER TWENTY-SIX

AFTER DINNER, JAYDEN AND PEGGY INSISTED on washing dishes, so Lissa thanked her hostess for the meal and stood to leave. "I better get home or Sorrel will be climbing the kennel fence."

Kurt smiled. "I'll walk you out. I need to check on Lady."

Lissa bit back the retort surfacing in her brain. *If you'd paid attention to details like this when you were in Afghanistan, we wouldn't have had to swim through such deep waters.* But even as the thought emerged, she shoved it back, breathless. Mouth dry, she resisted the urge to touch him. Kurt had proven himself today—rescuing Jayden, staying by him at the hospital, and comforting him on the way home. Kurt needed her praise. Her love wasn't far behind. He walked by her side, silent but for the crunch of his boots on the gravel drive. The air smelled sweet, redolent with juniper and prairie grass. The night sky sparkled with a thousand stars.

Lissa searched for something to bridge the chasm between them. "Is it my imagination, or do the stars on this side of the mountains seem closer than where we grew up?"

"No valley fog over here. The elevation is about four thousand feet higher." Kurt sounded distant, like his body stood here, but his thoughts were a million miles away.

"So they are closer."

"Yep."

Lissa waited for more, but Kurt only watched the night sky. "What are you thinking?" she asked.

"Wondering what's going to happen to Jayden." He lowered his chin, worry lines between his brows. "Today only confirmed my worst suspicions."

"Can't he stay here?" The night air grew colder, and Lissa drew her arms to her sides, grasping her elbows. She shivered.

"When George is released, he might come back, even if he gets a couple of years." Kurt slid his vest coat off and pulled it around her shoulders. "Melanie didn't persuade him to leave the boy alone the first time."

"But didn't she say George only took Jayden to pacify her?" Lissa drew the vest tighter around her. "I feel sorry for Melanie. She was a victim too. I doubt, though, she'll regain custody, considering what they did." Her teeth chattered.

Kurt reached out and pulled her next to his side, wrapping an arm about her shoulders. "You're as cold as butter fresh from the fridge." At her laugh, he stepped behind her, tugging her shoulders against his chest. His biceps ran the length of her arms, the warmth of him radiating against her back. As his shoulders engulfed Lissa's frame, he rested his chin on her head.

Her heart found a pocket in her throat to throb, the tempo reminding her of a racing horse. She stiffened, afraid Kurt could feel the erratic rhythm against his shirt. "Aren't you cold?"

"Afghanistan was so cold, I thought I'd lose my fingers from frostbite. This is Oregon in June. The elevation makes the nights colder, but nothing like what I endured over there." Kurt turned her around. The warmth of his breath tickled her forehead. "Besides, warming you up makes me feel alive again. Like I've rejoined the living." He drew back, sapphire eyes darkened in the moonlight like a midnight sky. "Jayden gave me purpose again. And having you this close is something I've wished I could do since the day I returned. I couldn't let myself love you until I felt I was loveable."

"And now?" Lissa dared to look up, afraid of what she would see. Could he be returning those feelings she'd yearned to feel coming from him?

"I'm waiting for you to finish telling me about the testing you had done." He pinned her with his gaze, his eyes narrowed, his chin tucked against his chest. "Before we were so rudely interrupted earlier."

"I didn't think you'd remember." Lissa inhaled, searching for words. "The truck chase made for an intense afternoon."

"You're skirting the subject." He rested his palms on her shoulders. "Does this involve Delaney?"

"Yes and no." The flutter in her midsection felt as uncomfortable as a nest of disturbed hornets. "She's a carrier for the gene that caused my mom's cancer. She'll need frequent tests to protect herself from the disease."

Kurt stepped back a pace, his gasp almost imperceptible. "Do you carry the same genes?"

"It's a possibility." Lissa shuddered. "And research said because I'm in my thirties, and childless, the potential risk was higher."

"What a terrible burden for you to carry." Kurt pulled her closer. "Why didn't you tell me sooner?"

She stepped back a pace and probed the depths of his eyes. "Because you've already suffered enough trauma, and I didn't want to resume our relationship, if we have one, if the effort would only end in another heartbreaking separation. . ." She swallowed. "Me in a hospital, or at the doctor, or in recovery. A lot of things could distance us, again, even though you are here and not in Afghanistan."

"I understand." He inclined his head. "But you said it *is* a possibility, as if it's still in limbo."

"You're focused, aren't you?" She turned and stood beside him so her shoulder touched his.

"It's a personality flaw. Being chased by enemy soldiers sort of puts you on your guard. I don't miss much."

"Yes, you're right. The test results came yesterday. They were inconclusive, so I have to be tested again." She peeked up at him, gauging his reaction.

"So you still don't know." He hugged her and stepped away, concern in his eyes. "Am I right?"

"I don't have any answers, but I thought you should know what I'm facing." Lissa straightened, searching for her resolve. "And why I'm reluctant to pursue any relationship."

"You can't live your life afraid of what might happen." Kurt searched her face. "No matter how we all try, something is bound to happen sometime."

"I watched my mother die. I watched my dad die with her, at least in spirit. I vowed I'd never knowingly put another man through that kind of torture." Lissa lifted her chin, daring him to challenge her convictions. "I intend to keep that promise to myself."

"But Lissa, the tests could be inconclusive again. How long are you willing to postpone your future?"

She chose her words, careful to make him understand. "Until I'm sure no one will be left grieving if bad test results follow."

"Can't I have a say in this?" Kurt pulled her shoulders toward him. "I've missed you more than you know. Waiting for a test to distance us even more will be torture for me."

"I don't want to hurt you."

"I'm hurting right now as you push me away. I want to explore where our relationship is going." Kurt's eyes pleaded with her to understand. "Can't you give me time as a friend?"

"As long as you accept that's what we are." Lissa widened the distance between them. "Friends."

"This friend is ready and waiting at the head of the line." He grinned. "Starting with this." He lowered his mouth to hers, brushing her lips. Like a man caught in a prairie fire racing for his life, he drew her tight against him, deepening the kiss as though he might not get another chance.

When he pulled back, Lissa felt weak in the knees, her heart bolting like a horse at the starting gate. "If this is how friends behave, I'm in big trouble." She looked at him. "Kurt, I'm serious."

"So am I." Kurt chuckled, his laughter vibrating through her torso. He drew her closer, squeezing her as if he'd never let go. "Oh, Lissa. I'm so sorry." His kisses brushed her temples and his cheek rubbed against her hair. "My entire world stopped when Foster died. It's taken so long to get to this point." He explored her reaction, as if drinking in her eyes. "And all this time you've been fighting your own war."

She returned his gaze. "But you made it. God chose you to live." She placed her hands on either side of his face. "Accept the life you've been given. Life moves forward."

"You've said that before." Kurt lifted his face to the stars above them. "I should have listened."

"At least you're learning." Lissa pulled his chin down to hers and kissed his lips. "I'll look forward to seeing you, McKintrick, and soon." She released him and stepped away. "I need to get home. Sorrel will be dancing the two-step if I don't hurry."

He grabbed her, wrapping her tighter in his arms, and kissing her like a thirsty man in a desert of sand. Releasing her, he smiled. "That ought to hold you for a while. See you tomorrow, *friend.*"

Her heart banging like a trip-hammer, Lissa strode to her pickup and climbed in. The engine shrieked as she twisted the ignition too long, making her jump. *Get your head in gear, Frye.* Kurt's wave in her rearview mirror brought joy to her soul. The future she'd feared only days before now rolled ahead of her like grass on a plain—long, endless, and beautiful—but she couldn't fully accept it until she knew. She hit the gas and hurried down the road, knowing she'd revisit this highway soon. *Please God, don't let me be dreaming. I want to go forward, not live in fear.*

Kurt whistled as he watched Lissa drive away. The noise brought Duke racing around the corner of the barn, tongue lolling and tail wagging as if he expected something. Kurt laughed and stroked the eager dog's head. "Can't a man whistle a happy tune? I think she's going to give me another chance."

"I knew she would." Jayden stepped from the shadows of the barn's lean-to. "She watches you when you're not looking."

"Does she stand in dark spaces like you do?" Kurt slanted his head, eyebrows raised, stifling the chuckle threatening to erupt. "Then jump out when the coast is clear?"

"I'm only telling you what I see." Jayden stopped before him. "She kept looking over at you while she worked on my mom's cuts today."

"How are you feeling tonight?" Kurt touched the boy's shoulder with care. "Sore?"

"A little." Jayden stepped up beside him. "And dog tired."

"You were very brave to do what you did." Kurt walked toward the house, Jayden matching his stride.

"I had to stop the truck." Jayden's voice broke. "George hit my mom, and she had bruises around her wrists. I've never seen her so scared." He hiccupped, as if remembering the day caused spasms in his diaphragm. "The only safe thing I could think to do was turn off the ignition and jump."

"I'm glad you weren't hurt." Kurt wrapped an arm about the boy's shoulders. "Lissa was pretty scared, too."

"Will my Mom be okay?" Jayden cocked his face toward Kurt. "He slammed her against the side of the truck."

"I saw bruising on her cheek, but she refused an ambulance, so I think she'll recover."

"I wish I could see her more." Jayden kicked at a piece of rock, then smiled at Kurt. "Lissa likes you."

"Well, if it's any consolation. I think you're right."

Jayden's smile filled his face. "You like her, too?"

"Yes. I always have. But life in the military has a way of discouraging romantic leanings."

Jayden nodded. "I know."

Kurt's mind replayed the roadblocks the last two years had thrown at him. He frowned, thinking of the burden Lissa carried, not only wondering what had happened to him, but also the added pressure of illness in her family's history. He intended to make it up to her.

"You're not a Marine anymore." Jayden grew serious. "Go after Lissa. She understands military."

Kurt stopped and faced Jayden. "Have you ever considered matchmaking as a career?"

"After witnessing marriage at its best and its worst, or so my mother has told me, I might consider counseling in my future." Jayden snorted. "My bill is in the mail."

"You're begging for another horse trough lesson, aren't you?"

"Another time, maybe, but I've got to report to Peggy. Her prayers are paying off." Jayden took off running, giggling as he reached the door and slipped through the screen. "It's your turn to beg."

Too late, Kurt heard the lock slip into place. "You stinker."

Jayden's cackle vibrated from within the house. "I'll let you in after you get a date with Lissa."

"How do you know I don't already have one?"

"Do you?"

"I'm seeing her tomorrow. Does that count?"

The lock clicked out of its hook. "I'll be checking."

Tired and in need of sleep, Jayden watched a spider crawl across the ceiling, images of the day replaying across his mind like a malfunctioning DVD—stops and starts and stops again.

His mother's behavior weighed on him the most. Her attempt to lure him into George's pickup felt like a kick to the stomach. She'd betrayed him. After all she'd been through with George, why would she agree to do anything with him? Her actions left Jayden confused. He'd always seen her as strong and determined, but today's actions proved otherwise. She'd risked both their lives. And for what? To keep George happy? Never happen. She should have been smarter than that.

Turning in his bed, Jayden pulled the pillow tight against his chest, fighting the unrest still churning there. He heard Kurt's words again: "Your quick thinking saved her." How strange was that? He was only a kid. His mother should have saved him, not the other way around. What would become of him now?

"God, if you are up there, we need to talk." Jayden glanced around the darkened room, afraid to bare his soul to a being he couldn't see. But Kurt talked to God as if he existed, and Peggy did, too. Even Lissa had prayed. Dad always had. And Mom had, too—before George.

Jayden slipped out of bed and knelt, leaning against the mattress. "I don't know what is going to happen to me after today. Mom's in big trouble for helping George kidnap me. She won't get me back for a while, if ever. Kurt is making goofy eyes at Lissa. If they get married, I'll lose him. Peggy is nice, but she misses her son. I'm feeling pretty alone. I need someone to hold on to."

Jayden bit his lip. Kurt had told him God had plans for his life. Loved him. Wanted to be his protector and guide. All he had to do was ask. "I don't know how to ask this, but I need you in my life. As Foster asked you in Afghanistan, please be my Savior, and stay with me."

He opened his eyes and examined the darkness of the room. The space hovered in silence. Everything remained as it was, except the feeling he was not alone. Warmth crept around his heart, working its way up his spine and into his head. Though not tangible, something indeed had happened. He couldn't contain his smile.

CHAPTER TWENTY-SEVEN

"NICE PLACE." KURT STEPPED THROUGH THE door of Lissa's home, the dinner date ahead propelling his nerves into high gear. Though he and Lissa had dated before, and their relationship had flourished in that brief time, this night represented a milestone, an evening of new beginnings. For Kurt, the next few hours would be a wall he hadn't thought he could hurdle. He held out a box. "I remembered you like roses."

"Thanks." Lissa extended her arm so he could place the flowers on her wrist, smiling as his fingers shook. She sniffed the blooms, fingered a petal, and closed the door before following him into the room. She wore a blue dress that whispered when she walked, and her hair fell in curls over her shoulders.

Though sparse, the décor danced with color, adding warmth to an otherwise barren space. The coffee table lacked adornment except for a single potted plant in the center. An eclectic assortment of books filled shelves hugging a corner, an opened tome waiting in silence on the nearby chair. As far as he could see, every surface shone, not one item out of place anywhere. "I can tell you lived on a ship for a while."

"I'm trying to decorate, but fifteen years of keeping everything put away so it wouldn't slide to the floor in a storm is a hard habit to break." She shrugged, her palms turned upward. "Plus, I'm not much of a decorator. Color is about all I care about." She beckoned him to the small kitchen that filled one wall opposite the living area. "Would you like a cup of something before we go?"

"Coffee made?" Kurt stared at the short length of the kitchen, so little space compared to Peggy's place.

Lissa pulled two mugs from a cupboard and walked to a coffee brewer on the end. "I've got espresso and dark roast."

"Dark roast sounds good." He kept his attention on the coffee maker and not on the beautiful woman making it.

"Cream?"

"A little sugar too." Kurt accepted the cup from her, the brush of her fingers notching his pulse a degree higher.

She swiveled to the cupboard behind them and removed a small, teacup-like bowl, along with a matching pitcher, which she filled with milk.

Ignoring his trembling fingers, Kurt spooned sugar into his mug and drizzled milk alongside, watching the white liquid form a design atop the surface of the drink. He sipped, savoring the flavor. "Good."

"I like the machine because it's fast and easy in the morning. Matthew makes the coffee at work, and you need a sledgehammer to stir it. Strong and bitter."

"A man's kind of fortitude." Kurt grinned. "Made for those with hair on their chests."

"Or stomachs of steel." Lissa tasted hers. "At least with this I don't need antacids."

"I guess working for the sheriff's office isn't much different than living on a ship full of men." Kurt hadn't served in a unit where a woman was present. Lissa had served on a carrier where men outnumbered women by scores. An odd sensation of jealousy swept over him. "Do these guys accept you as one of their own?"

"My job is different from theirs." Lissa set her cup on the counter. "I'm like a public safety officer. I chase strays. Not high on their priorities. The men run down the criminals."

"But you were involved in the search for Jayden, weren't you?" Kurt finished his coffee and set the empty mug next to Lissa's.

"Only because the filly and the missing boy were intertwined." She rinsed the dishware and set them on the drying rack. "The filly landed in my lap because she was a neglected animal. Jayden became a missing person, last believed to be destined for the Mueller ranch. That they showed up together popped me into the mix."

"Did you know Jayden is still bothered by things he saw at the ranch? Broken routines Mr. Mueller would never have forgotten?" Kurt searched her face.

"Like what?" Lissa's brown eyes flashed, a wrinkle forming across her forehead. "The autopsy didn't find anything out of the ordinary."

"Jayden said Bennie never left his pickup in the driveway." Kurt loved the way Lissa processed the information, her mouth angled to the left, eyes narrowed, frown lines beneath her wispy curls. "He wouldn't have left the horses in the dilapidated round pen either, which suggests a second party put them there."

"Really?" Lissa wiped her hands on a towel and leaned against the counter. "You're saying Mr. Mueller's daily habits and what we discovered at the ranch were inconsistent." She reached for a notepad sitting by the phone and made notes.

"That about sums it up." Kurt's stomach grumbled, and he patted it. "Sorry. Want to discuss this over dinner?"

"No, I don't want to take work with me tonight, but I'll let Matthew know tomorrow." She set the pad of paper on the counter and reached for her sweater. "Will I need more than this? I'm still adjusting to weather on this side of the mountain."

Kurt strode to where she stood and wrapped his arm around her shoulders. "I can always warm you up."

"I can think of a time or two where you left me cold." She glared at him, though the twinkle in her eyes gave away her teasing. "Why should I trust you now? Hmm?" Eyebrows raised, she twisted her lips into a pout. So adorable.

"Let's not go there and opt for dinner instead." Kurt grinned. "A friend I know told me life always moves forward."

"You're learning."

The unmistakable smell of jalapeños and cayenne pepper heightened Kurt's senses as the spicy mix wafted across the Mexican restaurant. A waiter escorted Lissa and Kurt to a table near an open hearth. Cantina music played in the background, while waitresses dressed in full skirts and white peasant blouses carried steaming platters of food to waiting patrons.

"Smells good." Kurt sniffed, his hunger growing with each inhaled breath. "Peggy said this restaurant is as good as it gets here in Burns." Kurt opened the plastic menu, studying the different offerings. "Look at the centerfold."

Lissa's eyes widened. She peeked over the top of her menu. "Are you up for the challenge?"

"Yep. I hustle stable waste for a living." Kurt flexed. "Got to keep those shovelfuls flying."

"What a vision you paint." Lissa held her nose and spoke with a nasal twang. "Sounds as if you enjoy your work."

Kurt laid his menu down and chuckled. "I do. The horses are wonderful companions. Foster knew what he was doing when he made me promise to help his mother. I think he realized I'd need healing after the trauma of Afghanistan, like the horses at the rescue center need time. He couldn't think of any better way to soothe my wounds than to send me home to care for his hoof-and-hide babies."

Lissa nodded. "When I ran away from home after Mom died, my best friend's family took me in and let me finish high school while living at their farm. The routine of rising early, caring for the animals before school, and learning to nurture something besides my personal pain helped me refocus and adjust to living with the emptiness inside me. I lost myself tending to the animals' needs."

"I'm sure Bennie Mueller understood that. He used his horses and Duke to help Jayden cope with his family situation." Kurt shook his head. "Jayden is so attached to the memory of the man."

"You think Bennie saw the abuse and tried to intervene?"

Kurt rested his elbows on the table. "He may have suspected problems within the family. Jayden told me Bennie let him spend most of his summer working on the ranch, and Jayden's mother never objected."

"That kind of attention from an outsider could fuel jealousy in a stepfather."

"You read my mind."

The waitress approached their table, order pad in hand.

Kurt placed their orders and the young woman swished away, the full skirt of the costume she wore rustling with each step.

"I wonder if those costumes get in the way of their work." Lissa followed the girl's retreat with her gaze. "Looks like endless yards of fabric hanging from the waistband."

"They're probably accustomed to working in them, even though jeans are what I'm guessing these girls wear when off the job." Kurt studied the dress Lissa was wearing. "I know I like seeing you in that shade of blue."

"Thanks."

"Does wearing a dress feel different than wearing your county uniform?"

"Wearing a dress transforms your self-image." Lissa's cheeks reddened. "I've worn slacks and a shirt for so many years, the dress makes me feel vulnerable."

"And makes you look feminine and alluring." Kurt soaked in the sight of her, letting his appreciation show as his eyes drifted across her shoulders and up her neck to her mouth. "You have my full and undivided attention."

Lissa's eyes sparkled, a hint of a smile on her lips. "Kurt, that sounds like a pass."

"Sweetie." Kurt leaned toward her. "It is."

Lissa stiffened. "Don't promise things you don't intend to deliver."

Kurt swallowed his laughter, pausing while the waitress set their food before them. As soon as she left, he rested a hand on Lissa's arm. "In that blue dress, you are a most tempting woman. And this Marine has gone a long time without seeing you. I'm fighting my instincts."

Lissa pressed her fists against her hot face and fell silent, her mouth tight-lipped, as if she were ready to fling her food at him. She couldn't keep up the façade for long—her twinkling eyes and a deepening dimple in her cheek gave away her ruse. He'd flattered her and, judging from the smile she tried to hide, she liked it.

"Shall we offer thanks?" Kurt held out his hand, and Lissa grasped it as she bowed her head. "For this food and for this companion, Lord, I give you thanks. Bless our evening. Amen."

The evening with Kurt passed in moments of laughter and a too full plate of aromatic food, leaving Lissa emotionally and physically sated. Her traitorous heart battled with her brain, one already forgiving this man while the other reminded her she'd been angry enough to shoot him when she first moved to Hines. What a difference a few days had made.

They rode home listening to a Christian talk show stressing the importance of finding a life partner who shared one's faith and followed God's precepts. Lissa couldn't help thinking how perfectly Kurt met those qualifications. But whether or not their relationship would grow to the possibility of a lifelong commitment, she couldn't pretend to know.

Kurt pulled into her drive and shut off the engine. "I enjoyed our time tonight."

"Me, too." Lissa memorized Kurt's face, moonlight highlighting his rugged cheekbones, shadows deepening the set of his eyes. She'd always thought him handsome, but tonight he looked every inch the rugged man he'd become in the wake of fighting a war and losing a best friend. "Tell Peggy she was right about the food."

"I will." Kurt reached for her hand. "I'd like to see you again."

Lissa's pulse raced, like an unseen force had stomped on the accelerator of her heart. Images of Kurt after he'd left her at the airport two years ago scooted through her mind. The sensitive places of her heart still ached from the bruises left by the last goodbye. Why did her head want to take this slow, and her heart revved as if it meant to win the Indy 500? "I'm willing to continue seeing you." Lissa paused. "Our friendship means a lot."

"I don't want friendship." In the shadows Kurt's face grew darker, his intensity filling the cab. "I want to return to where we were. Before Afghanistan stole my friend's life, before my mom married your dad, before we said goodbye at the airport."

"Give our relationship time." Lissa glanced at their clasped hands, then lifted her knuckles to his cheek. Rough whiskers ghosted his chin. If she wasn't careful, her heart would jump on the love express and carry her away. "That's all I can tell you. Time will make the difference."

"I can live with that."

Kurt slid closer, pulling her to his side. His other hand swept through her hair. Gentle fingers combed her curls, his tender touch easing her face closer to his. Even in the dark she could hear his labored breathing, see his grin widen. He inclined his head and brushed her lips with his, like an unspoken question hanging between them. She returned the kiss with a light peck and smiled at him. His mouth claimed hers, his arms wrapping her in an embrace. Strange flutters beat in her belly, rattling her resolve clear to her toes. Yes, she wanted to trust him.

CHAPTER TWENTY-EIGHT

PEGGY HUNG UP THE PHONE WHEN Kurt walked into the kitchen Monday morning, her shoulders rigid. He stopped and frowned. "What's wrong?" At her hesitation, he moved toward the coffeepot, waiting for an answer.

"The hearing for George Barnes is set for Thursday." Peggy leaned against the counter. "The child advocate called. She says the judge insists Jayden attend."

"What do you think the courts will do?" Kurt opened a cupboard door, retrieved a mug, and filled it. "As one who was part of the chase scene, I think George's punishment should be severe."

"Kidnapping a child held as a ward of the state is a serious offense. George is the stepfather, not the father." Peggy's attention skirted the room as if she were looking for answers. "He'll probably get jail time. Melanie may be charged as an accessory."

"Jayden's going to be devastated." Kurt set his mug on the counter. "On the campout he told me he missed his mother terribly, but he wouldn't go home if George was there."

"I'm in favor of visits. The boy needs to see his mother. What little I've learned from him is that his family was close before the father was killed in Afghanistan." Peggy brought her mug and filled it. "It's a wonder Jayden has survived intact with all that has happened."

"I knew his biological father. Great guy. So proud of Jayden. Knowing both of them makes me believe his dad instilled core values in his son before deploying." Kurt paused, thoughts of Foster resurrecting painful memories. "Jayden honors his father's name by being a younger version of the man—a Marine in the making. When Jayden dropped and rolled from that pickup, he said his dad taught him how. Amazing he remembers. As if every word his father said has been etched in his memory." Kurt swallowed another sip, the lump in his throat going down with the brew. "You should have seen the pride in that kid's eyes."

"He adores you, you know." Peggy retrieved a pan of muffins from the oven and set it on a dishtowel. "He told me you make him remember his dad."

Kurt ached for the hurting child. "Yeah, I heard that, too."

Peggy handed him a plate. "Help yourself. These are blueberry. I'll go see if our resident hero is awake yet." She headed for the door, then stopped and faced him. "Did you know the Mueller ranch is going on the market?"

"Really?"

"Yep. Bennie's will left the property to his brother, but according to the ranchers' rumor mill, the brother doesn't want it." Peggy tapped the door casing. "Think I should expand the rescue operation?"

"Are you serious?" A bigger operation meant more work, but more opportunity to help neglected animals and hurting kids. What did Peggy have in mind? "Expansion—as in more horses?"

"Maybe. And kids." Peggy cocked her head his way, a thoughtful expression on her face. "Of course, you might consider the idea as well." Peggy gestured again to the muffins. "They won't eat themselves." She turned down the hall.

Kurt hadn't considered owning property before, but being made part of the foster system through Peggy's involvement had forged awareness of what a good ranch life could do for a hurting child. After the kidnapping Jayden might not be allowed to return here. Too many knew of his situation. At some point in the future, George could become a problem again and Jayden's safety could be compromised.

But if Jayden needed new placement, Kurt could become a

foster parent and take him into his own home. Jayden was already ranch-savvy and could perform many useful tasks. Besides, Kurt already loved the kid. The last thing he wanted was for Jayden to be placed out of state. Peggy had said that was a possibility.

He had to consider Lissa as well. Though she remained verbally uncommitted to their relationship, she had kissed him the way he remembered from two years before. Hope filled his soul.

Perhaps Friday he could visit the ranch and have a good look. After that he'd deal with the rest of his plan. Lissa had forgiven him, and if she could overcome her fear, they'd move forward together. Owning a ranch was a dream they could share.

Jayden entered the courtroom Thursday with his caseworker, Molly, at his side. He surveyed the area, looking for a familiar face, having seen Peggy and Kurt waiting outside the chambers. He walked forward, only to be met by the narrowed eyes of his stepfather. Clean-shaven and dressed in a suit, George appeared shaken, as though he'd awakened this morning in a strange place and didn't know why.

Jayden's mother sat nearby, her arm in a sling, one eye bandaged. She waved at Jayden, her smile tilted to the left. Jayden resisted the impulse to run to her side, touch her hand, and smell the cucumber fragrance of shampoo lingering in her hair. Whenever she hugged him, Jayden pictured a flower garden engulfing him like a warm blanket. He longed to return to his old life—before war had destroyed his family.

Molly led him to a line of chairs behind the railing, only a short distance from where George sat with his lawyer. Jayden gulped. What if his stepfather broke into a rage and nobody stopped him before he landed a fist to Jayden's face? The man thought nothing of punching his own wife in the wild pickup ride last week.

The judge stepped into the courtroom, and they all stood. He sat down in his big chair, a stack of papers in front of him. He read for a few minutes before glancing up and studying George. "Mr. Barnes, please rise."

Jayden's stepfather and the attorney stood. George looked over at Jayden again, the meanness in the man's eyes making Jayden's stomach crawl like the caterpillars he used to catch and race. George sneered before he faced forward.

The judge continued. "You are charged with reckless driving, kidnapping a minor child in state custody, and aggravated assault." The judge rattled the papers. "You disregarded a restraining order as well. How do you plead?"

"Not guilty," George snapped, before his attorney had the chance. "My wife and stepson got in the truck on their own. Not kidnapping where I come from."

George's attorney laid a hand on his forearm, stopping him from saying more.

"Your stepson was placed in foster care to protect him from you." The judge's words were quiet, but firm. "Do you deny that?"

"I never hurt him. It's his word against mine." George talked to the judge the way he always talked to Jayden—like he wanted to start a war.

The attorney leaned closer to George, shaking his head. George muttered under his breath, loud enough to be heard, "He was always sneaking off to that rancher friend of his. Probably injured himself messing with that wild horse he loved. She was an uncooperative animal, I'll tell you that."

The attorney shushed his client, and Jayden gasped. George had been to the ranch? Jayden had never seen him there. He turned to Molly and whispered, "How does George know about the filly?

He's never seen her."

"Are you sure?"

Jayden nodded. "Never came around. Not the entire summer." The courtroom had grown silent, and Jayden realized his whispers were attracting attention. Molly put a finger to her lips and Jayden sank into his chair, catching the last of a quiet conversation between the judge and the bailiff.

"Jayden Clarke, would you please stand?" The judge looked at him as he rose to his feet. "Come forward."

Shaking like a bumblebee caught in a tin can, Jayden followed Molly forward. The clerk had him raise his right hand. "Do you promise to tell the truth, the whole truth, and nothing but the truth, so help you God?"

"Yes, sir." Jayden peered at the judge. "Am I in trouble?"

"I'd like to see you in my private chambers with your caseworker." The judge nodded at the sheriff and both attorneys. All three rose and followed Molly and him.

The judge closed the door and faced Jayden. "I see you're surprised by Mr. Barnes' statement." The man continued to his desk, sitting in a large, brown swivel chair.

Jayden felt tongue-tied, his knees knocking like loose bike tire spokes. "Yes, sir. I am."

"Why is that?" The judge leaned forward, his chin resting on his hand, kind grey eyes studying Jayden.

"I didn't think my stepfather had ever been to Mr. Mueller's ranch." Jayden's gaze skimmed the walls of the room, bookcases filled with fat books lining the perimeter. Had this man read all these?

The judge stopped to wipe his glasses. "And now you think he has visited?"

Jayden refocused on the man and nodded. "He couldn't know anything about the filly unless he had."

"Is she stubborn?" The judge seemed so kind, as if he understood Jayden's reluctance to say anything.

Jayden grinned at the mention of the filly's mulish disposition. "She's not crazy about halters and lead ropes." That was an understatement.

"And did your stepfather take you away in a vehicle without your consent?" The man relaxed into his chair and adjusted the shoulder seams of his robe.

"Mom called me to the fence, said she needed a hug. I was surprised she'd come in George's pickup. Then he grabbed me and shoved me into the middle of the seat and then pushed my mother in and drove away." Jayden's hands involuntarily flexed as the memory of the scene paraded across his mind. "He kicked my dog in the belly too." He steeled himself against an onslaught of tears. "He slammed me back against the seat and slugged my mom across the mouth."

"He took you from the foster home where you are staying?" The man's forehead wrinkled in a frown, his eyes troubled and mouth firm.

Jayden's anger tormented him, his need to make the judge see the real George causing his heart to pound in his chest. He nodded.

The judge glanced at Molly. "You can return to your seats."

Jayden followed the caseworker back into the courtroom and found his chair. George watched him out of the corner of his eye. Jayden shuddered, sliding backward in his seat as far as he could go. He'd told the truth. Now the judge would follow through.

Moments later the attorneys and the judge returned. He took his seat on the bench at the front and slammed his gavel. "We're back on the record. Will the accused and his counsel please stand?"

Jayden watched his stepfather get to his feet, along with his attorney.

"For kidnapping a child in the custody of the state, I order

George Barnes to be remanded to the Oregon correctional authorities to stand trial. In accordance with Oregon law, recommended sentencing for this crime is one year." He cast a brief look Jayden's way before addressing the district attorney and the sheriff. "Would either of you like to request anything further?"

The sheriff stood. "Your honor, I've requested permission before this hearing to examine Mr. Barnes about his knowledge of the death of Mr. Benjamin Mueller."

"Granted." The judge eyed George, head inclined to the side. "Need I remind you you're still under oath?"

George's mouth dropped open. Staring at his attorney, he whispered in a loud, panicky voice. "He's dead?" George paled, eyes darting like bees on a bush. "I shoved the man, but that's all."

The attorney laid a hand on George's shoulder. "Don't say anything more."

Visibly shaken, George pointed at the sheriff, his voice growing in volume. "Mueller was fine when I left him. I went there to talk. He accused me of neglecting my family. When I objected, he ditched his pickup in the middle of the driveway, threatened to get his rifle, and barged into the house. The horses were tied to a fence. When he didn't return, I put them in their pen and I left on a truck run. I know how much the man cared for his animals. The kid was always rattling on about that."

The judge banged his gavel. "We're going to adjourn, and you can continue your discussion at the sheriff's office."

George whirled around and pointed a finger at Jayden. "If you weren't always sneaking off, me and Mueller wouldn't have had words. I told him I didn't want you hanging around his place all summer. You needed to help your mother." George's face reddened, his voice nearly shouting. "You killed him by being a brat." George raised clenched fists, shaking them at Jayden. "I'll see that you pay for breaking up my family. You hear me? You'll pay!" George lunged toward Jayden, knocking a chair sideways.

The bailiff and another deputy darted toward George, subduing him with handcuffs as the man continued to shout. Jayden slunk into his chair when George was led away, still ranting over his shoulder.

Jayden couldn't control his shaking, and his stomach threatened to spill its contents. The awful truth slammed him. George had caused Bennie's death. Jayden didn't know how it happened, but he was certain they'd fought over him. Poor Bennie.

Kurt waited outside the courtroom once the proceedings were over, anxious to hear what the judge had decided about Jayden's placement. After the hearing, only Jayden and Molly were allowed to meet with the judge to decide Jayden's future. At least George was out of the picture for now.

The doors opened, and Jayden appeared with his caseworker. The boy's white face and quivering lip belied his fear. Seeing Kurt, Jayden broke away from Molly and ran into his arms, no longer the strong, confident Marine's son he'd been on the campout.

Kurt held Jayden's slight frame, trying to calm him as he buried his face in Kurt's vest. "Shh. You're safe with me, son."

Jayden pulled back and looked up at Kurt, his breath coming in sobs. "He hurt Bennie—I know he did. That poor old man." Jayden pressed his face tight against Kurt's side, the sobs growing louder.

Molly came to where they were, smiled, and rubbed the boy's shoulder. "Jayden, you're safe now. George isn't going anywhere until the investigation is finished." She spoke to Kurt. "It got pretty rough in there. Give Jayden plenty of TLC for me. I know you will."

Jayden pushed away from Kurt and wiped his face. "I get to go back to the ranch?"

"Absolutely. We can't have you missing out on the filly's progress and time with your dog, can we?"

Kurt smiled and shook her hand. "Thanks. Peggy and I were hoping for his return, but we wanted him safe, even if it took him away from us."

"I suspect George will be put away for a long time when this is all over." The caseworker checked her watch. "Melanie may resurface, though. She's next to be investigated, but I think she'll be cleared of wrongdoing since she was coerced. With George out of the picture, she can regain custody of her son."

Kurt gulped, already dreading the day those words would come true. "That's the way it should be. I don't think she's a bad mother, but she made a poor choice in second husbands."

"That's an understatement." Molly squeezed Jayden's shoulder, aiming a smile at Kurt. "Thanks for taking care of Jayden. He's a good kid."

Kurt stopped at a local hamburger hangout on the way home from the courthouse. "You feel good enough to eat?" He waited for Jayden's reaction and got a big grin and a thumbs up. The kid's appetite knew no end.

"Two hamburgers and a chocolate shake ought to do it."

"You are feeling better, I take it?" Kurt opened the pickup door and climbed out as Jayden exited the other side.

"I'm not scared with you." Jayden managed a lopsided smile. "George is the bad guy."

"George and I could both be considered bad guys by some

people." Kurt frowned as he said the words. "There are those who don't like military personnel. Marines accept it as part of their service."

Jayden's mouth quivered as though he was revisiting the anguish he'd experienced at the courthouse, each breath catching on a lingering sob. "Yeah, but you don't beat up helpless old men and leave them to die, or slap smaller people like me and my mom."

Kurt's gut wrenched at the pain he saw in the child's face as Jayden filled him in on George's unsolicited testimony. "I'm sorry you had to live in such a nightmare."

"I knew something was wrong when I saw Lady in that old pen." Jayden opened the door to the restaurant and held it for Kurt. "Bennie treated her like she was the queen of his barnyard."

"Because of George's admissions in court, there'll be a thorough investigation." Kurt gestured to the front counter. "That should shed more light on the case."

"Will Lissa be part of that?" Jayden slipped onto a stool and spun around to face the waitress. "Chocolate shake, please. And the largest burger you've got—minus tomatoes."

"I'll have the same." Kurt glanced Jayden's direction. "No fries?"

"I'd rather have another hamburger." Jayden peeked up, a sheepish grin on his face. "I'm super hungry."

"I'll have a side of fries and give him an extra hamburger, please." Kurt leaned toward Jayden. "Lissa probably won't be in on the investigation because she works mostly with neglected animals."

"But Lady was neglected."

"Yes, but the filly didn't harm Mr. Mueller in any way. At least we don't suspect she did."

The waitress returned, setting the shakes before them. Jayden stuck his straw in the creamy mixture and sucked up a mouthful. "Um! I so needed this. It's good."

"Let's thank God for the food." Kurt reached for Jayden's hand, then bowed his head.

"Here?" Jayden whispered. "You're going to pray here?"

"This is as good a place as any." Kurt smiled. "Other people need to know we believe in a heavenly creator."

"Okay. I know how." Jayden closed his eyes. "Jesus, thanks for bringing me back to the ranch, to Duke, and Lady, and Peggy, and Kurt. Help my mom heal. Tell her I love her. Amen."

Kurt stuffed his surprise in a corner of his heart and finished the prayer. "And Father, thanks for answering our prayers for Jayden and for this good food." Kurt squeezed the boy's hand, then socked him lightly on the shoulder. "This day's getting better by the minute."

"Almost perfect." Jayden clamped his lips around the straw. "The only thing missing is Lissa."

CHAPTER TWENTY-NINE

ON FRIDAY, HIS TRUCK IN LOW gear, Kurt followed the long, twisting driveway leading to the Mueller ranch, making mental notes of the terrain as he approached the house and outbuildings. When he and Peggy first came to pick up Lady, he'd been more worried the deputy sheriff meeting them would be Lissa. The property, the horse, and any other information pertinent to the rescue had paled in light of seeing her again. Now he approached the ranch with the mindset of a prospective buyer, a man hoping to please the woman he loved. She'd often said how much she enjoyed the wide-open terrain of Oregon's high desert country.

The house, barn, and outlying utility buildings stood in grim silence in the ranch's center. What remained of the fenced pasture spread outward like silk in a spider web, the barbed wire and rail enclosure mimicking the gossamer threads of the arachnid's handiwork. The house needed a roof, the fencing lay broken or leaning, and the barn could use a coat of paint. Hours of planning and manual labor would be required to create a home anyone might enjoy.

He parked the pickup and stepped toward the dwelling. He'd read the specifications—three bedrooms, one bath, den, and living area. He circled the perimeter, making note of the placement of windows and doors, looking for an angle where he might add on a master bedroom and bath. The shuttered panes made it impossible to see the interior layout or the size of the bedrooms.

When he reached a structure at the far end of the house, he stopped. A breezeway connected the unfinished addition to the house, and steps from the structure led to the house's side entrance. Another set of stairs ended at a door fronting the building's oversized attic. What had Mueller used the space for? Hobby room? Storage? The two stories could be converted into many different uses.

Perfect! Enclose the breezeway and build a master suite on the second story. An immense kid's room or a private bedroom would fit there, depending on what the other rooms in the main house looked like. Adding windows would provide a view of Steens Mountain in the distance, towering like a lone warrior over a wasteland of sage. Kurt basked in the magnificent scene. Lissa could share this with him, waking every morning bathed in the shadow of the massive peak.

Hold on, buddy. She hasn't said yes. Yet.

Kurt had reached the barn's double doors when he heard the sound of an engine idling at the top of the rise. He cupped his fingers over his eyes to shade them and watched as a sheriff's vehicle approached the house. A man dressed in tan and green stepped from the car and circled Kurt's truck. Kurt sucked in a breath. Was he trespassing?

"Officer?" Kurt loped to where the man stood, writing information on a clipboard. As he drew near, Sheriff Briggs waved and stuck out his hand.

"It's good to see you again, Sheriff." Kurt returned the handshake. "Or should I call you Matthew?"

"Matthew's fine. What brings you out here?"

"Peggy told me the ranch might go on the market. I came by to take a closer look." Kurt stumbled over his words, nervous in front of Lissa's boss. *Idiot. Try to say something intelligent.* "I'm interested in finding my own spread."

"I understand. This morning I received word from the judge that Mueller's death needed to be investigated further." The sheriff indicated the property behind them. "I'm here to re-establish a crime scene before the real estate agent comes in and destroys all evidence."

"So Jayden's testimony did make a difference." Kurt's heart warmed to think the boy had paid close attention to what he saw and felt duty-bound to report it. "I'm glad your department is on the scene."

"We owe it to Bennie Mueller." Matthew removed his hat and shook it before placing it further back on his head. "The man had a heart of gold."

"Jayden certainly holds fond memories." Kurt scanned the horizon, where a hawk circled in the distance. "Treated the kid better than his family did."

"That's not surprising." Matthew followed his gaze. "There's more than two-hundred acres here. You think you could run a spread this size? You'll have to rustle up a lot of capital."

"I thought of starting my own rescue center." The more he said it, the more Kurt liked the sound of the idea. "Perhaps make it a ranch for abused children."

"Is Lissa part of your plan?" The sheriff grinned like he knew more than he was sharing. "I only recently got her trained."

"The end of that story isn't written yet." Kurt suspected he had become the object of the man's curiosity by the glimmer passing through his eyes. "We're renewing our former friendship."

"Good. She's been alone too much." The sheriff gestured around him. "A lot of kids could benefit from living on a place this size." He dropped his pen into his shirt pocket. "And local people would rally to support such an enterprise."

"Thanks. I appreciate the encouragement." Kurt studied the landscape before him. "Right now, I'm only at the dreaming stage."

"Then I'd say you've got a lot of ground to cover." Sheriff Briggs extended his hand again. "Good luck to you."

Kurt surveyed the property one last time before he headed toward his truck. Jayden's observations might be paying off. The kid had good instincts.

Lissa hurried home, her day at the office over, anxious to change for her evening with Kurt and hear the news from Jayden's court proceedings. She eyed the clock above the window, deciding she had time for a shower. She and one of the other deputies had chased cattle out of a ravine today—bovine escapees from a nearby ranch overpowered a sagging wire fence and went looking for greener pastures. Dust and debris clung to her skin, the itch begging for a shower.

Half an hour later, she slipped an earring into place and fastened it the same minute a knock sounded at the door. The clock on her dresser told her she'd finished ahead of time, but Kurt had a tendency to show up at exactly the moment he promised, a habit borne of years in the military. Tonight he'd arrived early.

Pulling open the door, Lissa gulped, warmth creeping along her neck and into her face as Kurt whistled, his eyes shining as he smiled his approval. "Hello, gorgeous. Care to join me for a movie tonight?"

"Well, when you put it that way, of course." She giggled when he planted a peck on her cheek. "Have you decided what you want to see?"

"I'll surprise you." He winked as she shut the door, fumbling with the knob, her nerves causing her hands to tremble. "We can flip a coin when we get there. As long as I get to hold your hand."

She stepped to the closet and pulled out a short jacket. Opening her purse, she popped the house key inside, and smiled at her handsome date. "How did the court appearance go for Jayden?"

"You aren't going to believe what happened." Kurt opened the door and gestured for her to precede him. Pulling it closed, he checked the lock as it squeaked. His grip couldn't move the knob.

"Why? Tell me." Lissa followed him to the truck, heart throbbing in her throat like a drummer in a jazz band. "Did you lose Jayden?"

"I'll tell you on the way." Kurt helped her in, darted around to the driver's side, and started the ignition. "Your office will be busy the next couple of weeks."

Lissa listened, stunned, as Kurt recounted all that had happened with George and Jayden inside the proceedings. When Kurt drove into the theater parking lot, she sucked in a calming breath, her composure rattled. "So there's a good chance Bennie's death wasn't natural?"

"Your follow-up team will determine the outcome." Kurt offered his arm as they walked inside the building. "I imagine they'll be looking for fingerprints and blood stains with the possibility of a new assault now on the roster."

Lissa leaned into Kurt's warmth and gained strength from resting against him. To think she'd put him off only days before, and now they were acting like love-struck teenagers. Though they weren't back to the level in their relationship they'd shared two years ago, this rekindled attraction certainly held promise. With both of them out of the service, their chances for moving forward without interference became even better. Lissa smiled at the possibilities.

She refocused on Kurt's account of the afternoon. "I would never have guessed Mr. Mueller's death was suspicious. Or that George was involved."

"He acted as if he didn't know Mueller was dead." Kurt dug his wallet out of his hip pocket as they moved forward in the noisy crowd. "George actually turned pale. Makes me believe he didn't intend to harm the old man. Or Mueller was fragile, and the encounter triggered a physical response. That's possible." Kurt stepped up to the ticket window and paid their admissions. "Sure hope this movie lives up to its hype."

"We can always opt for a chick flick." Lissa nudged him with her elbow. "Aren't you up for unabashed flirting with a wiggle thrown in?"

"Please. I'll take a dragon movie any day over that." Wrapping his arm around her back, Kurt led the way into the theater lobby and flashed a twenty-dollar bill. "Popcorn and soda?"

"Sounds great." Lissa rested her head against his shoulder while they waited for the snacks. Having Kurt so near and attentive sent shivers up her arms. Her head spun. Her tummy fluttered. Secure. Safe. Beautiful. Sought after. If only this could continue. "So you think maybe George had words with Bennie and things got out of hand?"

"George is hot-headed and stubborn. Wouldn't take much to push him over the edge." Handing her a soda, Kurt grabbed the popcorn tub and his drink, nodding in the direction of the movie theater. "I've seen many a fist fight start with a temperamental personality who thinks he has to be right."

"Melanie insists he's a nice guy when he's sober. He couldn't be a long-haul truck driver if he behaved as he has all the time."

"I remember guys like that in the service, too. Good soldiers, bad drinkers."

"He'll be guilty of involuntary manslaughter." Lissa lifted her face to him, stating the truth she'd explored and wondered about since the trial.

"That's what I'm guessing."

Kurt still had the court proceedings on his mind when the movie finished. If George was proven guilty of manslaughter, given the kidnapping charges he already faced, the man could be sent away for quite a while. With George out of the way, Melanie could be reunited with her son. Kurt hated to think of Jayden gone. Losing the boy now…he couldn't wrap his mind around it. He forced the negative possibilities to the back of his mind and faced Lissa. "Dinner?"

"I can eat." Lissa smiled at him. "The popcorn didn't satisfy my hunger. I chased cows today."

Kurt couldn't believe what he'd heard. "Cows?"

"A small herd found a weak spot in the fence and moseyed their way across Steens Highway. We located the rancher and helped him persuade Bertha to lead her ladies home."

"Bertha?" Kurt fought the chuckle making his cheek twitch. "Is she the leading lady?"

"Yep. She wears the cowbell. The other cows go wherever the bell sounds." Lissa laughed. "Get along, little doggies."

"Then I'd say you need a steak dinner, complete with salad and roasted potatoes."

"I'd say you're right."

Kurt learned something new about Lissa every time they were together. The woman never ate more than half a sandwich in front of him. "You really are hungry."

"So why are we still standing here?"

"I had a wonderful time tonight." Lissa paused on her front porch, fishing the door key out of her bag. She dropped it, and the metal clinked on the cement. Kurt stooped and handed it to her. "Thanks for a great dinner, movie, and conversation."

"You're welcome." Kurt's attention inched across her face,

stopping at her mouth. "Thanks for putting aside our checkered past and giving me another chance." His hands rested on her shoulders, gently tugging her toward him. "I don't deserve it."

"I had my pistol ready." She trembled when he cradled her chin in his palm, drawing her face closer and caressing her lips with his thumb. His aftershave and minty breath tickled her nose. But when his lips claimed hers, his arms rippling about her like a suit of armor, the passion of his kiss made her heart race and her knees go weak. Ending the moment left an ache in her middle. "When can I see you again?" Kurt's hands slipped down her arms and grasped her fingers. "Would you enjoy a hike?"

"After chasing that herd today, a hike isn't at the top of my list. But maybe this weekend."

"There's a bowling alley in Burns." Kurt flexed. "Can you roll one down the lane?"

"That I can do." Lissa laid her palms against Kurt's shoulders. "Let's take Jayden. Think he's ever bowled before?"

"Only one way to find out."

Lissa inserted her key in the lock. "Care to come in for coffee?"

Kurt's countenance grew sober. "How about a rain check?" His smile didn't reach his eyes. "I'd be lying if I said I didn't want to. But I'd better play it safe and say goodnight."

Suddenly warm all over, Lissa nodded. "Understood." She grew shy at his confession. "It's nice to know you respect me enough to bow out."

Face puckered in a frown, Kurt tweaked her nose. "Good night, Lissa." The crunch of boots on the gravel and the roar of the engine as he sped away stirred up another nest of butterflies fluttering behind her breastbone. Heat crept along her collarbone and up her neck as his words registered with her heart. Tonight their relationship reached a new level of understanding. She hugged herself. *Bring it on.*

CHAPTER THIRTY

THE PAIN IN LISSA'S ABDOMEN THROBBED like a knife had been thrust through. She'd not yet had her morning shower, the minutes ticking by like time on a march, her need to get ready for her day uppermost in her mind. But she couldn't move. She tightened her grip on the bathroom counter, each breath catching as the ache sharpened. She'd rubbed the area with her palm, hoping to relieve the problem. She assessed her other symptoms. No nausea. No headache.

Convinced she didn't have the flu, she hobbled to the kitchen to take a pain reliever, only to have the ache stab her with greater intensity. Grabbing a coffee pod, she punched in a flavored latté on her brewer. She struggled to a nearby chair, trying to think if she'd overworked a muscle yesterday while chasing Bertha and her ladies. She'd been up and down the sides of multiple ditches and had to re-direct Bertha a dozen times, yanking the old girl's ears, but she didn't think she'd overdone it. Thank goodness she didn't have to work today.

She retrieved her drink and carried it to the table. The steam rose in fragrant wafts, and she breathed in deep whiffs of the decadent scent. Her fingers hugged the mug, the hot brew warming them through the ceramic.

Half an hour later, the medication kicked in and the sharpness of the throbbing dulled. She sat for several minutes, toying with the idea of calling Dr. James. If this was no more than a strained muscle, she'd be embarrassed. But if it was appendicitis in the early stages, she should have it checked. She wouldn't give voice to the other possibility, because that one threatened to upset her entire future.

As the ache continued, she picked up her phone and confirmed an appointment. Lissa hobbled to the shower. She prayed for strength, but her heart thumped in terror.

Three other patients waited in Dr. James' office when she arrived, two of them pregnant. She found a chair, nodding at a young woman whose slight form bulged with the swollen roundness of her belly. "Do you have much longer to go?"

The girl breathed deep. "Four more weeks. But between you and me, I'd be happy to have a C-section tomorrow."

Lissa cast her a sympathetic smile. "My sister had twins. She was miserable toward the end of the pregnancy, too. But having a little boy and girl to care for made her discomfort all worthwhile. Hang in there."

The young woman blew out an exasperated puff of air. "What else can I do?" She rubbed her abdomen. "This little one is taking his sweet time."

A nurse came to the door. "Heidi?"

The young woman stood. "My turn. Thanks for the encouragement."

As Heidi waddled away, her gait lopsided, Lissa watched in envy. If only she could have the chance to have her own child. The pain in her side seemed to intensify at the thought, mocking the desires of her heart.

"Lissa?" The nurse waited at the door.

She stood, her heart pulsing in staccato rhythm as she walked to the examining room. The catch in her side made her gait as uneven as the pregnant woman who'd preceded her. She slid onto the exam table, a groan escaping her lips as she straightened.

"Looks like you're hurting pretty bad." The nurse directed her to remove her shoes and took her coat. She whipped out the blood pressure cuff, her face a blank page as she took Lissa's vitals. "Blood pressure is elevated, too." She laid the chart on the counter. "Dr. James will be right here. Do you want to lie down?

"I'll wait." Any kind of movement jarred her side.

Dr. James entered a few minutes later, a fistful of papers in her hand, an unreadable expression on her lips. "Lissa! I'm glad you came in today. I wanted to see you." She laid the papers on the counter and picked up Lissa's chart. Flipping through the pages, she stopped, lifting the other set of papers alongside the first. "I have the results of your second round of lab work."

Here we go. Lissa couldn't hide the tremor in her voice. "Anything definite this time?"

Dr. James looked up at her. "Actually, yes."

Lissa shuddered, resisting the impulse to jump off the table and hurry from the room. If her side wasn't aching so badly, she'd have exited like a speeding bullet. She leaned forward, the movement making her groan.

"First, let's take a look at what brought you in here today." Dr. James offered a hand. "Can you lie down?"

Lissa sucked in a breath. "I'll try." With Dr. James holding her neck, Lissa lay back on the table, swinging her legs up as she went. She fought the moan seeking escape, but lost. "Owww! Ohh."

The doctor adjusted the pillow beneath her head, then placed her palms on Lissa's abdomen. "Tell me where it hurts the most."

"Right side of the pelvis. I chased a cow home yesterday and had to descend and climb several ditches. I thought I might have pulled a muscle."

Dr. James nodded, slowly massaging Lissa's lower torso. She pressed above the hip, then below, always coming back to the same spot on the right. Always finding the pain. "Here?"

As she nodded, Lissa watched the doctor's face for a hint about what she thought it might be. But any trace of what Dr. James had found or suspected, remained hidden from her patient while she probed. Lissa's pulse kicked faster.

Dr. James picked up her chart. "No temperature. Blood pressure is elevated. Do you feel nauseous?"

"Not really. Very full, though."

"Full?" Dr. James made a note on her chart. "Like you ate a big lunch?"

"Yes." Lissa couldn't remember eating anything this morning. "All I can remember having was coffee. That's unusual for me."

Dr. James hooked her stethoscope around her neck. "I don't think it's appendicitis, and because of where it is, I'm ruling out a pulled muscle." She offered Lissa a hand to sit up. "When is your cycle due?"

Lissa frowned. "This next week." She spotted a wall calendar. "Probably Thursday or Friday." She searched the doctor's eyes. "Can this be related?"

Dr. James picked up her charts. "Hop down and come into my office. We need to talk."

Lissa's hands shook as she slipped her shoes back on and grabbed her jacket. Once inside the office, she blinked several times, the alarm she felt raising monsters in her imagination.

Dr. James offered her a mint. "Your lab results are still inconclusive, but one panel revealed you carry the same gene as your sister. Which isn't surprising. Your last exam didn't show any unusual masses around your ovaries, but I believe this pain you have today is a cyst. Have you had cysts before?"

Lissa shook her head. "Not that I'm aware of. But I've spent fifteen years in the Navy aboard ship. You take a pain killer and report for duty. Still, I think I would have remembered a pain this intense."

"Probably." Dr. James settled back in her chair. "I'd like to send you to a specialist. Considering Delaney's recent procedure, I think it would be wise to have you re-examined. Women your age with your family history who haven't had a child are at greater risk of developing ovarian issues, simply because you've ovulated more. I know that sounds pretty far-fetched, but couple that with the fact you carry the gene, and you have the perfect combination for a problem."

"Where's the specialist?" She thought about her work schedule. "How long would I need to be gone?"

"I know of one in Eugene who'd be good, but you're looking at a drive over and a drive back. You'd have to stay at least a couple of days." Dr. James tapped her pencil. "Is there someone who can take you?"

"My father lives near there. He'd come and get me and I could stay with him."

"Perfect. I'll make the arrangements and give you a call. The sooner we do this, the better." Dr. James stood and extended her hand. "We'll focus on good results."

Lissa shook her head. "If this is headed where I think it is, I'd probably be better off rejoining the Navy."

"Don't jump to conclusions." Dr. James offered her a comforting smile. "This is only routine testing."

Saturday morning Kurt enlisted Jayden's help with hoof cleaning. He taught the boy how to lift each of Lady's legs and scoop out the dung packed around the soft frog. When Jayden asked what harm a little mud could do, he explained how an embedded rock could injure the foot and make her lame.

Jayden caught his tongue in his teeth as he focused on the fetlock squeezed between his knees. He struggled to balance the horse's leg while holding the hoof, his hands shaking, the cleaning tool wobbling while he pried loose the hardened debris.

Lady nuzzled the boy's backside, her lips wandering along his pockets as if looking for a forgotten carrot. When she didn't find anything to her liking, she shoved Jayden with her muzzle, sending him sprawling. The hoof pick slid across the floor and hit a nearby garbage can. The ping made the filly snort.

Kurt stifled his laughter and offered his hand to the boy. "I think Lady wants a piece of the action."

"If she could smell the stuff in her feet, she wouldn't be quite so curious." Jayden straightened, hands on his hips, and twisted his torso. "Her legs are heavy. I think she was leaning on me."

"Could be." Kurt retrieved the pick and lifted one of Lady's hind legs. "Let me finish." He cleared the back two hooves and gave Lady a pat on the rump. "Take her on out to pasture. I've got a surprise for you when you return."

"What?" Jayden's eyes widened.

"The pasture." Kurt thumbed the direction of the waiting gate. "Lady needs her exercise."

The boy slumped. "You know she's only going to get dirty again."

"You need something to do."

Jayden didn't appear happy with his comment but untied Lady and led her to the waiting field. The other two horses nickered their greetings, and the filly broke into a trot to join her companions. Jayden returned with the halter and lead rope and hung the tack near the stall, a frown on his face. "I told you so."

"Did she already roll?" Kurt scanned the pasture, catching a glimpse of the filly struggling to her feet near the creek bank. He bit his lip, not wanting to laugh at the boy's distress.

"In the mud hole." Jayden kicked at a bucket. "Makes me wonder why we clean them up only so they can get dirty again."

"You've learned a universal truth."

"Dirt is forever?" Jayden's mouth hung agape.

"Caring for another is a lot of repetitive action." Kurt pointed to the pasture where the horses grazed. "Lady goes out, gets dirty. You bring her in, clean her up. Tomorrow she goes out again."

"Sounds endless." Jayden leaned on the stall rail.

"Yep." Kurt tapped the boy on the arm. "Once you accept this as part of life, you will have taken another giant step toward maturity." He led Jayden to the barn door. "Besides, I think you enjoy working with that silly little horse." At Jayden's nod, Kurt continued. "Don't you want her to have fun?" He gestured to the house. "When you do a good job, you feel more important, and Peggy bakes more goodies."

Jayden rubbed his stomach. "You've got that right."

"Shall we go see what we can raid from the kitchen?" He raised his eyebrows.

Jayden darted ahead. "I get the chocolate ones."

In the kitchen, Kurt poured two glasses of milk while Jayden reached into the ceramic clown. When each plate held a stack of Peggy's homemade cookies, he directed Jayden to a chair at the table. His phone buzzed, and he winked at Jayden. "Hello, Lissa." He listened for a few minutes, her words making him frown while he watched Jayden down one cookie after another. "Are you okay?" He concentrated on the phone call. "Sure. Keep me posted."

"What's wrong?" The question came out muffled by a mouthful of cookie crumbs.

Kurt glanced up as he pocketed his phone. "Lissa wanted me to invite you to go bowling with us tonight. But she's not feeling well and has to cancel."

"That's the surprise?" Jayden snatched up another cookie and took a bite before he landed on the seat, scraping the floor with his chair.

"Yes. Ever been bowling before?" Kurt picked up a cookie.

Jayden's fingers paused mid-air, the morsel between them

inches from his mouth. "Like the guys on television who roll a ball and knock down those white things?" He shook his head. "I think we should wait for Lissa. I'd planned to steal her away." Jayden laughed, and cookie crumbs spattered the table. "Oops. Sorry."

Kurt leaned both elbows on the table and rested his chin on his knuckles. "She's not into younger men."

CHAPTER THIRTY-ONE

BY MONDAY, LISSA'S PAIN HAD SUBSIDED and she felt well enough to tackle work. Matthew had texted her the night before, telling her of a situation where animals were dying of neglect. Her boss deemed it an emergency, and that meant a long day of inspecting livestock.

The numbers were staggering. Lissa mourned for those that had suffered. Staying busy was good for her, allowing her to push aside thoughts of Kurt and the upcoming visit to the specialist. If Dr. James followed through, she would be spending next weekend with her dad and not at the Malheur Wildlife Refuge with Kurt. With the Fourth of July falling on Wednesday, she might get to take in the local fireworks show.

Her cell phone buzzed, Kurt's picture on the screen. She pressed it to her ear. "How was your outing with Jayden?"

"He wanted to wait until you could come with us." Kurt paused, his words clipped as if he feared asking his next question. "Are you feeling better?"

Lissa fudged her answer, not wanting to drag him into the drama that lay ahead of her. "A little. I'm headed for work. Matthew says we have an urgent matter to solve."

"Should you be at work?" Kurt's voice expressed concern. "You didn't sound good on Saturday."

"I went to see the doctor. She didn't think it was serious." Lissa chose her next words carefully. "But she does want me to see a specialist in Eugene, to be sure."

"When?"

"I'll probably drive over later this week." Lissa bit her lip, keeping the need for a driver to herself. "Which means I'll miss our hike to Malheur."

"Your health is more important. We can see Malheur another time." Kurt's disappointment resonated in his response. "Be careful." He stumbled over his words. "I don't want to lose you."

An hour later Jayden zipped through the barn door, Duke at his side. "Kurt?" The boy peered into the loft where Kurt had been pitching hay, eyes squinting through the hole. "Peggy sent me out to deliver this letter for you." He waved the envelope, making it rattle. "She said it looks official. Whatever that means."

Official? Kurt's throat constricted. Only one kind of letter could arrive with the dubious distinction of being called official: one from Uncle Sam. He groaned. "I'll be right down, buddy." He planted the fork into the opened bale, dusted off his jeans, and took the ladder rungs two at a time. His boots clunked on the hardened dirt floor of the barn as he jumped from the last step, the sound as heavy as the thud of his heart. "You want to go fetch Lady and bring her into the stall?"

Jayden's grin spread across his face. "Duke can help me."

"Let me know if you have any trouble." Kurt took the letter and followed the boy out the barn door. Watching Jayden run across the pasture, Duke at his side, Kurt leaned against the tractor wheel. He slid his thumbnail beneath the letter's seal, a sense of dread surrounding his heart. Where would he be sent this time? Timbuktu? Now, when he and Lissa were finally making strides? Like a fist to the gut, another tour would finish his relationship with Lissa. He didn't want to leave, but since he'd become part of the inactive ready reserves, the military owned him. At least for another three years.

"Is that what I think it is?" Peggy appeared from behind the tractor, carrying a basket of eggs. Her smile sagged. "I saw the return address."

"Stick around a minute." Kurt lifted the flap, pulled out the letter, and skimmed the contents. "July 8, three p.m., Portland airport. Bound for San Diego." Chest aching, he held the paper out. "I'm headed back to sand country."

"Oh, Kurt." Peggy set the eggs down, read the notice, and laid a hand on his shoulder. "You shouldn't have to go."

"You know the drill." He straightened his shoulders, folded the document, and replaced it in the envelope. "I wonder where this leaves me with Lissa."

"Won't she wait for you?" Peggy's gaze searched his face. "She's military. She knows your status."

"Yeah. She'll understand." Kurt stuck the missive in his shirt pocket. "This may only be a temporary call-up."

"And if it isn't, you should tell her how you feel." Peggy came around his side to face him. "She needs to know you're serious—that when you return, you want to marry her."

"Lissa deserves a wedding. White dress, flowers, cake. Even if I proposed, she might not say yes. We've got a lot of history to unravel before we head to the altar."

"At least let her know you're entertaining the idea." Peggy poked him with her index finger. "A lady needs to know where her man stands. Give her hope."

"She may not believe me." Kurt studied the ground. "I left her with hope the last time we parted and that ended badly."

"Don't let history repeat itself." Peggy's attention shifted beyond his shoulder. She pointed. "Look at that."

Coming up the field, halter rope in his hand, Jayden was leading Lady to the gate. Duke snuffled behind, nose to the ground as if covering their tracks. The filly plodded alongside, cooperating with the boy's lead. Jayden beamed. "I think she's hungry." He opened the gate, passed the filly through, and locked the latch. "She came right up to me without even a chase."

"Or she wants a friend, and you're it." Kurt waited until the filly stood beside him, then scratched her ears and rubbed the round curve of her jaw. "She needs a good grooming after spending the day in the pasture."

"I'm on it." Jayden clicked his tongue at the horse, and the three companions walked on into the barn, Duke's tail beating a rhythm against the stall gates as he passed.

Kurt followed the boy, horse, and dog with his gaze, nodding as they disappeared. "He's one good thing I've done since coming home. I've made a difference in his life."

"And in Lissa's as well." Peggy winked at him and headed to the house, calling over her shoulder. "Don't stop now."

Matthew had been right about the abuse. Sixty head of cattle and twenty horses were already dead when they arrived at the ranch where the animals had been neglected. Ten more horses barely clung to life, and only fifteen cows remained of the original herd.

Lissa could scarcely contain her anger at the loss of life. She and the other members of her team loaded the animals they could fit into trailers and transported them to a temporary holding station while she made arrangements for more permanent homes.

Lissa's next two days were twelve hours long; by Tuesday evening she was exhausted. Her phone buzzed as she headed home, grateful for a holiday tomorrow.

"Lissa? This is Dr. James."

She froze, her hand on the steering wheel turning into a vice grip. The next chapter of her life might be written in the next few minutes. "I'm driving. Let me pull over." She stopped on the shoulder of the road. "Do you have news?"

"Yes. You have an appointment on Thursday at the Women's Clinic for Reproductive Issues with Dr. Keller." The doctor paused. "Can you make that?"

"I'll call my boss and let him know." Lissa struggled to say more. "I already gave him a heads-up, and I've had to work extra-long hours this week, so I'm due comp time."

"Good." Dr. James sounded relieved. "Any chance you can pick up the paperwork today on your way home? If you can't, I'll fax it to Dr. Keller."

"I'm already out of the city. Please fax it."

Lissa returned to the road and continued home. Her heart banged in her chest like a warning gong. She forced herself to take deep, cleansing breaths as she drove. She'd call Matthew tonight and see if she could leave for the weekend. She'd also have to call her dad. The one call she didn't want to make was one she'd promised—Kurt. What on earth would she say to him?

Sorrow and regret haunted her as she thought of all the progress they'd made in their relationship. They'd been coming together as a couple again. Kisses of promise had passed between them. They shared a love for Jayden. The future stood wide open, waiting for them to step through its portals.

And now—this.

She clenched her teeth and gripped the steering wheel so hard she was convinced she could pull it from the steering column. This wasn't fair. Not to her. Not to Kurt. Not to life. She spoke to the empty cab. "God, I know you saved Kurt for a reason. I know that when we landed jobs close to each other, your divine hand was at work. All things, you said, all things work together for good for those who love you and are called by your name. But this? What good can possibly come of this?"

She pulled into her driveway and exited the SUV. Sorrel's bark welcomed her and she headed to the kennel to let the dog out. On any other day the dog's exuberance would have filled her with happiness, but today the wriggling, happy pet annoyed her. She wasn't in the mood. "Sorrel, sit!"

Sorrel deflated as if she'd been poked with a pin. She sat, her ears sagging, and her tail stilled, her dark brown eyes staring like deep pools in a rock-strewn stream.

Lissa's guilt weighed on her like a vest made of lead. The dog didn't deserve her mood. No one did. But knowing her life was about to take a serious turn at high speed, she couldn't control her terror. Nor could she think about what she would have to do.

Sitting in her living room, she made the calls. Matthew understood and promised to pray. Dad sounded concerned but encouraged her to stay through Sunday. When she dialed Kurt, she braced herself for an onslaught of questions. She'd tell him as little as possible, sparing him any worry until she knew more. Eventually, though, she'd have to do what she'd expected all along—set the man free.

She hit speed dial, waiting for the friendly voice on the other end. When he answered, she summoned her courage. "Sorry I couldn't call sooner, but we had a mess to unravel the last two days. A rancher left his ranch to manage itself, animals included."

"Did they have pasture?"

"Not enough for seventy-five head of cattle and a rodeo of horses. We transported what was left of the herd to a holding center." Lissa swept the images from her mind—the devastation imprinted as if she'd viewed an animal massacre. "Fifteen cows and ten horses were all that survived."

"Oh, man." Kurt's groan matched what Lissa felt. "How are you feeling?"

"Better. But there's something else. My doctor wants me to

have the muscle checked by another doctor. I'm driving to Dad's tomorrow morning." She closed her eyes and prayed the pain didn't return while she drove.

"Tomorrow? That's quick." Kurt sounded surprised. "I need to see you before you go. Something's come up." His voice held an edge to it. "It can't wait."

Something's come up here, too, Kurt. And you aren't going to like what I have to say. I can barely manage the truth myself. Oh God, why did this have to happen?

Lissa pressed her lips together, fighting the emotion that wanted to enter her voice. "We can talk after I see the doctor. I should be back Sunday." She grabbed a breath, searching for courage. "See you then."

"But Lissa . . ."

She clicked the phone before he could say more. After she saw the specialist, they could talk. Whether they wanted to or not. She didn't welcome the conversation.

The drive over the mountain seemed endless. Lissa didn't remember the journey taking this long before. Maybe it was because at every wayside she was tempted to turn the SUV around and head back the way she'd come. As the miles disappeared beneath her tires, the dread of what she faced built a wall of terror in her mind. Images of her mother dying by inches surfaced in every other thought.

Prayers bounced off the cab walls. Her terror at what she faced consumed her thoughts. The pain in her side threatened to sideline her a couple of times, but she willed it away. She had to make this journey even if the results spelled the end of her relationship with

Kurt. If she was at risk, she couldn't encourage him any further. She'd made a promise to herself and she intended to keep it.

She pulled into her father's driveway and parked next to his familiar pickup, letting out a moan of relief. She'd been foolish to drive alone. She opened the car door for Sorrel as Goobers came racing around the corner of the house, barking and tail wagging. A minute later her father appeared, pushing a wheelbarrow full of soil. Lissa feared the most what this diagnosis would do to him. He'd already suffered through one illness with her mother and had stood by Delaney as she worked through her procedure. What would a third stint of the same disease do to him?

"Welcome, dear daughter." Dad pulled off his cap and wiped his forehead with a rag. When he replaced the cap, a band of pale skin peeked below the rim, his tan line stopping where the cap usually ended. "Give me a hug."

"Thanks for letting me stay here." Lissa stepped into her father's strong arms and burst into tears. He held her close, letting her cry against his overalls. When she could find her voice, she sniffed. "Sorry. I'm just letting my panic overwhelm me."

He kissed her on the forehead. "Your doctor is doing the right thing by having this checked out. Eily and I are praying." He took her hands. "Come into the house. Eily's got lemonade and sugar cookies."

"Sounds wonderful."

Eily bustled around them as they sat at the kitchen table and talked. "We're going to the butte tonight to watch the fireworks. Hope you'll join us."

"I'd like that. I haven't seen a Fourth of July display in years." Lissa savored a bite of cookie. "I see the specialist tomorrow morning, so doing something fun tonight will keep my mind off the appointment."

"Would you like us to accompany you?" Eily brought more

lemonade to the table. "We're good for moral support."

Lissa shook her head. "No, I'm fine, I think."

Dad went to the desk. "I almost forgot. This letter came for you last week. I was going to forward it, but then you called and said you were coming, so I waited." He laid the missive on the table.

Lissa stared. *Office of the Navy.* She glanced at her father. "Wonder why the Navy sent it here?"

"Did you give them this address when you left?"

"I probably did, come to think of it. I didn't have a job or a residence yet."

The return address made Lissa shudder. What could the Navy want now? She'd left at the end of her tour, at a time the Navy was reducing the numbers of military personnel. After she'd served fifteen years, they offered her an early out, winding up in the Naval Reserves on inactive status. Lifting the letter out, she scanned the contents, dismay burning in her throat. With the world in chaos and terrorist cells increasing, intelligence officers like herself were being put on alert status. She'd known this could happen, never believed it would. Now, here before her eyes, the truth unnerved her.

When she'd finished reading the letter she looked up to find Dad and Eily both waiting for her to speak. "Well, this gives me something to think about."

"What do they want?" Dad couldn't hide the disappointment in his voice.

"They're offering a bonus if I come back and finish my commission. My early out was conditional, and they have the right to recall me."

Dad reached for her hand. "Can you say no?" He searched her face. "We haven't had any time with you."

"I'll have to see." Lissa's heart grew heavy with dread. Why now? If the tests weren't enough to keep her and Kurt apart, this certainly would be. Maybe this recall would provide the easy exit she might need after tomorrow. She stood, tucking the letter into her pocket. "I'll go unpack my bag. Thanks for the yummy cookies."

She closed the door to her bedroom and sank onto the bed. "No! God, I can't do this." Breathing the prayer more than speaking it, she continued. "I served my country, did my job. Please, Lord, find a way."

She pulled the notice out again, folded the page, and returned it to the envelope. She plunked the unwelcome letter onto her pillow. Disappointment vied with grief as she walked to the dresser and filled the drawers with her belongings. Sunlight burst through the window like a laser beam searching for its target, coming to rest on the unwelcome letter. She and Kurt had only gone on two real dates this time around—two chances to begin again. Their relationship could flourish before she'd be recalled, but what was the purpose? Tomorrow she'd see a specialist who could change her life forever.

She gripped the dresser, letting rage vent before she collapsed like a sack of potatoes against the sturdy drawers. Leaning her elbows on the dresser's surface, she cradled her face with her hands, praying God would carry her anger away and bring her some promise of hope. She'd climbed on a train named Despair with no available exit. Breaking glass sounded in her head as each of her dreams shattered in the wake of what she faced. The future she'd come home to claim had vanished.

CHAPTER THIRTY-TWO

THE NEXT MORNING LISSA ARRIVED AT the women's center a few minutes early. The receptionist handed her a clipboard with papers for her to read and sign. Apparently, Dr. James had made all the preliminary arrangements for her visit. All she needed to do was give her permission. She scanned the documents, pulse pounding against her breastbone. Words jumped out at her—laparoscopy, surgery, recovery—all indicators that Dr. James thought her test results merited the need for a specialist and an in-depth look at her physical condition. Her panic mounted as she read each successive page.

"Lissa Frye?" A nurse waited at the left of the reception counter.

She wobbled toward the woman, an elevated heart rate and breathlessness making her unsteady on her feet. The life she'd hoped to live upon returning to the States faded in her memory, the reality of the moment erasing her hopes like club soda dissolving fingerprints on glass. After the nurse took her to the examination room, recorded her pulse and blood pressure, and left, she braced herself for the coming encounter.

Lissa heard a knock at the door of the exam room, and in came a small, wiry woman with graying hair and a smile as wide as the mountain waterfall Lissa had passed on the drive here. "Good morning. I'm Dr. Keller." The doctor picked up her chart and scanned the entries. "Nervous?"

Lissa pressed her fingers together to keep them from shaking. "A little, I suppose."

Dr. Keller glanced up. "I'd say a lot nervous. Your blood pressure's climbed higher than it was at Dr. James' office." She patted Lissa's knee. "Relax. This is going to be very routine."

Lissa cleared her throat and forced a deep breath. "Routine?"

"Dr. James filled me in on your family history, your lab tests, as well as your hopes for the future." The doctor turned another page. "I'd say you're in line for a good one."

"Depends on what you consider good."

"Husband, family, home." Dr. Keller put on her glasses and peered over the top. "That cover it?"

Lissa let out the breath she'd been holding. "I don't dare dream of any of that at this point."

"After tomorrow, you might."

"What's tomorrow?"

Dr. Keller set the clipboard down and folded her arms. "I understand you drove over here from Hines. That's what, about two hundred and fifty miles?" At her nod, the doctor continued. "Not sure that was wise, considering your condition." The doctor gave her a knowing look. "And you'd like to get this over with, so you don't have to drive over again and again?" Another nod. "With this being a holiday weekend, I checked the surgical roster at the hospital and it seems there are several openings available. After I examine you, if I find what I suspect, I'd like you to undergo a laparoscopic procedure at the hospital. You'd be here a couple of hours, someone would drive you home, and you'd recover enough by Sunday to drive over the mountains." The doctor pulled her stethoscope from around her neck. "Sound like a plan?"

She stared at the doctor. What did she know? "Do you know something about my condition that I don't?"

"No." The doctor offered her a hand. "Lay back and I'll get a better idea." After a few minutes of probing the pelvic area and asking questions, Dr. Keller straightened and helped her sit up. "How's the pain you were experiencing?"

"It has subsided. I thought it might have been a pulled muscle since I often do strenuous work."

"Quite possible. But the mass I feel on your right side is suspicious. Dr. James thought so, too. The laparoscopic exam would allow me to make a definite diagnosis. I'd also like to treat the site while I'm there."

"Meaning?"

"Remove the mass and any surrounding tissue I deemed suspect, have it tested, and make recommendations based on what I find." Dr. Keller made a note in her chart. "You are so young, that if this proves to be what you fear, we are in all likelihood catching the disease before it has a chance to do any damage."

"But what if you have to remove the ovaries?"

"I would never do that unless both ovaries are involved and are proven cancerous, which, in your case, I highly doubt. You are a healthy young woman. Even with only one ovary, you can still have that family you want."

"But what about down the road? Can't I develop the disease later?"

"You can. You can also die in childbirth. Or be hit by a car crossing the mountains. Or eat too much and develop heart disease. The possibilities are endless." Dr. Keller smiled. "Life is given out one day at a time, not in doses. Enjoy the life you've been given and anticipate what lies ahead for you. Tomorrow is only one day. I want you in the short stay unit by 8:30. Bring a friend along to drive you home. I'll have a full report by the time you awake from the anesthesia."

She stuck out her hand. "Agreed. Let's get this done."

Saturday morning, Lissa played the lazy invalid, nestling in the covers of her old bed, relishing the warmth and comfort of the familiar surroundings. Her bandages pulled at her, so staying still seemed a wise choice. Childhood memories floated through her mind—long talks with her sister, laughter from the kitchen as Mom and Dad shared breakfast, the honk of the school bus as she pulled on her shoes and ran to catch her ride.

Yesterday's laparoscopic surgery had left her a little sore and the anesthesia had made her groggy the rest of the afternoon. Dad and Eily had driven her home, Eily insisting that she spend her day resting. Lissa didn't argue. Her new job had not afforded her many leisurely mornings to waste. The pampering revived her.

A dog barked, followed by another one answering back. She could only imagine what mischief Sorrel had gotten into with Goobers and dreaded the need to give her dog a long, sudsy bath before she could take her home. Dad and his dogs had always been part of the landscape, even when he worked at the high school as its principal.

A knock sounded on her door and Eily poked her head in the room. "Are you needing a mid-morning snack yet?"

She sat up and nodded. "Your breakfast left me full, but what did you have in mind?"

"I have a tray of Danish and coffee for you, if you'd like to lounge a little while longer."

"Oh, Eily, you spoil me. I won't want to go home."

Her stepmother laughed. "It's all part of the plan to make you forget that letter from the Navy. Your dad wants to keep you in the worst way."

Lissa sighed. "I'm sure he does. But the reasons I left the Navy are now different from the reasons that would keep me here." She forced a smile, searching for a change of subject. "I'd love a plate of pastries."

"I'll be right back."

She sank against the pillows, her mind picking its way through the reality of her situation. The time with the sheriff's department had been interesting work, and though much of it had been heartbreaking, she'd enjoyed many moments of satisfaction knowing she'd made a difference in a stranded animal's life. The strenuous part of the job she could do without, but maybe the cattle wrangling had been providential, forcing her to get a close-up look at her physical condition. Yesterday's surgery might not have happened had she been at sea tracking terrorists on a remote computer. The condition of her ovaries might have gone undetected for years.

The sound of a vehicle in the driveway met her ears. Had Dad decided to go somewhere today or did they have company coming? She ran her fingers through her curly hair, wishing she could pin up the unruly mass from a reclining position. But she couldn't. She'd have to stay hidden in the bedroom.

Eily returned a few minutes later, the tray emitting smells of fresh cinnamon rolls. A small carafe sat on the tray with a cup and saucer. "You still drink coffee?"

"Does the sun still shine?" She reached for the tray as Eily set it across her lap. Lifting the carafe, she poured coffee into her cup. "At home I make one mug at a time because I'm usually out the door before I can drink another. The coffee my boss makes requires antacids. That stuff is stiff enough to stand on its own." She took a sip. "Mmm. This is heavenly. Thanks."

"I'll be back to check on you, but I've got to go fix another plate." Eily turned toward the door. "There's a late arrival in the kitchen."

"I wondered if you had company. Don't worry about me. Take care of your guest."

Eily laughed. "Kurt's hardly a guest. But I still like to mother him when I can." She waved and hurried from the room.

Lissa set the cup down hard enough to splash. Why had Kurt shown up?

Kurt listened while Marshall recounted Lissa's timetable from the day before. She'd come to see a specialist. That's what she'd told him. But this doctor had already planned a procedure for her when she arrived, a course of action that landed her in the hospital and surgically explored her internal organs. "What's the prognosis?"

"I'll let you ask her." Marshall studied him for a moment. "She'll be as surprised as I am that you're here."

"I'm not here for a visit." Kurt pulled the letter from his pocket and handed it to Marshall. "My unit has been called up."

"No." The man shook his head as he read the contents. "I thought you were through."

"I still had time left to serve. My inactive status flew out the window because of need. The Marines have the right to recall me."

"Monday?" Marshall snapped to attention. "You leave Portland on Monday?"

"Yes, sir." Kurt exhaled. "I stopped to tell Lissa goodbye."

"She's resting in her room." Marshall went to Lissa's room and returned a minute later. "Go on in. She's decent."

Kurt entered the room on unsteady feet. Lissa was sitting up, pillows propped at her back, hair tumbling to her shoulders. He took a deep breath. She'd never looked more beautiful. "I heard you had a rough day yesterday."

"I've had better days." Lissa cocked her head. "You didn't drive two hundred and fifty miles to find out how I am, did you?"

"Yes and no." Kurt pulled up a chair and sat by the bed. "I needed to talk to you, but you took off before I had a chance to tell you the latest."

"What?" Lissa's eyes widened. "Has something happened to Jayden?"

"No. Jayden is fine." He scuffed the rug with his boot, scrutinizing the floor like he'd never seen hardwood before. "I've been called back to San Diego."

"The final straw." Lissa closed her eyes and leaned back into the pillows. When she opened her eyes, she cast him a sad smile. "It's an omen, of sorts. Isn't it?"

"What are you saying?"

"We weren't meant to be together." She wiped her eyes on the corner of the comforter. "This on again, off again relationship we've struggled to maintain keeps facing roadblocks we can't seem to circumnavigate."

"I know." Kurt leaned forward and put his hand on the comforter. "But this time I won't stop writing or texting or video chatting with you. I want to keep our relationship going."

Lissa's face grew serious. "The problem is, Kurt. . ." She looked out the window before continuing. "The problem is I can't give you what you want."

"What's that?"

For a minute she didn't speak. Sorrow hovered in her eyes, and her lips trembled. "When I was eighteen, I made a promise to myself that I would never put a man through the pain and suffering I watched my father experience as my mother died by degrees." She dabbed at her nose with a tissue. "My tests show I'm a carrier for the gene that killed my mother. Yesterday's surgery removed a mass from my ovary, along with other material left from previous cysts. Not only could I develop the same disease Mom had, my ability to have a family could be compromised."

"None of that matters—"

"Yes, it does. You deserve better. You need to be a father. To have a quiver full of little kids clamoring for attention at your feet. Sons you can go hiking with, daughters to adore you. Your future happiness shouldn't hinge on a woman who already faces significant challenges." She gripped the comforter in her hands until her knuckles hurt. "Whose very life could be shortened unexpectedly because of her lousy placement in the gene pool."

Kurt scooted to the edge of the bed. "However many years we have together is what God has planned for us. And the children don't have to be our own." He reached for her clenched fingers. "You've loved Jayden as much as I do, I know you have." At her nod, he grabbed both hands and leaned toward her. "Think of all the children like Jayden out there who only want someone to love them. If we can't have our own, we can love them."

Lissa freed herself from his grip. "No. You're overlooking the big problem. This disease is a killer. I've witnessed firsthand the sword it wields claiming its victims. Survivors last about five years. I won't risk your future with my health. I made a vow—I won't do it. I know what the disease did to my dad. I will not do that to you."

"You're letting fear affect your reality."

"No, reality has taught me to fear." She reached for her handbag at the head of the bed. "Besides, you aren't the only one with marching orders. The Navy wants me too." She handed him the letter. "If I die on the ocean, they can throw me overboard."

He opened the orders and read them in disbelief. "You're heading to San Diego too?" He handed the letter back. "Are you accepting their offer?"

"I'm considering it." Lissa tucked the envelope back in her bag. "The Navy would like to have me, and considering all that has happened in the last few days, I believe this is the path I'm supposed to follow." She pulled the covers up over her shoulders. "The problem has been solved, for both of us."

"You're not even going to fight?" Kurt clenched his fists and smacked his palm. "For us?"

"I've already told you once there is no us." Lissa turned away from him. "Goodbye, Kurt. Invite me to your wedding. I wish you every happiness."

He stood, watching as she buried her face in the pillows. She didn't want him to see her cry. If he weren't leaving on Monday, he'd stay and pursue the argument. But he had to get to Portland, make arrangements for his truck, and check in with the rest of his unit who would fly with him. He couldn't miss his plane.

He left the room, heart heavy. When he returned from San Diego, or Afghanistan, or wherever this call-up took him, Lissa would be gone. She'd made her decision without him. He mourned what might have been, but he could see her mind was set. She didn't want him to be hurt by something she might face in the future. She wouldn't let him stand by her side, something he ached to do. The chasm between them gaped wide and impossible to bridge.

Marshall and his mother were in the kitchen. He joined them. "I wanted to say goodbye."

"You won't stay for dinner?" Mom looked at him, a worried frown on her face. "Surely you have time to eat?"

He crossed the room and kissed her on the forehead. "All things considered, I think it's best if I fast-track up the interstate." He shook Marshall's hand. "Thanks for everything."

He turned and headed for the door. As he stepped outside, he glanced over his shoulder. Marshall had his hands on his mother's back as she leaned into him. She was crying.

Lissa listened as Kurt's truck started. Wheels sounded, growing fainter in the driveway. The emptiness of the moment threatened to hurtle her into hopelessness. She'd never see him again. Never feel his strong arms about her again, warming her when she was cold. Never press her cheek against his or feel his tender kisses on her neck. Never know what it was like to lie in his arms. Though her heart continued to beat, the hollow sound of its rhythm did little to warm her soul. How she wished she could have changed the past to preserve her future.

But letting him go was the kindest act she could perform. When her follow-up routine was finished and the preliminary test results from her procedure yesterday were confirmed, she'd head to San Diego, awaiting orders to return to her carrier. Kurt would be gone, trudging across some forgotten wasteland, his mind on terrorists and not on her. They were finished.

"What just happened?" Dad stood in the doorway, a scowl across his face. "What did you say to that young man to make him leave without so much as a look back?" He entered the room, hands on his hips. "He wasn't even willing to stay for dinner."

Lissa stared at her father. She'd never seen him so angry. "His unit has been called up. I've got marching orders." She plucked a tissue from the box on her nightstand and dabbed at her cheeks. "Couple that with my surgery yesterday and I'd say we've finished our tour. I told him goodbye."

"You sent him away?" Dad towered over her. "Kurt loves you. Why would you do such a thing?"

Lissa sat up straighter, ignoring the pull of her butterfly bandages across her middle, and gazed into her father's face. "I watched you die by inches while Mom lost her battle to cancer. I vowed I would never put a man through that kind of pain. I have an uncertain future. Kurt deserves better. He's handsome, loves little kids, and has a lot to offer a *whole* woman." She lowered her gaze. "I'm not that woman."

Dad sank onto the edge of the mattress. "Lissa, honey, what if your mother and I had decided not to marry because we knew she might get cancer?"

"You didn't know. That's the difference."

"No, it isn't." He reached for her hand. "Life is not about certainties. It's about trusting God to take you through whatever circumstances you face. If I hadn't married your mother, I would have missed twenty-two years of the happiest moments of my life. No memories of her, you, or Delaney and her family." He touched her chin and turned her face toward him. "I'd never abandon that part of my life because I wasn't willing to risk the pain of losing her. You don't want to wind up a gray-haired old lady with no memories."

Lissa fiddled with her comforter. "Kurt will have a better life with someone else."

"Maybe you should stop thinking like a naval intelligence officer and start letting your heart speak. If you did, I'm pretty sure all that love you are bundling up inside you would burst out. You wouldn't return to the Navy, and you wouldn't let Kurt get away." Dad smiled and patted her arm. "Baby, let love call you home."

"Kurt reports for duty tomorrow. He won't be back." She pulled the covers over her head. "It's better this way."

CHAPTER THIRTY-THREE

Six weeks later, Hines, Oregon

LISSA SHIFTED INTO LOW GEAR AND let the sheriff's vehicle rattle down the driveway of the Mueller ranch. She hadn't been here since she and Matthew had first discovered the neglected horses and Bennie Mueller's body in the house early this spring. Her only other visit had been to turn the filly over to Kurt and Peggy.

The August sun blazed overhead, highlighting the green pastures with a touch of gold. The mountains beyond rose sharp above the flatness of the terrain. The dreary shadows and weary forlornness that flanked the ranch buildings the first day she'd approached the property now scurried away in the scrutiny of the sun's rays, surrendering to the charm of the aging homestead. The serenity beckoned her, like a blanket she could snuggle into and catch a few winks.

She had returned to work following her surgery, finding no joy in her routine. Co-workers and Sheriff Briggs had noticed her grim demeanor, she was certain, but had let her grieve in peace. The sheriff had called her into his office yesterday with a new assignment: drive over to the old Mueller place and bring back the materials left over from the crime scene investigation. It would be an easy call, compared to the daily grind of rescuing abused animals.

The ranch property had been sold off, and the new owner had called the office to tell Matthew to send someone for the forgotten items. She'd wished he'd sent someone else—returning to the property only resurrected unhappy memories of that spring day when she and Kurt had met again after two years apart. She remembered that reunion as a chilly one—cold as an Oregon ice storm. Her fist punched the steering wheel. "He even called me sis."

She pulled to a stop in front of the ranch house. The windows were open, as well as the door, and the sound of a table saw met her ears. She climbed from the SUV and approached the front door. "Hello in the house. Sheriff's deputy here."

"Meet you outside." The voice sounded far distant, as if the owner were at the other end.

Lissa stepped into the yard, the glare of the August sun burning through her clothing. She straightened her shoulders, adopting her most professional stance to greet the newcomer. Whoever it was certainly had loud feet. The steps of someone approaching grew louder, and made her wonder if the new owner was a big man. Hearing him round the corner, she turned and smiled, but her smile faded as Kurt came into view.

"Kurt?" Lissa gasped, staring in disbelief. "What are you doing here?"

"Hello to you too." Kurt gestured toward the open door, stepping beyond her as he entered the house. "Let's get out of the sun, shall we?" Inside, he pulled up two chairs, brushed the sawdust from them, and offered one to her. "Peggy told me the ranch was going up for sale when your office finished its investigation. So I put in a bid and won."

"But you went to San Diego six weeks ago," Lissa sputtered, her surprise at seeing Kurt and not some stranger standing there, still not registering with her brain. "Didn't you?"

"My unit was called up for a training exercise. I'm back now until Labor Day."

"When did you have time to buy a ranch? Or find the money, for that matter."

"You might say I got a good deal. Bennie Mueller's brother was anxious to get the property off his hands. I made him an offer he couldn't refuse."

"What are you going to do with a place like this?" Lissa glanced around her. Judging from the walls torn open to the supports, Kurt had already done plenty. "You've been busy."

"Anger is a great motivator."

Lissa shuffled her feet, unwilling to look him in the eye.

"Come on, I'll show you." He led her to the end of the ranch house, pausing by the stairs that led to the extra building sitting there. "I think this was the original garage, but Mueller used it for a different purpose." He pointed at the stairs. "See how steps lead both to the second floor and down to the ground?"

Lissa nodded. "Makes you wonder what purpose the space served." Her gaze followed the rise of the building, a frown wrinkling her brow above her nose. "That's a lot of space."

"Well, I had a thought. Why not close in the breezeway and remodel the second floor into a large master suite and bath, and convert the first floor into a two-car garage?" Kurt pointed at the main house. "The kitchen is between the main entry and the bedrooms, so this would be like another bedroom wing." He pivoted toward her. "I could fill it with foster kids or my own children."

Lissa considered him, wide-eyed. "You've moved that far along?"

Kurt chuckled. "Well, no. A certain navy intelligence officer I know put a kink in my plans." He studied her. "But I learned you didn't leave for San Diego after you received your letter."

"I'm awaiting their decision." Lissa grew sober. "There's a chance I won't have to report."

"Perfect." Kurt turned back to the house. "My unit is on alert, and I may have to leave for a while, but I didn't want to abandon my dreams." He took a step toward the door. "Too many kids need this."

"Will you be able to foster children here alone?"

"Yes, I could. But I'd rather have a helpmate." Kurt stuck his hands in his pockets and rocked back on his boot heels. "So I keep praying the woman will change her mind."

Afraid to see his expression, she grew quiet. "You did all of this to share it with me?"

"That's the general idea." Kurt looked down, crunching a piece of dirt on the sidewalk with his toe. He hurried on. "After the war, Foster's death, and all I witnessed in the desert, this place draws me. The peacefulness of the ranch against the backdrop of the rugged mountains is inviting."

"What a dream." Lissa closed her eyes and let herself imagine the future. "This would be a wonderful haven for battered children."

"And rescue horses."

"Horses, too?"

He nodded. "But I can't do it alone." Kurt straightened, his sights set on the pasture. "Living here, I could help keep Foster's dream alive, but without a wife, it wouldn't be a family setting." He gestured for her to follow him. "Let's go count the stalls in the barn." When they reached the building, Kurt slid the doors open and they stepped into the darkened interior. Four stalls lined one side and a long, railed pen waited across the open aisle. "We could put dividers over there if we needed them."

"I had no idea you would ever settle on a ranch." Lissa couldn't contain the surprise his news gave her. "When I ran away after my mother died, my friend's invitation to live on her family's farm was the best thing I could have done. I know people can heal from this kind of setting. I'm one of their progeny."

"Can this setting heal you?" Kurt's eyes narrowed, his expression stoic as he posed the question.

"Oh, Kurt." Lissa breathed deep, the memory of their last

encounter making her feel embarrassed. "I don't have any cancer. My lab work came back clean." She swallowed, gathering courage to tell him how sorry she was. "I didn't think I'd ever get to tell you."

Kurt turned toward her, arms folded. "You sent me away because you feared you couldn't give me children. Though I might be disappointed, I still accept the possibility."

"You do? I can't imagine you without children of your own."

Kurt waved her off. "Do you think you could love another person's child if you couldn't have one of your own?"

Lissa struggled to understand what he was saying. She wanted children, kids they might not be able to have. But other youngsters, children like Jayden, needed parents to love them, too. Could her heart include those as well?

"I'm crazy about Jayden." Her voice dropped to a whisper. "What I can't believe is you still want *me*."

Kurt bent down on one knee and reached into his pocket. "Lissa, I can't get you out of my mind. You've stolen my heart and taken residence in my thoughts. I love you. With every breath I take, I say I love you. Will you marry me?"

Lissa cocked an eyebrow, growing suspicious of the scene unfolding before her. The moment to fulfill her dreams had come, yet it felt too surreal to comprehend. She couldn't resist teasing Kurt. "Have I been set up? Did Matthew know you were here?"

"Is that a no?" Kurt's smile wavered and his lower lip trembled.

"Oh, Kurt. You silly man. I thought I'd lost you forever. And here you are on one knee." Lissa giggled. "I'd be a fool to say no." She pulled him to his feet, and he wrapped his arms about her. She reached up and placed her hands on both sides of his face, pulling him down where she could kiss him. "Yes, Kurt, I will marry you. I love you with all my heart."

"What changed your mind?"

Lissa looked over his shoulder at the far side of the barn, the incident locked in her mind. "After I sent you away, my dad came in the room and asked me what I had said that made you leave so abruptly." Lissa angled her head back so she could look into Kurt's eyes. "I've never seen him so angry with me."

"Angry?"

"Yes. Furious."

"I like your dad."

Lissa laughed. "Me, too."

"What else did he say?"

"He told me I can't live my life on the what-ifs out there. The doctor in Eugene said the same thing. There are no guarantees for anyone, much less me. He said I should grab hold of my future, ask God to join me, and live my days with all the gusto I can find."

She studied the wonderful man who stood watching her with love still in his eyes. "But you know me, I never listen. Dad was right. I'll wind up a wrinkled, disenchanted old lady with nothing to show for the years I spent."

"So you're willing to give us a chance?"

"I can't wait to be your wife." Even as she spoke the words, Lissa's heart fluttered like a butterfly on steroids. "I've been so foolish."

He kissed her as if he were a man who had only recently discovered kissing was fun. When he broke away, Lissa gripped the side of the stall, trying to breathe.

"You're sure?" Kurt steadied her with his hand.

"Yes. I've never been more convinced. Thank you for sharing your dream with me."

"Our dream." From his shirt pocket he pulled a small velvet bag. Opening the drawstring, he tilted the bag upside down in his hand, allowing a gold band with a white center stone to drop on his palm. He held up the ring for her inspection. "This was my grandmother's engagement ring. The center is a moonstone encircled by a gold mounting. The gems on each end are diamonds."

"It's beautiful." Lissa blinked, enraptured with the detail of the ring. "How old is it?"

"The jeweler who inspected it said it was retro 1940s." He took her hand and cradled her fingers in his. "Aged to perfection."

"I'm honored you've decided I'm worthy to wear this. I've put you through enough heartache to send you packing."

Kurt slipped the band over her knuckle, stood, and kissed her forehead. "In my eyes, you outshine the moonstone."

"When did you want to get married?" Lissa admired the ring on her finger. "You said something about a church full of flowers?"

"What I asked is how set are you on a big church wedding?" Kurt tucked a strand of hair behind her ear. "I leave again the Tuesday after Labor Day. That's not much time to plan."

Lissa gulped. "You want to get married before we report for duty?"

"I'm not taking chances on losing track of you again." Kurt placed his hands on his hips. "I assume, if you're called up, you're destined for the *USS Ronald Reagan* in San Diego, and I have to report there, too. I figured we could fly there together and honeymoon until my unit either stands down or I deploy. Or you receive your orders."

"What an adventure." Lissa raised her hands skyward and twirled in a circle. "This will be a story to save for our grandchildren."

Kurt touched the end of her nose. "I like the way you think. We're engaged five minutes and you've already got grandchildren planned. Quite a mover and shaker, I'd say."

"Well, a gentleman recently told me I have two weeks to plan a wedding." Lissa fanned herself with her hands. "I better get on it, hadn't I?"

Setting his glass of milk on the kitchen table, Jayden lifted wounded eyes at Kurt, mouth agape. "You're going to marry Lissa? Before you leave again for San Diego?"

"Yep. I asked her this afternoon." Kurt stepped from the doorway where he'd made his announcement and let the screen door slam behind him. He grinned and wiggled his eyebrows. "She said yes."

Peggy scurried across the kitchen to where he stood, dropped the dishtowel she held, and wrapped him in a bear hug. "I'm so happy I could yodel from the hills right now."

Kurt stopped to pick up the towel and handed it to her. "I didn't know you yodeled."

Peggy laughed. "I don't. But your news could certainly make me try."

"Don't hurt yourself on my account."

Peggy snapped the towel at him and chuckled. "This calls for a celebration."

From the edge of the table where he stood, Jayden slumped into a chair. Mouth puckered and eyebrows sagging, his face focused on the floor.

"Jayden?" Kurt cocked his head to try and capture the boy's glance. "What's the matter?"

He spoke through quivering lips "What's going to happen to me?"

Kurt pulled out a chair and sat beside Jayden. "You and Duke and Lady will stay here and help Peggy."

"But my mother will get me back when George is sentenced." Jayden turned wary eyes on Kurt. "I'll lose my dog, the filly, *and* you." Jayden sprang from the chair and wrapped his arms around

Kurt. "I can't lose you. It would be like having my dad die all over again."

Kurt swallowed the lump in his throat. He grasped Jayden by the shoulders and held him at arm's length. "Even though my unit has been placed on ready alert, there's a good chance we'll be told to stand down."

"What's that mean?" Jayden studied his face, mouth slack, forehead wrinkled.

"It means we're no longer needed and can return to civilian life." Kurt ran a thumb along Jayden's cheekbones, wiping away a smidgeon of dirt hovering beneath his eyelashes. "I'm coming back here."

"But what about Lissa?" Jayden scowled and crossed his arms. "You can't marry her and leave her behind."

"No, but if Lissa is required to stay on her ship, I may not get to see her much." Kurt gestured for Jayden to sit back down beside him. "Military life can be tough on marriages." He caught Peggy watching them and winked. "I have a surprise for you."

"Another surprise?" Jayden's eyes widened, expectancy written across his brow. "What surprise?"

"We've purchased Bennie Mueller's ranch and plan to live there and make it our home."

Jayden jumped up and pumped his fist. "Awesome."

"I thought you'd like our plan. We want to become licensed foster parents and run a ranch for hurting kids."

Standing behind him, Peggy let out a contented murmur. "Wonderful." She squeezed his shoulder. "Foster would be so proud of you."

"Where will Duke stay?" Jayden looked between him and Peggy, then sat back down. "Will he stay here with Peggy or move back to his old place?"

Kurt rested his hands on his knees and leaned toward the boy. "I think Duke should stay wherever you are."

"Mom can't let me have a dog where we live." Jayden shook his head and slumped lower in the chair. "The landlord only allows cats." He rubbed his toe across the floor, hands in his pockets.

"Your mother may not return to that house." Peggy ran her fingers through Jayden's hair. "She might need to make new memories like you have."

"But the towns out here are so far apart." Jayden studied his shoes, one foot kicking at a table leg. "Moving in with Mom could take me miles away. I'd never see Duke, or Lady, or either of you." His face grew sober. "Duke's a herder. It wouldn't be fair to make him live in town where the only thing to chase is Mom's cat and an occasional coyote." The boy shook his head at Peggy. "No. I couldn't do that to Duke. He needs to be here with the filly and the other horses."

"Which is why I called your caseworker today." Peggy sat across from Jayden. "Your mom is going to have to answer for her part in the kidnapping, but once she's cleared of the charges, I am going to invite her to come live here."

"Here? On the ranch?" Jayden pondered Peggy's words, eyebrows lifted in wonder. "She's *not* a horse person."

"But with Kurt gone, I'm going to need more help running this place. Your mother cooks, so she can handle the kitchen for me. Which will free me up to do more of the administrative responsibilities the Herrick Valley Rescue Center board of directors expect. The handyman I hire will work with you, caring for the animals."

"Kurt taught me lots of things this summer." Jayden stood a little straighter, squaring his shoulders. "I'll know what to do."

"You are going to school in September." Kurt's no-nonsense tone sounded from where he'd stood and leaned against the kitchen sink. "You'll have to serve in an advisory capacity except on weekends."

"Sounds epic to me."

Kurt rapped the counter beside him. "For a young man, you're growing wise fast. I think a situation like this calls for prayer."

"Prayer?" Jayden's eyes narrowed. "After all this?" He raised his hands in the air, as if exasperated. "I thought God would take care of things. I told Him I needed Him and you. Now you're going away." He stomped toward the hallway. "God didn't listen."

Kurt caught Jayden's arm and pulled him against his chest. He cupped the boy's face, forcing him to look up. Jayden's lips quivered, eyes hard as he studied him. Kurt smiled at the feisty boy. "I'm only alive because God rescued me from the pits of war."

"I quit believing He hears me when my dad was killed." Jayden's chin rose higher, daring Kurt to respond. "Mom and I prayed for him every day. But he got killed anyway."

"What you don't understand is God promises to be with us through the bad and the good. He doesn't promise to reach down and scoop us out of harm's way." Kurt paused, searching for the right words. "Your dad and I were on the same patrol together. When I fell into the cave and found the stash of weapons, I was excited. But the Taliban showed up, and I had to hide for several days in the dark at the bottom of a cave. I kept praying God would get me out of there, but I was terrified. Both your dad and I were shot at. He was hit, I wasn't. I can't tell you why God called him to heaven and left me, but I know your dad was praying for you even as he died."

"How do you know?" Jayden raised his chin, eyes shuttered. Like a wild horse ready to flee from fright, the boy waited to spring from the room. "You were in a cave, remember?"

"I know, because your dad led us in Bible study every evening after patrol." Kurt smiled. "Jordan asked for prayer requests, and he always put you and Melanie at the top of the list."

"You lost your best friend too." Jayden's voice wobbled. "Were you praying for Foster?"

"Yes. And losing Foster almost cost me my life." He heard his voice crack. "For a long time, I felt responsible because I had the enemy in my sights and didn't shoot him. I didn't think I could go on."

"How did you?"

"Foster made me promise to come home and help his mother with the horse ranch if he was killed." He looked at the ceiling, searching for a response. "He said Peggy would need the help and I would need the healing."

Peggy squeezed Kurt's shoulder. "Foster knew what he was doing."

Kurt laid his hand over Peggy's and smiled. "Yes, he did." He spoke to Jayden. "And finding you in that barn gave me new purpose and a will to return to the living."

"Me?" Jayden didn't look convinced. "How?"

"Because you looked so much like the little kids in Afghanistan who have known nothing but war since they were born. I vowed I would make a difference for them. When I found out you were Jordan's son, I knew God had brought me home for a reason."

Jayden stood at attention, his rigid body every inch the small Marine his dad had impressed upon him. "You've kept my memory of my dad alive. I miss him so much."

"Come here." Kurt held out his arms. Jayden fell into them, his body shaking as he wrapped Kurt in a hug. "When I return, I will be in your life as much as your mother will let me."

"Promise?" Jayden's words were muffled as he spoke against Kurt's shirt.

"I promise."

"Well, believe it or not, God answered one of my prayers when

Lissa said yes." Jayden stepped back and sniffed. "I guess you better hurry up and marry her so you can report for duty and come home."

Kurt laughed. "I wish it was that simple. But our country is not at war, so my reporting for duty may simply be an exercise."

Peggy sighed. "I pray that's all it is."

Jayden nodded. "Me, too. Peggy and I will pray for you and Lissa while you're gone."

"Thanks, bud. I can't do any better."

"You're getting married?" Delaney's squeal burst over the phone line. "David! Lissa's getting married."

"I'm going to need a lot of help." Lissa loved her sister's enthusiasm, but planning a wedding on such short notice seemed an impossible task. "Kurt flies out of Portland the day after Labor Day, and he wants me to go with him to San Diego and await my orders there."

"How romantic. Like a World War II movie." Delaney's breathless laugh sizzled into the phone. "Ingrid Bergman and Humphrey Bogart, together at last."

"I'm serious." Her sister's lack of focus set Lissa's nerves on edge. "How can I do this?"

"I've got an idea." Delaney covered the phone and spoke to someone in the room. "David and I celebrated my recovery by hiring a landscaper for our backyard. David's been filling it with flowers while I lie on my back at Dad's. We even have a gazebo in the center."

"Sounds pretty."

"It is. Pretty enough for a backyard wedding." Delaney giggled.

"We can do a Dad and Eily wedding repeat right here. You and Kurt will be thirty minutes from the airport."

"Are you sure, Sis?" Lissa flopped back in her chair, thinking of the family-only wedding her father and his new bride managed to pull off on New Year's Day. "We might get fifty guests."

"We can handle it. Our patio is set up for tables. We'll barbecue steak kabobs or burgers or whatever you want for wedding food."

"Kurt's plane leaves at three o'clock. We'll have to do a brunch."

"No problem. Wedding at ten. Breakfast at eleven. Leave for the airport at one." Delaney's excitement abated as she lowered her voice and dropped into business mode. "Make the invitations. I'll call Dad and Eily."

"You are the most wonderful sister a girl could ever want." Lissa wished she could hug Delaney. "I'm getting married!"

"Buy your dress online. With flowers, you can use any theme for colors. I have a long peach silk gown I could wear as matron of honor." Delaney paused, the sound of a pencil scratching on paper coming through the phone line. Her dear sister, the list maker, was at it again. "Do you think Kurt's sisters will want to be bridesmaids?"

"Call Dad and see what he thinks. I don't want anyone excluded." Lissa smiled into the phone. "And if each of them wears a pastel long gown, it will add to the flavor of the flowers."

"I'm on it," Delaney cooed. "Go buy your dress. Kurt can wear his military uniform. What a wedding!"

"Should I hire a caterer?" Lissa's heart fluttered, thinking of doing this in fourteen days.

"Say no more." Delaney's voice grew more animated. "I have a friend at church who caters. I've helped her before. I have her brunch menu right here beside me." The sound of paper crunching carried into the phone. "How do you feel about pigs in a blanket, cocktail size? With fluffy scrambled eggs. And a fruit platter?"

"Sounds wonderful." Lissa's mind whirled with all she had to do. "Does she make wedding cakes?"

"Her sister does." Delaney could again be heard rustling paper. "You've come to the right part of the state."

"What will I do without you?"

"You were there for me. This is payback time." Delaney spoke again to someone in the room. She returned. "David insists."

"I'm so in love I barely function." Lissa wanted to pinch herself, but doing so might wake her from this dream and she'd not be planning a wedding after all. "I still can't believe we are doing this." She tapped the phone with her finger, assuring herself she was having a live conversation. "It's unreal."

"I've got calls to make and you have a dress to buy." Delaney's tone transformed again into one of all business. "You can sigh and giggle on your honeymoon."

CHAPTER THIRTY-FOUR

LISSA GAPED AT HER IMAGE IN the standing oval mirror Delaney's guest room provided. The long-sleeved, white lace mermaid gown clung to her torso, accentuating her curves to her thighs. The scalloped chapel train flared into a puddle of satin and lace around her feet. The neckline draped across her collar bones, plunging to her waist at the back.

Delaney adjusted the shoulders. "This is the most gorgeous gown I've seen." She stepped back and considered Lissa head to toe. "Kurt is going to start panting the minute you step into the garden."

"Probably from the sun." Lissa twisted back to the mirror. Her hair hung in ringlets around her face, the cluster of little curls creating a mane that fell midway to her shoulder blades. She lifted the chiffon veil and pressed the tiara holding it into her hair. Behind her Delaney spread the filmy fabric across her back, letting the cascade of the veil join the train of the dress.

"You are a beautiful bride." Delaney winked at her in the mirror.

"I could never have pulled this off if it weren't for you." Lissa pivoted to face her sister. "The gardens, the tables, the brunch." She wrapped Laney in an embrace. "Thanks for making my day so special on such short notice."

A knock sounded at the door, and Lissa's father peeked into the room. "Are you decent?"

"Hey, Dad. Ready to give your Navy officer away today?"

His eyes grew warm as if delighted as he took her in. "You couldn't be any lovelier. I'm one proud papa." He spoke to Delaney as well. "You and David have outdone yourselves on the grounds. Eily and I thought we had a garden, but your yard is spectacular." He kissed Delaney's cheek. "You and Lenna look like two flowers in your pretty peach gowns."

"Thanks, Dad. Lenna wore her dress to the prom this spring. She's always loved my evening dress, so she wanted one in a similar shade of peach."

"With her blonde hair and brown eyes, she could be your twin as well as her brother's." Dad put his arm around Lissa. "Kurt is shaking like a leaf. He's afraid you're going to cut and run. He says he deserves it if you do."

"I'm not going anywhere." Lissa hugged him back. "I started dreaming of this day with Kurt when I first met him two years ago. He's been through a river of hurt since then and emerged on the other side more patient and thoughtful than any man I've ever met."

Dad nodded, clearing his throat. "Kurt had my attention the first time I met him. I'm glad the two of you were able to work out your careers and trust issues in order to make this day happen. I am so happy for you." He leaned in close and whispered low. "And the Marine uniform isn't bad, either. He looks like a movie star."

"I'll take him any way he comes." Lissa couldn't wait to stand by her groom's side. She could only imagine him in uniform dress blues.

Dad reached inside his vest pocket. "I brought you a gift to go with the 'old, new, borrowed, and blue' part of weddings." He held out a long velvet box. "These were your mother's."

Lissa opened the box and discovered a triple strand of pearls and teardrop earrings. Lifting the necklace from its case, she struggled for words. "Dad. . ."

"I conspired with Delaney. With all your stuff packed, we figured you probably wouldn't remember jewelry. Your mother would have wanted you to wear these."

"They're perfect."

He took them from her fingers and placed the strands around her neck. Turning her by the shoulders, he sought her eyes, loving tenderness in his glint, and landed a kiss on her cheek. "Now you're ready."

Another knock sounded, and Kurt's three sisters, Kathryn, Madison, and Zoe, entered, each dressed in a pastel floral gown. Though invited to be bridesmaids, they'd opted to serve at the reception table.

Kathryn gave a thumbs-up to Lissa. "The brunch is going to be fabulous. Your friend is a genius at this. My sisters and I wanted to come before the wedding and welcome you to our side of the family because we'll be busy serving your guests afterward."

"Thank you." Lissa breathed in deeply. "I know Eily and Dad's marriage legally made us stepsisters, but I still feel as if I'm gaining an entire set of siblings by marrying Kurt."

"You weren't there for their wedding." Zoe hugged Lissa. "You didn't get to know us as family until you left the Navy."

"I still don't know you as well as I hope to."

Madison covered her mouth, catching a giggle mid-air. "Well, as soon as you say 'I do' you're stuck with us. Better run now, because we can be pretty crazy."

"I can't wait to find out." Lissa thought of all the days she'd spent aboard ship. "Living on a Navy vessel where you are one of a handful of women doesn't allow for a lot of girl talk and craziness. If Kurt gets stuck overseas, and I come home, I expect a McKintrick sisters' sleepover."

Kathryn raised her palm and flashed her fingers. "You're on. Bring your nail polish and your facial, because we work on beauty treatments all night."

"While we watch old movies and eat popcorn by the gallon." Zoe puffed out her cheeks.

"Don't forget potluck." Madison waggled a finger. "We stuff

before we stuff."

Lissa didn't know what to say. "I can't wait to get home and I haven't even left yet."

Kathryn turned to Delaney. "You need to join us too. We're all part of the same clan now, you know."

Delaney accepted the invitation with grace. "I'll look forward to it."

Dad cleared his throat, holding up his watch. "Girls, it's time to get this wedding started. We don't want to keep Kurt waiting any longer than we have to."

Zoe, Madison, and Kathryn headed for the door, Zoe glancing over her shoulder one last time. "We'll see you out there. My brother is going to faint when he sees how beautiful you are."

"Thanks." Lissa gulped. "I can't wait to see him, either."

Kurt's knees knocked as he made his way toward the gazebo where the chaplain from his unit waited. Ahead of him his veterinarian friend, Damon DeLorme, and Lissa's boss, Matthew Briggs, led the procession.

White folding chairs followed the line of the heart-shaped patio, coming to a perfect point at the opening to the wedding area. Beyond the patio, manicured lawn stretched to the fence line. Clusters of rose bushes, marigolds, and zinnias bordered the green grass, while pots of petunias ringed the serving tables. A string quartet, which included Lissa's nephew Liam on the bass, sat off to the side playing Brahms.

As Kurt passed the guests settled on either side, he nodded to a few men he recognized from his unit seated on the aisle. The men had turned out in military dress for this occasion. He would not be the only one among his band of brothers who would leave for San Diego today.

He smiled at the rest of the guests. His diving buddy, Rudy Taylor, sat with his new bride, McKenna, in the middle. Kurt moved forward to the gazebo, gaze fixed on the trailing white roses climbing about the structure in clusters like snow.

Both Damon and Matthew were former military personnel and each wore the dress colors of their branch—Damon in Army dress and Matthew in Coast Guard blue. They stopped at the steps leading into the area where the chaplain waited.

Kurt advanced to the first step of the gazebo and turned to face the audience. He smiled at his mother, sitting where the bride's family usually sat. Lissa had asked Eily to sit in her mother's place. Marshall would join her after he gave his daughter away. Kurt couldn't think of any way Lissa could have honored his mother more—the gesture symbolized the complete bonding of the two families.

Kurt's three sisters, who'd fussed over his dress uniform like mother hens, were escorted by their husbands to spaces on the right side of the seating area. Dressed in pastel shades that highlighted their individual beauty, each of them drew glances from the audience as they found their seats. His nieces and nephews occupied a row behind them, the older cousins caring for the little ones. He dreamed of the day he and Lissa might add to the growing numbers of cousins. His nephew Peter, now a hulking eighteen-year-old, looked the image of Kurt's own father, Kenny, who had died ten years before. Kurt blinked. *Dad, I wish you were here.*

The string quartet keyed into a musical bridge that increased in volume and changed melodies. As the viola struck three distinct notes, the quartet broke into an arrangement of "Whither thou goest, I will go." As the soloist sang the age-old hymn, Delaney and Lenna stepped up the aisle first, their peach-colored dresses shimmering in the breeze as if imitating the riot of color blooming in the garden scene around them. They joined Kurt at the gazebo, taking places to his right.

Jayden entered next, carrying the rings and casting a brief glance at his mother, who was seated at the back with Peggy. Melanie Barnes had been released from jail and cleared of all charges. She and Jayden would soon be reunited at the rescue center. She beamed as she watched her son join the groomsmen, finding his spot next to Matthew on Kurt's left.

The music changed again, and Kurt focused on the spot where Lissa would appear any moment. His mother stood and turned toward the aisle, the guests following her lead. Kurt breathed in deep, fighting the need to shout as Marshall, dressed in a navy blue suit, walked across the lawn with Lissa at his elbow. After what seemed a lifetime, the father and daughter duo came to the patio area. They stopped and waited. Lissa's blush covered her face as she caught his attention, her dress outlining every curve of her body. Kurt's pulse raced, his mouth dry and palms sweaty. How had he ever captured the heart of such a beautiful creature?

To Kurt's surprise, the men in his unit who had occupied seats on the aisle rose together as one and turned, facing each other. Withdrawing swords from their scabbards, they raised them in the air, forming a bridge of blades over the path as Lissa glided on her dad's arm to the podium. When Lissa and Marshall reached the gazebo, the men lowered their weapons, returned them to their sides, and then saluted Kurt. He saluted back and nodded his thanks.

The chaplain stepped forward and directed a comment to Lissa. "It appears Kurt's men weren't about to let you get away." Laughter drifted across the audience as they took their seats. "Marshall, are you ready to give your daughter to be married to this handsome guy?"

"I am." Marshall kissed Lissa on the cheek and found his seat beside Eily.

Kurt offered his elbow, and Lissa stepped to his side. Her eyes shone as his hand covered hers. A few more minutes and they would be husband and wife.

"We are here today to join this man, Kurt Kenny McKintrick, and this woman, Melissa Renée Frye, in holy matrimony by order of God's laws and according to His teachings."

Airport security waved the military men through to their waiting plane as Lissa followed Kurt up the ramp. Her Navy dress uniform felt large on her frame after wearing the form-fitting wedding dress this morning. She gazed at her left hand, watching the stones of her wedding ring glitter in the sunshine like freshly polished silver on a table of marble. Traveling as a new bride on a plane full of Marines, Lissa waited for the catcalls and innuendos to begin.

Kurt found their seats and gestured for her to take the window. "After you, Mrs. McKintrick."

She started to slip past him, but he caught her cheek with his palm and leaning in, kissed her fully on the mouth.

Whistles erupted around them. "Hey, McKintrick, get a room."

Lissa hurried to her seat, the telltale heat of flushed cheeks creeping along her neckline. "Why did you do that here?"

Kurt followed her into the assigned spaces. "I'm a married man. Comes with the territory." Once seated, Kurt wrapped his arms about her shoulders and pulled her close. "They won't bother us. I issued a warning before we got on the plane."

"They're *guys*." Lissa raised an eyebrow. "You know they're waiting to pounce."

"Don't worry." He reached into his jacket and produced a wad of papers. "Brought you a little reading material for our journey."

"What's this?" Lissa unfolded the packet and scanned the top page. "Is this what I think it is?"

"Yep." Kurt kissed her forehead. "The papers for the Mueller ranch. Now that you are my wife, I had you added to the deed."

Lissa read the document. She couldn't suppress the frown forming across her brow.

"What's wrong?"

"I was thinking about George Barnes. The forensics team found evidence he'd gone inside Bennie's house, as far as the bedroom. From there everything is pretty sketchy. There may not be enough to convict him of causing the old man's death, but he'll get time for the kidnapping, and that will keep him locked up for a while."

"Does it bother you that Bennie died in his house?"

"A little. But he died being a rancher, doing what he did best. That counts for a lot." Lissa smiled at him. "And we'll continue his legacy when we get back from our deployments."

"Sounds like a great future." Kurt's lips brushed her temples.

Lissa handed him the documents. "The ranch is ours?"

"All you have to do is sign on the dotted line and we can close the transaction. I saved it to surprise you. It's my wedding gift for my beautiful bride. When you come home from San Diego, you'll have a ranch waiting. Think you'll like living there?"

"I'll like living anywhere you are, Kurt." She breathed in, her happiness lodging itself in her throat. "You are my happily ever after."

"God made this happen. *He* is our happily ever after." Kurt's eyes narrowed, the hunger she'd seen many times before taking residence in his irises. He leaned closer, the scent of his aftershave wafting to her nose, making her tingle. His breath warmed her cheek as his mouth sought hers.

She surrendered to the kiss, the intensity of it shaking loose a thousand butterflies in her stomach, all fluttering like petals driven by a strong wind. When he drew back, she couldn't hide her grin.

"Hey, McKintrick—I think we need a room."

Study Questions

1. Lissa has returned home seeking a change of career, but her reaction to the phone call that first early morning suggests she hoped the caller is Kurt. How sincere was her quest for a new career? What do you think she really wanted?

2. Kurt is haunted by his Afghanistan experiences, but he seemed to rally to answer inquiries about his war experiences. When do you first suspect he's struggling to cope with this side of the war? How has his faith enabled him to persevere?

3. Have you ever known a man like George? How do you feel about someone who manages to stay sober for his job, but surrenders his weekend to the bottle? Could his wife have done anything to help him break the cycle besides giving in to it?

4. All of Lissa's plans crumble in light of Delaney's health news. Have you been faced with that kind of setback? How did you cope? Should Lissa have continued with her plans in spite of the risks she faced?

5. Jayden is devastated by the death of his friend Bennie Mueller. How does Mr. Mueller's history with Jayden make you think the man might have suspected more about the Barnes family than he revealed? How involved have you been with children who are starving for love at home? In what ways can the average citizen help? What should be a Christian's response?

6. Communication between Lissa and Kurt suffered when Kurt lost Foster Blake, but when they started talking again, things seemed to

head in the right direction. How often have you allowed a failure to communicate shape your opinion of someone you cared about?

7. How did the state's refusal to allow Jayden to return to his mother affect you? How justified was the state in keeping the boy away from his home until George was contained? Have you known children in similar circumstances?

8. Have you visited a horse rescue center? A ranch for abused children? How do you think Kurt and Lissa will fare when they return to their ranch and begin living their dream?

Now a Sneak Peek at
A Kite in the Wind

CHAPTER ONE

THE SLAM OF A DOOR CAUGHT Claire Simpson's attention as she watched snow fall on the small patch of beach barely visible beyond the Yaquina Bay Elementary breezeway. Even though she stood close to the parking lot, she hadn't heard the pickup drive in. She was surprised by its arrival, since school officials had cancelled classes earlier to avoid the onset of a severe Pacific storm.

A well-groomed man, his uniform suggesting military personnel, climbed from the truck. Trench coat flapping about his knees as the wind played tag, he opened the doors of the extended cab, and lifted first a girl, then a boy from the back. The little boy ran toward the playground, exuberance oozing from his busy body. He pointed to the beach, but the blunt sound of an angry voice turned him around. He walked bent over toward the truck, head hanging like a scolded dog.

Claire didn't recognize either child, but perhaps they attended school elsewhere. The man might be here to pick up his wife. She hadn't met all of the staff's spouses. The threesome entered through the main doors and disappeared. She returned her attention to the storm, mesmerized as the churning ocean slapped at the edge of the sand, daring the falling snow to encroach its mighty waters. The waves seemed to laugh as the fragile flakes vaporized in the rush of the wind.

She hadn't grown up on the Oregon coast and assumed the

north Pacific was all surf and sand. She'd never have guessed the shore could be covered in white, nor had she seen it this way, even in pictures. Mounds on the beach turned into oversized marshmallows. Driftwood transformed to fanciful fences. Did this happen often? On the sand? In November?

Yet here snow fell—sloppy, fat flakes fluttering down like a curtain of white fairies on a theater's stage opening night. The quiet drift of the airborne dancers made her pulse race, their presence evoking memories from her past—images she'd tried to forget.

A brisk whack of wind chilled her. She turned to the school where for the last two years she'd filled her days as the learning specialist. Except today. The voices of children were missing in light of the unusual snow day. The swings jingled in the breeze, their black seats responding to the swish of cold air driving the storm inland. The silvery slide no longer shone, its curved form home to pockets of wintry slush instead. When the squall landed shortly after nine, the superintendent ordered the buses back. High winds were expected, along with freezing rain, and maybe the snow. She glanced down at the little stretch of beach peeking through the housing project surrounding the school. Cross off the maybe. Snow still fell.

She checked her watch. Staff members were free to leave at noon. She should be packing up for the day. Grocery shopping lay ahead. The errand meant she'd brought her car. Any other Monday she'd have walked the short mile from her duplex to the school. But providence had smiled on her, so she wasn't stuck walking home in the storm.

Claire scooted in through the side entrance and headed to her office. The family she'd seen a few minutes before stood talking with the principal. The man, gesturing with his hands, spoke as if agitated. The children clung to his pant legs. She watched them a few minutes, then realized her gawking might be considered rude and entered her room. She couldn't put a finger on her angst, but something about the scene bothered her. Perhaps the father had had a bad experience elsewhere.

She lifted the stack of files she needed to work through tonight, stuffed the papers into a canvas tote, and set it on the floor. In her position, paperwork never ended. Individual education plans had to be evaluated quarterly. Goals set for the disabled student needed to be addressed, assessed, and re-addressed.

She grabbed her coat, buttoned the front, and headed to the door. Grabbing the tote, she locked her office and followed the red tiles toward the entrance. The man she'd seen earlier still stood talking with the principal. Acknowledging them with a nod, she veered to the left.

"Claire?" The principal's voice caught her by surprise.

She turned and faced the superintendent, the woman's smile forced as if she were dealing with an obnoxious student. Claire eyed the two children, noting the little girl slumped on a chair by the wall. Sandy blonde hair tumbled over her forehead, hiding her eyes. The little boy, arms folded and a frown on his face, stood beneath his father's hand, the man's fingers firmly planted on the top of the child's head. "Hello."

"Claire, this is Montgomery Chandler. He and his children recently moved to Newport." The principal gestured to the boy. "This is Mason. His sister is Mia."

She held out her hand. "Claire Simpson. I'm the learning specialist." She smiled at Mason, then Mia.

Mr. Chandler let go of Mason and shook her hand.

The twins studied her, shy grins on both of their faces. The boy, hair like his sister's, had eyes the color of dried walnuts. The girl looked up, and Claire noticed her eyes were blue. Claire glanced at the father. His clear blue eyes scrutinized her like a bug under a microscope and confirmed who the little sister favored. Her cheeks burned in the intensity of his stare. "Twins?" She never liked to ask that question because people often took offense in the obvious, but since this pair were brother and sister, she decided to risk it.

"Yes." Mr. Chandler drew the boy back toward him, and placed a firm grip on the child's shoulder. "Both of them were doing well in school when we left Seattle."

"It's nice to have you join our community." No mother had been mentioned, but Claire decided this was not the time to ask. She could access the children's files easily enough. "Will they start tomorrow?"

Montgomery stiffened at the question. "I had hoped they'd start today, but the weather had other ideas."

The principal gestured as she spoke. "Usually these storms are only wind and rain. When snow threatens, we have to think of the safety of our students traveling in buses on slick roads."

"Mia and Mason will arrive by car. My sister will pick them up."

Claire found the defensiveness in his voice curious. More than ever she wanted to read their file.

The principal pressed her fingers together. "Tomorrow, then?"

"Tomorrow." Mr. Chandler nodded at Claire. "Nice to have met you, Mrs. Simpson, even though my children will have no need of your services."

Claire stifled the urge to correct the man. He was wrong on two counts. She didn't have a married name, and his children, of the many she'd met at this school, already seemed likely candidates for her expertise. She hadn't met many second-grade girls who still sucked their thumbs, and the little boy's unspent energy threatened to explode from beneath his jacket, despite his father's firm hand. Parts of the family's puzzle appeared to be missing. What those pieces were, Claire didn't know, but to do her job, she needed to

find them

He turned, and with a grip on Mason's coat jacket, extended his other hand to Mia, who scuffled to his side sucking her thumb. The threesome walked to the door, the man's brisk strides making the children hustle. As the door opened, Mia glanced back, her sad eyes searching the hallway. When she found Claire standing where she'd left her, she lifted a pudgy hand and waved.

Time for Claire to fill in the gaps of the puzzle.

Montgomery slid his two children into the back seat of their crew cab, fastened the seatbelts, and hurried to the driver's side. As the engine warmed, he looked over the little grey building where his children would attend school. The large red letters naming the structure seemed out of proportion to the building's size. Beyond the long, boxlike exterior, a larger addition rose from the back, a space he guessed to be an auditorium or gymnasium. The playground extended behind, newer looking play structures and sturdy swings filling the fenced recreational area. He glimpsed a limited span of the ocean in the distance, the view obstructed by a housing development that graced the school's perimeter.

"Is that a kite? A kite flying in the snow?" Mason's voice rose from the back, high-pitched and excited. Like a ballerina pirouetting on a stage, the kite lifted into the air, reaching a lofty space and dashing toward the ground again.

"Yes, the person holding the string must either be frozen or nuts to brave this wind and the cold." Montgomery watched, fascinated by the strange dips and turns of the kite's dance across the beach. He hadn't flown a kite in years. He understood Mason's enthusiasm.

"He might be cold, Dad." Mason leaned as far forward as his seatbelt would allow. "But think of all the fun he's having."

"I hope he doesn't catch pneumonia down there." Montgomery put the truck in gear and reversed out of the small parking place. "I need to drop by the NOAA headquarters and let them know I've arrived. After that we'll go see if your Aunt Ellen is home yet." He glanced in the rearview mirror for a response. Mason, nose pressed against the glass, sat watching the kite. Mia, thumb stuck in her mouth, had collapsed in the corner of her seat, fast asleep.

He sighed. His sister Ellen had her work cut out for her with these two. Had she known what she was doing when she volunteered? He wondered if he should have accepted her offer. But the transfer from Seattle left him few alternatives. If only Marissa could have beaten her illness last spring, she could have transferred with him. Illness gave her no say in the matter, but he couldn't help wishing she had. The kids so needed her. He needed her.

Mason shrieked. "It got away, Dad. The kite flew away."

Mia, startled by her brother's scream, awoke and started crying.

Montgomery fisted the steering wheel and closed his eyes. Why did it feel as if everything they did ended in a crisis? How had Marissa smoothed each squall into an ocean breeze? Calm every fear with a quiet word? He had no answers. He hadn't been home enough to learn. How would his family survive without her?

Claire shivered as she walked into her apartment. She set the groceries on the kitchen counter, hurrying to start the flame in the front room's standing fireplace. The little electric hearth, with its counterfeit blaze and glowing logs, had been a gift from her mother. The fireside might not contain a real fire grate and burning coals, but in minutes it could heat her kitchen, dining, and front room area to a comfortable seventy degrees. In this coastal climate, with the windy days and rain-filled nights, she welcomed the warmth. The snow today made the device even more appreciated.

By the time the apartment lost its chill, Claire had put away her purchases, made a cup of hot chocolate, and settled down at her desk to study the paperwork she needed to finish. Two of the teachers had registered a complaint against a second-grade girl who continued to sneak cigarettes into the girl's restroom and smoke them before dropping them in the toilet. The girl's foster parents didn't know where she might be getting the packs, but considering the child's history of pandering on the streets for her drunken mother, the illegal possession of smokes didn't surprise Claire. Figuring out a way to change the girl's attitude toward what she was doing became the goal. Claire had no clue how to proceed. What eight-year-old had already learned to smoke?

The telephone interrupted her thoughts and she picked it up.

"Hi, Claire." Her mother's voice sounded strong and healthy.

"You must be feeling better." Claire settled deeper in her chair. "Your flu bug made its exit, I take it?"

"Pretty much. I still have a residual cough." Her mother stopped and cleared her throat. "But I'm on the mend. How was school today? Did I understand the news correctly? You had snowy roads?"

"Yep. I saw snow near the water's edge. I'm used to flurries in the valley, but I've never seen snow falling on sand before." Claire remembered Montgomery Chandler and his two children, the father upset that his son and daughter didn't get to start school today. "The students were sent home because of slick roads."

"Better safe than risking trouble."

Claire listened to her mother ramble for a few more minutes, waiting for the inevitable question she always posed.

Mom didn't disappoint. "I saw Jamie's mother at the grocery store, and she asked about you."

"You two are never giving up on us, are you?"

"You came awfully close to tying the knot, Claire. I haven't forgotten. But I also understand why you wouldn't want to try again."

"He left me three days before we went to the altar. For reasons I find unacceptable. I'm trying to forget."

"I don't blame you, though I thought it was only a misunderstanding at the time." Mom paused. "But you obviously had your mind set. Running away to Pennsylvania sealed the deal."

"What was I supposed to do? Sit around and wait for him to come crawling back?" She sipped her hot chocolate. "Angie and Brennan had space for me. And the teaching program at Penn State was excellent." She set the cup down. "I believe I landed on my feet after Jamie's debacle."

"You did. Quite well." Her mother sighed. "Any new men in your life?"

Claire smiled at her mother's question. Mom's mission, it seemed, centered around getting Claire married. Mom had almost accomplished her goal when she and Jamie Duval, an Olympic hopeful, became engaged. The wedding guests had returned their RSVP's when Jamie sent her a note saying he'd changed his mind. He'd been invited to compete in a slalom at Aspen and couldn't pass up the opportunity. The event might have been his ticket to the next Olympics.

Only Claire understood the real reason for his departure. Though betrayed, discovering this side of Jamie before she repeated her vows had been a godsend. He'd dumped her with the wedding expenses, the embarrassment, and a future forever carrying the burden of their past in silence. To save face, she'd opted to live with her married sister, Angela, in Pennsylvania. She spent the year there finishing her degree, earning her teaching credentials and healing from the brokenness Jamie's departure created. Time well spent.

When she returned to teach in Newport, he had the audacity to make a reappearance, pleading with her to forgive him. Once she might have considered it, but she'd discovered the truth behind his absence. Another woman had caught his attention. That she couldn't forgive.

Her mother still waited for an answer. "No, Mom. This is a coastal town. Single men are usually here for the weekend, looking for a good time before they hurry back to jobs in the valley. Those who are permanent wear rings on their left hand or, so far, haven't interested me, when I've had the opportunity to meet someone new." She raised her chin in defiance, as if her mother could see. "But I'm happy in my job, glad to be free of Jamie's control over me, and enjoying my enduring single status. What Jamie and I had is over. I'm not going back there again. Ever."

"I know. I'm only thinking of your happiness."

"I am happy, Mom. I discovered a new life after Jamie walked out. I found out God loves me as I am. Past mistakes are forgotten in His eyes. My slate has been wiped clean. That in itself made me happy. It has nothing to do with my broken engagement or marital status." She checked the clock. "Anyway, I'm midway through a pile of papers I need to complete before tomorrow. I'll have to say goodbye for now."

"I admire your dedication to your students." Mom sniffed and blew her nose. "You've done well with your education."

"Thanks. Stay healthy. Praying for you."

"Oh, I almost forgot. Angie asked me to have you call her. Apparently Fallyn has been having problems. She thought you might have some insights into her behavior."

Claire swallowed hard. "I'll call her soon. Thanks for the heads-up."

Fallyn, had problems? Her five-year-old niece held a special place in her heart. She'd give up her life to help the child.

A cold shiver passed over her. *Fallyn* ...

Made in the USA
San Bernardino, CA
20 February 2018